MOTH TO A FLAME

PRAISE FOR THE BUTTERFLY ASSASSIN

'[A] dark, enthralling thriller'
The *Guardian*

'An immersive, fast-paced thriller'
The *Irish Times*

'With a complicated heroine, richly-drawn characters and
pulse-pounding action, Isabel's story had me racing through
the pages, gasping for breath. What an electrifying debut!'
Chelsea Pitcher, author of *This Lie Will Kill You*

'Sharp and layered, with a bright beating heart. It will lure
you deep into a fascinating and dangerous new world.'
Rory Power, author of *Wilder Girls*

'A heart-in-your-mouth thriller that grips you
from the first page until the very last.'
Benjamin Dean, author of *The King is Dead*

'A bold, jagged and uncompromising thriller that
will keep you guessing all the way to the end.'
Tom Pollock, author of *White Rabbit, Red Wolf*

'Dark, vivid and uncompromising – an
utterly addictive story. I told myself "just one
more chapter" well into the night.'
Emily Suvada, author of *This Mortal Coil*

'Fierce, thrilling, and impossible to put down.
Packed full of amazing friendships, plot
twists and a desperate fight to survive'
C. G. Drews, author of *The Boy Who Steals Houses*

MOTH TO A FLAME

FINN LONGMAN

Simon & Schuster

First published in Great Britain in 2024 by Simon & Schuster UK Ltd

1 3 5 7 9 10 8 6 4 2

Simon & Schuster UK Ltd
1st Floor, 222 Gray's Inn Road
London WC1X 8HB

Simon & Schuster: Celebrating 100 Years of Publishing in 2024

www.simonandschuster.co.uk
www.simonandschuster.com.au
www.simonandschuster.co.in

Simon & Schuster Australia, Sydney
Simon & Schuster India, New Delhi

A CIP catalogue record for this book
is available from the British Library.

PB ISBN 978-1-3985-2342-5
eBook ISBN 978-1-3985-2344-9
eAudio ISBN 978-1-3985-2343-2

Typeset in Times by M Rules
Printed and Bound in the UK using 100% Renewable
Electricity at CPI Group (UK) Ltd

MIX
Paper | Supporting
responsible forestry
FSC
www.fsc.org
FSC® C171272

For those working to repair harm,
not perpetuate it.

'THESEUS: Stop. Give me your hand. I am
                  your friend.
HERAKLES: I fear to stain your clothes with blood.
THESEUS: Stain them, I don't care.'

Herakles by Euripides

(translated by Anne Carson in
Grief Lessons: Four Plays by Euripides)

MAP OF ESPERA

NW
CHECKPOINT

GANTON

SHERBURN

HESLERTON

FOXHOLES

WEAVERTHORPE

NEWTON

LUTTON

GRINDALYTHE

9

COWLAM

10

SLEDMERE

LANGTOFT

WATCH
TOWER

4

SW
CHECKPOINT

5

DISTANCES

NW CHECKPOINT TO SW CHECKPOINT
——— 7.5 MILES

NW CHECKPOINT TO
EASTERN TRADE ENTRANCE
——— 15 MILES

 COMMA

 HUMMINGBIRD

 CIVILIAN

NEUTRAL ZONE

 INDUSTRIAL: MANUFACTURING

 INDUSTRIAL: FARMING

 BOROUGH BOUNDARIES

 MAJOR ROADS

STAXTON

FLIXTON

HUNMANBY

FORDON

EASTSIDE GATE

WATCH TOWER

1

BURTON

7

2

REIGHTON

EASTERN TRADE ENTRANCE

8

CENTRAL ESPERA

GRINDALE

RUDSTON

SWAYTHORPE

BOYNTON

3

KEY

1 – SECRET WAY INTO CITY
  (UNDER WATCHTOWER)

2 – ABOLITIONIST SAFE HOUSE

3 – COMMA / COCOON COMPLEX

4 – WATCHTOWER

5 – GARRISON OUTSIDE SLEDMERE

6 – RONAN'S HOUSE

7 – FORMER GUILD HOUSE

8 – CENTRAL COURT

9 – COMMA OFFICES

10 – CEMETERY ENTRANCE

ANTAŬPAROLO (PROLOGUE)

A girl, running.

A dark tunnel: an artery for the blood she trails, a road to the unknowable, her only chance. When she stumbles, there's nobody to see her fall, or hear the faint sobbing gasp of her breath. *Dead.* She's left them all behind. Her city of death, her lost friends, any safety she's ever known, and now she runs towards a world she doesn't believe in, not knowing what she hopes to find at the other end. It's a gradual abandonment, leaving behind her name and her self. Each step stitches the thread of her footprints into the black seam of the unlit tunnel, binding her to the earth.

It's endless, interminable, unbearable. And then it isn't. The faint glimmer of light through a manhole cover, reflected on the rungs of a ladder screwed into the wall, is a blinding sun. It sears her eyes and heart with undeserved hope, her bloodstained hands almost too weak to grip the rungs. She

1

tries anyway, climbs anyway. It takes three attempts to shift the hatch.

The girl emerges into the world like a maggot from a corpse, grotesque and unwanted. The corpse makes a final attempt to claim her, tugging at her exhausted knees, but she stumbles onwards on a pilgrimage to nowhere. One foot in front of the other, survival by unwilling degrees, bloodied feet on potholed tarmac roads. Lost and losing: memories, strength, the will to continue. The place she's left is a nightmare, vague and terrifying. The place she's going is an emptiness, unfathomable.

They find her in the end. The darkness first, and then the people.

She falls again, and this time it's a relief.

1

PERDITA (LOST)

She wakes nameless and fragmented in an unfamiliar room, her fingers clenched around weapons and blood sticky and persistent on her hands. The air conditioning bites, stripping her of her skin one layer at a time and leaving her flayed and exposed, and the sound of approaching footsteps thunders like her heartbeat in her ears. She lashes out, protecting herself, but the blade in her hand is an illusion and a memory, dissolving inches from the stranger's throat, and she's unarmed and helpless to resist as they pin her arms and wrap thick restraints around her wrists.

'And I thought you said she wasn't dangerous, doctor,' says a voice.

'While she was unconscious,' says another voice, 'she

wasn't.' The doctor, she presumes. Here to cut her up and slice her open to find out what it is that made her a monster. Maybe if they peel off enough of her skin, they'll see her rotten core; maybe they'll see the damage on her, written into her bones.

She doesn't know where she is. Barely knows *who* she is. But she knows she's not there any more, wherever *there* was, trapped in a crowd that hated her. Nor is she out on the road, running, running, trying to outrun the need to kill anybody else because there's enough blood on her hands already. All she remembers is the tunnel, dark and endless, and the thought that she might really be dying this time.

But here she is. And there's a doctor watching her, and restraints around her wrists, and she doesn't have a weapon.

She considers opening her eyes and demanding to know where she is, who they are, what they want – but that would require curiosity, and the ability to care about the answers. And that's gone, lost somewhere along the road to the exhaustion and the blood and the hollow inside her where her name should live.

'Is she awake?' says the first voice.

'Oh, I think so.' The doctor sounds vaguely amused. She would resent that, if she had the capacity to resent anything. Instead, it washes over her as a fact of her current situation: she is here, and she is being watched, and they will not let her fight back. 'But we can wait until she's ready to talk. There's no rush.'

A laugh from the first voice. 'True. She's not going anywhere.'

And maybe that should frighten her. But fear, like curiosity, requires her to care about consequences. What can they do – kill her? Everybody else is already dead. She should have joined them, given her scars to the earth and her bones to the dust, and now, here, it's impossible to remember why it is that she didn't.

Eventually they tire of watching her. She hears them walk away, leaving her to the bed and the restraints and the images behind her eyelids.

They're all dead. And it's her fault.

The next time she wakes – an hour later, or a week, or anything in between – she's alone in the room. She knows this instinctively, but she takes the time to double-check, listening for breathing and all the soft noises the living can't help but make. Nothing. Only the faint buzz of electronics and the sound of rain against a closed window.

She opens her eyes.

The room is as grey as her thoughts, washed out and made meaningless. She's still restrained, tied to a simple metal bedframe. She can't see her hands from this angle, but they feel clean. Dry. Somebody washed off the blood. Took her clothes, too, by the feel of it, and the scratchy T-shirt and trousers they've given her instead are abrasive against her skin.

The window – she can see it if she cranes her neck – is a small, high pane of clouded glass, firmly closed, letting in no sight of the outside world.

Outside. Is that where she is? Maybe. She remembers running. She remembers leaving everything behind.

Leaving every*one* behind.

She'd thought, because of the doctor, that this might be a hospital, but it looks less like a place where people are brought to get better, and more like a place they're left to be forgotten. There are worse fates, she thinks, than being forgotten; she might even welcome it. Maybe, if she tries hard enough, she can forget herself.

You are not allowed to forget, her brain tells her, ever-cruel. Forgetting is a luxury reserved for those who aren't monstrous, who haven't committed atrocities. Her mind denies her the knowledge of her name, but it gives her this: the memory of her hands wrapped around necks, holding weapons, lathered in blood. An endless parade of deaths in high definition.

The door opens. She can't see that, either; it's in the corner, beyond the narrow line of sight her restraints allow. But she hears the steady tread of comfortable shoes across linoleum flooring, and closes her eyes pre-emptively before the blow lands.

It never does. A voice – the doctor – says, 'I know you're awake.'

She doesn't answer. She wouldn't know how to speak even if she wanted to, her words swallowed deep in her dry throat.

The next question: 'Do you know where you are?'

No. She can guess, from the room, their unfamiliar accents, the wariness with which they approach her. She guesses that she got out, or someone got her out, and they brought her here: a holding place for the fugitives nobody wants. Perhaps they've been waiting for her to wake so they can send her back. They won't want her if they know who she is, and they must know. They must have seen her, and the blood, and the knives she carried.

Maybe they know her name.

She might have asked them that, if she had her voice, and if the words would obey her. But she's not sure she wants it back. She's crawled out from under her name, and she sees no reason to go clawing to retrieve it. Let them have it. Let them take all the words people use to explain her, to make her, and do what they like with them. She'll stay here, grey thoughts in a grey room, and wait to be allowed to follow the others.

The others. Her fault.

'You've been asleep for several days,' says the doctor, as though volunteering this information might encourage her. 'You were dehydrated and suffering from blood loss. There were a dozen injuries—'

She opens her eyes. The doctor stops speaking, lips parted expectantly, waiting for her explanation. She doesn't have one. She's not sure she knew she was wounded.

The doctor is not grey, which comes as a surprise. Blue, instead: pale blue scrubs and cap, like this is a real hospital and not a forgetting-place. He wears an expression of professional interest, not concern. To him, she is an anecdote more than a person.

She thinks perhaps she's okay with being a story, if only somebody will let it end.

'We have some questions for you,' says the doctor finally. 'When you're feeling up to answering.'

She closes her eyes.

The next bout of wakefulness brings light but not clarity, the room lanced with sharp beams of filtered sunlight streaming through the dirty window. Around her is the babble of words she can't understand, her grasp of English fragmenting under the weight of pain and grief as the threat of memory grows in her shattered mind. Questions – she knows they're questions by the inflections, and some part of her wants to explain that she doesn't understand, can't answer them, but the rest of her only wants to close her eyes and wait for the darkness to claim her again.

Nokto. *Night*. It was always her home: softer than day, sharper than morning.

Their daylight's no use to her now, and their words mean nothing.

The first thing she notices is that the restraints are gone.

No. Not the first thing. The first thing she notices is that she is no longer alone in this room. The second thing is that this is a different room. And the third thing, after all of that, is that the restraints are gone, which she notices because her hands have curled into defensive fists even before she knows that she's afraid.

In this room are other beds, neatly spaced with a small locker in between. The beds closest to hers are empty, but the sound of raspy sleep-breathing from the corner near the door confirms a second occupant. The walls are as grey as the last room, but perhaps that's her, her weak incurious vision filtering out the unnecessary colours that might tell her whether or not she's alive.

She knows, though, that she's alive. She resents it. She resents the fact that she's grateful, hates herself for the small relief of drawing breath. The rest of them don't get this. Why should she? Just because she ran? Just because she killed? She hasn't earned her survival.

She knows this with a certainty she lacks about all else. Her name, their names, their faces, are nothing more than the memory of a knife in her hands and the pounding of her heart and the need to *run*. But she knows she doesn't deserve this.

Footsteps. A figure stops just out of sight at the end of her bed. She'd have to sit up to see them, and her exhausted body won't allow that. She's made of rocks and lead, so heavy she's surprised she hasn't sunk straight through the mattress and deep into the ground.

They ask her a question. She doesn't understand the words. She tries to tell them this: *I don't understand you.* But her tongue's as leaden as the rest of her, and the words won't take shape. Her mouth is sandpaper-dry.

'Akvon,' she manages, in a rasp of a voice. 'Akvon, mi petas.'

They say something else, but the blackness is already creeping back in. She closes her eyes and waits for it to be over.

The next thing she knows, something is being held against her lips. Her first instinct is to recoil, until she realises it's what she asked for. *Water.* Greedily, she latches onto the bottle, swallowing in great gulps. They pull it out of reach, a note of warning in their voice, but she doesn't care if it'll make her sick. She needs water.

With the water comes a clarity she's lacked these last few times she's woken. She blinks grit and sleep from her eyes and sees the person the voice belongs to, their grey clothes blending in with the room. They wear a lanyard and a staff badge with a logo she doesn't recognise. It tells her nothing of use, and their expression is unreadable. But they gave her water.

'Dankon,' she says, her gratitude genuine.

They give her the bottle. She holds it herself in shaking hands and tries to ration it with care. She fails, is sick on the floor beside the bed, and sinks back into unconsciousness because it's easier that way.

Gradually, she comes back to herself. Still no name. Still not sure she wants one. She senses that it's *there*, somewhere, inside her head, waiting to be claimed, but it's tangled up in a world of hurt she doesn't dare to touch. When she prods at it, she remembers nothing but death, and fear, and flight. There'll be no kindness in the memory of herself.

She learns that these people keep her alive out of duty, not care, and that they're only waiting for her to be well enough to speak. Sometimes her mind cooperates, sifting meaning from their words, but sometimes English abandons her, and she's left with only fragmentary Esperanto, Russian, German – nothing that belongs here – to package her scattered thoughts.

She's not sure if she's a prisoner or a patient, but that, at least, is a familiar state of affairs.

Finally, there comes a day when they take her from her bed

and along grey corridors to a room, where they sit her on a chair and shackle her hands to a table and say, 'Are you ready to talk now?'

She's got enough English today to ask them what she's supposed to be talking about.

'Espera,' they say, and she—

She remembers.

Espera. City of hope, city of fear, city of death. Walls and art and murder. Her whole world playing out within a few dozen square miles, the outside as unknowable as eternity. Espera that made her and Espera that would have unmade her again.

Remembering the city means remembering the rest of it.

'Papilio,' she says. The word tastes strange on her tongue and she tries again. 'Noktopapilio.' It comes with the rotten scent of something forgotten, but this, this is the closest she can get to her name.

The Moth. Trapped now and burning.

In the end, she talks.

They tell her it's the only way she'll be allowed to leave this place, and though she's got no interest in the world beyond these grey walls, she still feels them closing in on her, the ceiling heavy and ready to crush her hateful body. She's got nowhere else to go, but this is not a place where anyone can live, and she's not sure she's ready to die.

They ask a lot of questions. She didn't realise how many answers she'd be able to give them until they come spilling out of her. There are gaps, lacunae, languages layered over each

11

other until meaning is lost, but she can give them enough to keep feeding the wolves. Enough to earn herself a brief walk around the grey courtyard they call a garden. Enough for a glimpse of the sky.

She keeps talking, and all the while a part of her mind whispers, *you will pay for this*, says, *they will kill you for this*, says, *traitor traitor traitor*, but she can't think about who she's betraying without remembering who she is, and she's got no interest in remembering who she is, remembering her guild and the blood on her hands. It comes back anyway. Comma. Ronan's face in her dreams, smiling as he makes a weapon of her. Nightmares of Daragh crumpling to a bloody hospital floor, the doctor unmade in a place of healing. Running, trapped and cornered, knowing the whole city wants her dead.

But she's not in Espera any more, and she doesn't truly know why she ran.

Coward.

Too afraid to die. Let everyone else do it and couldn't bear it for herself.

The names come back one by one, when she lets them. Mortimer is next; she remembers his smile and his carpenter's hands before his name, but she gets there eventually. Laura she puts off as long as she can, not wanting to recall the look on her flatmate's face when she left her behind in her hospital bed, but she can't hide from it for ever.

One day she remembers Leo, and for the first time it occurs to her that she might not be completely adrift in this strange, unfriendly world.

'Leo Jura,' she says, tentative. 'In this city?'

They don't know what to do with that. She tries to clarify, scrambling for details that might help – *he's a librarian, he left Espera, he's good, please find him* – but her English is slipping away again. The Esperanto always comes back first, a relic of a childhood spent learning to kill before she ever learned how to live. So in the end she can only beg them: 'Leo Jura. *Mi petas.*'

She doesn't really think they'll find him.

When he comes to visit her for the first time, the kindness in his eyes undoes her.

'Isabel,' he says, and just like that, as though it's easy, he gives her back her name.

There is a lot of paperwork involved in being saved.

They've explained it to her, expressions serious and words heavy with technicalities: *defector, asylum, conditional, responsibility.* Isabel sits silently beside Leo and nods when she's supposed to, pretending she understands, but she heard nothing after they told her she'd be leaving this place. She's not alone. Leo is here, and he came for her.

Now Leo's filling out the forms, acres of them, occasionally looking up to ask her for a detail. His voice is gentle, and his pity flays her open: when he asks her for her date of birth and she admits that she can't remember, beyond that it's in April, the look in his eyes almost unmakes her. She can't explain how entirely she's lost herself, jettisoning every piece of information that seemed inessential. If he hadn't come, maybe she would still be nameless.

There are only three things she knows for sure:

Her name is Isabel Ryans.

She's a killer and a coward.

Everybody else is dead.

In the end that's all that matters.

2

MALHELA (DARK)

The corners of the room are dark and full of shadows.

The main light is on, washed out by the pale grey lampshade. Isabel crosses the room and turns on both the lamps, angling them so that they chase away the darkness. It doesn't work. She can still see it in the corner of her vision. Is still consumed by it every time she closes her eyes.

She can't fall asleep because it feels too much like dying.

This room – the spare room of the house Leo shares with Ant and Sam, fellow Esperan fugitives – is softer and darker than the hard edges and fluorescent glare of the detention centre. It should be comforting, and isn't. Isabel sits on the edge of the unfamiliar bed, unarmed and useless, and waits to forget the terror of closing her eyes, or for sleep to overtake her before she can think long enough to panic.

'Isabel.' Leo opens the door a little way, lingering on the threshold. 'I saw your light was on. Do you need anything?'

She shakes her head. 'Foriru.'

He doesn't go away. The open door casts a rectangular stain of darkness on the carpet. 'Can't you sleep?'

'Vi permesas la ombrojn eniri.' *You're letting the shadows in.*

'You can't stay awake for ever, Isabel,' he says, coming into the room.

'Tro malhele.'

'You've got every light on.'

She looks up at him, fights her shattered mind for the English to make him understand. Says, 'It's too dark when I close my eyes.'

Leo sighs and sits down next to her on the bed. 'You're scared,' he says. 'I get it. And I'm sorry I didn't come for you sooner. If I'd known you were there ...'

But he didn't know, because she didn't know how to ask for him.

Isabel doesn't want to talk. Talking is exhausting, language betraying and abandoning her, and Leo, though he understands her Esperanto well enough, seems reluctant to speak to her in it. Maybe he wants to pretend they can leave Espera behind, but she can't do that without leaving herself behind, too.

He puts his arm around her. She wants to shudder away from the touch, but it's helpful to him, so she doesn't. 'I understand how you're feeling,' he begins.

'I'm not feeling anything,' Isabel tells him, and she thinks it's true. All that's left is emptiness. Too much emptiness even to inject any emotion into the monotone of her voice, or to know what she hopes to achieve by telling him this. 'Foriru. Mi petas.' *Go away. Please.*

Leo doesn't go away. He's got it into his head that he should help her, too noble to leave her to suffer alone like she deserves, so he says, 'Tell me what I can do that will help, and I'll do it.'

Her voice is flat, but the words burn her throat. 'Bring Laura back,' she says. 'Bring Daragh back. Bring Mortimer back. Kill my mother a thousand times over. Unmake me.'

'Isabel—'

'Unmake me, so that I was never the Moth, and they never died, and none of this happened. Pull me apart and make me into something and somebody else, because—'

'Isabel,' he says, more sharply. 'Haltu.'

She stops. If Leo wants it enough to ask in Esperanto, she'll oblige. But she says, 'Why?'

'Because you're only making yourself feel worse.'

Again with the feeling. Again with the assumption that there's anything left inside her except rot and ashes. He's casting a shadow on the floor that the lamps can't chase away, bringing darkness into the over-bright haven of her room. She tries not to look at the shape of him thrown across the floor and walls like an insubstantial corpse. Too dark. Too dark. Like she's half closed her eyes already.

'You can't be unmade,' he says, very gently.

'Shows how little you know.'

'Isabel.' He keeps saying her name, as though to remind her who she is. It won't work. She's gone lost somewhere on the road. 'None of this is your fault. If they're dead, it's—'

He breaks off, and all she hears is that word *if*.

She hadn't told him they were dead. She hadn't told him what happened. She didn't mean to do it like this: throw her grief in his face and leave him to draw his own conclusions. Something that might be regret worms its way through the hard shell around Isabel's heart and trickles like acid through her veins.

'Mortimer?' he asks finally, her saviour made supplicant as he looks at her. 'He's dead?'

'They're all fucking dead.' She should soften it, but she doesn't know how. They were friends, Leo and Mortimer, since before she knew either of them, and she – she *forgot*, so wrapped up in her own grief it didn't occur to her that it might hurt Leo to find out like this. But it's not like there's a way of saying it that'll make it better, undo the damage. And Daragh ... Leo knew Daragh, too, worked with him at the Sunshine Project. Isabel just keeps *taking* people from him. 'They beat Mortimer to death,' she says at last, brutal and efficient. 'Hummingbird. He never regained consciousness, but it still took him days to die. My mother shot Daragh – at least that was quick. And Laura ...'

Laura she abandoned to the mercy of Comma and Hummingbird, injured in a hospital bed and entirely lacking in allies. Isabel didn't see her die, but she hopes it was quick.

18

Mortimer, Daragh, Laura: none of them chose to get caught up in her shit. She's the one who tangled them in this sticky web of death, and she didn't deserve to escape it. Maybe if Leo understands her culpability, he'll stop looking at her like she's worth pitying.

'It's not your fault,' says Leo, but he sounds less sure this time, grief pulling certainty away from him and cutting him down to size.

'They'd still be alive if it weren't for me. Suzie would still be alive.'

His expression shifts from lost to bewildered. 'Who's Suzie?' Still that gentle voice, like she'll spook if he asks too loudly.

'A girl. A Hummingbird trainee.'

He sighs. 'Don't think about—'

'I killed her, Leo.'

'You killed a lot of people. I'm aware of that.' He doesn't know the half of it. He might understand academically that she fought her way out of Espera – they'd have told him that when he came to claim her at the detention centre, their explanations pieced together from her fragmentary confession. But he didn't see it, the bloody wretch it left of her by the end. If he did, he wouldn't still be sitting here. 'That's the past, Isabel.'

Isabel looks at the floor, her bare feet pale against the carpet. The month she spent in that place gave the bruises and blisters of her journey time to heal, but she still feels the ache of them. 'She was twelve.'

Leo goes still. 'What?'

'She was twelve years old, and I killed her. That's why ... that's why I had to leave. She was a *kid*.'

'She was my sister.'

There's a shadow on the floor that wasn't there before. Not quite as dark, not quite as defined. They both look up at Sam, standing in the doorway in her oversized pink pyjamas, the colour clashing with her red hair. It's the first time Isabel's seen her since arriving here, and she'd almost convinced herself it wouldn't feel like looking at Suzie's ghost. She was wrong. Sam's shorter than her twin, slender, a hacker rather than a fighter – but she still wears a dead girl's face.

It hurts, in the numb, distant way that things hurt these days.

'Sam, you should be in bed,' says Leo automatically, well settled by now in his role of surrogate parent to the young abolitionist criminal he helped escape from the safehouse under the library after Isabel blew their cover.

'I heard you talking.' Sam looks at Isabel, fearless. 'Suzie was my sister.'

'Yes.' She says it hesitantly, as though unsure of the facts, but of course she's sure. Of course she knows. 'Your twin.'

Sam nods, takes a step further inside. 'You know, you saved her once. Or thought you did.'

Isabel frowns. 'I saved her?' she echoes, thinking of the girl with her cloud of red hair and the scissors clutched in her hands, and then she remembers – all of a sudden – another redhead, a lifetime ago. Shielding a child with her body. Trying to get her out. 'That was her,' Isabel breathes. 'That

20

was her? Katipo?' But she got that girl out. She blew up her parents' guild and she got the children they were training *out*. They were meant to be safe. Emma died so that that girl could be safe. 'But you ... you weren't there, were you?' Surely she would remember.

Sam shakes her head. 'They didn't want me. I wasn't as strong as Suzie.' Her tone is matter-of-fact. 'Then Hummingbird took her when we were ten. I didn't see her again. I thought maybe she was dead anyway.'

Isabel hasn't got the words for what she's trying to say, in any language. She saved that kid – the one good thing she's ever done, the one selfless thing – only for her to be dragged right back into the same lethal trap. And then Isabel killed her. Without even *knowing*.

'I didn't know,' she manages. 'That she was yours. Or that she was—' *My father's.* But she knew the girl was her mirror. It just hadn't seemed to matter at the time.

'You killed a child,' says Leo. It would be easier if he sounded disgusted, or better, furious. Instead, he's carefully stripped all emotion from the statement until it's neither an accusation nor a question.

'I wasn't given a choice.' The lie Isabel tells herself. She had a choice – a choice to kill Suzie, or face the wrath of a city with every reason to hate her, exposed by the very man who made her a monster. A choice between murder and death, the same choice she's always had – just as she had a choice between leaving Laura to die and staying to fight. *I always choose the wrong one.* 'I didn't ... want to.'

As if that fucking helps.

Sam nods, expression unreadable, and turns to leave. Isabel can't tell if her calm is grief or fury or both, but neither would be any less than she deserves.

Leo watches Sam go, his expression torn as he wars with his conscience about whether to follow.

'Iru,' Isabel tells him. *Go.*

'No,' he says, without conviction.

'She needs you more than I do.' Isabel pulls her legs up onto the bed and wraps her arms around them, trying to keep warm. She's been cold ever since she stumbled into this city, blood-soaked and helpless, like the ghosts of all the people she's killed have crawled into bed with her and are draping themselves over her skin. 'And I'd rather be alone.'

'You didn't tell me—'

'That I killed a child? Somehow I didn't think that would convince them to let me stay here with you.' He's bringing all the shadows back in, letting them crawl from the walls towards her, and soon they'll slither across her face and inside her nose and mouth until she chokes on them and – and – *they're not real, Isabel.* She knows they're not. That it's only the light shifting with Leo's agitated movements.

They look real.

'Or that Mortimer's dead. Or Daragh.' His grief makes him sad and quiet. She wishes it made him angry, wants him to rage the way she can't.

'Do you think I'd be *here* if they were alive back in Espera?' she asks.

'I just meant—'

'Leave me alone, Leo.'

'Isabel ...' He looks at her, shakes his head. 'Twelve,' he says. It's still not a question, but he wants an answer, and nothing she says will fix this.

'No blood,' she tells him. 'Cleanest job I ever did. She'd have barely felt it.' A bitter smile. 'Guess I'm good for something after all.'

Now she's made him uncomfortable. He's trying to find something to say that will make this okay, and he can't. He wants to tell her she's wrong, even though he knows she's telling the truth. *I'm a monster, Leo. Stop trying to pretend otherwise.*

The dancing shadows grin with delight, and she can't look away for fear that they'll laugh at her.

'I'm next door if you need me,' he says eventually. 'Try to sleep. Things will be better in the morning.'

'Will they?'

'You're out of Espera. You've got a whole world now to make a future in, all the choices you never had.'

Out of Espera. Out of water, a helpless fish. 'Sure.'

'You'll be all right.' His smile is unconvincing. 'I should check on Sam.'

Always ignoring his own grief to help somebody else. Isabel watches Leo leave and, when he's gone, closes the door as firmly as she can. At least now the shadows are predictable, locked within the box of her room instead of creeping in from the corridor. They can't sneak up on her. They're all here already.

All her shadows. All her ghosts.

Isabel hardly notices her eyes closing; the dark has rushed in on her, settled itself around her neck like fear. She's curled in a tight ball, tense with the instinct to run, and only when she hears the bedroom door open does she realise she's not watching it any more.

Ant. He stands in the doorway, as crumpled and grey as the day she met him in the secret room at the library, and doesn't attempt to comfort her. He watches for a second, silent even when she scowls and spits a few profanities in his direction.

'Leo told me what happened,' he says eventually, when she's run out of unearned insults to throw at him. 'Sounds like Comma used you for jobs they shouldn't have been doing in the first place.'

It makes no difference. 'I didn't say no.'

'The guilds have ways of making your answers not matter at all.' He keeps his distance. She's grateful. This way his shadow barely touches the edge of the bed, and the lamps soften its outlines. 'You're scared.'

'I'm not anything. Just empty.'

'You're scared of the dark.'

Isabel looks up at him. 'How ... ?'

'How do I know? You're flinching at shadows. They've made a moth of you after all, haven't they? Sent you fleeing towards flames.' Ant sounds like he doesn't care if it's her wings or all of her that burns. 'There's no point hiding. The shadows are already inside you.'

He's gone. She wants to reply, but he's gone. The door's closed, and there's no sound of footsteps. It's like he's vanished.

Like he was never there at all.

I'm seeing things.

And the shadows mock her and keep dancing, dancing, dancing, until eventually they dance across her vision and force her down into a sleep she can't resist.

3

KOMPATA (MERCIFUL)

'I made you breakfast.' Leo nudges the door open, precariously balancing a tray. 'You didn't eat much last night.'

'I'm not hungry.'

'Your body still needs fuel.' He puts the tray on the bedside cabinet. Toast, tea, a glass of juice. Nothing special, but more than Isabel deserves after last night's confession.

'I can't eat that,' she says. Leo opens his mouth to argue, so she clarifies: 'The toast. I can't eat wheat.'

'I know,' he says. 'I bought special bread for you. Please.'

Isabel eyes the toast again. It looks different here, less like cardboard. Another thing she should be grateful for, she supposes, but all she wants is to go home.

She sips the tea, though, for Leo's sake. It washes away the dry, bitter taste of sleep and chases some of the cold from her body. 'Thanks.'

Leo takes this as an invitation, sitting down on the end of the bed as though he plans to stay until the breakfast tray is empty. He says, 'Do you remember what medication you were taking, back in Espera?'

Isabel blinks at him over the edge of the mug. 'What?'

'I know your immune system is ...' He waves a hand vaguely. 'Fucked. From the poison. I need to know what meds to get for you.'

It hadn't occurred to Isabel that some of her ongoing nausea and disorientation might be withdrawal disrupting the delicate equilibrium of her damaged body, which is possibly the longest she's managed to forget about her misfiring immune system since the day she barely survived her father's poison. Amidst the complete loss of all familiar routines, her medication was a small absence, easily overlooked. But of course Leo would remember.

She takes a mouthful of toast to buy herself time, then lists the medications she recalls, all the pills that do the jobs her body can't do any more. Leo makes a note of them in his phone, frowning down at it when she's done.

'Okay,' he says eventually. 'I know who can get you the HRT; she's already getting my T. I'll have to ask around for the others.'

Isabel chews uneasily, swallows the toast, and then says, 'You're not going to ask ... them? The doctors?'

A pang of guilt crosses his face. 'I thought perhaps you'd

prefer as few people as possible to know about your ... vulnerabilities,' says Leo, so maybe he understands her after all. 'And it's easier to get black-market meds here than in Espera. Don't need to smuggle them across the walls.'

If she'd wondered whether he still had contact with the smugglers, that would be all the confirmation she needed. Of course he hasn't abandoned Espera and his friends there – he cares too much for that. But Isabel, who's got nothing to go back to, is meant to be making a clean break.

And she doesn't want to.

As if he's read her mind, Leo says, 'I've been thinking about what you should do next.'

'Does it involve getting out of bed? Because I'm not interested.'

He sighs. 'Look, that paperwork I signed was a commitment to ensuring you make some level of effort to integrate into society.'

Isabel puts down her half-eaten toast. 'I don't *want* to integrate into society,' she says. 'And society doesn't want me.'

'Society's going to have to get over it,' says Leo. 'And you need to look like you're trying, because otherwise ...' He trails off. He doesn't need to voice the threat: Isabel already knows they'll take her away from him, back to the detention centre, if she doesn't jump through their hoops. 'It's in your best interests,' he finishes instead. 'If you want to stay in Leeds, with us, you've got to try.'

Leeds. He's probably told her the city's name before, but it feels like the first time. Isabel mouths the word, tasting it, but it means nothing to her beyond *not-Espera, not-home, not-mine.*

'Go on then,' she says. 'Get it over with. What are you suggesting?'

'I don't know yet,' says Leo, in the patient tone of voice he used to use on irascible library patrons when they worked together. 'You haven't got much work experience, and you've got fuck all qualifications. We could enrol you in adult education classes, but . . .'

'Don't waste your money.'

'Yeah, I thought you'd say that.' He watches her fiddle with her breakfast. 'Have you got any ideas?'

'Funnily enough, I didn't do much career planning while running for my life.' The toast is nearly cold, but Isabel forces herself to finish it. 'I don't want to do anything. Don't really want to exist, to be honest.'

'Yes, well, that's not an option.' Leo folds his arms. 'You've been given a second chance, Bel.'

'Don't. Don't do that.'

'Do what?'

Call me Bel, like you're Emma, like I deserve that friendship. 'Act like this is a good thing, like good people didn't die so that I could live.'

Leo says nothing for a while, so she focuses on finishing her tea, ignoring his pensive look.

At last he says, 'What are you good at?'

'Killing people.'

He doesn't flinch, she'll give him that. 'Apart from that.'

29

Developing poisons. Running. Lying to everyone she meets. Making enemies. 'Knowing when you're avoiding talking about something because if we actually discuss the fact that everyone's dead, you'll be forced to face the idea that you were wrong to help me.'

'I'm not *avoiding* it,' he says, a tiny flare of anger in his eyes. *Finally.* 'I'm still . . . processing, okay? You're not the only one who's lost friends.'

'So then ask me.'

'What?'

'Ask me what happened to Mortimer.'

'Isabel, I don't need—'

'Ask me about how they used his own furniture to beat him. Ask me what I did to make Hummingbird want revenge that badly in the first place. Ask me about how he never woke up and he didn't know, nobody told him, I couldn't tell him I was sorry, I just *left him*, because I leave everybody, I fail everybody. Just like I failed Emma. I left Laura, when I could have stayed to fight, and now – now I'm here, buried in second chances I don't want, and she's dead, she must be dead, they're all dead. I should have stayed, and instead—'

'There was nothing you could have done,' interrupts Leo. And maybe he's not wrong, but it doesn't matter, because she's alive when she shouldn't be and he's refusing to accept that.

'So that's why you don't ask,' she says. 'Because you think you already know.'

He watches her for a moment. 'You're more coherent this

morning,' he says at last. 'Last night, I was worried that you were . . .'

'Crazy?'

'It seemed like you weren't sure what was real and what wasn't.'

Isabel doesn't ask if Ant genuinely came to talk to her, in case it turns out he didn't. 'Are you hoping I hallucinated Suzie? Because you're out of luck there.'

'I know.' That even tone hides a dozen emotions. 'I talked to Sam.'

She wonders if Sam's plotting revenge. 'You'll have to face it eventually. Decide whether I'm worth sacrificing your principles for.'

Leo picks up the now-empty tray. 'My principles,' he says, 'tell me that people deserve a shot at redemption. Even people like you. No matter how little you want it.'

It's smothering, this mercy of his, the way he refuses to encompass a possibility that isn't loving. She wants his hatred far more than she wants to be *redeemed*.

Being hated is a much more comfortable feeling than being loved.

'How about you take a shower?' he says, before she can respond. 'You'll feel better when you're clean. And we'll get you some new shoes soon, too. I know the ones they gave you at that place aren't much to speak of.'

That place. Leo hasn't asked her about the detention centre. She wonders if he was taken there too when he arrived, or if turning up with a child and smuggled papers allowed him to skip that step. A civilian with abolitionist contacts is a much more sympathetic candidate for asylum than a fucked-up ex-assassin who arrives armed and covered in blood, regardless of the technicalities of law that protect defectors from the consequences of their Esperan history.

'My knives,' she says. 'Will I get them back?'

'Probably not,' says Leo, half apologetic. 'They're a murder weapon, Isabel.'

It's not murder inside the walls. Just guild business. Always just fucking guild business. 'That was Espera,' she says. 'That's none of their business. I want them back.'

'Why? You're not allowed to use them here.'

Like she doesn't know that. She's not even allowed *scissors*, though maybe Leo thinks he's being subtle about removing the tags on the new clothes he gave her before she'd be in a position to need them. 'I want them back,' she repeats.

'Because you don't feel safe without a weapon?' Leo leans against the door frame. 'It's different here, Bel. You don't need blades to look after yourself. I know it'll take time to adjust, but . . .'

'They're mine.' What doesn't he understand about that? 'They're all I've got left. They're *mine*.'

'I know.' Maybe she's getting through to him; there's something like sympathy on his face now. 'I'm sorry. But this is for the best.'

He leaves with the tray, and Isabel sits numbly, surrounded by the crumpled sheets of her unsettled night in a room that doesn't belong to her. Maybe he's right about getting up and into the world, but this bed is warm, and comfortable; it gives her something to hold and a place to hide from the sharp, cold air of the room and the unknown world outside.

Despite the caffeine slowly spreading through her system, she curls up again, pulling the duvet up to her chin and defiantly closing her eyes. The shadows, the darkness – they don't scare her today, not the way sunlight does. The familiar smiles of the dark are a comfort, like an old enemy in a crowd of strangers.

'You can't stay in bed for ever, you know,' comes Sam's voice, and the bed dips abruptly beneath her weight as she sits down, narrowly missing Isabel's feet. 'Especially since we're going shopping.'

'No, we're not,' says Isabel. With her face buried in the pillow, it comes out as an incoherent grumble.

'Oh, so you *don't* want any shoes apart from those shitty plimsolls?'

Not really. Shoes are for leaving the house, and she doesn't want to leave the house, although they'll probably make her eventually.

Isabel cracks one eye open to look at her tormentor. 'Did Leo put you up to this?'

'No,' says Sam squarely. 'Actually, he told me to stay out of your way for a bit, but I thought that would only make things worse.' She regards Isabel, looking older than her years. 'He doesn't get what it means that Hummingbird took Suzie. When he thinks about sisters, he only thinks about Emma and Jean. I tried to tell him it's different, but he wouldn't listen.'

Isabel rolls over and stares up at the ceiling. 'Is it different?' she asks.

'You know why I hacked Hummingbird?' says Sam, and doesn't wait for an answer: 'To find out if she was dead. Three times I did it, and I couldn't find a trace of her. So I assumed she must be, and that made it easier.'

'Why, because dead's better?' Isabel's hyper-aware of the girl perched on the edge of the mattress. She wants to be alone, but she's lost the ability to make people leave. Funny. She used to be good at that. 'Better dead than like me, is that it? I don't blame you.'

'Will you *stop* trying to tell me what I'm feeling?' Sam snaps. 'She was my sister. Of course I wanted her to live. But I saw what it was doing to her. After you saved her, the first time ... she didn't want Katipo, and when she came back, she was different. She didn't want Hummingbird either, but they took her anyway. I lost my sister when we were eight and I lost her again when we were ten and I was never going to get her back. I just didn't want to think she was suffering.'

Isabel closes her eyes. *She didn't want Katipo.* Her father said the children were grateful, and she never believed him, but she wanted to. She wanted to think maybe they'd chosen it. 'Didn't your parents care?'

'Our parents are dead. We lived with our aunt, and the guilds paid better than the council did.' Sam's voice is flat. That's a hurt she's learned to squash over the years, but that doesn't mean it's gone. Only means it's pressed down into a hard little ball inside her, ready to be used as a weapon.

'There wasn't anyone to fight for us, once they decided they wanted Suzie.'

'Still,' says Isabel, because she's a masochist, 'dead isn't better. At least being part of Hummingbird, there was always a chance she'd get out.'

'Just like you got out,' says Sam. 'Right?'

Leo doesn't understand Isabel, or the way she left part of herself behind. But Sam does, even though she's just a kid and shouldn't know what it's like to be this broken. She looks at Isabel and sees straight through to the shackles that still bind her to the guild, making butterflies of her heartbeats and knives of her breath. Sees the girl who never got out. Will never get out.

Maybe, deep down, there's still a part of Isabel that's twelve years old, too.

'What do you want from me, Sam?' she asks, laid bare by the girl's understanding. 'Do you want me to tell you your sister was screwed either way and it didn't matter if she lived? Because it mattered. It matters that she's dead and it matters that I killed her.'

'So you regret it.'

'Of course I fucking regret it,' says Isabel. 'I didn't want to do it in the first place. They told me – they told me if she died that Mortimer would live, but he didn't, he died anyway, and I killed her for nothing. Fuck, I regret that Hummingbird had her at all, that she didn't ... that she wasn't safe, even after Katipo. But it doesn't matter. My regrets won't fix it.'

Sam gets up. 'I liked Mortimer,' she says thoughtfully. 'I

35

don't know if I'd have chosen him over my sister. If they'd asked. But nobody asked me.'

This would be so much easier if Sam was angry. 'If you want to take your revenge,' says Isabel, 'do it soon, will you? Don't drag it out.'

Sam seems genuinely bewildered. 'Why would I want revenge?'

'Why wouldn't you?' retorts Isabel. 'I killed your twin sister. Most people would consider that grounds to smother me in my sleep.'

'Right, because killing people has solved our problems in the past.' Sam shakes her head. 'You saved her once. I know you didn't choose to get to the point where killing her felt like the only option.'

Everyone in this house seems determined to offer her mercy. Everyone wants to point out some speck of goodness as though it makes up for the rest. But they're ignoring the truth, which is that she's fucked up in the head and rotten to the core. Why would they bother to save her, when this is all there is?

'They broke you, Isabel,' says Sam. 'They hurt you so much that they ripped all the kindness out of you.'

Maybe they did. Maybe they knocked it out like teeth and it'll never grow back. 'I deserve whatever you'd do to me. No one would blame you.'

'I know,' says Sam. 'But I'm not going to be the kind of person who does it.'

Not forgiveness, but kindness. A moment of grace.

Isabel watches Sam walk towards the door, and then says,

'I can't say I'd make a different choice now, if given the same options. But I . . . I *am* sorry.'

'I know.' So certain of everything, when Isabel's sure of nothing at all.

Sam leaves while Isabel's still hunting for a response. Would it have changed anything if she'd known who Suzie was when Ronan gave her the assignment? Did *he* know – did he remember the girl she saved when she was barely more than a child herself?

Would it have mattered to him?

That was Espera. That's over now.

But that's the thing about death: no amount of running and no amount of wishing will ever make it *over*.

4

NEVOLATA (UNWANTED)

Three days later and Isabel is perched on the deep windowsill in the front room, looking out at her new world. The street is red and black and grey: a shabby terrace of narrow houses with their crimson bricks; black railings around the gardens and black detailing on the windowsills and porches; grey concrete pavement. She misses the colours of Espera, the shifting solar panels of the roads and the street art covering every surface. This place looks the way grief feels: blood red and washed out and fading under the pale sun.

In the kitchen, Leo and Ant are arguing. The closed door does little to muffle their voices, and the threads of conversation drift through along with the scent of cooking.

'You need to claim it,' says Ant, with the tone of somebody who has said this before.

'You know I can't.' Leo. Tired. He always sounds tired. He works too much: days at a nearby bookshop, long hours into the night for the smugglers, in whatever role they need him to play.

'Why not? In Espera, sure, anonymity was the only option – but we're safe now.'

'We don't know that.'

'It would help, Leo.' A crash, like Ant's punctuated this by slamming a saucepan onto the hob. 'A named author's way more convincing than an anonymous source. Plus it's evidence that you're an abolitionist. That we're *all* abolitionists. And after that picture of Isabel—'

'It's not her fault,' Leo cuts in, leaping instinctively to her defence.

'It's not about whose fault it is. The fact remains that when people think of Espera, when they think of us, that'll be what comes to mind first.'

The picture. They showed it to Isabel at the detention centre. She didn't realise it was being taken, but she was beyond realising anything much by that point. It shows her when they first found her, before the van and the detention centre and trying to remember who the fuck she was and how she got there: squinting in the sunlight after days in the dark, covered in blood and delirious with dehydration.

Isabel's got to admit, it's not her best angle.

'But we're civilians,' says Leo. 'And they know that. They know it's not the same.'

'Do they?' says Ant, cynical as ever. 'They've got no idea what it means to be Esperan. As far as they know, we're all killers.'

'We've got papers.'

'*You*'ve got papers. Me and Sam have got the best forgeries that twenty-four hours' notice could provide, and yours are hardly legal, anyway.' Ant sighs heavily, followed by another thump. 'Look, I can't make you claim it. But I think you should.'

'It's not just my work.' A pause, and then: 'You could claim it, if it matters so much. I don't mind.'

'You're a better option,' says Ant. 'I'm a hunted man, Leo. Wouldn't take much digging to find out why. But you – pacifist adoptee library assistant with a tragic backstory? Even an outsider couldn't be afraid of that.'

Isabel hears a dull *smack*, like Leo's punched Ant in the shoulder. 'Not so much of a pacifist that I can't do that,' says Leo, but his tone is light. 'And I was fostered. Not adopted.'

'Even better. They'd eat it up. *And* you're Black. *And* you're trans.'

'Oh, fuck off, Ant. Don't tell me you're buying into their shit about that.'

'Outsiders care about that stuff,' says Ant. 'Might as well take advantage of it.'

'They care in the wrong way,' says Leo, the humour fading from his voice. 'It would only make me a target.' The pots and pans clatter. 'I'll think about it. But Sam doesn't need the attention at school, and with Isabel living here ... well, that won't help our image as abolitionists, will it? Better not to draw attention to ourselves.'

'So she's staying, is she?'

A deep sigh from Leo. 'I signed the papers, Ant, we agreed—'

'You decided,' Ant interrupts. 'You decided to take her in. She killed Sam's *sister*, and you—'

Leo cuts him off. 'I didn't know about that.' He sounds wretched, wrecked, because Ant's right: Isabel is fundamentally unworthy of Leo's help, and she'll only bring more trouble. If she had anywhere to go, she'd leave right now, save them the awkwardness of kicking her out.

But she's only here in the first place because she's got no other options, so Isabel stays curled up on her windowsill, half listening, half staring out at a world she doesn't recognise.

'Well, don't come crying to me when it bites you in the arse,' says Ant. 'Where is she, anyway?'

'Front room,' says Leo immediately. Isabel's surprised; she didn't think he'd noticed her here. 'Probably listening to every word we're saying. Which reminds me.' There's a scrape – a pot being dragged across to another hob. 'Keep an eye on this for a minute, will you?'

Footsteps. The kitchen door opens, and a moment later Leo comes into the front room. He gives Isabel a small smile. 'All right?'

She shrugs in response.

'I brought you a present,' he offers, and holds up his rucksack. 'Thought it might cheer you up.'

41

That seems unlikely. But she says, 'What is it?', because showing interest will make Leo smile again.

It does. He rummages through the bag and produces two small paperbacks, which he puts on the windowsill next to Isabel. 'Here. These are for you.'

Classic Leo, still thinking books can fix everything. She regards them for a moment, then picks them up. One is in German, the other in Russian. They're a little battered, their barcodes hidden behind discount stickers, but they're a gift. Hers. Something she owns, in a world where she has nothing.

'I remembered you were good at languages, before,' he says. 'Couldn't remember the whole list, but those two came in today . . .'

The bookshop pays him a pittance, but he loves it: she sees his old passion for stories in his face as he watches her examine the books.

'When did I tell you I spoke Russian?' Isabel asks, flicking through the first book. A long-neglected part of her brain stirs into life as she tries to puzzle out the language. She's rusty, unable to pick out more than a few words, but it'll come back. That kind of thing always does.

'You didn't,' he says. 'Jem did. Said it was why she hired you.'

Jem – the librarian who gave Isabel a job, and a brief taste of a normal life. That feels like a lifetime ago. 'How do you even remember that?'

Leo shrugs. 'I figured it was worth a try. Knew I could always return the books if I was wrong.'

Instinctively, Isabel grips it a little tighter. *Hers*. 'You … you weren't wrong,' she says, stumbling on her gratitude. 'Thank you.'

He's still watching her. 'See,' he says. 'You're good at something other than killing people.'

Isabel considers asking him why he thinks her father taught her half a dozen languages, constantly testing her to ensure she kept them sharp. But if he hasn't figured out how far the guilds' power reaches, she won't be the one to break it to him. 'Still haven't got any qualifications.'

'True,' he admits. 'Maybe you should talk to Emily about that.'

'Emily?'

'Your caseworker. You've got a meeting tomorrow.' He perches for a moment on the arm of the nearest chair, pretending to settle, unwilling to commit. 'She might have some ideas.'

Isabel had forgotten about her caseworker, let alone that she was called Emily and that they've got a meeting tomorrow. She listens to the muffled sound of Ant swearing in the kitchen and then looks at Leo. 'What is it he wants you to claim?'

'So you *were* listening,' he says, looking faintly pleased to be proved right. 'You remember our history book?'

Isabel nods: the illegal, unlicensed history the abolitionists wrote and began distributing across Espera is half the reason they're here, since Leo's part in writing it is what made him a fugitive.

'Well, it's a pretty different perspective on Espera than

43

anything these outsiders have got access to,' he continues. 'Civilian history, you know? They barely even know Espera's *got* civilians. So the smugglers were helping us distribute copies out here, trying to raise money to keep the Free Press afloat, but it's begun circulating beyond that.'

The Free Press is the voice of the radical abolitionist underworld in Espera, its newssheet their main way of coordinating resistance and its publications the home of their ideologies. It's how Leo and Mortimer met, and it's a good reason why Isabel should never have been friends with either of them. It was the Free Press who published her identity and ensured she'd never be safe in Espera again – the Free Press who forced her to run.

But the Free Press is also Leo, and Leo is all Isabel's got left in the world.

'The book's still anonymous, isn't it?' she says, piecing together Leo's words and the argument she overheard. 'And Ant thinks it shouldn't be.'

Inside Espera, claiming authorship would have got them all killed. Outside, it might still: if the guilds think they're influencing global opinion of Espera, they could easily send an external operative to eliminate them. Escaping the walls doesn't mean escaping the threat.

'Right.' Leo shrugs. 'I'd prefer to stay anonymous. But there've been doubts about its authenticity, and about our status as abolitionists. Once people know we're from Espera, they tend to automatically assume we're a threat – Ant's right about that much. So we'll see.'

Isabel swallows her instinct to beg him to keep it secret and leave the guilds hunting for an author inside the city walls. 'Is he right about me, too? About the photo?'

He frowns, like he hoped she'd have conveniently missed that part of the conversation. 'No,' he says decisively. 'Ant's being a knob. Besides, they didn't print your name, nobody knows you're living here, and nobody will recognise you now that you've showered. Forget the photo.'

But Isabel can't, because it's proof. Proof of how she got here, proof that it wasn't a nightmare. 'I didn't mean to cause trouble. When I asked for you. I just ...' *I didn't want to be alone.*

'Never apologise to me for that,' says Leo. 'You said you'd follow me one day, and you did. That's it. That's all there is to it.' There's so much more to it than that. 'But you can do me a favour, if you want to be helpful.'

Isabel can't imagine what she can do for Leo, when she's useless and he's carrying the weight of the world already. 'What is it?'

'I need you to take Sam to her book club on Saturday. I've got work and can't rearrange.'

Panic rushes in on her. 'I can't.'

'She knows the way. She just needs someone to go on the bus with her. You can wait in the library café until she's done.'

It's Tuesday now, and Saturday is too soon, too sudden. She hasn't dared go further than the garden path since she was brought here, and the thought of taking a bus across the unfamiliar city triggers choking fear. 'Why can't Ant do it?'

45

'He's working too. It'll be fine, Isabel. I know you can do this.'

'Can't she . . . can't she go by herself, if she knows the way?'

'She's twelve,' says Leo, as if that's an answer. 'We're supposed to be responsible guardians.'

Isabel isn't a responsible guardian for anyone, not even herself – though perhaps Leo's trying to be kind by pretending she's not the one who needs looking after. She wants to agree, to take some of the weight he's carrying, but her old fearlessness is long gone and the task seems impossible. She's lost, rendered helpless by the strangeness of the city.

She leans her head against the window and looks out. All those people, walking unafraid beneath the empty grey sky. People who can go anywhere, be anything, and if that means turning their back on the walled city to the east and pretending they're not witness to its atrocities, they'll do so readily and without a twinge of conscience, because it's easier that way.

'I know you're scared,' says Leo, and she doesn't bother to deny it. 'But Sam will be with you, and it's only a library. This will be good for you.'

Good for you. Like a vitamin, or an exercise regime.

'Leo?' calls Ant from the kitchen. 'Something's burning.'

Leo swears, then calls back, 'I don't know how you survived in that basement if you're this bad at cooking.' He looks at Isabel. 'Will you eat dinner with us today?'

He's been patient, bringing her a plate and letting her pick at it on her own, away from prying eyes. But after nearly a week in this house, it's about time she started pretending to function. 'Okay,' she says, unwillingly.

Leo smiles in triumph and pushes himself up from the chair. 'Then I'd better go and rescue it,' he says. 'Come through in a few and see if I've succeeded.'

Isabel nods, and watches Leo head back to the kitchen. Very carefully, she stretches out her legs and places them on the floor. They're stiff, and her feet have forgotten how to bear her weight. As soon as she's upright, she's conscious that she needs to pee, and wonders why her body didn't tell her that sooner.

My body doesn't care any more, she thinks. *It'd kill me if it could.* But that's not news; she's been fighting a long, quiet war with her body since she was seventeen and her father's poison turned it against her.

The bathroom means confronting the horror of the mirror and a face she hardly recognises. Her hair's getting longer, the turquoise dye faded; she uses one of Sam's abandoned hairclips to pin it back from her face, though that doesn't disguise the state of it. The zip of her hoodie is only pulled up to her sternum, and the tattoos twined around the scars on her collarbones and chest are easily visible. It doesn't matter outside Espera. She doesn't have to hide here.

But without the masks, she's not sure she can bear the sight of herself. That girl in the mirror – that's Isabel Ryans, Isabel before the Moth, a girl who died at seventeen now resurrected and wearing her face. A girl who is scared, directionless and broken.

At least the old Isabel knew what she wanted. Now she's

got the escape she dreamed of, it feels like another kind of captivity.

It's a relief, after that, to close the bathroom door and go into the kitchen, where Leo is spooning food onto plates. It only looks slightly charred, and she doesn't need to ask to know that he's made sure it's safe for her.

'Ah, good,' he says, at the sight of her. 'Will you call Sam, please? She's upstairs.'

Sam's bedroom is in the attic, tucked under the eaves. The door is open, the sound of her music drifting out, and she's sitting at the little desk in the corner, ostensibly doing homework. Even from the doorway, it's clear she's struggling to focus, drawing spirals in the margins of the page.

'Dinner time,' says Isabel.

Sam jumps at the sound of her voice. 'How long have you been there?'

'About three seconds. How's the homework?'

She throws down her pen in disgust. 'Boring and pointless. I know all this stuff already. I don't see why I've got to do it again.'

So that you'll have more choices than the rest of us, thinks Isabel, but Sam's heard it all before. 'So you can prove to them how clever you are,' she says instead. 'Now come and eat. Leo's waiting.'

5

OBEA (OBEDIENT)

Isabel spends Wednesday morning wrestling with the first chapter of the Russian novel Leo bought her, noting down unfamiliar words to look up later and trying to muddle through without them. The years have stolen more of her Russian than she realised, and the novel's vocabulary is frequently unfamiliar, being less acutely concerned with the specifics of arms dealing and poison manufacture than her father's lessons. She should have known she didn't have the skillset for a civilian life.

She lets the book and her eyes close for a moment, but the doorbell startles her awake. Ah, shit. Emily.

Reluctantly, Isabel makes for the front door. She might have forgotten her caseworker's name, but as soon as she sees

Emily's face, she remembers her from the detention centre: dark hair, light brown skin, oversized glasses and a smile she doesn't seem to know how to turn off.

Emily unbuttons her coat and hangs it up without asking permission. 'Where are we headed then, Isabel?'

Isabel gestures awkwardly. 'Living room?' She spends most of her time there, perched in the window, and it's a communal space – less of a violation than inviting Emily into her own room.

Her caseworker accepts this choice wordlessly and settles herself in an armchair, scanning the room as though it'll offer some clues about how to deal with Isabel. She's worked with Esperans before, but it's usually civilians who defect.

'Kiel vi fartas, Isabel?' Emily asks, when she's completed her survey of the room. *How are you?*

Now she remembers why they assigned this woman to her: because she speaks Esperanto. Emily's got it into her head that this will set Isabel at ease – an understandable conclusion to draw, since she spent a lot of time at the detention centre not speaking anything else, too shell-shocked and exhausted to manage English. But hearing it now, with that strange outsider's accent, doesn't help at all.

'Fine,' lies Isabel, in English, and perches on the settee across from Emily. Replying in Esperanto feels like ceding territory she doesn't want to give.

Emily capitulates easily, switching back to English. 'What have you been doing since I last saw you?'

'Not much.' Sleeping. Doubting the evidence of her own

eyes. Second-guessing herself. Emily wants more than that, though. She manages, 'I'm still adjusting.'

'To living here with your friend, or to the city?'

Maybe she should've chosen the windowsill; then she'd have somewhere to look that isn't a pointed avoidance of Emily's gaze. 'Both. Mostly the latter.'

'It's a difficult transition,' says her caseworker sympathetically. 'Everyone I've worked with from Espera has needed time to adjust. But they've all made very successful—'

'I get it,' Isabel interrupts. She should wait this out, pretend to be the person they want her to be, but she *can't*, not when they're acting like she's no different from every civilian who ever fled the city. 'They're all functional, productive members of society. Good for them.'

Emily's lips tighten, but she doesn't reprimand her. She's too nice for that, sympathetic no matter how unlikeable Isabel is. It would be easier, Isabel thinks, if someone would just snap and yell at her. She knows how to deal with that.

Emily says, 'Have you had any more nightmares?'

Isabel's grip tightens on the arm of the settee. She woke up screaming every night in that fucking detention centre, watching them all die over and over again. Or it's her mother, or Ronan's knife at her throat, or – on rare nights, when her mind is being particularly cruel – her father's lab, like nothing's changed at all. The nightmares are well-documented in her file, so of course Emily knows about them. Doesn't mean Isabel wants to talk about it.

'Not since I came here,' she says, half truthfully. The

51

nightmares persist, but they wake her less often these days. It's the daytime memories she dreads, the way they force themselves in without warning and rip her away from the present.

'So you're doing better, since you came to live here?'

A leading question if she's ever heard one, and Isabel doesn't want them to take her away, so she nods and doesn't mention the shadows, or the hallucinations. If it *was* a hallucination.

Emily writes this down. 'Is that your book?' she asks.

With some surprise, Isabel follows her gaze to the coffee table, her notebook of new vocab tucked inside the Russian novel as a bookmark. 'Yes. Leo bought it for me,' she adds, in case Emily thinks she stole it.

'You speak Russian?'

Isabel shrugs. 'I did. I'm rusty.'

Emily's smile is slightly uncertain. 'That's great, Isabel. That's a really useful skill.'

Isabel narrows her eyes. 'Then why do you look so nervous about it?'

Her caseworker laughs awkwardly, embarrassed to have been caught. 'I'm not nervous. It's just . . . well, Russian is . . .'

Ah. So Emily's made the connections Leo didn't. 'You think it'll look suspicious that I speak Russian. Like I might start hiring out my services now that I'm no longer bound to the guild.' Leo's so trusting – it wouldn't have occurred to him that Isabel's language skills could be anything except an asset. But this world will never stop seeing her as a threat.

'I'm not saying that,' begins Emily, but it's unconvincing.

'I think it's good that you have language skills. I'm only apprehensive about how it might be perceived.'

Isabel leans over and retrieves the other book from the windowsill, holding it up. 'Kafka,' she says. 'German. How are the optics on that?'

'Better,' Emily acknowledges. 'And believe me, I'm not suggesting there's anything wrong with reading Dostoyevsky, but in your specific circumstances ...'

'Yeah, I know. Everyone thinks I'm waiting for an opportunity to assassinate the Prime Minister or whatever.' She drops the second book on the coffee table next to the first. 'Like anyone would hire a defector.'

This was the wrong thing to say. Emily's cheerful face creases into a concerned frown. 'Isabel, you need to understand the position you're in.'

Isabel abandons the settee and the pretence of calm and goes over to the windowsill, hopping up lightly and curling her legs to her chest. 'I understand,' she says, staring determinedly out of the window. 'Nobody wants me here. *I* don't want me here. They'd rather deport me back to Espera, right? That's why you're here, to check I'm *integrating* properly and take me away if I'm not. Well, I promise you this – if I wanted to make connections with the Russian government, I wouldn't be using *Notes from Underground* to do it.'

'I know that.' Emily exhales and sits back, visibly trying to order her thoughts. 'Isabel, I'm trying to help you. You're considered high risk. It's only a technicality in the Esperan treaty that means a guild defector can be treated as a refugee and not a terrorist – and some people are advocating for revising that. I'm trying not to give them a reason.'

Isabel contemplates this. She thinks again of the photo of herself, the blood, her bad reputation casting its shadow over her civilian housemates. 'And if you decide I'm a danger to others?' she asks, giving Emily a once-over – she doesn't look fragile, but she's no match for Isabel.

There's a long silence, and then Emily says, 'Right now, I'm more concerned that you're a danger to yourself.'

The words hit Isabel one by one and sink like lead. She wants to refute the point, but she's got no evidence to support her argument. *I'm not going to kill myself*, she tries to say, but the words are strangled by the reality of feeling every night like it would make things easier if she never woke up.

She says, 'If the city doesn't want me, it shouldn't bother them if I die.'

Too late, she realises this is the worst thing she could've said if she's trying to convince Emily that she's not actively suicidal, but she can't take it back now. Emily leans forward, as though that makes a difference when Isabel's still perched halfway across the room. 'I want you to see a therapist,' she says. 'You're grieving, and you have PTSD. I think it would help you process things.'

Isabel shakes her head. 'No.' Her mind's the only thing that's her own. Her mess, her trauma, but hers to deal with, hers to break down and put back together. And no outsider therapist will ever understand what it means to have come from Espera. To have come from the guild.

'I thought you'd say that.' Here come the threats. Can they *make* her see a therapist? She doesn't know what the rules are here, or what they can do to her. 'I'm going to give you the business card of somebody I trust, someone who might be able to help. If you decide you want help, call her, and tell her I referred you. Okay?'

Not a threat. Isabel blinks in surprise as Emily places a card on the coffee table next to the books. 'You're not going to make me?' she asks, before she can stop herself.

Emily sits back. 'Therapy tends to work best when you're willing to put the work in,' she says. 'You need to feel safe before you can heal. Forcing you to do something you're not ready for is unlikely to help.' She inclines her head towards the books. 'It's good that you're reading. Maybe I can recommend some books that might help with what you're going through, until you're ready to talk about it.'

She killed her way out of that Comma hospital, can't even begin to guess how many bodies she left in her wake. Isabel highly doubts there are self-help books about that. But—

'Okay,' she says, because cooperating is how she stays in this house and not in a cell or extradited back to Espera. And she thinks that's what she wants – to stay – because she's not allowed to want to go home. There's nothing to go back to, anyway. But for the sake of honesty, Isabel adds, 'I won't promise to read them.'

Emily smiles, a real smile this time. 'Okay. Shall I give the titles to Leo?'

Right, because Isabel's life is filtered through proxies these days. After years of fighting for her independence, she's reduced to relying on others to do the simplest tasks for her – and Leo never asked to be anyone's parent.

'I can get them,' she says. 'I'm taking Sam to the library on Saturday.'

Emily smiles again. She doesn't ask who Sam is, so that must be in her notes too. 'That's great,' she replies, as if she means it. 'Tell me more about that.'

Isabel shrugs. 'Nothing to tell. She's in a book club. Leo's working and asked me to take her instead. I can get the books then.'

'I'm really proud of you, Isabel.'

Isabel looks away, embarrassed by the praise, unwilling to admit she's terrified of fucking this up the way she's ruined everything else. Such a small thing to seem so impossible. 'Be proud of me after the fact,' she says. 'Don't know yet how wrong it'll go.'

'I have faith in you.'

She does, doesn't she? Funny, that. Maybe it's because the other Esperans she's worked with have been innocent civilians, and they've all turned their lives around and become thriving citizens once given the opportunity. Emily doesn't understand what it means that Isabel is different, doesn't comprehend the violence she's lived with for the last twenty years.

Doesn't know the details, either. Doesn't know about Suzie, doesn't know how many people she's killed, doesn't know that in a city full of murderers, Isabel's the one people hated the most.

'Yeah, well,' says Isabel, staring out at the front garden again. 'We'll see.'

Emily doesn't press the point. Instead, she says, 'I've got a few forms for you to fill in. Do you want to do them together?'

Isabel shrugs. 'Sure.' She can't imagine caring enough to complete them by herself.

Her caseworker retrieves the papers and a pen. 'Easy questions first. What's your full name?'

'Does it matter?' That's genuine curiosity, not resistance. 'I haven't got any valid ID. You could put anything on there and they wouldn't be able to argue with it.'

Emily pauses. 'What would you like me to write?' she asks. 'If you think choosing a new name might help you, we could discuss that.'

For a brief moment, Isabel considers the idea of becoming somebody else. Maybe she really did leave Isabel Ryans in that tunnel below the city, a shattered corpse of her past self. She could walk into the world as somebody new, and never hear her old name again.

But she'd still have all her scars.

'No.' Isabel Ryans is written into her skin, down into her bones, all the way through her. She moves the way Comma taught her to move, speaks with an Esperan accent, carries her parents' cruelty in her body. 'Isabel Ryans. That's it. That's all there is.'

'No middle name?'

'No.'

'Okay.' Emily writes it down. *Isabel Ryans*. Black ink,

white paper. Indelibly a part of this new-old world beyond the walls.

But no amount of paperwork can make her into someone who belongs here.

6

KOLERA (ANGRY)

Saturday, and panic looms.

Clothes. That's step one. Getting dressed. She can do this much, has done it before, is familiar with using clothes as armour.

Isabel stares at the open wardrobe and feels acid sting her throat as her fear makes itself known. Stupid, pointless fear. All she's got to do is pick up the clothes and put them on and—

and lace her shoes and leave the house and take the bus and go to the library and take Sam to her club and find the titles Emily gave her and get a library card and say as little as possible so nobody asks about her accent and be normal and pretend and leave the house and leave the house and leave the house—

Just the clothes. She's not allowed to panic about the rest until she's dressed.

With shaking hands, she grabs one of the T-shirts Sam and Leo picked out for her and pulls it over her head before she can second-guess the choice. She doesn't look down; she doesn't want to see herself. Being embodied will only make it worse. Then she rummages until she finds a pair of jeans and pulls those on, too.

Step one done. That wasn't so hard, was it?

Sam's waiting downstairs with her book bag and a wallet, which Leo wanted to give to Isabel. She refused it: she doesn't understand the money here (hasn't tried, for all Leo promises her it's easier than Esperan pounds, shillings and pence) and anyway, Sam's the more trustworthy of the two of them. The kid looks up and smiles at the sight of Isabel.

'You ready?' she asks.

No. 'Nearly.' Her only shoes are the plimsolls they gave her at the detention centre, flat and ugly and lacking in arch support, but if she laces them tightly enough, they'll do.

Sam eyes them with distaste. 'We have *got* to get you some boots,' she says. 'It's like you're naked without them.'

Isabel wishes she wanted her boots back. Her boots and her leather jacket – the fierce front she showed the world. But she'd rather hide, like a creature pulled from its shell, spineless and unarmoured.

At least boots would have taken longer to lace. With her shoes on, there's no reason to delay walking out of the front door, and while that shouldn't be a big deal – she's been in the front garden twice this week, on Leo's orders – it still feels unbearable.

When did you stop running, Isabel? When she lost the will to go on.

Sam doesn't stick around to watch her cross the threshold. She races up the garden path, swinging the gate aside, so that Isabel is obliged to follow her, and holds out a hand when Isabel reaches the pavement.

Isabel eyes it. 'I don't need you to hold my hand,' she says uncertainly.

'Maybe I need *you* to hold *mine*,' says Sam, which is such a charming attempt at a lie that Isabel eventually gives in. The warmth of Sam's grip is comforting, grounding her even as the grey sky above them balloons into an unfathomable expanse and threatens to crush her.

She keeps her eyes trained on the cracked paving slabs and lets Sam lead her to the bus stop. The bus: another challenge. The first vehicle she remembers since her escape is the blacked-out van that took her to the detention centre. They kept her bound in the back, feverish, dehydrated, and sticky with blood; she passed the journey in a haze of nightmarish confusion, not entirely sure she wasn't dead. The second vehicle was the taxi she and Leo took when he got her out, and by that point, she was too numb to process anything much, head pounding and eyes sore from weeks under relentless fluorescent lights.

She doesn't know how she'll react to being on the bus, surrounded by other people. She wishes she had a knife and she's glad that she doesn't, because the weight of it in her hand would be comforting and because she doesn't trust herself not to use it.

When the bus eventually pulls up, Sam hands her Leo's bus pass – 'Don't lose it,' she warns – and shows her how to swipe it. It's half full on board already, but there are a few seats left towards the back.

'Want the window seat?' says Sam.

The window seat means being trapped, unable to get to the aisle, but it also means Sam as a barrier between her and the rest of the world. Isabel nods and slips in, pressing herself up against the glass. Sam drops into the seat beside her.

The window shakes as the bus pulls away from the kerb and into the Saturday traffic. Isabel pretends that's the only reason she's trembling. 'Tell me about your book club,' she asks Sam, trying to keep her voice steady.

'Oh, well, Leo made me join.' Sam's voice is a tether to reality and a distraction from the world around her. 'Thought I needed some friends my own age, and people at school think I'm weird, so I wasn't going to find them there. At first I wasn't sure about it, because, like, I *lived* in a library. But the books here are different. There are so many of them.'

'No censors,' manages Isabel.

'No censors,' Sam agrees, and chatters on about the books they've read together already, each session another hour of discussion, with biscuits at the end. 'And, I mean, the biscuits are mostly why I go. But I'm glad. That he made me join, I mean.'

Isabel takes this as an unsubtle reminder that this whole excursion is supposed to be *good for her*, and wonders again why everyone's trying so hard to rehabilitate her. She wouldn't have bothered.

She spends the rest of the journey staring out of the window at interminable terraced streets, churches on street corners, and a vibrantly striped building that Sam tells her is a mosque. Another reminder that she's no longer in Espera: religion, out in the open.

Just as the motion of the bus is becoming unbearable, Sam tugs on her arm. 'This is us,' she says. 'Come on.'

The red bricks of the residential streets are nowhere to be seen. Sam's pulling her towards an edifice of a building: brown stone, columns of pinkish granite either side of the door, wrought-iron fences adorned with owls of blue-green oxidised copper.

'*This* is the library?' Isabel was expecting a small flat-roofed building and the smell of worn carpet, not this temple to bibliophilia and civic pride.

'Yep,' says Sam. 'Hurry up, or I won't be able to get you a library card before club starts.'

Isabel follows her up the steps. Inside, they pass through glass security gates, but otherwise it's like no library Isabel has ever seen. Sam heads straight through the wooden doors ahead, ignoring the vast, intricately carved archway overhead and the stained glass splintering the afternoon light into a multitude of colours, but Isabel follows slowly. Not since Espera has she seen colours like this: the tiled walls, the goldish stone of the carved archways, the floral motifs of the stained glass in every window. Ahead is a more familiar sight: grey carpet and low, pale shelves crammed with colourful books. But when she looks up, she sees the colonnades and arches of the higher floors, all the way up to the skylight in the roof. Even the stairs are tiled, the steps a mosaic of colour, as though ascent itself is an art.

'You didn't tell me,' she says to Sam, without pausing to consider whether the words make sense. 'That it looked like this.'

Sam grins. 'Wait until you see the café,' she says. 'Now come on. We need to get you a library card.'

With one last glance around, Isabel follows her. Sam is fearless, marching up to the inquiry desk to ask about registering a new member – but she would be, wouldn't she? The vaulted ceilings and ornate stonework might be nothing like the dark basement where Sam spent the last couple of years, but she was still practically raised by librarians, a feral child among crowded shelves.

The librarian asks for proof of address, and Isabel's heart sinks. But Sam's come prepared: from her bag, she retrieves the document authorising Isabel to live with Leo. The librarian gives both it and Isabel a curious look, but she pushes the form across the desk for Isabel to sign without further questions.

Isabel does, and takes the card she's handed with a strange sense of relief, like she's been given a small piece of herself back.

'Okay,' says Sam. 'This is where I leave you. I'll meet you in the lobby at four, yeah?'

'I—' Of course she was going to be left alone. That was the whole point. But the library's so *big*, and she's got no idea where to start looking for the books on Emily's list.

'You can ask Oreolu if you need help,' Sam tells her, gesturing to the librarian. 'I'm sure she'll help you find things. And you can use the computers if you want.'

Isabel eyes them warily, clutching her new library card so tightly it digs into her palm. 'Sure,' she says. 'I'll see you later.'

Sam gives her one last encouraging smile, not fooled by her attempt at nonchalance, and leaves her. Isabel takes a moment to breathe in the familiar smell of paper and plastic and carpet and people. It's a library. She can do libraries. It's going to be all right.

'She's right, you know,' says Oreolu, startling her. 'You can ask me for help. Are you looking for anything in particular?'

The librarian is hardly intimidating, with her fuzzy, pale green jumper and her short natural hair forming a cheerful cloud around her head, but Isabel still doesn't want to show her Emily's list of recommendations, the titles weighed down by words like *trauma* and *bereavement* and *violence*. She doesn't want to watch Oreolu's expression become one of pity and concern for the broken creature in front of her; she'd rather remain a stranger with a brand-new library card and no history.

So, after too long a pause, Isabel shakes her head. 'Just browsing.'

'All right. Let me know if you need a hand.' The librarian gives her a friendly smile, but Isabel can't shake the feeling that she somehow failed the interaction.

At first it's all she can do to wander among the shelves, taking in the colours of the books. After so long with little to look at, the sheer quantity is overwhelming. It takes time for her eyes to focus on the titles and the signage, but eventually she finds her way to the non-fiction section, and from there to self-help and psychology.

Nobody is looking at her. Nobody cares which books she slides surreptitiously off the shelf, so there's no reason for the hot flush of shame pooling in her stomach as she scans the titles. But it's there anyway, her chest tight as she skims the blurbs. *Trauma. Abuse.* Can you even call it that, does she deserve those words, after everything she's done? *Healing. Recovery.* Is she worthy of that? Is she allowed to want that?

Kneeling beside the shelf, she sinks back onto her heels, staring at the volume in her hands. The title blurs, and she swipes angrily at her tears before it registers that she's crying, for the first time since ... since when? Since she fled the city. Since they all died. Since she lost everything.

The book creaks as she opens it, the protective plastic cover too tight around the spine. *You are not a victim*, says the first page. *You are a survivor.*

That's as far as she gets. The book falls from her hands and she curls instinctively into a ball, leaning against the shelf so that the bite of it against her spine reminds her that she's here, that she exists in physical space. She can't do this. It was stupid to think she could do this: come to a place like this, a public place, and open up all her old wounds, the ones buried so deep she could almost forget about them. And anyway, she doesn't deserve to, because these books were written for people who got hurt, not people who hurt others. When they talk about *child abuse*, they're not talking about her, a child capable of killing.

And everyone's dead, and she's here, and she's got the audacity to think she's fucking *traumatised*. At least she's alive. At least she got out. She's grateful, right, that she got out? If she didn't want to live, she wouldn't have run. She wouldn't have abandoned Laura, left Daragh's body on the floor, left Mortimer. Wouldn't have left Emma's grave untended and run without knowing where she was going because she was too much of a coward to stay, and – and anyway, her mother's dead, she shot her, she doesn't have anything to be afraid of any more, she escaped, so why is she—

'You all right, duck?'

Isabel looks up and sees Oreolu with a cart full of books to shelve and a concerned smile.

It's too late to cover the titles of the books piled next to her, but she's not going to talk about any of this to a stranger. With considerable effort, she nods. 'Thank you,' she manages, when what she wants to say is, *please go*.

The librarian leaves, reluctantly. Isabel's grateful. It still takes her several long minutes to convince her muscles to relax, to emerge from her tight little ball, to stand up. Her body refuses to believe she's safe, no matter how far she runs.

The library hasn't got every book Emily recommended, but it's got enough. Isabel makes a little pile of them and goes in search of the self-service machine, tucking them into her bag as soon as they're checked out. Only when the last of the titles is hidden away can she breathe freely again, and there's still time to kill before she can collect Sam and go home.

She makes her way upstairs, trailing her hand along the tiles as she goes. From the mezzanine, the stonework and stained glass are more beautiful than ever, but Isabel forces herself to keep climbing, making her way up, and up. She pauses at the entrance to the Art Library, thinking wistfully of Emma, but she's fairly sure she'll break down if she spends any time there, so she keeps going until she reaches the nearly silent reading room of the Local History floor.

It's another grand room, the kind Espera has never known: all high ceilings and archways and a wood-panelled balcony running around the room, researchers working diligently at long desks in the centre. The shelves are filled with weighty tomes: bound newspapers, voter records, historic maps.

And then she sees it.

Espera, 1915–present.

It's a small section, perhaps four shelves in one of the room's overly grand alcoves, but Isabel wasn't expecting it. How could people – outsiders – write books about Espera, when they've never seen it, and don't know what it's like? The fact that Leo's wretched history book is causing drama even here made her think they knew nothing of the city.

But these books say otherwise. Lurid covers with grandiose

titles like *The Dark Flight of Death* jostle for space with sober, academic tomes. Isabel pulls out a book at random: *From Hope to Fear: The Changing Face of Espera in the 20th Century*. She shoves it back onto the shelf.

They know. They've always known. Of course they have. It's the outside world that enables Espera to exist – buying its weapons, hiring its agents, trading with the guilds. They knew what they were facilitating, and they did it anyway.

She takes down book after book, skimming the blurbs, flicking through the pages. Few of them seem interested in the inhabitants of Espera, always its first victims; they're more interested in the impact on *their* world. *Chemical weapons created by pioneers in Espera were instrumental in exacerbating conflict in Northern Ireland*, one of them tells her, and she can't read any further because she's thinking about Daragh and Ronan, their grandmother fleeing that same conflict and finding shelter in 'neutral' Espera. So much for neutral. She's willing to bet every refugee who found safety behind those walls was running from a war the city had fed and encouraged.

Abruptly, Isabel realises that she's angry. It's been so long since she felt anything except grey and tired, she thought she'd lost the capacity. But here on these shelves are all the lies of her city exposed, and all the proof that they were abandoned deliberately. No doubt the people of this country excuse their government's atrocities by pointing to Espera and saying, *well, it could be worse*, like they're not the ones allowing it to be worse.

Everyone in this city is complicit. Everyone in this *country* is complicit.

Even through the fog of grief clouding her thoughts, Isabel has seen enough of this world to realise one thing: no matter the darkness inside her, no matter how rotten her core, she would never have become what she is without the city that shaped and moulded her. Maybe some part of her is fundamentally broken and would never have been kind the way Leo manages to be kind; maybe violence was always in her nature. But this outside world would have sanded down her edges, and instead Espera sharpened them into points and sent her out to do as much harm as possible.

And these people, all of them, let that happen. And they've got the nerve to consider *her* a threat.

Anger doesn't chase away her grief, but it lights it up, crimson and sharp and demanding to be heard.

7

BELA (BEAUTIFUL)

When Sam finds her, Isabel's sitting on one of the mezzanines, her back against the wrought-iron railing that separates staircase from open space, tracing the mosaic floor with her fingertips. The girl eyes her, trying to gauge her mood, before giving up and asking, 'Are you okay?'

Isabel shrugs. She's not sure that word ever applies these days, but she's calmer than she was an hour ago. The fire of her anger has faded, leaving her with bitterness and nothing to keep her warm. At least now she knows she's still capable of feeling something.

'Got some books,' she says, nudging her bag with her foot.

Sam seems pleased. 'Want to see the café?'

Isabel frowns. 'Is there much to see?'

The kid laughs. She grabs Isabel's hand, pulling her to her feet with surprising strength. 'You'll like it,' she promises. 'It's the same colour your hair used to be.'

Isabel snatches up her bag and lets herself be pulled through the building until they reach the café. She can hear the clatter of crockery and the din of overlapping voices, and her dread builds. 'I'm not sure if I can—'

'Just long enough to look,' says Sam. 'Then we can go.'

Isabel takes a deep breath. She can do that. She'll look at whatever Sam wants to show her, and then she can leave.

But the moment she sees the room, the noise fades away like it was never there at all.

The colours strike her first. The walls: textured blue-green tiles, broken up by a border of red and gold blocks. The floor: scuffed parquet in a thousand shades of brown. Tall, elegant windows cast the day's brutal sunlight across the room, and columns support a barrel-vaulted ceiling covered in hexagonal tiles of gold and blue and green and white.

Isabel's still staring at the ceiling, its gentle curves and vivid colours, when Sam tugs on her hand. 'We're blocking the entrance,' she says, pulling Isabel to the side. 'Here, sit down. I'm getting something to drink.'

She hardly notices Sam leaving, though it leaves her surrounded by strangers and noise. Sam's right: the walls match the blue-green she used to dye her hair. Up close, Isabel sees the floral motifs embossed on the tiles, and the way the hexagons of the ceiling form their own flowers and honeycombs, the shapes of nature made ceramic in the fabric of the building.

She wishes suddenly that Emma could have seen this, could have known that buildings like this one existed in the world, because it was Emma who first taught Isabel to see beauty, and she should have had the chance to witness it herself. Isabel can only stare at it, hollowed out by grief.

This building is the first beautiful thing she's seen since leaving Espera.

'Here.' Sam puts a pot of mint tea on the table in front of her. 'So you like it then?'

With difficulty, Isabel looks away from the ceiling and down at the tea. 'There's no need to sound so smug about it,' she says, but the bitter edge in her voice has given way to humour for the first time that she can remember.

Sam grins. There's definitely some smugness there. 'You can come back with me next time, if you want. I'm sure Leo won't mind. It means he doesn't have to bring me.'

Does she want to come back? Take the bus journey again, deal with the crowds and the fear? *Yes*, whispers a voice immediately. Yes, because at the end of it all is this building, with all its colours. And all its books. Maybe eventually she'll have the courage to read what they say about Espera.

'We'll see,' she says, not committing to anything, but Sam's expression tells her the kid thinks she's already won.

The journey home is easier, though the bus is more crowded, wheezing its way up the hills and away from the city centre. Isabel sits by the window again, looking out at the maze of red-brick terraces. It's almost familiar enough to feel like homecoming, and the journey lulls her into something approaching sleep; when they reach their stop, Sam has to nudge her alert. She stumbles over her feet as they disembark, still dazed, still thinking about the colours. In Espera, beauty is external, splashed defiantly across walls like a manifesto: *We will claim our city for art*. But it's transient, destroyed by weather and the hoses of the borough councils and the next artist to come along with their paints. This is different: hidden away, locked inside buildings, but permanent, solid, made to last. Art with history, meant to endure into the future for any who know where to look for it.

Isabel hadn't known where to look for it. But it was there all along.

Back at the house, she stows her bag of library books carefully under her bed. She can't face taking them out now, but she retrieves *Notes from Underground* from the living room and loses herself in muddling through the Russian until she hears the front door slam closed and Leo asking Sam: 'Successful trip?'

She can't hear Sam's answer, but Leo doesn't come thundering upstairs to check on Isabel, so it must be positive. He doesn't ask her about it at all, actually, even later, when they're eating dinner together. Maybe he's letting her process it, or waiting for her to say she won't take Sam again and he shouldn't have made her do it.

She doesn't. She says, 'It's a bit nicer than our library.'

His mouth quirks. 'Just a little. I think nineteenth-century architects had grander ideals than guild contractors in the fifties.' Nineteenth century. That thing the outside has, along with religion: history. Remnants of the years gone by that Espera, little more than a century old, can't replicate. 'I hear you borrowed some books.'

Isabel nods. He doesn't ask what books, and she doesn't tell him, some unknown fear stopping up her voice. It's not that she can imagine Leo looking at a book about PTSD and telling her she's not allowed to use that label, not when Emily used it – and she knows they talk about her – but she's still not ready to claim it. She can't articulate how she feels about the word *trauma*, and she doesn't think he'll understand that, because he's never been the one who did the damage before.

'No Ant this evening?' she asks instead, trying to steer the conversation into safer waters.

'Working late. He'll be back around three.'

Isabel still isn't sure what Ant and Leo do for the smugglers, except that it involves raising money to keep the Free Press running. They often have tense, whispered conversations in the kitchen when they think Isabel and Sam are asleep, so she knows all is not well, but they keep the trouble to themselves and only pass on the good news – that Jem and Beth are well, that the library team sends their best wishes ...

It's unlikely these are meant for Isabel, but she hoards them anyway, secretly: a fragile connection to a life she can never go back to.

Whatever Ant's doing, it often keeps him out of the house, and gives Isabel time alone with Leo. She finds that easier; Leo's presence is soothing, undemanding, even if she can never quite let go of her guilt about Emma. Ant is polite to

Isabel, but he never wanted her here, and she can sense it in every careful interaction.

Isabel's quiet for the rest of the meal, half listening to Sam and Leo talk. She's almost cleared her plate when Leo says, 'Will you punch me if I say I'm proud of you?'

It takes her a moment to realise he's talking to her, not Sam. 'For what, leaving the house?'

'Yes.' He gives her a lopsided smile.

'Then, yes.' She's been itching to hit something all day, and she's not allowed to fight anyone else, so Leo needs to watch himself. 'I'm traumatised, not five.' But secretly, it *does* feel like an achievement: that she left, that she brought Sam safely home, that she saw something beautiful.

'Guess I won't, then,' he says lightly, and exchanges a conspiratorial look with Sam. 'But I am, you know.'

Isabel pushes away her now-empty plate before embarrassment can dissolve her calm. 'I'm going upstairs, unless you need me.'

'No, go ahead.' Leo gestures magnanimously. 'You're free to go.'

If only.

In her room, the anxiety returns. She's hyper-aware of the pile of library books, their waiting words demanding to be read, asking why she borrowed them if she was only going to hide. She can't answer that, but she's not going to look at them today.

Instead, Isabel curls up in bed, and is surprised when sleep comes easily.

Normally, when she dreams, it's of the deaths: of accusation in Mortimer's expression when they come for him, betrayal in Laura's. But tonight, she dreams of the library on Chartrand Street, shabby and small by comparison with the building she saw today. Like a ghost, she crosses the empty room, the door to the basement giving way beneath her touch, and follows the stairs down into the depths of the building, through the stacks and the secret door, into the maze of shelves behind. It's silent, bereft of the usual gurgle of tired pipes and the whine of electronics.

Isabel emerges into the meeting space, where a circle of chairs surrounds the old stained coffee table, but there's no sign of Ant, or Sam, or any of the regulars.

She turns to go, and almost runs directly into Kieran. 'Hello, little Moth,' he says, wiping blood off his hands. 'Stubborn, these new friends of yours, aren't they? Pity you weren't here earlier.'

'Where's Sam?' she tries to ask, but the dream steals her voice and strangles her words.

Kieran smiles like he knows what she meant to say. 'Ronan will be pleased to know we've eliminated some of those Free Press bastards. Oh, don't worry, I'll make sure you get the credit.'

She reaches out to – what? Hit him? Grab him by the neck and demand answers? But he's already dissolving into nothing and she wakes with the taste of tears on her lips and the utter certainty that Sam is dead.

It takes several minutes of carefully counted breaths before her heart slows, and still the certainty won't shake itself, though logic tells her it's not true. Eventually, she abandons her bed and pads silently up the stairs to Sam's attic room.

The door is slightly ajar, as always. Isabel nudges it open with her foot, and the light from the stairwell shines on the bed. Red hair against the pillow. Sleeping. Of course she's sleeping; it's the middle of the night.

She *is* sleeping, isn't she?

Isabel steps closer, Suzie's ghost haunting every movement. Her foot knocks a small stack of books that have been left on the floor, and they topple. It's a tiny sound, deadened by the carpet, but Sam opens her eyes.

She looks up at Isabel with exactly no fear. 'What's wrong?'

Afterwards, this will be what sticks: that it never crossed Sam's mind that Isabel might mean her harm.

'Nightmares,' Isabel confesses in a whisper, slumping down beside the bed. 'I thought you were dead.'

Sam nods and shuffles across the mattress towards the wall, pulling aside her duvet. 'Here.'

Isabel looks up at her in bewilderment. 'What?'

'Get in. That way you'll know I'm not dead, even if you have more nightmares.' She doesn't say this like it's at all remarkable, but nobody has ever offered to sleep beside Isabel before, or tried so readily to soothe her anxiety. She's afraid to accept, worried she'll violate some unspoken etiquette she never learned. 'Come on,' says Sam. 'Your feet must be cold.'

They are. Isabel climbs into the little single bed – it's lucky they're both on the small side – and Sam drops the quilt over them. One of Isabel's chilled feet brushes against the kid's, and she laughs and squirms.

'Keep your cold feet to yourself or I'll kick you out again,' she threatens.

Isabel dutifully tucks one foot under the other leg and tries to keep herself to herself, staring up at the glow-in-the-dark stars stuck to the sloped ceiling. It's several minutes before she realises the girl is watching her.

'You thought I was dead,' says Sam at last. 'And that was a nightmare.'

'Of course it was a nightmare,' says Isabel, not understanding. 'You're fine. I can see that. I just . . . needed to check.'

'Not what I meant,' says Sam. 'I meant that the thought of me dying upset you enough to count as a nightmare.' She sounds like she's smiling. 'See. You're soft on the inside, no matter how much you try to hide it.'

Isabel turns her face away. 'Sure. Keep telling yourself that. Let's pretend it's not just guilt.'

Sam pokes her in the back. 'For an emotionless super-assassin, you sure feel a lot of that. Has it ever occurred to you that it's a good thing? Maybe it might contradict some of your self-loathing ideas about your own evilness?'

'Evilness isn't a word.'

'How would *you* know? You dropped out of school to kill people for a living.'

'You're twelve,' Isabel retorts, because it's easier to treat

Sam like a child than listen to what she's saying. 'Go to sleep. Babies shouldn't be up this late.'

Sam prods her again. 'You're the one who woke me up,' she says, but she subsides into silence, and a little while later her breathing evens out as she falls asleep.

Isabel stares up at the constellations on the ceiling for a long time, finding shapes in the random arrangement of stars, listening to Sam breathe beside her. Not dead, not even close: more alive than Isabel's ever been.

She doesn't remember falling asleep, but she doesn't wake until Leo comes in with a morning cup of tea for them both.

'No more nightmares?' says Sam.

'No more nightmares,' Isabel agrees, and is surprised to realise it's true.

8

MALPLENA (EMPTY)

The books are supposed to help.

That's why Emily recommended them. They're meant to dig inside Isabel's head until they find the rotten parts, and then cut them away. Like therapy, without the awful part where she'd have to talk to another human being about her feelings.

But so far, all they're doing is highlighting the deep hollow inside her where all the emotions they're describing are meant to be.

One asks her to write down her feelings, being as specific as possible, and she falls at the first hurdle. She doesn't *know* what she's feeling, unless *empty* counts as a feeling; the anger she experienced at the library has faded back into the same apathetic greyness, and without it, she's as lost as before.

Maybe she's grateful, but she's not sure if she's *feeling* that, or if she just *thinks* it's what she should be feeling in her current circumstances. She's not even sure she knows the difference between feeling an emotion and thinking about it.

She can't shake the nagging sense that she's doing it wrong somehow. Exactly *what* she's doing wrong is harder to pin down. Trauma? Grief? If there are criteria for processing the shit she's been through, she isn't meeting them. Apart from her breakdown at the library, she hasn't cried, which feels wrong. Everyone she knows is dead. A better person would have cried.

One of the books talks about the stages of grief. But she's not in denial, because of course they're dead: she's been pre-emptively mourning them from the moment she started to care, because anything good always gets taken away. And she's not bargaining, because she's made enough blood-soaked deals for a lifetime. Anger, yes, maybe: anger at Espera, at the world, at herself for being alive when they're not. But the fire of it's gone, and she doesn't know how to coax it back to life.

So it's depression, then. That seems reasonable. She heard Daragh talk about depression, and knows this grey emptiness fits the bill, but since it's an entirely logical response to her circumstances, it doesn't feel temporary, like a phase that will pass over. It's not like her friends will stop being dead.

Isabel drops the book on the floor next to the bed and tries another, this time with the knowledge that she's probably clinically depressed, so most of their emotion shit won't work for her. But like all the books, it seems determined to make her into a fragile thing, belly exposed, and she can't bear it. The walls she's built are the only reason she's still alive. Maybe it's a coping mechanism, but without it she wouldn't cope. That's the whole fucking point of it, after all.

She hasn't let herself touch the books that involve thinking about what her parents did to her. She's not ready to open that can of worms; she doesn't know why she borrowed them, when they'll be due back to the library before she ever brings herself to read them.

Her door opens, and she flinches upright, but it's only Leo.

'It's very quiet up here,' he says. 'You all right?'

What's he expecting her to do in her bedroom, take up tap dancing? 'Fine,' says Isabel, shoving the book off the bed to join the others.

Leo's gaze drifts to the pile. 'Emily told me she'd recommended some titles,' he says carefully. 'I'm glad you're . . .' But he doesn't seem to know how to finish that sentence.

'Glad I'm *trying*?' suggests Isabel. 'Or glad I picked something that won't have the world suspecting me of being a Russian spy? Because apparently that was on the table.'

He pulls a face. 'She told me that too. I'm sorry. That never occurred to me.'

'That's because it's bullshit. Also, isn't it racist, to assume that because I speak Russian, I must be a spy?'

She's still getting her head around the outside world's concept of racism. Espera wasn't free of prejudice, but it looked a little different, the closed borders imposing a weird, shitty equality on its citizens. People found distinguishing features and ways to split themselves up into *us* and *them* regardless:

83

Grindale civilians looking down on Lutton civilians, guild loyalties and political allegiances visible in the papers people read, a dozen meaningless borders drawn throughout the city. You learned to see them, growing up there; she hasn't yet learned to see this world's fault-lines and categories.

'I think that one's xenophobia,' says Leo, attempting a light tone; he, of all of them, has been shoved into new boxes and faced with bigotry he doesn't have an outsider's thick skin to protect against. 'But probably.'

So fucking complicated, and she should never have needed to learn it. Isabel gestures to the books. 'Well, I'm trying. But it's not going well, so don't hold your breath that I'll magically transform into somebody mentally stable any time soon.'

Leo smiles ruefully. 'You're already doing better, if you're joking about your mental health now.'

Is she joking? Maybe. The bar for improvement was on the floor, though, so he should hold off on the celebrations. 'Let me know when they write a book called *The Murder Detox* and then we might get somewhere.'

His smile fades. 'Is it . . . I mean, it was a job, wasn't it? Are you saying . . . ?'

What he's trying to ask is, *Are you addicted to killing people?* Which would be funny if it wasn't symptomatic of how fucked up she is that he even needs to ask.

'That was a joke,' she assures him. 'Though there *is* a gap in the careers advice market when it comes to switching industries after three years as a state-sanctioned murderer.'

'I see.' Leo's smile hasn't quite returned, and his expression

84

is tight. Right. Because he pretends he's okay with her being who she is, but only as long as he can forget what that actually entails. And there's nobody left she can make those jokes with. No more sarcastic remarks to Laura about the relative merits of assassination compared to waitressing. Time to lock them up inside her and pretend she's disgusted by it, just like everyone else.

'I'm fine, Leo,' she says pointedly. 'You don't need to check on me. There are limits to how much trouble I can get into in a room this size.'

'I know,' he says, but he doesn't leave. 'Still. I really am glad that you're trying to process ... everything. And if you need anyone to talk to ...'

'Emily gave me the number of a therapist,' she tells him, then adds, 'I won't be needing it.'

'If you say so.'

When he's gone, she ignores the books and lies face down on the bed. It would be easier, she thinks, if she could make jokes about it. *Surely* there's something funny about a girl who was raised to kill people and now isn't even allowed a pair of scissors. There's got to be a joke in that, because otherwise it's extremely fucking tragic.

Isabel is very tired of being a tragedy.

But she sure looks like one, spending every day doing her best impression of a slug inside her duvet, and neither self-help nor Dostoyevsky is improving her mood, so it's time to take more drastic action. Do something – anything – to remind herself that she's alive.

(It's a bitch of a reminder, but she's got to keep throwing it at herself until it doesn't sting so much when it hits. Maybe, eventually, she'll make peace with the concept. *Hey, loser, you're alive. Now get the fuck up.*)

Going to the library hasn't conquered her fear, but it's punctured it, let some of the air out. She can do it again, can't she? Leave the house, this time alone. There's the spare key Leo pointed out to her when she first came here, on the nail behind the kitchen door. She's *allowed* to go out; he told her she was.

The first time she tries, she hardly makes it further than the front gate, her lungs crushed by panic almost as soon as she steps out onto the pavement. The second time, she gets as far as the end of the road. It's easier in the evenings, when the sun is low and the light softer, and she doesn't feel like an insect pinned to a board beneath the endless sky. Her world expands to the next street along, the pub on the corner with raucous punters spilling out onto the street, the meagre little park beyond that. Sometimes Leo watches her go, but she always comes back, so he doesn't say anything – even when she only manages ten minutes before she flees for the safety of four walls and a ceiling. He probably thinks it's good for her, like it's driven by a desire to 'integrate' and not by the need to walk until she outruns her own shadow.

It gets easier, even if Isabel can't bring herself to cross the threshold of a shop. She lingers near the pubs, where people crowd onto picnic benches outside to drink and chat, and listens to the unfamiliar tones of their local accents until they start to sound less alien. After a week or two, she knows the streets well enough that her solitary walks are no longer haunted by the fear of not being able to get home.

Emily is delighted by Isabel's progress, when she eventually manages to tell her caseworker about the library and her walks. She doesn't mention the books she borrowed, which remain abandoned in a heap under her bed, and Emily doesn't ask. The meeting goes downhill, however, when the subject turns to Isabel's contribution to the household, and the prospect of trying to get a job triggers a panic attack that she entirely fails to hide. Leo's home by then; he takes over, ushering Emily from the room and keeping her in the kitchen while Sam brings Isabel a drink of water and sits with her until she can breathe again.

It's stupid. But she remembers what happened last time she tried to have a day job, and even with Sam beside her, the nightmare of Kieran invading the sanctuary of the library basement still lingers.

When Emily's gone, Leo gives Isabel the latest book he's acquired from the bookshop's second-hand 'foreign languages' section, and she takes it with a watery smile. She finished *Notes from Underground* a couple of days ago, but she hasn't started the Kafka yet, unable to face it. Maybe what looks like a shitty French fantasy novel will be easier. And less relatable.

Then he checks the calendar on the wall – Ant's working late again – and says, 'How about we get fish and chips? I'm too tired to cook.'

So Sam's dispatched to the chippy around the corner, and returns with greasy paper packages and the promise that the chips are safe for Isabel, fried separately from the batter. They're hot and well salted; Isabel's anxiety seeps away, back into the familiar apathy.

Leo's got a knack for this, she's learning. He knows when to draw attention away from Isabel, and how to bring her back afterwards – not to normality, but to something she's never had: family. Sam is usually the one to help her breathe, but Leo grounds her in their new life. She wonders if he learned that from looking after Emma, when she was newly fostered and afraid and waiting to lose everything again.

But it still hurts to think about Emma, after all this time, so Isabel tries not to. Maybe it even hurts more now than it did in Espera, because she's seeing things her friend never got to see. And if she lets herself, she starts wondering about Emma's biological parents, the ones who abandoned her. Are *they* somewhere in this city? Have they got caseworkers, jobs, new lives as ordinary citizens?

Do they know the daughter they abandoned is dead?

So, no, she doesn't think about that.

The nightmares don't disappear completely, but gradually she gets better at pushing them away when she wakes, and rarely needs to check on Sam. Once or twice the kid comes to Isabel's room instead, seeking reassurance from her own fears; Isabel's not sure if they're real or if it's a ploy to make her feel better, but it works, because she never feels stronger than when she's able to convince Sam that they're safe.

You saved her once. She remembers sheltering Suzie with her body at Katipo. She remembers going back for the kids because there was no way she could have left them behind. She remembers her fury, her determination to protect them.

When did she lose that? How did Comma twist her into someone who would kill a child instead of save them? How can she have allowed Ronan Atwood to make such a monster of her? She was never a good person, but they made her so much worse.

She will never forgive them for making her worse.

Sometimes, when the emptiness threatens to overwhelm her and she needs to feel something – anything – Isabel lets her mind drift to the governments who buy the city's weapons. The rage is simple and cleansing. Did they know her father's poisons were tested on a child? Would they still have bought them if they knew?

Maybe, she thinks, they'd pay extra for that. For the cruelty inherent in the making.

She takes Sam to the library the following Saturday. Goes straight upstairs to the local history section and tries to find a book – one book, one single book – that will tell her there's a justification for how the world treated the city's inhabitants. Like maybe lives were saved by leaving Espera alone, maybe it had a purpose, maybe there was some value in it and she just doesn't understand the situation properly.

But the more she reads, the clearer it becomes that it was only ever about money. No wonder Leo's book's causing such drama: an insider's view, a reminder that there are people

89

inside Espera and they're more than collateral damage ... how the world must hate being reminded of that.

That night, Isabel can't sleep. She lies flat on her bed, staring up at the ceiling, and feels the anger taking hold of her again. Fury comes easier than sorrow, and maybe that's another sign that she's doing it all wrong – because there's no doubt in her mind that she is, somehow, performing mourning incorrectly – but if that's the case, she might as well keep going. This gut-deep desire to hit something, to fight something, is better than the empty void and the days where the only emotions she can muster are 'tired' and 'sarcastic', which she's not sure are emotions in the first place.

But there's nothing here for her to fight, no way to release her rage.

Isabel rolls out of bed and listens to the noises of the house. Ant's out and won't be home until late; he's on night shifts again. Leo got home an hour ago and headed straight for bed. Sam's fast asleep in her room.

There's nobody to stop her.

She pulls on her clothes and creeps down the stairs, palming the wallet from the kitchen table and easing the spare keys from the hook, careful not to let them rattle. The door closes noiselessly behind her, and she steps out onto a street transformed by night and weather. The weak orange streetlights cast pools of warm light, illuminating flecks of falling rain.

She's never been out after dark here before. With no solar panels in the roads to guide her path, the difference between

Leeds and Espera is starker than ever, but night has always been Isabel's territory. She slips down the streets like the shadow she was raised to be, neither knowing nor caring where she's going.

The closer she gets to the city centre, the more lights there are: illuminated signs glaring above shops shuttered for the night; neon lights outlining the entrances to clubs and bars beloved by the city's student body. Isabel watches a crowd of already-pissed revellers stagger up to one of them and attempt to convince the bouncer they're sober enough to be let in. The wallet in her pocket is burning a hole.

She takes a detour down a side-street next to the club, where a fire escape spills smokers onto a rooftop balcony, the door invitingly propped open with a brick. Isabel lets herself in without anybody noticing and disappears into the noise.

It's nothing like an Esperan club, and not only because the music is unfamiliar. It's the way people behave around each other, fearless and free. Isabel watches them for a moment, their bodies in motion, dancing like it's a fight they're trying to win. It tugs on her instincts, urging her to move with them.

First things first, though. She heads for the bar, and is surprised to be served without difficulty, despite her unprepossessing outfit. When it comes to paying, she taps Leo's card against the reader and holds her breath until she knows it's worked. The drink is strong, flavour obliterated by bitter alcohol; she tosses it back, uncaring.

'Break-up?' says a voice next to her.

91

Isabel looks up. The speaker's a girl maybe her own age, though it's hard to be sure with the dramatic eye make-up and elaborately styled hair. The light catches on a silver piercing through her lip. 'What?'

'I was asking if it was a break-up that had you sitting here drinking like there's no tomorrow.'

Isabel shrugs. 'Technically,' she says, 'it's already tomorrow.'

The girl laughs and slides into the empty seat beside her. 'True. You seem surprisingly sober for someone who just downed that in one. How many have you had?'

'This is the first.'

'But not the last,' guesses her new acquaintance, and orders them both another drink. 'Where's that accent from?'

Isabel's surprised she can hear well enough over the music to notice that she doesn't sound local. 'Espera.'

The girl's eyes widen. 'Shit,' she says, giving Isabel a once-over in the light of this new information. 'You're ... you're her, aren't you? I saw you on the news. Oh my god.'

Isabel takes the drink the girl paid for and downs it, because if she's going to get ogled by strangers, she's going to be drunk when it happens. 'Maybe.'

'I wondered what you looked like under all the, you know, blood.' The girl's next look is appreciative. 'You clean up well.'

Isabel snorts dismissively. She's wearing jeans and a plain T-shirt, and she looks as out of place in this club as she feels in this city – but maybe the standards for 'cleaned up' are lower for fucked-up former assassins.

'Wouldn't have expected to see you here, I have to say.'

Somehow there's another drink in front of them both. It takes the edge off Isabel's mood, shaves its edges down into something less violent, but that wasn't what she wanted. The fire's meant to stay, not subside again into the ash of depression. She can't let it fade, can't go back to feeling nothing – fuck, the alcohol was a mistake, this was the opposite of her plan, insofar as she had one at all.

Isabel looks out at the dancefloor, the urge to move still tugging at her gut. There's something about the crowd she can't put her finger on, distracted as she is by the lights and the brightly coloured banners on the walls.

'I mean,' continues the girl, who could apparently hold a conversation with a brick wall, given how much feedback she's getting from Isabel, 'I didn't exactly expect to see you anywhere. But if you asked me to rate on a scale of one to ten the likelihood of running into the assassin girl in a gay club, it definitely would've been near the bottom.'

Isabel turns her head. 'This is a gay club,' she says. It was meant to be a question, but it doesn't entirely come out that way.

'Uh.' The girl seems wrong-footed. 'Yeah. Wait, you didn't know that?'

If there was anything like a gay club in Espera, Isabel didn't know about it. She can understand why it might appeal, to people for whom that sort of thing is relevant, but as she's never been one of them, she never sought out these spaces, or the communities that inhabit them and the labels they use.

Esperans had their own words, she suspects, overlapping with but distinct from the identities these people claim with their banners and their pin-badges, but she never looked for those, either.

'Came in the back door,' Isabel says, by way of explanation, jerking her thumb towards the fire escape. Then reconsiders her words in light of the context. 'No pun intended.'

That makes her new acquaintance laugh, although she's got this weird surprised look on her face that Isabel doesn't like, because it means she's being weighed against some expectation for how the 'assassin girl' from the photographs would behave.

'So, are you only here to drink terrifying amounts of overpriced vodka?' asks the girl. 'Or do you want to dance?'

Isabel looks out at the dancefloor. It's a long time since she was last in a club, and she's never been much of a dancer, but it's not that different from fighting. It's only bodies in space: only power, and control, and everything she craves.

And these couples, draped over each other, bodies so close it's hard to see where one person ends and the other begins, they come here for a reason. They find something in this that she's lacking. Why shouldn't she? Who's to say she can't have what they have?

'Sure,' she says, and downs the last of her drink. 'Let's dance.'

9

SCIVOLA (CURIOUS)

'Kate,' yells the girl over the music, as they move away from the bar. It takes Isabel a second to realise she's introducing herself. 'Forgot that part.'

'Marie,' Isabel replies, pulling the name from nowhere. The news reports didn't identify her, so Kate can't call her out on the lie, and she doesn't feel like being herself tonight.

'Seriously?' says Kate, and for a second Isabel thinks she miscalculated, but then the other girl laughs. 'Not what I'd have expected with all the knives and blood and whatever. Marie. Sounds like my nan.' But she doesn't accuse her of lying, just grabs Isabel's hand and tugs her closer.

Even with alcohol dulling her paranoia, it takes everything in Isabel to quell her instinct to twist free of Kate's grip and disable her before she can press herself any closer. She knows she's tensed, and forces herself to relax and lean into the slide of Kate's hands across her skin, her hips, the small of her back.

She used to keep a knife there. It's gone now, and Kate's hands have slipped beneath the hem of her T-shirt. It's intimate, and she hates it. It's physical, and she loves it, wants to throw herself into this like it'll kill her if she doesn't, to drop all her walls and let the world in, because maybe if she does, she'll be able to feel something again.

Kate doesn't seem to mind that she's a shitty dancer. There's not enough space for it to matter, anyway, and Isabel lets her take the lead, ignoring every single one of her brain's warning signals, because there's nothing anyone in this room can do that's worse than what's already happened to her.

Gradually, she becomes aware that they're drifting away from the dancefloor, towards the shadowed edges of the room near the toilets. Kate's make-up is smudged with sweat, but her smile is luminous and feral under the lights. She's so ... *vibrant*, like all her feelings have been turned up to eleven. Isabel's starving for it, desperate for the palest imitation of that luminosity. She lets Kate back her up against the wall, which is sticky with sweat and fuck knows what else, and doesn't flinch when the girl kisses her.

So this is kissing, thinks Isabel. *This is what they all talk about.*

She's never kissed anyone before and never wanted to, but books have led her to believe that around now she should be overwhelmed with passion, a primal instinct kicking in and taking over. Except nothing about this feels natural, and no instinct makes itself known: she's aware of lips and tongues and teeth and a fumbling terror that she's doing something wrong, because nothing about this appeals or makes sense.

It must be the rest of it that people like.

Isabel brings her hands up to hold Kate, trying to mimic how the other girl is touching her. The stud in Kate's lip clinks against her teeth, and she captures it, sucking gently, which seems to be the right thing to do: Kate pushes her harder against the wall, hands moving under her clothes to press against the bare skin of her hips. So it's her, then, there's something wrong with *her* that this does nothing for her – that makes sense.

In answer to a question Isabel didn't ask, Kate grabs her hand again and tugs her towards the nearest door, pulling her through it and locking it behind them. It's a single-stall bathroom, barely big enough for the both of them, the sink pressed up against Isabel's back, but she doesn't complain. She lets Kate drag her T-shirt up, her palms against Isabel's skin, her scars, the thin fabric of her bra, and is about to return the favour when Kate stops and pulls back.

'Holy shit,' she says.

She might be talking about the tattoos. The web of artwork covers Isabel's skin, hours of pain financed by other people's deaths, decorating and disguising everything that's been done to her and taking back a little of the power she's always been denied over her body. Her skin is a poor canvas, damaged and scarred, but the artists who worked on her knew their shit:

97

the lines are clean and the colours strong, even in the crappy lighting of this club bathroom.

But then Kate reaches out and rests her fingers against the butterfly-shaped burn on Isabel's chest, and it becomes apparent that it's not the tattoos she's interested in after all.

'I knew you were from Espera, but Jesus Christ,' she says. 'What happened to you?'

The warmth of Kate's fingertips has gone from a pleasant fire to an acid discomfort. Isabel pulls away, elbowing the soap dispenser as she tries to put distance between them, backed up against the tiled wall.

'It doesn't matter,' she says. 'It doesn't—'

Kate's between her and the door. The locked door. Fuck. She let her guard down and now she's trapped in this tiny fucking bathroom with a stranger who's seen her scars, and the worst part is that it's not even pity on Kate's face, or disgust, either of which would be easier to bear than this weird hunger, this insatiable curiosity, like there's something illicitly thrilling about Isabel's damaged body.

'Is the city really like people say it is? Like, with assassins and stuff?'

'Pretty much.' And she would never have been in this situation back in Espera because in Espera she would *always have a knife*, and she doesn't have a knife, she's not allowed a knife, and Kate's between her and the door.

Kate stops touching her chest, finally, but she doesn't move out of the way. 'Have *you* killed people?' she says.

Isabel needs to get out of here. 'You called me the "assassin girl",' she says, with difficulty. 'Doesn't that answer your question?'

'I don't know,' says Kate. 'Does it?' She takes Isabel's silence as an answer and moves closer again, capturing Isabel's hand in hers and entwining their fingers. 'How many?'

Maybe if she tells the truth, Kate will leave her alone. 'I don't know. I didn't keep count. It was my job.'

Kate should recoil. Should be afraid. Instead, she says, 'Did you ever kill people with your bare hands?' and takes one of Isabel's hands, bringing it up to her own throat. 'Without a weapon?'

It would be so easy to hurt her. To kill her. Then Isabel could leave this bathroom, and she'd be gone before anyone knew she was ever here. She's good at that. It's the only thing in the world she's good at.

But—

Isabel pulls her hand away. 'I've got to go,' she says, fumbling around for her abandoned T-shirt and tugging it over her head. 'Sorry. I can't do this.'

'Wait—'

'Please let me out. I've got to go.'

Kate stares at her, hurt. 'Jesus. What did I say wrong? I didn't mean—'

'It's not you.' It is. That fucked-up desire in her eyes when she saw Isabel's scars, the unhealthy fascination that made her put a murderer's hands around her throat. This whole encounter was something the real Isabel would never have done – but that's the point, it was meant to be different, a chance to escape the inside of her own head and convince herself it's a good thing she's alive.

But Kate doesn't want any stranger, isn't interested in Isabel's charms or her looks. She wants the 'assassin girl', she wants a story, and Isabel thinks she'll be sick if she doesn't get the fuck out of here *right now*.

'Please,' she says, biting off the word. It's taking every ounce of her restraint to keep her violence locked up tight inside her. 'Let me past.'

'Shit,' says Kate, as though only now realising she's blocking Isabel's escape. 'I'm sorry, I didn't—'

She moves away from the door, and Isabel's already gone, Kate's apologies drowned out by the music flooding back to deafen her as she disappears into the crowd.

She pushes her way through the club, shoving people aside with no regard for their outraged squawks. Out to the fire escape, past the smokers and the sweet, artificial scent of their vapes, down the metal steps, into the street.

Jesus Christ, said Kate, the blasphemy easy on her lips. Isabel tastes it on her own, an unfamiliar way to swear, and tries very hard not to go to pieces.

She can still feel Kate's throat in her hand. The delicacy of it. It would have been so fucking easy, and she didn't do it, *she didn't do it*, even though Kate wouldn't stop touching her, and even though she made a colossal mistake getting herself into that situation in the first place.

Fuck.

The night's warm, so it doesn't matter that she forgot to

bring a jacket; at least Leo's wallet's still in the pocket of her jeans. She can feel sobriety rapidly returning as she stumbles towards the main road. *Have you killed people?* Like it was some delicious novelty. *How many?*

Too many. Enough to drown in all the blood. But Kate wouldn't see that, would she? It's all a story to her, Espera little more than a fantasy world and Isabel's scars just another exotic detail, a costume.

Isabel's furious with herself, even as she feels violated by the encounter. What the fuck was the point of giving herself a fake name – *Marie*, fuck, Kate's right, it sounds like somebody's grandma – as if she could ever leave any of it behind? It's no good trying to be somebody else when it'll always be her body they're touching.

When her stumbling feet finally bring her home to Leo's house, she's surprised and dismayed to see a light on in the front room, ruining her hopes of a surreptitious return. She'd expected them all to be asleep – it's nearly three in the morning. Somebody must have noticed she was gone.

Isabel takes a deep breath, and lets herself into the house.

Ant's sitting on the settee in the front room, Leo pacing up and down. Sam's curled in the armchair in her pyjamas, wrapped in a blanket. All three of them look up as Isabel enters.

Leo speaks first. 'Where the *fuck* have you been?'

She returns the key to its hook and unlaces her shoes, keeping her movements steady. 'Out.'

'Out,' he repeats. She's never seen Leo angry before. It's unbearable; she throws up all her emotional walls, trying to keep it away from her. '*Out*. Isabel, we were scared to death. Ant was about to call the police.'

'That seems like an overreaction.' She places the wallet on the table. 'Sorry. I bought a drink. I hope it wasn't too expensive.'

Leo makes a small, strangled noise as though she's robbed him of the ability to speak.

Ant gets up and puts a hand on his arm for comfort, before turning to Isabel. 'You can't just disappear like that without telling anyone where you're going, especially late at night,' he says. 'What made you sneak out?' It's easier for him to be calm, she suspects, because he cares a lot less about her than Leo does.

'I didn't *sneak out*,' she says. 'You were out, and the others were asleep, and I needed air.'

'More air than you could find in the garden?' he says mildly. 'You've been gone at least ninety minutes, given that that's how long it's been since I came home and found the spare keys gone and your room empty.'

Well, that explains how she got busted. 'Sorry. I didn't think anyone would notice.' Her body still feels strange, her mind dislocated from physical sensations, like she's existing a few inches to the left of herself. 'I won't do it again.'

'For fuck's sake, Isabel,' says Leo. Then he seems to remember that Sam's there and looks apologetic about his swearing, although he doesn't take it back. 'You should go back to bed,' he tells the kid. 'Isabel's safe. No need for you to be up.'

Sam looks mutinous, but she's too sleepy to argue, and soon she disappears back upstairs, trailing the blanket.

When she's gone, Ant says, 'So are you even going to attempt an explanation, or is *out* all we're getting?'

'I needed air,' says Isabel again. 'I just went for a walk.' And she's sore from it, sore from the dancing and the touching and the long journey home through unfamiliar streets.

'And you bought a *drink*?' says Leo. 'Where exactly did this walk take you?'

She shrugs. 'A club. I don't know what it was called.'

Ant leans close and sniffs. 'Are you drunk?' he says uncertainly.

Isabel shakes her head. 'Not any more.' If the alcohol ever did anything more than blur the edges of her sobriety a little, the haze has passed, the fresh night air leaving her glass-sharp. 'I said I was *sorry*,' she adds resentfully. 'Can I go to bed now?'

For a second she thinks Leo might hit her, and she braces herself, the fear undercut by a thrill of satisfaction that she's managed to trick him into being something other than perfectly loving and forgiving. But then the moment passes, and he's back to being tired and worried.

'We care what happens to you, Isabel,' he says. 'You do realise that, right? You nearly gave us all a heart attack.'

'I'm sorry,' she says again, and she is, even if she doesn't know how to make it sound convincing. 'I really didn't think you'd notice I was gone.'

He sighs. 'How many drinks?' he asks, inclining his head towards the wallet.

'One.'

'And that was enough to get you tipsy?'

'I didn't pay for the others.'

He accepts this without asking for details. Maybe he doesn't want to know. Understandable; Isabel would also prefer to forget tonight ever happened. 'Go shower,' he tells her. 'Then bed. Okay?'

Isabel's too relieved that the interrogation is over to object to being treated like a child. 'Okay,' she says, and makes good her escape.

The shower is a familiar ritual, at least, but the memory of Kate's touch is harder to wash away than blood.

10

DETRUA (DESTRUCTIVE)

Isabel wakes later than usual after a few hours of uneasy sleep, still aching from the night's exertions. Halfway down the stairs she pauses, listening to the raised voices coming from the kitchen.

'We *need* more money. If people are starving, they'll break the strike. And we're losing supporters constantly now the media here is publishing anti-Esperan bullshit every other day, so—'

'We don't know the book would change their minds.'

'But it's something. *Anything* to get people's attention. Leo, they're starving.'

'I know, but ...' Leo sounds anguished. 'Why do *we* have to fix it? Haven't we given enough?'

'Who else is going to?' Ant responds. 'Come on. You're better than this.'

Carefully, Isabel creeps back upstairs to hide in her room until the conversation is over. She can't handle anger today, or the sad, quiet mood Leo's always in after arguing with Ant. It's not long until she hears the tell-tale slam of the door that promises Ant's absence, but by then she's lost her nerve, too much of a coward to face her housemates after last night.

By the time she emerges, at least an hour later, Sam's in the kitchen with Leo, and they're finishing up what looks like an epic baking session. The kid's giggles merge with Leo's deeper laugh, and Isabel hesitates on the threshold, unwilling to interrupt their moment of peace.

Leo catches sight of her and turns. 'Ah, you've rejoined the world of the living,' he says. 'Just in time. We've created a mountain of washing up.'

Mutely, Isabel accepts this as her penance and heads for the sink, where a number of bowls are soaking. She doesn't mind the chore: it gives her something to do with her hands, and a reason to be in the room without the others feeling they need to include her in their activities. But part of her can't stop sneaking glances at Leo, trying to gauge how angry he is with her.

Except he wasn't, really, was he? He was worried, and then disappointed. It hurts more than she'd have thought, disappointing Leo.

Isabel dumps the utensils Sam hands her into the water and says, 'Is something happening in Espera?'

Leo hesitates. 'You heard me talking to Ant.'

'He mentioned strikes.' She doesn't remember the city ever taking collective action before – the very idea that it's possible is a revolutionary shift. 'So? Is something happening?'

'A few things,' he admits. 'I've been trying to keep you both out of it.'

'Why?' asks Sam, looking up from prodding the cakes already cooling on the counter. 'It's our home too.'

'Because—' He breaks off. 'Because it's messy, and complicated, and we only know about it because of the smugglers, and most of what we do for them isn't legal on this side of the wall either.' He helps Sam retrieve the last batch of cakes from the oven and decant them onto the cooling rack, and then looks back at Isabel. 'It was Project Emerald first. People were angry about Hummingbird training minors. Then the Free Press leaked your identity—'

'I know about *that*,' says Isabel. 'I was there.'

'But it might not have gone anywhere if not for the fight inside Comma, which weakened the guild.'

'A fight inside . . .' It's a moment before Isabel realises what he means. 'At the hospital? But that was—'

'A big deal,' says Leo. 'People are angry, but fear of the guilds would usually stop them from acting on it. Except Comma had retreated to lick their wounds, and you'd already weakened Hummingbird.' He says this without flinching, which means someone told him about the Hummingbird massacre a while ago and he's had time to process it while pretending he didn't know. Isabel's not sure how she feels

107

about that. 'That emboldened people. The *Gazette* and the *Echo* both published pretty scathing critiques of Project Emerald and demanded to know whether Comma ever ran a similar programme.'

She doesn't remember the last time the civilian papers actively criticised the guilds like that. 'What happened?'

'Nothing,' says Leo, and spreads his hands: *you see?* 'Nothing happened. The journalists weren't killed. Everyone expected Comma to send the Moth after them, so when they didn't ... well, civilian feelings have shifted a lot, and it doesn't look too good for the guilds. Some of the factories have downed tools. The Free Press is holding the line, supporting the strikers, but we're struggling to raise enough cash to keep getting supplies in.'

Well, shit. That's ... that's a big deal. That's a *Huge Fucking Deal*. 'And Ant thinks admitting authorship of your history book will help.' He might not be wrong. A named author gives the book legitimacy, proves Leo and Ant's credentials as abolitionists, *and* the extra publicity would draw attention and sympathy to the plight of Esperan civilians. If that's what their cause needs, it's a simple way to get it.

'Yeah,' Leo says, a little reluctantly. 'That's the gist of it.'

'Are you going to do it?'

Sam's watching Leo carefully too, the cakes forgotten. He diminishes under the scrutiny, shrinking in on himself. 'I don't know. It ... it might not be safe. Drawing attention to this household. You know?'

Because of you. Because Isabel's the face of everything the world hates about Espera, and she'll only bring trouble down on their heads if people realise she lives here. 'Right.'

'Isabel ...' begins Leo, as she plunges her hands back into the washing-up water and scrubs the spoons, sending them clattering into the cutlery drainer. 'I'm trying to do what's right for all of us. I just don't know what that is yet.'

'You took me in,' she reminds him. 'You *chose* to take me in. And if I'm messing things up for the Free Press—'

'It's not like that,' he says, but it is. She's a problem. She's always been a problem, forcing her abolitionist friends to compromise their values to help her, when they should've left her well alone.

'Maybe you should've left me in the detention centre,' she says caustically. 'Ant would've preferred that, I'm sure.'

'But I wouldn't,' interjects Sam, and Isabel looks at her in surprise. 'I like that you're here. Look, we made you these.' And from the kitchen table she takes a plastic box, placed well away from the baking mess. 'We did them first so they wouldn't get contaminated.'

Isabel opens the box to reveal half a dozen fairy cakes. 'Are they ... ?'

'No gluten, no dairy, no anything that might poison you.'

They made her cakes. She snuck out in the middle of the night to get fucked up somewhere across the city and had them all scared for her life; she's screwing up everything about their careful revolutionary existence; and they made her *cakes*.

Isabel hastily puts the box down before her shaking hands

deposit the gift on the floor. 'I ...' she manages, before she chokes. 'Thanks. I've got to—'

She flees upstairs to the bathroom, locking the door and sitting on the closed lid of the toilet. They made her cakes.

It's not fire she feels now, but something else, welling up inside her, too big to encompass with words or thoughts. She wouldn't know what to call it, if somebody asked. Not gratitude, exactly. Bigger than that.

Isabel puts her face in her hands and cries.

It's a long time before she dares emerge from her hiding place, and she can't face going back downstairs. She retreats to her room instead, leaving the door ajar so she'll have prior warning if anyone comes upstairs to talk to her, and curls up in bed.

Part of her wants to confide in Leo about last night. About Kate. Another part of her already knows what he'll say: *you're not broken, Isabel, just because you don't like all the same things other people like.* She wishes it was easier to believe that – and she wishes she'd actually got the chance to find out for sure whether she liked any of it. Probably, it was a mistake. Probably, it would have been a mistake even if Kate *wasn't* just looking to sleep with the 'assassin girl' for the novelty of it, but Isabel deserved the chance to make it, on her own terms. She hates her scars all over again, for taking that from her, denying her youth and rashness and the opportunity to experiment, to make misjudgements that don't get anyone killed. Instead all she gets are these shitty reminders that her past will follow her wherever she goes, and no attempt to lose herself will ever truly succeed.

So she keeps it to herself. It feels too personal to discuss, anyway, a private humiliation nobody else should witness. And Leo, for his part, says nothing further about her nocturnal excursion. They pass the week in careful avoidance of the topic, his quiet disappointment gradually giving way to his usual care. He doesn't claim authorship of his book, either, and his conversations with Ant become sharper and shorter, until they hit a stalemate and stop talking entirely. Isabel stays out of the way, unwilling to get between them.

The following Saturday, she takes Sam to the library again to swap out her books. This time she steers well clear of the history section, losing herself instead in poetry she doesn't understand. She sits back and lets the words happen to her, the taste of them in her mouth crisp and new even when the meanings are beyond her.

But the emptiness hasn't gone. If anything, it yawns wider now she's had a taste of how to fill it, however momentarily. The chasm gapes, and if she lets herself stop moving for more than a minute, she fears she'll fall in and never emerge.

So she goes out.

She makes sure Leo knows she's going, and he lets her take the wallet. In town, she haunts the streets looking for a distraction, and finds homey pubs and seedy bars, clubs full of students and restaurants full of businessmen. Enough alcohol to take the edges off but never enough to forget herself entirely.

Night after night, Isabel wanders the city, learning its bright lights and dark corners. She lets unfamiliar hands touch her skin, tracing her body, marking out the boundaries of her existence and transgressing them, but she never lets them see her scars.

Maybe she takes risks. Maybe, occasionally, she accepts the pills somebody passes to her, but Leo doesn't have to know about that, because she never spends his money. Only ever takes from those who won't ask for that kind of payment. Ignores every boundary, everything that might be called a comfort zone, pushing herself further and further as though if she finds her limit, she'll finally know who she is and why the fuck she's here.

She doesn't feel more alive. Just a little bit less dead.

She must be out most nights of the week. There's always someone willing to buy her a drink – they see something in her, and it doesn't matter that she doesn't see it in them, because it's all the same: the performance of flirting, the physicality of touch, the hasty encounters in grimy pub bathrooms or forgotten alleyways behind a club.

And this time, when they ask where she's from, she says: *around and about*, she says: *not here*, she doesn't say: *Espera*, and she doesn't take off her shirt, and she never, ever gives them her real name. And if they tell her she looks like someone they saw on the news, she laughs and tells them it's the shitty lighting in here, because she's never done anything newsworthy.

It's a mistake, probably. It's an abnegation of her self. It's a punishment and a poison and the only fucking release she's going to get from all the tension inside her. Sometimes she kids herself she wants it, and nobody ever guesses that she doesn't.

It gets easier with time; she grows to crave the lights and the drinks and the touch that used to make her skin crawl and now just reminds her that she's *got* skin.

There's one bar she finds herself going back to. It's not much more than a converted garage, the main door a rolling metal shutter and the inside lit by scavenged fairy lights and old neon signs. Away from the self-conscious glamour of the queer student clubs where she found Kate, it's the kind of place where nobody asks too many questions. Mostly, it's populated by a cluster of twenty-somethings with as many tattoos as Isabel and almost as much rage at the world around them. They come here to drink and to stand on tables and yell about the government, politics, the future – big brave impassioned rants that Isabel barely understands – and then, when it's over, they dance.

Maybe they recognise a kind of kinship in her, or maybe they're just encompassing her within their general policy of 'to each according to his need', but either way, they've taken her under their wing and they're generous with what that entails. She can usually score at least a couple of drinks without anybody asking for anything in exchange, and nobody here ever treats her as anyone other than *Natasha*, the name she gave them the first time she stumbled in.

There's a woman here, not much older than Isabel. Maggie, her name is. All biceps and smiles and impeccable eyeliner above a tight black vest and sturdy cargo trousers. The first time Isabel came here, Maggie was more than receptive to her flirting, but the second time she tried it, Maggie looked her right in the eyes and said, 'Not like this, Tashie,' with such unfathomable kindness that Isabel was tempted never to come back.

But she came back. She keeps coming back. And every time, Maggie gives her a nod, and pushes a drink along the bar towards her, and they don't touch. Which probably makes this the safest place in the city for Isabel, on nights like this, trapped in her self-destructive spiral. The perfect place to get herself fucked up beyond all functionality, and know that nobody will take more from her than she'd want to give them, even if she were sober.

Sometimes she doesn't want safety, though. On those nights she goes elsewhere.

She's careful about timing things to avoid getting home at the same time as Ant – she doesn't want him to see the state of her. Leo doesn't ask where she goes, but she sees him watching her when he thinks she's not looking. She knows he's worried, and she ought to care, but she's too lost in the small bliss of anonymity and decadent self-erasure.

It helps, a little; it distracts her, enough.

She should've known it couldn't last.

11

MALJUSTA (UNFAIR)

For once, Ant is home for dinner, and he and Leo seem to have called a truce. The mood's still electric, prickling with tension, but it no longer feels like there's a thread between them on the verge of snapping.

It's Leo who sounds ready to break when he says, 'Sit *down*, Sam,' because the kid's still dancing around the kitchen, even though their food's on the table.

Sam sits down, scowling furiously. Isabel says, 'Is this ... what's happened?'

She's waiting for Leo to say, *I claimed authorship*, or confront her about what she's been up to lately, but he says, 'So you know how I told you there was a certain amount of unrest in Espera?'

'The strikes,' says Sam, trying to redeem herself by proving she was listening.

'The strikes,' Leo agrees. 'And the anger about Project Emerald, and about Isabel. Well ...' He falters, glancing at Ant for help.

Ant takes over smoothly. 'Until now, news about this has been firmly contained within the walls of Espera. Our contacts inside have kept us updated, but there are limits to what they can share, and nobody outside the walls really grasps what's happening. But me and Leo have been helping connect them to outsiders, strengthening their support networks out here, and that's given the Free Press a chance to begin sharing intel outside the city firewalls.'

'We thought ...' says Leo, looking uncomfortable, 'if people here knew more about Espera, they'd be willing to support people there, especially those fighting for abolitionist causes. And we need money and support, if we're going to help the workers on strike.'

'Since Leo doesn't feel like making himself the face of the resistance—'

'Since I'm *understandably hesitant* to become a figurehead, we've been trying to do this another way,' says Leo, cutting Ant off before he launches into another rant. 'But it's had some unintended consequences.'

Sam's looking down at her phone in mounting concern. 'You mean the part where the Free Press leaked Isabel's identity to the entire internet?' she says. 'That kind of unintended consequences?'

They *what*? 'Wait, fuck, what do you mean—?'

'They don't know you're here,' Leo assures her hastily. 'They shared the *Bulletin* article, the one from before you left, that said Isabel Ryans was the Moth. They haven't admitted you left Espera.'

'They didn't *know* you'd left Espera,' adds Ant. 'We never told them you were here. But once your picture hit the internet, it didn't take long for people to connect it to that photo of you ...'

The 'assassin girl' photo. Isabel as an exhausted, blood-soaked refugee, photographed without knowing she was even being perceived. 'Shit,' she breathes.

Sam is still grimly scrolling. 'Basically the only thing they don't know about you is your address, at this point. And that won't take long. There's already a website where people are reporting sightings of people they think are you. *Called herself Marie, but she told me it was her in the pictures, and—*'

Isabel snatches the phone out of Sam's hand before she can read the rest. She only ever used that name with Kate, and she doesn't need to know what else the girl would have said about her. 'Fuck,' she says. 'What do we do?'

'I don't know,' Leo admits. 'It's not ... it shouldn't make a difference, if people in Leeds know you're the Moth. You were always a curiosity, your status as a refugee was always in question, and your picture was always online.'

'But it does make a difference,' says Ant flatly. 'Before, people didn't know for sure that you were a murderer – only that you looked like one. Combined with the Project Emerald news, and the death of Suzie Davies …' He glances at Sam, but she doesn't react to her sister's name.

'You're not popular,' finishes Leo. 'It's only online right now. The mainstream media never publishes stuff from within Espera. But the more momentum it gains, the more likely they'll report on it eventually.'

Sam tugs insistently on her phone until Isabel is forced to release her grip. 'These can't all be real sightings,' says the kid, scrolling through the website. 'Not unless you've been spending a lot of time in gay clubs.' Whatever Isabel does with her face gives her away. 'Wait, you have? But I thought you were ace?'

Isabel doesn't know what that means, and doesn't want to admit it. 'I can go where I like,' she says. 'I'm a grown adult, aren't I?'

'You're barely a step above a wanted fugitive at this point,' says Leo, who also looks surprised, although he's doing a better job of hiding it than Sam. 'I don't think you should go out alone any more. It's not safe.'

Isabel can practically feel the walls closing in on her as he speaks. 'It's safer for me on my own than with you,' she says. '*I* can look after myself. You being seen with me only makes it more likely they'll figure out where I live.'

'Even so—' begins Leo, but Ant cuts him off.

'No, she's right. If they see us together, they'll realise she's not the only Esperan in this area, and it won't be long before they triangulate our address. We all need to be careful.'

'And Espera?' asks Sam, finally putting her phone away. 'What's happening there, now they've got the news out?'

'I'm not sure,' admits Ant. 'One of my contacts hasn't checked in for a couple of days, so either he's in transit to another safe house, or the guilds aren't as weak as we think. I'll—' He breaks off and swallows, his only concession to concern. 'I'll follow up tomorrow, see what the latest is. But if things continue like this, everything will change.'

Isabel knows it's a fuse that was laid a long time ago, explosive with a century of cruelty behind it. But it still feels faintly surreal that Project Emerald, or Suzie Davies, could be the catalyst to set it alight. That *Isabel* could be the catalyst, however indirectly, and through whatever monstrous acts.

She never set out to start a revolution. She was only trying to survive. But if what the city needs is a figurehead to rally against – well, maybe her villain status is good for something. Perhaps that'll be a comfort, when they eventually hunt her down.

'I'm not hungry,' she says, pushing her nearly untouched plate away. 'I'm going to my room.'

'Isabel,' begins Leo, but she's already shoved back her chair. She can't sit here calmly, knowing the world is turning against her for what she did in Espera. Soon she won't just be the nameless assassin girl, a fun curiosity for people who've never met a killer before. Soon they'll want to hold her *accountable*, and she doesn't even know how she'd begin to take responsibility for everything she's done.

'Don't come after me,' she tells them firmly, and goes to her room, the only safe place she's got left.

It catches Isabel out, how much it hurts to think of her new life going to shit. She's hardly been doing a great job of making it work, even if she's getting better at pretending. But now, with the possibility of building a future here fracturing around her, all she wants to do is peel off her skin and scream, because it isn't fair.

She knew she couldn't leave the Moth behind in Espera. Kate proved that, for fuck's sake. But she thought she'd have longer before it caught up with her, before everyone knew.

One thing's for sure: she can't stay in this house all night, not with fear and anger buzzing beneath her skin. She waits until the household has gone to bed, writes a note for the others in case they wake up before she's back, and lets herself out of the front door as quietly as she can.

Most of her usual haunts aren't safe any more, but she thinks she'll be okay down at the garage bar. The crew there, with their welcoming smiles and general disdain for authority, are unlikely to turn her away or use her new infamy as an excuse to gawp.

It's late; the speeches and politics are over for the night, if they happened today at all. Isabel spots a few familiar faces, and Maggie's propping up her usual end of the bar. The bartender – a guy she thinks she's heard others call Dan – gives her a nod of welcome and slides a shot across the bar before she's even asked for it. It's almost like belonging.

It seems to take longer than usual to get the half-drunk buzz that makes the coloured lights and questionable music of this place bearable, though. Dan slides her another shot, and another. She's losing track of her alcohol tolerance, always needs to push further to get half as far, and maybe that's what fucks her up, or maybe the pills Jo slips her when she ventures onto the dancefloor aren't what she took before, or maybe, maybe it's just her old damaged body reacting wrong, the way it so often does. Doesn't matter. All she knows is that the world is green and gold and soft, her fear and anger giving way to mellow contentment. She hardly notices when somebody grabs her by the arm and drags her out into the muggy night air.

'Hey!' someone yells. Maggie, she thinks, bold and bright and revolutionary as ever. 'Leave her alone, you sick fuck, can't you see she's high? Tashie, come on, come back inside—'

'I'm not—' begins a familiar voice, but someone's already yanking her away. 'Wait, please, I'm trying to help. I'm her housemate.'

Leo.

Shit.

Leo can't be here. Leo can't see her like this. Isabel tries to tell him to go away and she tries to run and neither works because her words have abandoned her and her legs are rooted to the ground. He takes her arm and begins to lead her away, making reassuring promises to Maggie and the others, but she wants to beg him to let her go back, let her be Natasha for a little while longer . . .

When they're completely out of sight and earshot, Leo says, 'Christ, Isabel, there's going out on your own and then there's ending up in a place like that. What were you *thinking*?'

The fresh air is beginning to sober her up, enough to turn her head and ask him, 'A place like what?'

He doesn't have an answer to that, not one he's willing to say out loud. And she's glad, because right now her grasp of language isn't strong enough to defend the bar and the people there. He puts her arm over his shoulder and his own arm around her waist, half carrying her, and then says, 'I knew you were drinking, but this . . . how long has this been going on, Isabel?'

How long has what been going on? The world? Herself? The flickering lights inside her head? She's pretty sure she could have a conversation with her own kneecaps right now, but she can't seem to fathom the words to answer Leo. Maybe because he, unlike her skeleton, doesn't understand the backwards tongue of the inside of her head.

'Jesus, you're out of it,' he says. 'How did you – you know what, I don't want to know how you're paying for drugs. I'm pretty sure that would make me an accomplice.'

''ccomplice is for crimes,' Isabel manages. 'No crimes.'

'No *crimes*?' Leo repeats. 'You're high as fuck right now, your friend admitted it. Whatever you took was definitely not legal, and I'd have noticed if you were paying for it with my card.'

She shrugs, which proves quite difficult to do in her current position. 'Not everyone wants money,' she gets out.

Whether or not he understands the implications of this, he doesn't comment. He hails a cab and bundles Isabel into it, giving the driver their address and leaning over to buckle her into her seat to keep her upright.

He's silent the rest of the way home. Isabel leans her head against the window and ignores the way it jolts whenever they pass over a bump in the road. She's only half awake by the time the taxi pulls up outside their house and Leo heaves her out, helping her stumble across the threshold.

Inside, he sits her down at the kitchen table, pours a large glass of water, and places it in front of her. He takes her special bread from the cupboard and slots two slices into her toaster.

She stares at the glass for a long time before she manages to take a sip. By the time she's drunk half the water, Leo's putting a plate of toast down in front of her. 'Eat that,' he says. 'Maybe then you can explain this to me.'

'There's nothing to explain,' she says resentfully, but she eats the toast. It soaks up some of the alcohol, even if it can't touch everything else currently turning her brain inside out.

Leo takes a seat across from her, arms folded. He doesn't look impressed. 'I know you're upset,' he says. 'I get it. But this doesn't seem like a one-off. So tell me: how long has this been going on?'

'How long has *what* been going on?'

'This.' He gestures to her. 'The drinking. The drugs. Whatever the fuck you're doing to pay for it – I don't want to ask too many questions about *that*.'

'Don't be a bigot,' she says, words a little slurred, and wishes she had her radical friends here to explain to him why it's not like that and why he doesn't have to look at her like she's dirty, before it occurs to her that maybe he thinks she's been killing people. And that – well, she can't tell if she wants to laugh or cry, but it doesn't matter, since right now she can only prop her head in her hands and wait for the lights to stop flashing.

'This isn't about my opinions or beliefs,' says Leo, still frighteningly calm. 'This is about you being severely traumatised and apparently entirely unconcerned with your own personal safety. So I'm going to ask you one more time. How long has this been going on?'

She shrugs. 'Not that long.' It's not like she's kept track. It wasn't a deliberate thing in the first place; she barely knows how it started. With Kate – is that where it began?

'Do you know why I was out there looking for you tonight, Isabel?'

She shrugs. 'Because you thought people might come after the Moth?'

'Because you're a fucking mess,' he says, and sits back. 'I've been trying so hard to give you space. You're gone every night, you never talk about where you've been, and, yes, you're an adult, and you can go where you like, but I'm worried, Isabel. You're going to get yourself killed.'

She thought she was doing okay at hiding all the ways she's falling apart, but Leo's always seen straight through her. 'I can look after myself.'

'Can you?' he says. 'Because right now, it looks like you're doing the opposite.'

She frowns at him. 'I wasn't ... I wasn't hurting myself. I was having fun.'

'Fun,' he repeats. 'Did you forget, somehow, that you're immunocompromised and on a bunch of meds that don't mix well with alcohol and recreational drugs? You've got no idea what's in those things. You could've gone into anaphylaxis at any time, if they'd destabilised your mast cells. Does that sound like fun to you?'

'I'm not—'

'If you're about to tell me you're not immunocompromised, don't try it. I talked to Daragh, Isabel. I know enough about your medical history to know your body is a mess. The fact that we've got two toasters should make that pretty damn clear.'

Isabel needs him to stop caring so much about her, and to stop throwing reminders of that care in her face.

She swallows hard and repeats, 'I wasn't trying to hurt myself.'

'Then what were you doing?'

Filling a void. 'I just … wanted to be someone else for a while.'

Leo looks at her for a long moment, and then he pillows his head on his folded arms on the table and stays there for a long moment, a position of absolute exhaustion and defeat. She reaches out to pat his shoulder, then thinks better of it.

Eventually he raises his head. *'Please* tell me you haven't been sharing needles.'

This, at least, she can be honest about. 'Haven't taken anything that used them.'

He passes his hand across his face. 'Okay. Well. One less thing for me to worry about. And have you got yourself tested at all since this whole … misery porn trip started? Or were you just going to let your body take its chances?'

'Tested?' she asks, unsure what he means.

'I'll take that as a no. Christ.'

How quickly he's adapted to this world. How easily their words fall from his lips, as though he's shed Espera like so much dead skin.

'I didn't mean to worry you,' she says in a small voice. 'I . . . I left you a note.'

'A note,' says Leo, and laughs, faintly hysterical. 'Sure. That would've helped, if something happened and you couldn't get home.'

She doesn't have a *home*. Home was Espera and home is gone. 'I'm sorry.'

'You know I've got to tell Emily about this? Legally, it could screw us over if I don't and it comes out anyway.'

For the first time, Isabel feels afraid. 'Will they take me away? From you?'

'I don't know. Depends if they think I'm a fit guardian once they know I let this happen.'

'It's not your fault.'

'Doesn't matter. I didn't stop you; that's all they'll see. You'll probably have to agree to some kind of treatment, at least, likely inpatient, and maybe that'll convince them you're committed to turning your back on this particular episode, but—'

'Inpatient?' Isabel repeats, as panicked as she can be when her mind still feels like it's operating on another plane of existence. She's spent too much of her life in hospitals already; she can't bear any more.

'You're an addict, Isabel.'

She shakes her head. 'No. No, I'm not. That's not what this is about.'

'Then what *is* it about? Because that's the best explanation I can come up with that'll make them cut you some slack, and unless you've got a better idea . . .'

'I'm not an addict,' she repeats. She doesn't have a better explanation for him. 'I'm just . . . lost, Leo.'

He sighs and gets up, filling the kettle and flicking it on. 'Then, okay, we take the mental health angle. God knows you need the therapy, though I hoped we'd reach the point where you'd feel safe enough to choose it yourself. But that won't be enough, and with all this Moth stuff coming out . . .'

The softness of the drugs is wearing off, and the world around her feels sharp and unfriendly. 'You're trying to send me away?'

'I'd rather not, but I don't see that I've got much choice. There'll be somewhere that can help you, I'm sure, but if you stay here . . .'

'If I stay here at least I'm not surrounded by strangers who've got no idea what it's like to come from Espera!'

'But I can't look after you, Isabel!' he says, putting a mug down on the counter so hard it cracks. Leo stares at it for a few seconds, startled into silence by its fragility. When he speaks again, his voice wavers, breaking. 'I thought I could. That's why I filled in all those bloody forms. But clearly what I'm doing isn't enough, because I *saw* what people said on that sighting website, and I didn't think it was true, but it is, isn't it?

All of it. I know you, Isabel, I know that isn't what you want. So whatever this is, self-harm via shagging or—'

'Don't,' says Isabel, because it sounds so much worse coming from Leo, but he's not listening to her any more.

'You need help. *Real* help, real doctors who know what they're talking about.'

She doesn't want doctors. She doesn't want anyone poking around inside her head, especially if it means being separated from the only people she's got left in the world. 'Please,' she says, not knowing what she's asking for, only that she needs it in a way she hasn't needed anything for a long time. 'Please, Leo.'

He keeps his back to her as he makes his tea, stirring carefully and placing the teaspoon precisely down on the counter so that it forms a perfect right angle to the sink. 'You could have died, Isabel,' he says finally. 'You could have died, because nobody would've known how to help you, and I'd have had to go and identify your body. Did that ever occur to you at all?'

She wants to say: *maybe that would be easier for both of us.*

And because she's too numb to think better of it, she does.

Leo doesn't turn, but he stills, muscles tensing, hands gripping the edge of the counter. 'I lost my entire family,' he says. 'Both my sisters. My mum. I lost them *all*, one after the other. Don't tell me that losing someone is *ever* easier than having them there.'

But Isabel's not his sister. She's a mess.

'Then don't send me away,' she says. 'Please. Give me one more chance. I'll – I'll do better, I promise.'

He stares into his mug for such a long time that she thinks he won't answer her at all. She draws patterns in the condensation left by her glass and waits for something, anything, to break the silence.

Finally, he sighs, letting out his breath in one long stream. 'Go to bed, Isabel,' he says. 'We can talk about this when you've slept. And when you're actually sober.'

Sobriety won't help, but she knows better than to argue with him when he's like this.

Isabel goes to bed.

12

KURAĜIGA (SUPPORTIVE)

They don't talk about it.

Leo leaves an array of pointed pamphlets on the table before he heads out to work: 'Sobriety and you', 'Support in bereavement', 'Low-cost counselling'. Isabel ignores them and swipes the spare key from its hook, noting that Leo has taken the wallet with him, or put it somewhere else. Well, that's fine. She doesn't need it.

She heads back to the garage bar (if it has a name, it's not painted on any sign or awning). She tells herself it's because she owes them an explanation before she disappears, and maybe that's true, but she's there for more than duty, still craving the freedom of being somebody else and the glory of a willing self-destruction.

She's never been here in daylight. The rolling metal door is down, the shutter painted in bright colours by somebody with more enthusiasm than skill. Isabel hesitates. There must be another entrance somewhere, a door she can knock on . . .

'Oi! Tashie!'

The voice comes from above. Isabel looks up, startled, and sees Maggie on the building's flat roof, leaning over the small parapet. She waves tentatively. Maggie waves back, then climbs over the parapet and lets herself drop, hanging from the wall until she's in position to fall neatly to the ground.

Isabel would have done it with more elegance, but it's not bad for a civilian.

'Thank fuck you're all right,' says Maggie. 'I've been regretting not chasing after you since you left last night. Felt sure the next time I saw you would be on the news reporting your murder. That guy—'

'Really is my housemate,' Isabel admits. 'And as for what the news is saying about me . . .'

Maggie purses her lips. 'Yeah,' she says, so she's heard. *Tashie* is a kindness, pretending she's still Natasha, pretending she was ever Natasha in the first place. 'I wasn't gonna bring it up if you didn't.'

An awkward half-shrug. 'Some of it's true.'

She waits for Maggie to ask which parts, whether she really killed a child; to turn her away once she knows. But she only says, 'Why are you here? We don't open 'til this evening.'

'I . . .' Why *is* she here? It feels remarkably presumptuous to admit she came to say goodbye, as though they'd care if somebody who never paid for her drinks stopped showing up to claim them. So she looks at Maggie and says the only honest thing: 'I'm not okay.'

Maggie regards her. 'Yeah,' she says again. 'I figured that one out. What do you need?'

Of course she figured that out. There's a reason she stopped responding to Isabel's flirting, recognising it as the self-destructive impulse that it was. 'I . . . my housemate . . .' Isabel stares down at the cracked concrete pavement. 'He wants to send me away. Make me get sober, get therapy, I don't fucking know, but I . . . can't, okay? I can't.'

There's a long pause. Then Maggie walks over to the garage door and hauls it open with a thunderous metallic roar, gesturing for Isabel to follow her inside.

In daylight, the place is grimier than ever: mismatched chairs and tables around the edges of the room, a bar that isn't quite level with the ground. The mismatched fairy lights are off, but here's a lamp on behind the bar and Dan's there, cleaning.

He glances up when Maggie pulls out a stool and indicates for Isabel to sit. 'Hey,' he says. 'No afternoon dates on stock-take day, you know that.'

'Not a date, Danny boy,' says Maggie. 'I'm cutting her off. Got a wristband?'

Dan shoots a look at Isabel, but rummages in a drawer behind the bar and emerges with a plastic wristband, black and red. He gives it to Maggie, who slips it snugly around Isabel's wrist and fastens the clasp.

'If it breaks, tell me. If you decide to cut it off, tell me that, too, and I'll talk you into having another one.'

Isabel looks down at the wristband. It feels like a shackle. 'What's it for?'

'Means no one here will serve you alcohol, even if you ask for it. Or drugs,' she adds, as an afterthought. 'God, I gotta talk to Jo about that anyway.' She waves away the thought and focuses her attention on Isabel, eyes like searchlights. 'So. You're fucked up. What is it, grief? That's gotta be part of why you left, right, lost too many people?'

She's seen the news. She knows who Isabel is. Still, it feels wrong, talking about this here in a place where she's only ever been made of lies. 'That's part of it.'

'The bit where you're a notorious murderer and half your city's after your blood would be the other part, I guess,' says Dan, tone too light for his words.

Maggie glares at him. 'Great, Dan, really helpful, that's exactly what she needs right now.'

But weirdly, it's a relief to hear it said out loud: to know where they stand, and how much they know. It might be a game to them, a distant fantasy they can joke about because they don't know the taste of blood, but at least she doesn't have to lie. 'Yeah, that's pretty much it,' Isabel admits.

There's a moment's silence. 'Well,' says Maggie, rallying, 'can't help with that bit. But grief – you're not the only one. Self-destructive impulses – we're experts. And not wanting to let psychs inside your head – that's basically our entire ethos. So.' She reaches across the bar and takes the pen from

Dan's shirt pocket, ignoring his yelp of protest. 'Give me your hand.' Isabel stretches out her arm. Maggie grabs it and writes something on the back of her hand, the careful pull of Isabel's skin under the nib of the pen the closest she's got to meaningful touch in months. When she lets go, Isabel sees that it's an address and a time. 'What's this?'

'Support group. Mondays, Wednesdays, Fridays. Come to one or all, whatever suits.'

'James won't like it,' says Dan, a warning tone in his voice. 'Or Meera.'

'Fuck them. Tashie needs us.' Still *Tashie*. Still that warmth and that unbearable kindness in Maggie's face. 'Got it?' she says, looking back at Isabel. 'Tell your housemate it's AA. It's not, because none of us vibes with the higher power thing, not to mention finding the whole one-strike-and-you're-starting-over approach unreasonably punitive, but maybe it'll put his mind at ease.'

Isabel's got absolutely no idea what she's talking about, but she recognises when she's being thrown a lifeline, a way to prove to Leo that she's trying and he doesn't need to send her to a hospital so they can poke around in her brain and fix her the hard way. 'It's ... therapy?' she says.

'It's community,' corrects Maggie, and gets up. 'I'm making a cuppa. Want one?' Isabel nods, tentatively. 'Dan?' He nods too. 'All right. Back in a mo.'

She heads out through a door at the back of the bar. Isabel's left alone with Dan, who goes back to straightening up the bottles behind the counter.

'How long have you known who I am?' she asks.

He doesn't turn around. 'Thought you looked faintly familiar the first time I saw you, but you were screwing Mags, so I figured it was none of my business. Then Pher sent me the Free Press leaks and I joined the dots.'

She can't read him at all; can't tell if he hates her or likes her or doesn't care. 'Pher,' she repeats, rather than deal with the rest of that pronouncement.

'You'll have seen him dancing. Small guy. Too much hair. Bad fashion sense.'

Isabel takes his word for it. 'And you don't . . . mind? You're not afraid of me?'

Now Dan does cast a glance over his shoulder, evaluating her. 'Mind?' he repeats. 'Sure, I think the whole thing's fucked. Pher's been on at us to care about Espera for ages, but most of us were only humouring him, 'til now, with that book . . .' His gaze narrows. 'You got anything to do with that?'

'I know the authors,' says Isabel carefully.

'Jesus. Pher'll be delighted. Well, anyway, can't say any of us are pro-murder, but, y'know, shit's complicated, the book made that clear. And somebody who's fine with it doesn't drink the way you've been drinking the last few weeks, so seems to me you're not particularly pro-murder either. Least not these days.'

This is not what Isabel would have expected him to say. 'So that makes it okay?'

'No,' he says, turning back to his work. 'Of course it doesn't. But you know that, don't you? If you didn't, you wouldn't be here, looking tragic at Mags. And as for being afraid of you, well, you've had plenty of chances to hurt us and never taken them. So.'

So. As if that's the end of the conversation. Maggie's got the same quirk, their friendship apparent in their shared gestures and phrases. Maybe something other than friendship, actually, now that Isabel considers them in daylight: Dan with the same dark hair and hazel eyes as Maggie, the similarities made more apparent by Maggie's business-like crew cut. She can't gauge how old they both are, perhaps early twenties, but there can't be more than a couple of years between them.

'You're siblings,' she says aloud, not quite hiding her surprise. 'Aren't you?'

Dan snorts a laugh. 'What, they don't have those where you come from? No need to sound so astonished.'

Isabel feels her face grow hot. 'I didn't realise, that's all.' She's not sure how she feels about his dismissive *you were screwing Mags* remark now she knows they're related: does that make it better, or worse? Leaving aside the part where it's barely true, and was only the once in any case.

'Maggie's my little sister. *Little* being the operative word,' he adds. 'I've got eleven months on her, even if she does her best to pretend it's the other way around.'

'You just can't get over me being taller than you for three whole years when we first started secondary,' says Maggie, emerging from the back room with three mugs of tea in her precarious grip. She distributes them with care. 'Here.'

'So you own this place?' says Isabel, wrapping her hands

136

around the mug. The day is cool for July, but still the heat of the tea feels momentarily overbearing, sticky and too much.

'Run it,' says Dan. 'Technically speaking the lease is in our uncle's name, but he lets us do what we want with it. Maggie's been filling it with radicals since the beginning.'

'I've been filling it with my *friends*,' Maggie corrects. 'Just because you don't have any, doesn't mean the rest of us are similarly afflicted.'

'And this support group . . .'

Dan huffs out his breath. 'I'm still not sure this is a good idea,' he says. 'There's people there who won't be pleased to see you.'

'Ignore him,' says Maggie immediately. 'You belong there as much as anyone else. Look, it's not therapy and it's not rehab, but it's people who've been through some of the same shit you're going through, and sometimes, not being alone with it is what matters most. I can't promise it's a judgement-free zone, but it's a hell of a lot friendlier than getting sectioned because you freaked your housemate out one too many times, okay?'

Isabel will try pretty much anything if it'll mean Leo doesn't send her away.

'Okay,' she says, and takes a sip of her tea, just in time to see the siblings exchange a look she can't read.

Maggie wins whatever unspoken fight they're having. 'Great,' she says, turning back to Isabel. 'I'll see you there.'

13

NEBONVENA (UNWELCOME)

The address Maggie gave Isabel is a community centre about half a mile from the bar. Leo's got work, so he doesn't accompany Isabel to the door, but she can tell he wanted to; she's not convinced he believes her about where she's going.

Inside there's a circle of chairs, half filled. Some of those present look faintly familiar, as though she might have seen them before in poor light and while significantly inebriated; others are strangers. They're young, mostly – student-aged, probably gathered from Maggie's friendship groups. Isabel takes a seat facing the door so that she can watch the later arrivals, and waits to be asked what she's doing here, but nobody questions her.

Maggie arrives shortly after that, and then Dan. They sit

on opposite sides of the circle, but both of them flash her a welcoming smile, which she appreciates.

When the seats are nearly all filled, a woman stands up, introduces herself as Catharine, and invites those gathered to share how things are going. Isabel stays quiet, staring at the floor, as people speak – talking about addiction, recounting a good week or a bad one, a shaking voice describing the anniversary of a death. She gets why Maggie invited her, but she doesn't know what she's meant to do now that she's here. She doesn't *know* these people, and she can't help them, nor can they help her. She shouldn't have come.

Turns out she's not the only one who feels that way. 'What I want to know,' says a rough voice, 'is why the fuck *she's* here.'

Isabel looks up.

The speaker is a young man she noticed when he walked in. Military, she'd say, from his posture, his close-shaved hair, plain clothes like he doesn't want to worry about choice because he's used to wearing a uniform. He's in his mid-twenties at most, and he's pointing straight at Isabel.

'James,' begins Dan, a warning tone in his voice.

'No, I saw her on the news, I know who she is, she's from Espera.' He pushes forward, out of his seat, and Isabel tightens her muscles. They've got an audience: everyone in the circle is focused on them, curiosity and anger and distaste on their faces as they look at her. 'Your city killed my friend,' he tells Isabel. 'Blew him to pieces half a metre away from me. What do you have to say about that?'

For a moment, she wonders what this outsider's friend did to

139

warrant an Esperan hit, and then her tired brain puts the pieces together – *military, PTSD, support group* – and she realises it was nothing as personal as that. Just one of thousands of bombs the city's exported into every combat zone in the world. For once, an Esperan crime for which she can't be held responsible.

She says, oddly calmer now that somebody's angry with her, 'That was nothing to do with me.'

He scoffs. 'Bullshit.'

Isabel keeps her gaze steadily on him. 'I was a field agent,' she says. 'A soldier. Like you. I didn't make explosives. I'm not responsible for your friend's death.'

'You're a murderer.' He turns to Catharine, who seems to be vaguely in charge. 'She's a murderer. Why the hell is she here?'

Maggie cuts in before Catharine can speak. 'We let *you* in, didn't we? She's here for the same reason you are.'

James turns to scowl at her. 'I'm not—'

'You were in the fucking army, mate,' says Dan. He looks relaxed, slumped in his chair with his arms folded, but there's a core of steel beneath his mild tone. 'Pot, kettle. Leave her the hell alone and sit down.'

Isabel sees James's instincts warring: his feelings versus a direct order. In the end, the order wins. He sinks reluctantly into his seat, and Maggie gives Catharine an apologetic nod.

'Sorry, Cath,' she says.

Catharine rolls her eyes. 'You could've warned the group, Mags.'

'Wasn't sure she'd come. Didn't want to get you all excited about nothing.' Maggie winks at Isabel. 'Sorry about that. You might want to introduce yourself now.'

She doesn't want. She doesn't know what name to give them. *Natasha. Isabel. Bella.* She doesn't know who she's trying to be.

But everyone's looking at her now, and she can't let James's anger be the only thing they know about her. So she says, 'Isabel. I'm from Espera. And I . . . can't go back.'

'What does that mean, *field agent*?' says someone. 'What do you mean by that?'

Isabel glances at Maggie, but apparently she's had all the help she's going to get. She twists the plastic wristband around and around, feeling the edge bite into her skin when she tugs on it too hard. 'I was a guild contract killer. And,' she adds, a little vindictively, because if they're going to hate her they might as well have the truth, 'I was very good at it.'

There's uproar at that. Isabel stays in her chair and lets them yell at each other over her head. Telling Maggie it's antithetical to the group's values to invite someone *like that*. Or that it's *really fucking inconsiderate, actually*, considering what others present have been through. Asking why they're condoning the military-industrial complex by letting one of its tools into their space.

It goes on for a while.

Finally, Maggie says, 'None of you lot have got to stay if you can't handle it. But she's grieving, and she needs help. Isn't that what we do? Isn't that the whole fucking point of this? Can't ask people to turn their backs on the system if we're gonna abandon them too.'

And Dan says, 'Half of you have been dancing with her for weeks and she never killed any of you, so for fuck's sake, give over.'

And Catharine says, 'All of you, sit down, now. You absolute *children*.' As the room quietens down, she turns to Isabel. 'Why are you here?'

Fuck if she knows. Clearly nobody wants her here either. She tugs on the wristband again. 'Maggie invited me. Said it would help. My housemate was going to send me away. I'm ...' None of that's enough. She says, 'Nearly everybody I care about is dead. I haven't got anywhere else to go. I haven't got anyone else who'll fix me.'

'Ain't anyone who can fix *you*,' says somebody in the circle; she doesn't raise her head fast enough to see who, but Maggie snaps, 'Quit it, Ali.'

'Is that what you want?' asks Catharine gently. 'Someone who can fix you?'

Isabel shrugs. Right now she wants to be gone from here, to have never come in the first place, to not feel them watching her. 'I'm not okay,' she tells them, just like she told Maggie, and then the part she hardly dares admit to herself because she doesn't deserve it: 'I want to be okay.'

Catharine, she sees now, is wearing a red-and-black wristband too. 'We can't fix you,' she says, still in that gentle voice. 'We can't fix ourselves, either. But we can give you the space to talk about it, if that would help.'

She doesn't know what she's supposed to be talking about. If she wanted therapy, she'd have let Leo send her to a hospital. Instead, she's sitting in this room, the eyes on her still hostile, James glaring at her from across the circle. A soldier. He's a murderer too, she'd bet, blood on his hands just the way there is on Isabel's. Maybe he'd understand, if he could stop blaming her for five seconds because it's easier than looking himself in the eye.

Isabel doesn't say any of this. She says, 'I came because Maggie invited me. I don't know what I'm meant to be doing.'

Maggie says, 'Tell us about Espera. There are a lot of rumours, but most of us don't know what's true and what isn't.'

'If it's violent, it's real,' says Isabel.

'The book,' says one of the others in the circle, a boy of about eighteen with too much hair. 'It talked about an abolitionist movement.'

'The book's unverified, Pher,' somebody else begins, but Isabel says, 'Yes. They were the ones who wrote it. I ... I know them.'

'Holy shit,' says the boy – Pher. 'You *know* them?'

'Let's not stray off topic,' says Catharine. 'Why did you leave Espera, Isabel?'

Another shrug. 'Couldn't stay. Everyone I cared about was dead, and everyone else wanted me that way.' *Dead* is such a simple, rounded little word for the way they were taken from her, the way she watched them die. She was holding Emma when she died. She watched Daragh fall. She— 'I couldn't bear it any more. I didn't want to be the person the city was making me.'

'And you came here, and tried to lose yourself.'

Catharine is looking at the wristband Isabel can't stop playing with. Isabel feels crushed beneath the weight of her gaze; it's no easier for knowing that Catharine's been a recipient of the same mercy from Maggie and Dan.

'Turned out not to be very good at it,' she says. 'My housemate gave me an ultimatum. Sort my shit out or I wouldn't be allowed to stay with him any more, because they'd say I wasn't *integrating*.' She can't hide her disdain for the word. 'So I'm here.'

'See,' says Maggie, and when Isabel glances up, she realises this is directed at James. 'Told you she was here for the same reasons as you.'

'Fuck off, Maggie,' says James, but some of the fury in his voice has faded.

Catharine gives them both a tired look. 'That's enough,' she says. 'Thank you for sharing, Isabel. I hope we can help you find yourself again, if these clowns will stop bitching about it long enough to remember the whole point of this support group was to help *everyone*. And if they don't like it, they're welcome to leave, because I'm the one who books this hall.'

There are mutinous mutters at this, but nobody argues. Isabel's grateful. She doesn't want to have to be the one who leaves, not when it took all her courage to come here in the first place.

She keeps quiet for the rest of the session, and when it

finally draws to a close and everyone flocks towards the tea and snacks at the back of the room, she gathers her bag and prepares to make a hasty exit.

But Maggie catches her before she can flee. Says, 'You used to work out a lot, didn't you? Back in Espera?'

Isabel blinks at her. 'What?'

'You have the look of somebody who used to exercise a fair bit.'

Used to. A small knife to use against her. Once again she's trapped in this body. Living in it while it tries to die and she refuses to let it, dragging it back up, keeping it strong as though that'll protect her – except she can't even do that these days, because she's not allowed to train, not allowed weapons, so she's getting weaker all the time and she hates the feeling of wasting away, the endless sense of diminishing.

'I guess,' she says finally. 'I used to train.'

Maggie nods like she expected that. 'There's a gym here, you know. Cheap. If you joined . . .' She hesitates, then gestures to her arms, her sleeveless tee showing off her muscles. 'I figured out a couple of years back that if you channel your angst into weights, you get great biceps, and then you're both less stressed *and* you're hot. Think about it, will you?'

Cheap isn't *free*, and Isabel doesn't have any money that isn't Leo's. She can't ask him to pay for something extra, not after everything he's done to keep her alive so far. But the thought of reclaiming some control and remembering how to exist in her own skin *does* appeal, in a way that coming back to this support group doesn't.

'I'll think about it,' she says.

Maggie gives her a comradely punch in the shoulder. 'Good,' she says. 'And sorry about James. I knew he'd be like that. Would've warned you, except I thought if I did, you wouldn't come.'

Astute. She's got Isabel's measure, even though they hardly know each other. 'Yeah, well, it's not like he's wrong. I don't belong here.'

'Bullshit,' says Maggie. 'You're not the only person in that room who's killed. You're not the only person who was trapped into a life they didn't want when they were barely more than a child. And you're certainly not the only one who was abused.' She sees Isabel's startled look and says, 'It doesn't take a genius to figure out. You're way too young to have been an adult when things started, and somebody who was cared for doesn't have a scar like that one on your hand. I'm willing to bet you've got others, too.'

'I . . .' Isabel swallows hard. She doesn't like the idea that she's that easy to read, though on some level it's a relief not to have to say any of it herself. 'I'm the only one from Espera.'

'You're not responsible for all of your city's crimes, though.'

'James seems to think I am.'

'James has let grief make him bitter and his feelings aren't your responsibility. And—' Maggie bites off whatever she was going to say. 'Look, he's not the only one who feels that way, I won't lie to you. Come on Friday and you might meet Meera, and she's got her own grudges against the city. But that's not on you.'

146

'Were you intentionally trying to piss them off when you invited me to this support group?' says Isabel, with a trace of humour. 'Or was that just a fun side effect?'

Maggie pulls a face. 'I – look, I love James, really, I do. I'm the one who invited *him* into the group. And I worked damn hard to justify that to everyone, when they're all anti-military, fuck the army, etc. I pointed out that giving a shit about veterans and survivors is exactly what pacifism looks like sometimes, and eventually they caught on. I did *not* have that fight with them for James to do the same to you.' She jerks her head towards the rest of the group. 'Give them time. We caught them by surprise today. Next time will be easier.'

Next time. As though Isabel wasn't planning to run away and never come back. But Maggie will be disappointed if she doesn't turn up, and Leo will make her go to real therapy, and everyone here will think James scared her away – so she'll have to come, won't she?

'I should go,' she says, softly, like she's apologising. 'I . . . I'm babysitting later.'

Maggie's eyebrows go up. 'Babysitting?'

'My other housemate. She's twelve. She . . . honestly, she looks after me more than I look after her, but Leo doesn't like leaving her alone. So.' There she is, borrowing their phrasing: *So.* Like everything that needs to be said has been said.

'So,' agrees Maggie. 'Think about the gym. It might help. And if you ever want to dance, you know where to find us. We have lemonade on tap, and you wouldn't be the only one sober.' She says this like it's her last chance, like she might not see Isabel again. Maybe she really *does* understand her, and the deep instinct in Isabel's gut that's telling her to run away so she never has to sit here and talk about her feelings again.

'Okay,' says Isabel, and offers her half a smile. 'Tell Catharine I'm sorry about the chaos.'

'Oh, that,' says Maggie dismissively. 'Nah, that's on me, if it's on anyone. I'll make it up to her. Drama comes with the territory.' She crosses her arms. She's right: those biceps *are* impressive. 'I know things were a bit rough, but I'm glad you came today. I hope you're not regretting it either.'

Isabel needs a moment to think about that. Regret has become such an immovable part of the fabric of her existence, she can't quite separate it out from anything else. But: 'No,' she says, and thinks she almost believes it. 'I don't regret it.'

She's not okay. Maybe she never will be. But at least she's not quite so fucking alone with all of it now.

14

SIMILA (ALIKE)

A couple of days pass before Isabel is able to ask Leo about the gym membership; he's working every hour of the day and half the night, coming home frazzled and short-tempered, although he tries not to take it out on Isabel and Sam. When she finally finds a moment to bring it up, a complicated expression crosses his face, and he says, 'I should have thought of that. I'll look into it.'

'Thanks.'

'You're going back, then? To the support group?'

She didn't go back yesterday. She might go tomorrow, if the air is feeling friendly, if she can convince herself to step outside the door. 'I was going to try.'

He nods. 'And you'll be here with Sam tonight?'

She's here with Sam every night. She hasn't gone back to the bar this week, even with the wristband to keep her sober. Isabel's not sure if the sudden babysitting responsibilities are a sign of trust or the opposite, but they're making it difficult for her to do anything Leo wouldn't approve of. 'As always.'

'I appreciate it.' He looks exhausted. She should ask him about that, about how bad things are getting in Espera, whether the strikes are succeeding. But she doesn't know whose side she's meant to be on, and asking might force her to decide, so she doesn't. 'Sam appreciates it too, you know. She likes you.'

Which is mystifying, given everything. 'That's because I let her go to bed later than you do.'

Leo manages half a smile. 'Oh, well, now it all comes out.'

It's a game. A pretence of friendship, a mask over the cracks in their relationship. Something broke that night Leo followed her to the bar: his trust in her ability to keep herself alive, her trust in his willingness to put up with her shit. Now he's waiting for her to relapse and she's waiting for him to abandon her, and the tension's killing them both.

'The gym membership . . .' she says. 'If we can't afford it, I get it. I know I'm not contributing anything.'

'I'll look into it,' Leo promises her again, and he doesn't say it's okay that she's a parasite, but he doesn't tell her to get a job, either. Evidently he's resigned to the impossibility of her finding gainful employment now the city knows she's a murderer. 'I've got to go. I'll be back late; I'll see you tomorrow.'

The next day is Friday, and Isabel spends the morning mired

in indecisive self-pity before she resolves to drag herself to the support group again. They meet at one p.m.; she can see why evenings wouldn't be viable for Maggie and Dan, and maybe the others work in bars and clubs too, but it does rather interrupt the day.

The group is smaller today, and mostly unfamiliar. Dan and Catharine are the only people Isabel recognises, and a young woman she hasn't met before immediately objects to her presence. Meera, it turns out; Maggie mentioned her. She's got a halfway-justifiable grudge against Espera, as the manufacturer of the rubber bullet that blinded her father at a protest, but that doesn't mean it's got anything to do with Isabel.

Without Maggie to defend Isabel or Pher to take the part of Esperan civilians, the ensuing arguments are unpleasant, albeit informative. Outsiders are so *clueless* about life inside Espera – they might think they understand the city's murderous legacy, but they can't grasp the idea that its first victims have always been its inhabitants. To hear them talk, all Esperans are the same: the face of the arms industry, equally guilty, unworthy of being freed from the prison that a warmongering world trapped them in.

Eventually, Catharine gets them back on track, and Meera subsides into glaring. Isabel ignores her, and spends the session hoping nobody asks her to speak. She's afraid they might ask her about Espera again, and she'd feel she owes them her stories because she's the only chance they'll get to learn the truth about the city, but then they might say, *Do you miss it?*, and she doesn't know how to answer that.

Yes: she misses her home. She misses the solar roadways and the lights that guided her path at night; she misses catching glimpses of Emma's art on the walls as she wandered the streets; she misses the colours that serve as a living monument to a city that's alive and thriving despite the death at its heart. She misses the library, and feeling like she belonged.

But more than that, she's realising, she misses killing.

Well. Not killing. Not the deaths themselves, which always hurt, no matter how hard she worked to pretend they didn't, and not Ronan's orders, either. But there's violence inside her and Comma used it, tamed it, gave it a purpose, channelled it until she could almost believe it was their fault and not hers. Leeds can't give her that. Can't – *won't* – use her as a vessel until she doesn't have to hold herself responsible any more. She's left with nowhere to channel that violence except inwards, and Leo stopped that, so what now?

She hates that Comma made her dependent on them, formed her into a thing that can't exist outside the guild. She hates that violence is still, always, her first instinct and basest need, written into her since childhood. She wishes she could grasp this new opportunity for peace with both hands and cling tight to it, the way Leo wants her to.

But that's not who Isabel is. She is what they made her, and they made her a killer, rotten to the core.

She can't say that to these people, though, or to Leo, who would only worry more about her. So she keeps her head down and doesn't speak, although she feels the weight of Catharine's expectant gaze. When the session ends, she makes a hasty exit, heading home before anyone can talk to her. She doesn't know whether this is helping – sitting in that room, listening to other people's unfathomable problems – but the alternatives are sitting at home hating herself or going to actual therapy, so she'll endure it. Doesn't mean she'll endure small talk.

That night, Leo makes it home in time for dinner, and he slides a small green card across the table towards Isabel. 'Got you a present.'

She picks it up. 'Is this . . . ?'

'Gym membership,' he confirms. 'Called by on my way home.'

So he could check the place out, she suspects; verify that the support group really exists and the gym isn't a cover story for another way of self-destructing. But she can't be angry when he's given her back this small freedom: a chance to work her weakened muscles and reclaim some power over a body she used to trust to protect her.

Isabel closes her fingers around the card. 'Thank you,' she says, and means it.

'It's probably not as well equipped as what you're used to,' he warns. 'It's a community centre, not the guild, so target practice is out. But they've got cross-trainers, treadmills, that kind of thing.'

Isabel nods. She doubts they'd let her near any throwing knives even if they had them. 'Any rules?'

'On their part? Probably the usual. Wear clothes. Wipe down the equipment. Don't do anything stupid. On my part ...' He hesitates. 'Let me know when you're going out, okay? So I don't worry about you.'

Leo is by far the kindest jailer Isabel's ever had, but she still resents needing to account for her movements every minute of the day. She does as he asks, though, making sure he knows where she's going before she heads out on Saturday morning, when she hopes the place won't be too crowded.

It's a little busy, but she finds herself a quiet corner near the weights rack and starts to ease herself back into the unfamiliar sensation of physical exercise.

'Hello, little murderer,' says a voice, and she turns to see James, a towel around his neck and a water bottle in his hands. He looks as though he's most of the way through his workout.

'Hello,' says Isabel, and pointedly returns to her bicep curls.

'You're not even going to deny it?' There's a gruff, hoarse quality to his voice, like it's been ruined by smoking or screaming.

Isabel raises her eyebrow. 'I am a murderer,' she says baldly; most people nearby are wearing headphones, and even if somebody overheard, it's nothing that's not already public knowledge. 'But I didn't kill your friend, and I didn't make the bomb that did. You, though ...' She regards him for a second. 'How long were you a soldier?'

She's not expecting James to humour her with answers, but maybe exercise mellows him. 'Eight years,' he says, so either he's older than he looks, or— 'I was sixteen when I enlisted.'

Oh. 'I didn't ...' Isabel begins, hunting for the words. 'I didn't know the army here ...'

'It's not uncommon,' he says flatly, and takes a set of weights from the rack. So he's not going to leave her alone, then – but at least his hands are occupied, so if he wants to hurt her, there'll be a delay. 'I had shitty grades at school and no sense of discipline. Couple of years' training before they'll ever send you into a war zone – why not, right? Everyone thought it would be good for me. And it was, until . . .' He trails off, eyes refocusing on Isabel. There's something sharp and knowing about his expression. 'How old were you?'

'Seventeen,' she says, and then adds, 'or twelve, or nine, or . . . I don't know. I was born into it.'

There's a long silence, broken only by the endless roar of gym equipment and the pounding of other people's feet on the treadmills. It's not a sympathetic pause, but it's an understanding one. The anger she saw in him at the support group has diminished; it was surprise, she thinks, and fear, that fed the outburst. Maybe Maggie's talked to him, or maybe the past few days have given him a chance to reflect on how fucked up Isabel must be to have ended up where she is.

She says, 'You've killed, haven't you?'

James's expression tightens. 'If you're hoping to compare numbers, forget it. Not all of us take pride in our work like you do.'

Isabel puts down her weights for a moment, resting. 'Would you go back, if someone asked you to?'

She can tell he wasn't expecting this follow-up question; he doesn't seem to know how to answer. Then he says, 'Have you ever watched a friend die? Suddenly and violently?'

'Yes.' Emma. Daragh. Would be more if she wasn't a coward, didn't keep running away.

James puts down one of his weights, picks up another, puts it back. 'Has it ever been your fault?'

Now it's Isabel's turn to be surprised. 'I thought you said it was mine,' she says, without animosity.

He doesn't look at her. He seems younger then, diminished by grief, as lost as she is. 'Tom was my best mate,' he says. 'Met him in basic, basically inseparable after that. No head for strategy, but he was the bravest man I ever knew. Always felt safe with him watching my back, and always knew he'd follow where I went.'

Isabel keeps quiet, waiting for the tragedy she knows is coming.

'I ...' He has as much trouble with words as she does, it seems, like language fails grief. 'I made a bad call. Thought the enemy had set up near us, prepping for another assault, so I authorised my team to take them out. With all the shiny new weapons our commanders had ordered for us.'

Esperan weapons. Always on the side of profit, whatever the conflict.

'They were – the camp was – it ...' He looks down at the weight in his hand like he forgot he was holding it, and puts it back on the rack. 'You know, I haven't even talked to Maggie about this?' he says, and gives Isabel a fleeting, bitter smile. It fades, and he continues, 'They were civilians. I fucked up. And when Tom realised, he wanted to go in there. Get people out, help survivors, because we'd just bombed a fucking village,

156

because I had bad intel, because I didn't double-check and my squad trusted me too much to think I might've made a mistake. Of course I went in after him. God, I'd have done anything to undo it, I'd never made a call that bad before. Only not all the bombs we dropped had exploded, and Tom . . .'

'You watched him die,' says Isabel, sparing him the effort of finishing the sentence. 'Collateral damage.'

'Jesus,' he says. 'Yeah. Basically.'

Cautiously, she asks, 'How long ago did this happen?'

''bout a year. I spent the first six months blaming everyone except myself. The bad intel. The bomb that didn't go off.'

'Espera,' says Isabel.

'Espera,' he agrees heavily. 'Then I spent the next six months drinking myself into oblivion trying to forget it ever happened. I'd been discharged, obviously,' he adds. 'They were nice about it, pretended it was medical leave, but I knew I was being punished. Except I'd got nowhere to go back to, after that. Been in the army since I was sixteen, and I'm shit at being a civilian. Don't know what to do with myself without someone telling me what to do, without orders to follow and a routine to make the days a little more predictable. If I hadn't met Maggie, I'd probably be dead by now.'

He doesn't apologise for having a go at her the other day, for which she's grateful; neither of them wants forgiveness from the other. Nor does he say that he blamed her because it was easier than accepting responsibility himself, because she's not his therapist and neither of them needs to voice their self-analysis out loud to understand it.

Uncertainly, she says, 'My best friend died because of me, too.' All her closest friends have died because of her. 'I couldn't save her.'

'And you've killed civilians too, I'm guessing,' he says, this time without hostility.

'Basically everyone I killed was a civilian.' She picks up her own weights again; her arms are sore, but it's easier if she's got something to do with her hands. 'We were both following orders, you and me, but I guess you thought you were on the right side or something. In Espera, there are no sides. No moral justification for any of it. Deaths for profit, that's all it is, and I was good at it, so I made my guild a lot of money. I killed a sixteen-year-old,' she adds. 'And I never knew what he did to make someone call a hit on him, but I eventually tracked down the name of the guy who commissioned it, and . . .' She's never told anyone this. She doesn't think even Ronan knew she had that information. 'Well. Everything I found on him suggests he's an absolute bastard, so the kid was probably innocent. Killed to cover up something the guy had done.'

'Shit,' says James.

'His name was Oliver. Oliver Roe.' The name is important; it reminds her that he was a person. 'And then there was Suzie.' Isabel swallows hard. 'She was twelve.'

She expects him to walk away then, disgusted, but maybe there were bodies in that bombed-out village that were too small, too, because he just lets out a long, slow breath and says, 'I heard about that. So it's true, then.'

Isabel looks sideways at him, surprised. She knew the Free

158

Press leaks were spreading, but somehow she thought if he'd read as far as Suzie, he wouldn't have stopped to talk to her. 'I wish I could tell you it wasn't.'

James gives her a curious, evaluating look. 'Why'd you do it?'

Isabel weighs up her answers. *I didn't have a choice. I was trying to save a friend of mine. I'm evil and rotten to the core.* Finally, she says, 'Because I was afraid, and it was easier than the alternatives.'

James exhales steadily. 'Yeah,' he says at last. 'Sometimes I think that's the only reason any of us does anything.' He takes his towel from around his neck and passes it over his face, momentarily hiding his expression. Then he says, 'Coming to group on Monday?', in a tone that could almost be mistaken for an invitation.

'Maybe,' says Isabel.

He nods: brisk, efficient. 'Then maybe I'll see you there,' he says, and walks away, his straight-backed military posture not quite concealing the weight of his loss hanging heavy on his shoulders.

15

KATARSA (CATHARTIC)

The support group doesn't magically become helpful now that Isabel has formed an uneasy truce – it would be an exaggeration to call it friendship – with James, but she goes because it makes Leo happy and because Maggie gives her that bright flash of a smile every time she shows up. Mostly, she sits in silence while others talk about problems she can't relate to: their dead-end jobs, their complicated love lives. Even when their problems taste more familiar, tinged with grief and guilt, she doesn't feel she can speak. *It wasn't your fault*, people in the circle tell them, and for the others, that's usually true. Not for Isabel.

But the gym helps. Only a few days and she already feels the difference, her body getting stronger, feeling more like hers. She trains like she's punishing herself, and maybe she is: for what she's done; for the fact that she's here, alive, and everybody else is dead.

James joins her, as much because he shares her preference for the gym's quieter hours as because he wants her company. They don't speak often; that's fine. They don't need to.

But one day, when they've both drifted out onto the little patio outside the gym because it's swelteringly warm inside and there's sweat running down both of their faces, he says, 'Did they call it survivors' guilt for you too?'

Isabel glances at him, surprised. 'Who's *they*?' she asks, putting off the rest of the question.

'Doctors. Therapists. I don't know.'

She huffs a laugh. 'I've made a point of not seeing any of those.'

James gives her a sideways look. 'You astonish me,' he says drily, and takes a seat on the bench looking out over the scrubby car park-turned-garden. He leaves enough space for Isabel.

Warily, she sits down. 'Everyone thinks it's grief,' she says. 'My housemates. Maggie. Even Catharine, and she only knows what I've said in group, which isn't much.'

'What is it, then, if not grief?' he says, without judgement.

It's loss, sure. But *grief* doesn't come close to touching it, doesn't include the guilt and blame and culpability. *Grief* takes no responsibility for her own monstrosity, so it's never enough.

'I'm grieving for deaths I'm directly responsible for,' she

161

says. 'For people who died because of what I did. That's ...'
She hesitates. 'Well. I guess you'd know.'

'Yeah,' he agrees, and she thinks that's probably why he
started this conversation, because he does know, and nobody
else in that room gets it.

Isabel scuffs the floor with her shoe. 'We're not the same,
though,' she says, a little reluctantly. 'You were a soldier.
I'm ...' Again she hunts for words. 'Different.'

James makes a small, noncommittal noise that may or
may not be agreement. 'What do you think is the difference
between us?' he asks, and she's not sure if he's asking for his
own sake or hers.

'You made a mistake,' she says. 'One mistake, which haunts
you. I made choices.' And he already knows about that, but she
needs to say it. Properly, this time. 'I killed a child. Knowingly
and on purpose and looking into her eyes as I did it. Not
because I made a mistake or had bad intel or didn't know she
was there. The twin sister of the girl I'm currently living with,
the girl I've babysat every night this week – I went into her
room and I killed her.'

There's a long silence. Then James says, in a tone of
absolute incredulity, 'They're letting you babysit her *sister*?'

'Fucked, isn't it?' says Isabel, with grim humour.

'You can say that again.' She waits for the judgement, the
anger, but it doesn't come. He says, 'You're right, I made a
mistake. I didn't mean to kill those people. I definitely didn't
mean to kill Tom. But I did intend to kill someone. People I
was told were acceptable targets.'

Isabel raises one shoulder in a half-shrug. 'It's still not the same.'

'If you say so,' says James, in a tone that suggests he disagrees. After a pause, he adds, 'You don't seem like the kind of person who'd have done that for the fun of it, though. They had something on you, didn't they?'

It doesn't matter that they did. Everyone seems to think it matters, and in their determination to believe the best of Isabel they're refusing to let her be monstrous. Boxing her in, always, making her something they can label: 'patient' or 'traumatised' or 'victim', it doesn't matter what they call her. It all means the same thing.

They're taking away from her the choices she once had. Making it something that was done to her. And she wants them to recognise the agency she had in her own atrocities. She wants them to acknowledge, for once, that she could have taken a different path and she didn't. Because if nobody will give her that, how can she believe they'll give her a choice this time?

'I'm not a victim,' says Isabel, and then adds, with a cynical smile, 'I'm a survivor. I did what I had to do and I chose it, every step of the way.'

James lets out his breath and leans back, stretching his legs out across the gravel of the patio. 'Say that's true,' he says. 'I can tell you believe it, at least. But it didn't start where it ended, did it?'

No. Once, she tried to save Suzie. She doesn't think she can put into words how much worse that makes it.

'Tell me where it started,' suggests James.

'What are you, my therapist?' she asks him, half joking, half sharp.

He only shrugs. 'Maybe I'm trying to make myself feel better. No matter how fucked up I am, I'll never be as bad as you.' His smile softens the sharp-edged words and, weirdly, it does make Isabel feel slightly better. Talking about this for the sake of her own healing or catharsis would be unbearable. But talking about it to convince James he's not the most fucked-up person in this city? Sure. She can do that.

She doesn't know where to start, so she keeps going back, all the way to the point where she started having choices. Ian Crampton, the burglar. That's where it began, isn't it? Her chance to walk away, and the instincts that dragged her back in.

By the time she gets to Suzie, she's hoarse from speaking. James takes her water bottle inside to the fountain and refills it; she takes it from him gratefully, the cool water giving her the strength to continue. So: Suzie. And then Laura. And the final bloody mess of it all, and the decision to run instead of fix it.

She's about to stop, but that's not where her story ends, is it? This city didn't take her choices when it took her knives. So: Kate. And the others, the nights she only half remembers, all those desperate aching attempts to feel something. Maggie, who looked at her and saw what the others missed or didn't care about, recognising her self-destruction for what it was. Leo's ultimatum, which brought her here.

And finally she's done.

James says, 'Jesus,' and there's a moment of reflective silence. Eventually, he adds, 'Well, I was right, I definitely look functional and relatively unfucked up next to that, so, thanks for the validation.'

Isabel laughs emptily. She feels hollowed out, as though in telling him this she's paid a tithe in blood, but it helps that he doesn't immediately smother her in pity. Maybe she could only say this to him because he still faintly dislikes her, and that dislike is insulation, keeping her story at arm's length.

There *is* a certain catharsis in admitting all the ways she's not okay, though – and it feels right that it's James. James who was sixteen, and got chewed up and spat out and made a killer by a reflex of the same system that destroyed her; James who lost his best friend, and is haunted the way she's haunted. They're not the same, but they're alike, and that helps.

Maybe the reason Emily's self-help books did so little for Isabel is that they were aimed at civilians, and that's not who she is. It's a strange thought; she never conceptualised the guilds as a military organisation, despite the weapons they made. To be a soldier implies an enemy to fight against, a cause to fight for, and she ... well, she let them make a killer of her without any of that.

But she recognises herself in James, both of them still learning to accept that nobody will give them orders any more, and that any decisions they make from here are their own.

'I told you,' she tells him. 'I made choices. Mostly really bad ones.'

'Yeah,' he agrees. 'Didn't give you many good ones, though, did they?'

And that's true enough, though she can't blame Espera for the decisions she's made since she escaped. She wouldn't say she *regrets* what she's done, because she saves regret for the things that actually matter, but she's got sufficient distance now from the encounter with Kate to be angry about it, and to want to protect her past self. And with the clarity of hindsight and two weeks of bitter sobriety, she knows Leo was right to be worried about her. Any of those unregulated pills could've killed her with an unexpected ingredient, and she never thought twice about it.

Daragh, she thinks, would be *extremely pissed* if she killed herself that way. *What a waste of all my overtime*, he'd have said, *what a waste*.

(It's easier to think about him angry and disappointed than to think about him devastated, because she's never been comfortable accepting that people care about her. But she can't help thinking he'd have wanted this for her. Not the grief and the self-destruction, but the gradual healing, and the slow process of learning to express her feelings. He always tried to make her talk about it, always said she'd break down if she didn't. And he was right, but she didn't talk to him, and now he's dead, and she never will.

Of all the things she can't forgive her mother for, Daragh's death is pretty high on the list.)

James lets out another sigh and says, 'I should go. I'm meeting Maggie for coffee. You could come,' he adds, quickly.

'You always rush off after group. She was saying she never gets to talk to you these days.'

Isabel's leaden with exhaustion after her workout, ready to go home and shower and collapse into bed, but the emotions stirred up by their conversation are still buzzing under her skin and she doesn't know how else to rid herself of the lingering anxiety, so she says, 'Sure. I'll come.'

His smile looks genuine. 'Okay,' he says, and heaves himself off the bench, holding out a hand to help her up. Isabel takes it, amused by the gesture, and pulls herself upright, gathering her towel and her water bottle.

The coffee shop should be about ten minutes away, except that the main road has been unexpectedly cordoned off for a charity run. They look bleakly at the unending stream of runners, trying to judge how long it'll be before they can cross.

'Fuck this,' says James eventually. 'I know a short cut. Come on.'

It turns out to be more of a long cut, weaving through back streets past everybody's bins, but at least they're heading in the vague direction of Leo's house, so Isabel's journey home will be shorter.

'Just around here,' says James cheerfully, and raises his leg to step over a pile of rubbish strewn next to a wheelie bin. 'People really need to stop leaving their crap everywhere, it's— holy shit.'

He stops in his tracks, and Isabel stops too. What she'd taken for a bin bag is a raincoat, crumpled and sticky with blood. And inside the raincoat . . .

167

James's voice is tight. 'I'm going to need you to tell me you're seeing this, or I might start thinking I'm having a flashback, and I thought I was done with those.'

'I'm seeing it,' says Isabel. 'And that's definitely a dead body.'

16

FAKULA (EXPERT)

Isabel's seen a lot of corpses, but it's been a while since she encountered one that wasn't her fault. Whoever killed this person – white male, fifties, nondescript clothing, blood on his hands like he tried to put pressure on the wound in his chest – made a mess of it, and there's something shocking about the rough abandonment of the body. She'd expect this in Espera, not here, in this place where she's supposed to be safe.

'Okay,' says James, breathing heavily. 'So there's a dead man here. We should call the police.'

They probably should. A civilian would – but Isabel's not a civilian, is she? Her professional instincts kick in as she evaluates the scene. No visible weapon, so the killer took it with them. That also rules out suicide, if the placement of the wound and the look of terror on the man's face didn't. Messy, amateur, but effective, and if the killer took the weapon, they're still armed, which means they're still dangerous. As for the victim …

Isabel crouches to take a closer look at the body. A single stab wound, badly angled for a quick death; clothes in disarray, suggesting a struggle; jacket sliced open near the pockets like the killer took something from the body. No calling card. Of course there's no calling card, she's in fucking Leeds, not Espera. But—

'What are you *doing*?' James asks her, urgently. 'Get away from the body, we—'

'In a moment,' says Isabel, still looking at that pocket. Was it theft? An opportunistic killing, a fight that got out of hand? That might explain why the killer fled the scene without even trying to hide the evidence.

'Please,' says James, his voice thin with stress, 'get away from the body before you contaminate the goddamn crime scene and let me call the police so they don't think we're fucking *suspects*.'

He's right, and she won't learn anything else from this body. Isabel pushes herself to her feet, but as she steps back, her shoe knocks against something metallic. It rolls until it hits the bottom of the dustbin with a gentle *ting* and comes to rest on the ground. A coin, that's all, just a coin, but when she leans down to pick it up …

'Shit.' Isabel withdraws her hand and steps back. That's not just a coin. That's an Esperan shilling, last year's issue, and a shiny new Esperan shilling next to a dead body in Leeds is nothing but bad news. 'Shit, shit, shit.' Before, the body was a curiosity and a surprise, but now a heavy rock of dread is settling in her stomach, and she tastes fear in the back of her mouth.

'What is it?' asks James.

'An Esperan coin,' she says, and backs away from the body. 'Could've been dropped during the struggle. Fallen from somebody's pocket. Which means either this man or his killer had connections to Espera.'

It takes James a beat to get it, and then: 'Oh,' he says, and, 'Shit. We really need to call the police.'

'We can't,' says Isabel, already mapping her route home. 'If they find me here, they'll think I did it. They'll take me away.' Maybe she can take the coin, get rid of it. Hide the evidence, but—

'If you run, you'll only look guiltier,' James points out, and he's right, but her fear defies logic. 'You're the expert. How long has he been dead?'

She glances at the body again. 'A couple of hours, I'd guess,' she says. 'The killer missed his heart, so it would've taken him a little while to die. Can't tell if they stuck around to watch or if they left him to it, so they might have been gone longer than that.'

James looks nauseated, but he says, 'Then you've got an alibi. You were at the gym, with me. The CCTV will confirm it.'

It should be a comfort, but it relies on anyone being willing

171

to give her a fair shot at defending herself, and Isabel never gets that lucky. 'It won't be enough,' she says. 'If I take the coin, if I hide it—'

'No,' says James firmly. 'Jesus. You are *not* stealing evidence from a fucking crime scene, Isabel!'

'But they'll think it was me!' And they'll take her away and they won't let her see Leo or Sam, and everyone will think she's exactly what she always was and she's not, she knows she's not, she didn't *do this*.

'No, they won't,' he insists, with unwarranted faith in the justice system. 'I'll vouch for you. But if you run now, they'll never believe you didn't do it.'

Fuck. Isabel looks from James to the dead man and then back again, forcing down her panic. She's a professional. She knows better than to go to pieces. 'Okay,' she says finally, not exactly calm but at least in control of herself. 'Call the police. And then call Maggie and tell her we're not making it to coffee.'

He doesn't even manage a smile; he's more upset by the body than he's letting on. 'Don't touch him, or that coin,' he says firmly, taking out his phone. 'Just. Stay right where you are.'

Isabel does as she's told, hands stuffed firmly in her pockets. Her gaze drifts back to the shilling. A coin that new is no relic or heirloom. Whoever dropped it had a direct, *recent* connection to the city . . .

'Police are on their way,' says James, a little while later. His hands are shaking, and it takes him three attempts to put his phone away. 'I had to . . . I told them you were here. Your name. They're calling in a specialist.'

'A specialist?' echoes Isabel, mouth dry. 'What the fuck does that mean?' *Somebody to take you away, somebody to lock you up—*

'I don't know, but—' James breaks off and takes several deep breaths. 'You've got an alibi. We've both got an alibi. Everything's going to be fine.'

I've got an alibi, she tells herself, over and over again, but that coin is Esperan, and they're sending a 'specialist', and she shouldn't be here.

But it's too late to run now.

Isabel doesn't meet the 'specialist' until she's been at the police station two hours already, sitting alone in a tiny room, unsure whether she's under arrest or whether this is standard practice. With every minute that passes, her muscles tighten, anticipating the moment they send someone in to restrain her – or to take her out. Will they have her killed here, or send her back to Espera to meet her fate inside the city walls? That would be less paperwork, she imagines, but it would give her more of a chance to fight back, too . . .

When the door finally opens to admit a middle-aged blonde woman in a floral blouse and dark skirt, it's such an anti-climax that Isabel's panic begins to feel absurd.

'My name is Talia Weatherby,' says the woman, sitting on the other side of the table. 'I'm an Esperan Liaison Officer. Do you know what that means?'

Isabel shakes her head. She doesn't want to underestimate the woman, even if it doesn't look like she's carrying a weapon.

'It means I'm responsible for consulting with defectors when crimes like this are committed,' says Talia. 'I advise you to cooperate. It may affect your residency and asylum claims if you don't.'

No weapons, just threats. Isabel swallows hard and says, 'I didn't kill that man. I was at the gym, with James. There's CCTV.' She sounds desperate, even to herself, and wonders whether she should have asked for a lawyer. Maybe that's why they left her alone so long, so she'd be frantic enough to incriminate herself with hasty words.

'I know.' The woman's lips are a thin, unimpressed line. 'You're not a suspect at this time. Nevertheless, there is information you can offer us.'

'I'm not?' says Isabel, caught between relief and surprise. 'A suspect, I mean? And James isn't either, right?'

'CCTV confirms your story. You and Mr Reeve are not being considered suspects.' She couldn't sound more grudging about it if she tried. 'We do, however, have some questions.'

'Questions?' says Isabel. 'But I don't know any—'

'Miss Ryans, according to our records you were a Comma field agent for the best part of three years. Is that correct?'

That is ... not something Isabel wants on her record, but clearly the police already know, so she can't deny it. 'That's correct,' she says, reluctantly.

Talia's expression doesn't change at all. 'Please give me your professional opinion on this murder.'

It's the last thing Isabel expected to be asked. 'My ... my *professional opinion*?' she repeats.

'You were a killer,' says Talia evenly. 'You know guild work. Is that what we're looking at?'

Isabel blinks again, trying to process the question. 'No,' she says, honestly. 'This kill was messy. Slow. There was a struggle. If either of them dropped the coin, it was an accident, not a calling card. A guild kill would have been efficient and subtle, unless they were trying to cause a scene, and in that case they would have staged it properly, not abandoned the body in an alley. Whoever did this was an amateur.'

Talia nods, as though this is what she expected. 'So this was a murder, not an assassination.'

'As far as I can tell,' says Isabel. She adds, 'Who was he? The dead man?'

The officer pauses, like she's not sure how much to disclose, before she finally says, 'His name was Martin Thompson. He was a journalist.'

The name doesn't ring any bells, but Isabel doesn't follow the news particularly, so this is hardly a surprise. She tells Talia this, and watches her write it down.

'That will be all for now,' Talia tells her, standing. That was it? They threatened her for that – her perspective on the crime scene? Anyone could've given them that. 'Thank you for your cooperation, Miss Ryans. Would you like a cup of tea?'

She doesn't want a cup of tea. She wants to go home, shower – her sweat-soaked gym clothes have dried against her skin in a distinctly unpleasant way – and spend the rest of the day alone in her room, away from these glaring overhead lights and the smell of somebody's microwaved lunch. But she's cooperating, so she nods, politely requests tea with no milk, and takes the lukewarm Styrofoam cup she's offered a few minutes later with her best attempt at a smile.

'Is James still here?' she asks.

'I can't tell you that.'

'But—' Isabel swallows the urge to argue and tries a different tactic. 'If he is, can you make sure he's okay? He's got PTSD. I think finding the body really freaked him out.'

Talia gives her a slightly odd look, but something in her expression softens. 'He's a friend of yours, is he?'

This is probably part of the questioning too, but Isabel can't see the harm in telling her. 'We go to the same support group.'

'Ah, yes. With Catharine Hancock.'

She wonders exactly how many members of Maggie and Dan's crew the police have got under surveillance. 'Please can you just ... check he's okay?'

She's used to corpses, to questioning, to being left in miserable little rooms until she's ready to talk just to get out of there. James isn't. She saw his hands shaking, heard the tremor in his voice.

The officer watches her for a long time, as though trying to work out what Isabel's ploy is. Finally, she nods. 'I'll check on him,' she says, and that's that. The interview's over, and Isabel's alone again in the miserable little room.

Nobody comes to ask her anything else. The hours stretch out, tedious with worry, and she's just beginning to wonder whether they'll leave her here overnight when the door opens and Talia returns.

176

'Leo Jura's here to collect you,' she says crisply. 'Don't leave the city. Remain available in case of further questions. And don't talk to the media.'

Isabel had no plans to leave the city *or* talk to the media. 'That's it?' she says. 'You're letting me go?'

'For now,' says the officer, and holds open the door.

'Is James—'

'He's fine.'

'But—'

'Now, Miss Ryans,' says Talia, and the edge to her voice suggests arguing would be unwise. Mutely, Isabel follows the woman through to the lobby, where Leo is waiting.

He's holding her gym bag, which they must have given him; his face is drawn tight with anxiety. At the sight of her, it only relaxes a little. 'Isabel,' he says. 'Thank fuck. I thought—'

'Let's go,' she says, cutting him off before he says anything incriminating – or worse, emotional – in front of the police officers at the desk. 'I'm starving. And I'm absolutely *desperate* for a shower.'

17

SUSPEKTATA (SUSPECTED)

Leo's borrowed a car from the smugglers, and they drive most of the way home in silence. Two streets from their house, he says, 'When they called me and said there was a murder and you were at the station, I thought ...'

'You thought I did it,' says Isabel bluntly. From anyone else, it would be unremarkable; it's what she deserves. Coming from Leo, though, it hurts – a lot more than she'd expected it to.

'What was I meant to think?' he says. He's gripping the steering wheel so tightly that his knuckles strain against his skin. 'After everything – the sneaking out, the drugs ...'

He makes it sound so sordid. 'You could have trusted me,' says Isabel, aiming for reproachful and hitting *tragic* instead, her voice unsteady.

'I know,' he says – sighs, the word a long exhale. 'I'm sorry.'

But the damage is done. Something between them fractured the day he dragged her out of that bar, and can't be repaired.

When they reach the house, he parks the car but makes no move to get out. 'My alibi's not as strong as yours,' he says finally, lightly – too lightly. 'I was at home with Sam; they've only got her word for it. So we'll probably have to deal with that eventually.'

Isabel stares at him, trying to make sense of his words. 'You mean you're a suspect? Why?'

His laugh is hollow. 'Not yet,' he says. 'But I will be. Because I'm from Espera, and because ... because Martin Thompson was about to out me.'

'To out you?' She knows people here care a lot more that Leo's trans than anyone back in Espera did, but it's not like he keeps it a secret. Unless he means ... 'The book?'

'Yeah,' Leo says heavily, and lets his head fall back against the headrest. 'You know anything about this guy?'

Isabel shakes her head. 'I don't read the outsider news.'

'Well, he was a prick.' His smile is crooked and humourless. 'Hated immigrants, hated refugees, and hated Espera most of all. Had a bitchy little column in one of the tabloids and then continued his screeds on his blog. Ant's been desperately trying to get *any* journalist to give a shit about Espera, but he wouldn't touch Martin Thompson with a ten-foot barge pole, because even if he could be convinced to support us, it would do more harm than good. He had an absolute field day when that photo of you came out, and he's spent weeks trying to discredit our work, because believing that Esperan civilians are suffering contradicts his narrative that we all deserve to die.'

It doesn't sound like Leo will be mourning this particular death too much. 'But how did he know you wrote it?'

'I've got absolutely no idea,' he says. 'Nor do I know what he hoped to gain by naming me, though perhaps he figured if I hadn't claimed authorship already, there was a reason, and it was something he could use against me. He sent a letter to the bookshop threatening to expose me – I guess he didn't have our address, which is something. It arrived this morning. I was trying to figure out whether to report it when they told me he was dead.'

Isabel swears. Leo's an abolitionist, a good man – but people out here don't know that, do they? They look at him and all they see is Espera, and the damage it's done. And the timing of this, the clear motive it presents ... 'Does anyone know about the letter?'

'Not yet,' he says. 'But no doubt once they search his house they'll find whatever intel he's got on me, and that'll be enough to implicate me.' He hits his head once, twice, against the headrest. 'Ant was right. If I'd claimed the book weeks ago, nobody would think I was trying to hide it, so they couldn't accuse me of killing Martin Thompson to protect the secret. Now, though ...'

'But you weren't there. You—' Isabel breaks off. Being caught with the body was bad enough; this is worse.

'Don't tell Sam, will you?' says Leo, inclining his head

towards the house. 'That I might be a suspect, I mean. It would upset her.'

As if that'll work. 'She'll figure it out. She's cleverer than me. She's probably already hacking into the police database.'

'Fuck, I hope not,' he says, with a ghost of a smile. 'But I mean it. I'd rather keep her out of this as long as I can.'

That explains why they're having this conversation in the car, and not in their house.

'I'll try,' says Isabel doubtfully. 'She can always tell when I'm lying, though.'

This evokes another deep sigh. 'There's something else,' says Leo. 'I didn't tell you because ... well, because it was unverified, and because you had enough on your plate with the whole "getting sober" situation—'

'It's not like that,' she interrupts, already bracing herself for whatever bad news is coming her way, but Leo ignores her.

'But I guess at this point, you probably need to know. Some of the news coming out of Espera is ... troubling.' Leo releases his seatbelt at last, looking down at his lap; he seems to have swallowed his words. Finally, he manages to say, 'In the past month, there have been three high-profile hits by the Moth.'

Isabel stares blankly at him. 'No, there haven't.' The Moth hasn't killed anyone. She's the Moth and she's *here*. What's Leo implying, that she's been going back to Espera in secret? That's absurd.

'It's what the reports say. Three dead, all claimed by Comma, all attributed to the Moth.' He bites his lip. 'I don't know if they've replaced you, or if it's just rumour, but if it's intended to quell the resistance, it's failing. The strikes have spread from the industrial boroughs to some of the guild factories, and abolitionist groups are blockading the export of weapons. We've been helping them coordinate with pacifist organisations outside the city to prevent the guilds from trading. We haven't managed a complete cessation, but there's been progress.'

'You've what?' She knows Leo's been working ten thousand hours, but she thought he was fundraising, helping smuggle in money and supplies. Trying to stop the guilds from trading is a step beyond resistance and into *revolution* – something she thought would never happen.

And Mortimer, who dreamed of this, will never see it.

'Isabel, they sent the Moth—'

'Not the Moth.'

'—to try to wipe out the strike leaders, and it *didn't work*. Your disappearance is what emboldened people and made them think it was safe to act, so Comma thought they could undo that by sending someone back in under your name. But we've already gained too much momentum. They're losing.'

His eyes are bright with fervour, and she thinks, again, how absurd it is that anyone in this city could suspect Leo of murder, when he's never been like her. 'But the Free Press leaked my identity, and people figured out I was in Leeds. Doesn't everyone in Espera already know I'm gone?'

'Getting info in is harder than getting it out,' he says. 'The pictures of you from out here haven't made it into Espera, or haven't spread if they have. They know the Moth is you, but they don't know you're gone. Not for sure. And now somebody else has taken your place – somebody convincing.'

Somebody else. She never knew much about the guild's other field agents: if they weren't in Cocoon, she never met them in training, and they rarely crossed paths after graduation, to protect everyone's identities. But she read the Esperan papers, same as everyone else, and she knows there was no one as good as her. And to be convincing now that the Free Press has put her identity on blast, they'd need someone who can pass for Isabel in terms of age and build, and that definitely limits Comma's options.

'You said they're killing strike leaders?' she says.

'And abolitionists. A couple of Ant's contacts were targeted. He's . . . taken it hard.' That explains why she hasn't seen him around much. 'But it shows the guild's rattled. They wouldn't bother unless they thought the strikes were a threat.'

It's typical of Leo to see the bright side in a situation like this, but for once, Isabel agrees. Lashing out like this is risky for Comma. It shows they've let the protests get under their skin, and that means they're working, which will only encourage people.

'Well,' she says, 'shit. How long have you known about this fake Moth?'

'A couple of weeks,' he admits.

She doesn't blame Leo for not telling her sooner: she was too unstable to be any help and too volatile to trust, lost in herself. But she still feels guilty that he was dealing with these huge, world-changing events in Espera while she was clueless.

Maybe, she thinks wryly, she's been doing a better job of 'integrating' and leaving Espera behind than he has. Abandoning her city one more time, not even paying enough attention to know when it started to rise up and shake off the shackles of a century's murderous rule.

'And let me guess,' she says. 'The media's still not reporting on the protests and the strikes.'

'Nope. Ant's been cold-calling every journalist he can find, but none of them will break the media blackout. If they talk about Espera at all, it's only to argue about whether Esperan refugees should be allowed to stay – usually spearheaded by people like Martin Thompson, firmly arguing for "no".'

And now there's been a murder, and that single shilling's going to bring the whole country's suspicions down on their heads.

'This is going to be messy,' says Isabel. 'Isn't it?'

Leo glances at the house, and she knows he's thinking of Sam, and the better life they were trying to give her. 'Yes,' he admits. 'Whether they suspect me or not, whether the killer was Esperan or not, there'll be consequences for this, and it'll be Espera that suffers first.'

Isabel swears, stringing the profanities together for greater effect, enjoying the taste of them on her tongue. Then she looks down at the red-and-black wristband she's still wearing and considers, for a moment, asking Leo to slice it off for her – because if shit's about to go down, she's going to want a drink.

Hot on the heels of that idea, though, is the thought of Maggie's disappointed face if Isabel showed up without it.

Isabel pulls her sleeve down, hiding the band. Whatever crisis is coming, it looks like she's facing it sober and fully present in her skin, no matter how little she wants to.

'What if we could prove to them it wasn't someone from Espera?' she says, fumbling for anything that might put hope back on Leo's face, because she hates seeing him despair. 'Made it so you weren't a suspect, made the papers realise we're not the enemy?'

'How?' he says. 'Unless we can find the real killer, there's nothing we can do. And that— No, Isabel.'

He's seen the look on her face. The dawning light of inspiration. *Unless we can find the real killer.* Somewhere in this city is someone with a knife, a grudge, and a willingness to kill – and that, more than anything else in the outside world, is something Isabel understands.

For the first time since she arrived in Leeds, it feels like there might be a reason she's here. A way to be something more than an inconvenient burden with no useful skills to offer anyone.

Sometimes, catching a murderer is a murderer's job.

'Isabel,' repeats Leo. 'Stay out of this. It'll only cause trouble.'

'If I can find them,' she says, 'if I can prove they're the killer ...'

'You'll get yourself killed,' he says, pleading.

'No, I won't.' Isabel gets out of the car. 'I'm going to find them, I'm going to solve this, and I'm going to clear your name. And then,' she adds, 'I'm going to make the people of this city come crawling on their knees to apologise for suspecting you.' She gives Leo her widest, most upsetting smile. 'Watch me.'

18

POLITIKA (POLITICAL)

Isabel hasn't got a phone, which means she hasn't got James's number, and can't text him to check he's all right after their ordeal. So with Leo's blessing, she heads back to the garage bar on Sunday afternoon, hoping there'll be someone there who knows where to find him.

Maggie is once again on the roof. She hails Isabel cheerfully, then says, 'There's a ladder around the back, if you need it.'

Isabel eyes the wall, calculating angles. It's been a while since she did this, but it's an easy jump: a short run up, pushing off the opposite wall, getting her hands around the parapet and dragging herself up. It's not the most elegant transition she's ever made, but she receives a round of applause anyway – which makes her realise Maggie isn't alone.

There are five of them up there: Maggie, Dan, Catharine, James and Pher. They've dragged a couple of deck chairs onto the roof, and Maggie and James have claimed them; James looks tired, but otherwise okay, raising a hand to Isabel in welcome. Pher's sprawled on a pile of cushions, and Dan and Catharine are leaning against the parapet with their legs stretched out in front of them. Next to them is a plastic cooler. Dan rummages in it and tosses Isabel a bottle of lemonade.

'Thanks,' she says uncertainly, catching it. 'I didn't come to drink. I wanted to check James was all right.'

They all turn to look at him. 'I'm fine,' he says, scowling at the sudden attention. 'It's Dan and Maggie you should be worried about. They had a police raid last night.'

Isabel's heart sinks. 'What?'

'*Raid* is exaggerating,' says Maggie, but her expression is pinched. 'Fortunately, Dan finally sorted out our licence last month and nobody was actively taking drugs, so they couldn't hold anything against us. They claimed it was because of the murder, but they've been looking for an opportunity to bust us for ages. You know what they're like.'

Isabel doesn't, particularly, but she can guess; no surprise if their revolutionary politics aren't popular with the authorities. 'Was anyone hurt?'

'Our pride?' says Dan, with a grim little laugh. 'Ruined the vibes of the dancefloor, probably turned a couple of regulars off . . . but no. We're safe.'

'Bet you're glad you were at the Roxy instead,' says Maggie.

'There's a limit to how many cops anyone wants to deal with in one day, and I reckon you'd hit it, right?'

Isabel glances around to see who Maggie's talking to, but they're all looking at her. 'At the Roxy?' she echoes, bewildered. 'What do you mean?'

Maggie frowns. 'The club down by the station? Catharine said she saw you there.'

'I thought I did,' says Catharine uncertainly, when Isabel turns a confused expression on her. 'I was out with Meera. She wasn't thrilled to see you. But we lost you in the crowd.'

'No, I was at home,' says Isabel. 'I was with Leo.' Half joking, half unsettled, she adds, 'I've got an alibi.'

'Weird,' says Catharine. 'I'm sorry. I must've mistaken someone for you. Didn't mean to besmirch your reputation by suggesting you'd be at the Roxy on a Saturday.'

'Frankly, I'm astonished you'd admit to it yourself, Catharine,' says Dan. 'And with Meera, of all people. Your standards have well and truly declined, haven't they?'

His comment dissolves the odd tension lingering in the air. 'Oh, get fucked,' says Catharine, but she's laughing.

'Talking of alibis,' says James quietly, 'they checked the CCTV at the gym. In case they didn't tell you that. We're clear.'

Isabel nods. 'Yeah, they admitted that much, eventually.'

Maggie raises her bottle in a toast. 'Here's to living in a surveillance state,' she says. 'May it always get our friends off murder charges.'

Friends. Isabel swallows hard, and refrains from mentioning Leo, or Martin Thompson's threats. She twists the cap off her lemonade and joins the toast, sitting cross-legged on a spare cushion.

Pher's watching her, and after a moment, he says, 'James said you found an Esperan coin there.'

The others all roll their eyes. 'Here we go again,' says Maggie. 'Kitten, we know you love playing detective, but—'

Isabel cuts her off. 'Yes,' she says, focusing on Pher. 'Why do you ask?'

He shrugs. 'Just doesn't seem like very much evidence, that's all. Not enough to justify the trade sanctions.'

Isabel's blood cools. 'Trade sanctions?' she repeats.

'You haven't heard?' He rolls off his pile of cushions and sits upright, crossing his legs. 'They announced it this morning. Retaliation for the murder, which they're treating as *connected to Esperan interests*. The government's ordered a complete halt on trade with the city of Espera: nothing in, nothing out.'

Well, shit. The abolitionists might want to halt the weapons trade, but *everything* is a problem. 'But people will starve,' she says, mind racing. 'Our food – most of it's imported. They can't do that, they can't *starve* civilians because one person got killed. Fuck, that coin could have been Thompson's, for all we know, it's—' She breaks off. 'Sorry.'

'No, this is what I'm saying,' says Pher. 'It's not the guilds who will suffer because of this, is it? It's everyone else. And collective punishment's meant to be illegal, anyway. But nobody out here cares about Esperan civilians. I've been trying to spread the word about the book, but . . .' He hesitates. 'You said you know the authors.'

'I can't tell you who they are,' she warns. 'Not without their permission.' Especially now, with that information in Martin Thompson's dead hands.

'Can you get their permission?' he asks. 'Because everyone I talk to, they're like, oh, it's unverified, it might be propaganda, you can't spread that. But if there was an *author* . . .'

'I . . .' Isabel doubts it's within her power to convince Leo to do anything he doesn't want to. But trade sanctions will kill people, especially if it prevents the smugglers getting supplies and money into Espera. The strikes will crumble first, then the rest of the city, and everything they've been working for will be lost. 'I'll try.'

Pher's expression lights up. 'If you can, that'll change everything. Really, you can't understand, we didn't know—'

'That's enough, Kitten,' says Maggie, seeing that Isabel's getting overwhelmed by his intensity. 'Tashie, are *you* okay?'

Isabel shrugs and takes another swig of lemonade. 'Could've done without the hours at the police station.' There are noises of sympathy from the group. 'And my housemates might be suspects, and they didn't even *do* anything. It . . . it makes me angry, that people will assume it was us, just because we're from Espera.'

'I call that the Martin Thompson Effect,' says Dan grimly. 'Talk enough shit about Esperan refugees, people start believing it. And then when the man himself is killed . . .'

'Doesn't look good,' acknowledges James. Then he adds to Isabel, 'If you hadn't been with me, can't say I wouldn't have suspected you either.'

Suspecting *her* is one thing. She's a killer and a mess, and while it stings, she gets it. But Leo? How *dare* they?

'What I don't understand,' she says, fiddling with the lid of her lemonade bottle rather than looking at them, 'is why this is the line in the sand. One dickhead journalist is murdered, *maybe* by an Esperan, and they're imposing trade sanctions? The city's been killing people for years.'

There's an awkward pause, and then Maggie says, 'Well, we didn't know.'

'You did,' says Isabel. 'Don't give me that bullshit. There are *history* books written about the city. Even if you ignore everything happening inside the walls, they've been doing outside jobs for decades.' If the outside world was going to act, they should've done it the day Espera closed its gates, not now, when so much of the damage is already done.

'Okay,' says James; his tone suggests he's humouring her. 'We knew. The world knew. What should we have done – invaded and knocked the walls down?'

'Spoken like a soldier,' says Dan, at the same moment Isabel says, 'They should've stopped them being built in the first place.' But a world where Espera was never founded would be a world where Espera could never have thrived, a world that didn't think having bigger and better weapons was the path to power and war the route to justice. And this is not that world.

'But now that the walls are there,' says Catharine, 'what do we do? Say we invaded and took over the city. What happens after that?'

192

'Get rid of the guilds,' says Isabel, well aware that this is easier said than done.

'And what about the people who worked for the guilds?' says Maggie, watching her. 'What about the people who never killed anyone themselves, but made the parts for the bombs that killed Tom, or screwed together the bullet that blinded Meera's dad?'

'All right,' says Isabel, feeling cornered. 'I get it. So you figure out . . . a trial system, or something.'

'And the people who are guilty?' says Pher. 'Do you execute them?'

She feels like she's stuck in the middle of the bar on one of their political evenings, arguments thrown from all sides, the details fogged by drink. 'I don't know,' she says. 'Maybe.'

'Congratulations,' says James. 'You've just reinvented the guilds.' He shrugs when Isabel stares at him. 'Pretty sure killing people you disagree with is what got Espera into this mess in the first place.'

But what's the alternative, prison? Somehow she doubts mass incarceration would build a better future for her city, either. 'You were a soldier,' she retorts. 'Isn't killing people in the name of politics your whole thing?'

She's worried for a second that she's gone too far, and from the sudden tense silence among the group, they feel the same way. But James just raises an eyebrow and says, 'How do you think I learned that it doesn't work?'

Maggie crows with victory at that. 'Knew you'd come around eventually, Jim,' she says.

Isabel's beginning to wonder whether Maggie ever calls *anyone* by their real name. *Tashie, Danny boy, Kitten, Jim.* She gives out nicknames like sweets, like friendship is cheap.

Isabel takes a swig of lemonade to buy herself time and wrestles with the problem, turning over the concepts in her head as though that'll give her the perfect solution. 'Well, at the very least, civilians should get a chance to decide who rules them,' she says eventually.

'I agree,' says Catharine. 'But self-determination's messy. If that's what the city's fighting for, they'll need to have thought it through.'

Maybe they have, all those Free Press philosophers and political abolitionists gathering in their meeting houses to write pamphlets and spread revolution. They must have done. They wouldn't be dying on the picket lines if they didn't have a plan for what comes after the strike.

But they're right, too, these radical friends of hers: what happens to the people who work for the guilds, when all of this is over? She can see them letting the adjacents off. The teachers and the medics and so on, they'll be fine. Even some of the scientists might be, if they can pledge their abilities to a well-funded cause.

But the field agents?

The Moth?

They'll never forgive Isabel. If the city takes the guilds to trial, she'll be the first on the stand, and she doesn't think there'll be many people testifying in her favour. Not after Suzie. She should be trying to sabotage their plans, end the strikes, destroy the revolution, because it's the only way she'll ever get away with any of it.

Should she get away with it, though? Doesn't the city deserve justice?

I deserve justice too, she thinks, and she doesn't even know what that would look like.

'I think Espera deserves ...' She hunts for the words. 'A chance, I guess. The city was built for war and it's like it never ended. And we were born there and grew up there and being Esperan is part of us, but we should get to decide what that means.'

She wants *I'm from Espera* to mean something other than murder. She wants to know what the art could do, if it spread beyond the city walls. All that defiant beauty – how far could it go? She's known so many people who are better than what Espera gave them, and they deserve the chance to live that life. In Espera, or outside it, but it should be a choice.

'And *that*,' says Pher triumphantly, as though wrapping up a presentation, 'is why I think the coin is a red herring. Or, if the killer *is* from Espera, it's not the abolitionist cause they're fighting for.'

Not the abolitionist cause. Isabel's almost certain it's not a guild killer, but could it be somebody else, some other faction she hasn't identified? Maybe. But the only way to find out is to track down the killer themselves.

Which won't be easy. She can't go back to the crime scene, and the police won't share notes: all she's got are her initial observations, her suspicions about Martin Thompson's blackmailing habits, and a stubborn determination to clear her housemates' names.

It's not much to go on, but she doesn't plan to do this alone.

James's gaze is on her. 'What are you planning?' he asks, like maybe he actually cares.

'I'm going to solve it,' Isabel admits. 'Figure this out. Find the actual killer.'

She's expecting disbelief, or mockery, but they all take this pronouncement at face value. Maggie says, 'Are you sure that's safe? If the murderer figures out you're poking around . . .'

Isabel can't help herself: she laughs. 'I'm from Espera,' she points out. 'Pissing off a murderer is an average Tuesday for me. This is the most at home I've felt since I came to Leeds.'

Nobody laughs at her joke. Maybe they know as well as Isabel does that, somewhere deep down, it's the truth.

19

STRATEGIA (STRATEGIC)

If Isabel were a good babysitter, she'd keep Sam out of this, but she's a terrible one, and the kid already spent two years living in a basement doing crime, so it would be a waste not to consult her. She needs all the help she can get to solve this, and every piece of news that trickles in only makes her more determined – every whisper of the trade sanctions, every new worry line in Leo's forehead.

But Leo absolutely won't approve, so Isabel's spent several days waiting for him to be safely out of the way so that she can talk to Sam behind his back.

Fortunately, getting Sam on board takes all of two minutes.

'Does this mean I get to hack into the police database?' she asks, and Isabel is tempted to say yes.

'Leo would prefer it if you didn't,' she says instead. 'Let's focus on what we do know. Was the coin Martin Thompson's, or did it belong to his killer?'

'His killer,' says Sam immediately, and pulls a face; she, like Isabel, knows this is bad news for all of them. 'There's no way he had Esperan contacts. He hated us. He'd never have spent time with someone who arrived recently enough to have a coin that new.'

This was Isabel's thinking too; it helps to hear it from someone else. 'So his killer had an Esperan connection. Do we know who else he targeted in his rants? Besides us, that is?' Maybe he was blackmailing somebody other than Leo – someone with worse secrets, so the police would have another suspect.

Sam shrugs. 'I went through his blog, but it's been a while since he focused on anyone specific. More big picture. I think it's harder to sue him for that.' She opens up the news reports again, but it's nothing new, just the same self-congratulatory guff they've been peddling since the murder about the need to respond decisively in the face of a threat. Politicians are loving the atmosphere of fear and hostility; it's perfect for them to launch their soundbites about the necessity of the trade sanctions.

Isabel's trying very hard to stay calm about that. *People will starve*, she wants to say, *children will starve, innocents will starve, they had nothing to do with this—*

But of course nobody would listen to her.

'How do I find the Free Press leaks?' she asks Sam, tearing herself away from hate-reading the bigoted headlines.

'They won't mention the murder,' Sam warns her. 'They don't get outside news.'

'I know,' says Isabel. 'But still. How do I find them?'

Sam pulls up another website. 'Here.'

It's uncomfortable reading. The site is an online archive of everything the *Bulletin* has published in the past year, and she only has to run a search for the Moth to be reminded how much the abolitionists hate her. Only their ideological opposition to the death penalty stops them calling for her head.

The newer articles are more interesting, but they're limited. She imagines they've got people on the ground with cameras, but it must be harder to get pictures past the firewalls, because the articles are mostly text-only: hasty dispatches about the current strikes; a polemic against the food rationing the guilds have just announced; emotional obits for comrades lost.

Isabel pauses on these, scanning for familiar names. When she finds none, her attention drifts back to the news. Leo was understating it, she realises, when he said some of the factories were on strike. There's a labour crisis across all of the industrial boroughs, one factory after another downing tools, cutting off the manufacturing chain for the city's essential supplies. And the munitions workers have walked out too, leaving weapons disassembled as they join their civilian neighbours on the pickets. If this list is up-to-date, nearly forty per cent of adjacent workers have joined the movement.

And that's *before* the food rationing has kicked in.

To borrow a phrase from her new neighbours: *Jesus Christ.*

'Is this the only leak?' she asks Sam. 'The only site from Espera?'

Sam's mouth twists. 'Well . . .' she begins uncertainly. 'It's the only one the Free Press is running.'

'But?' prompts Isabel.

'But I found this one too.' She leans over and enters a new URL. The website that loads looks unofficial. It looks old, to be honest: the interface is dated, barely more than plain text and entirely anonymous.

'What is this?' Isabel asks, but as soon as she starts to read, it becomes obvious. Esperan data. Bare facts and figures. Names. Names of the dead who never got obits, and the dates they were killed. And then, going back years: every death published in *La Revuo*, with the pseudonym attached to it.

It doesn't take long to find the Moth. There they are, in black and white: all her kills, all the way back to Oliver Roe. It's a longer list than she cares to acknowledge, but the dates—

These are the kills Leo told her about, she realises, looking at the end of the column. The fake Moth, the one who's replaced her, the one people should know can't be her. There are more of them than he admitted. They start around the time she left the detention centre and came to live here, and they just keep going, all the way up to the tenth of July.

It's the twenty-second now; Martin Thompson was killed on the sixteenth. Presumably the fake Moth is still out there. Still killing. Still using her name and her reputation to terrorise the city she abandoned.

'Who runs this site?' Isabel asks Sam.

'I don't know yet,' says Sam. 'I've been poking around the code, but they're not stupid. They're hiding behind, like, seven layers of proxies; I can't even figure out if they're in Espera or outside it. It'll be easier if I can catch them when they're updating it, but so far I haven't got that lucky.'

'So far?' echoes Isabel. 'How long have you been trying?'

Sam's cheeks flush pink. 'A couple of weeks,' she admits. 'Since before the murder. I ... I've been worried about Ant and Leo. The work they do for the smugglers isn't legal, you know that? They're not supposed to have contact with people inside Espera, it's one of the conditions of our residency. It's meant to show we're not ...' She hesitates. 'Doing sedition. Is that the word?'

'It's *a* word,' says Isabel. 'You mean they could get deported back if anyone finds out?' She'd thought, somehow, that this end of the smuggling operation would be above board, even if the other end is shrouded in crime. No wonder Leo's stressed.

'Maybe, yeah.' Sam tucks her hair behind her ears; it immediately escapes. 'The bookshop's a front, you know. Leo's good at it, so they let him work there as if it's legit, but it's not a real bookshop. Just the respectable face of the operation.'

What is it with smugglers and books? Isabel will never look at a library or a bookshop the same way again. 'I ... shit, so all his jobs are actually crime?'

'Yeah.' Sam gestures to the website. 'Whoever manages this has got guild data, Esperan data, Free Press data – but they're not Free Press. If they were, we would know about it.

That worries me. I want to know who they are. And I think there's communication happening between Espera and Leeds that we don't know about – the murderer's coin tells us that much – which *also* worries me, because if the guilds are still looking for Leo . . .' She chews on her lip, looking her age for once. 'I want to *help*,' she says. 'I want to be useful. And Leo just keeps telling me to go to school because I'm too young to get caught up in it, but I've *been* caught up in it, for *years*. This—' She jabs at the screen. 'Monitoring stuff like this, I'm good at that. And it's safe. Well,' she adds. 'Safe enough.'

Isabel can't argue with that. 'So you think you can figure out who runs it?'

'Eventually,' says Sam. 'It's harder than anything I've done recently, but it's not going to be harder than the guilds.'

Isabel isn't particularly tech-minded, but she knows anyone who can break through guild encryption and steal their files is good at what they do. 'Seems to me it's worth doing,' she says. 'But can you show me that other website, the one from before? With the . . . with the sightings of me?'

So far, the media hasn't cottoned on to the fact that she found Thompson's body, but once they figure that out, she'll be back in the public eye and subject to their scrutiny. She needs to know what they're already saying about her, and how likely they are to keep punishing her for what other people have done.

Sam gives her an odd look, but pulls up the website. 'Here.'

There are a lot more entries on there than there were last time Isabel saw it. She grimaces, but skims the page. Around thirty per cent of the sightings are fake – or, to be charitable, mistaken – but the other seventy per cent are definitely her, and reading through them feels like a masochistic act. Her fake names litter the comments: *Marie, Elinor, Katy, Liz, Anna.* Not Natasha, though. At least some of her 'friends' had the decency not to gossip.

The list goes on and on, and with her whole self-destructive drinking tour of the city laid out in front of her, Isabel can't blame Leo for worrying about her stability: it looks so much worse from the outside, even when you take out the erroneous sightings. She's lucky he didn't force her to go inpatient and get real therapy.

But the list doesn't *end*, she realises. The most recent sighting was yesterday.

'What the fuck?' she mutters to herself, because it's *convincing*, the description, the way the girl they're talking about behaved. It's got a ring of truth to it that the other entries are lacking, a level of detail that's hard to fake. A girl with dyed hair, half-healed piercings, who spoke with an Esperan accent and moved like a threat. A girl drinking shitty vodka and flirting with strangers and lying like she believed it.

They could have made it up. But if Isabel didn't know full well she wasn't at a club last night, she'd think this entry was about her. *Lily.* It almost sounds like a name she'd use.

I thought I saw you, said Catharine.

She doesn't want to leap to conclusions, join dots that were never in the same constellation, but she finds herself reading the entry over and over again. A man is dead, killed by someone with an Esperan connection – or somebody pretending to have one. Isabel stumbled on the body, and only luck and CCTV stopped her from becoming a suspect. Leo's under scrutiny, their household a target.

And here, in Leeds, is somebody who could be – has been – mistaken for Isabel. Are they doing it on purpose? Planting clues, building up to the moment when they'll frame her? If they can fool Catharine, who actually knows her, it wouldn't be hard to fool the city – convince them she's a mess, and can't be trusted . . .

But if they really want to frame her, then Thompson's death won't be a one-off. Someone else will die, and this time, Isabel won't be able to prove she was at the gym.

She swallows hard. Maybe she's catastrophising. Maybe it's not as bad as it seems. 'Do you think—?' she begins, but she's cut off by a loud notification sound from the computer.

'Sorry,' says Sam, leaning over to dismiss it. 'I've got an alert set up for when the papers are talking about Espera. It's usually nothing, but . . .' She trails off. 'Oh.'

'What?' says Isabel, looking over her shoulder. And then: 'Oh.'

Leo's face stares out at her. Below it, the caption reads: *Esperan refugee and revolutionary historian Leo Jura speaks out about growing up in the City of Death.*

'He did it,' Isabel says wonderingly. 'He claimed authorship.'

'So he's not at work right now, then,' says Sam, and rather than surprised, she sounds fed up. 'I'm going to *kill* him. I can't believe he did this without me.'

20

SIEĜITA (BESIEGED)

The journalists arrive before Leo does.

The first one to ring the doorbell catches them by surprise, and Isabel makes the mistake of opening the door. A blinding flash sends her reeling back, disoriented – a camera, she realises too late. *Fuck.* She slams the door shut and bolts it, but the damage is done: now they know the 'assassin girl' is a member of Leo's household, and they've got a clear picture of her face to boot. All the ingredients needed for a tabloid storm.

After that, the floodgates open: journalists and protesters alike crowding the street, photographing the house and yelling questions and insults. Sam closes the curtains, but it doesn't seem to discourage them.

'How do they even know our address?' asks Isabel.

Sam shrugs. 'That's what they do, isn't it? Poke around where they don't belong.' She's agitated, constantly returning to the laptop as though she expects the news story to have changed. 'I can't believe Leo didn't tell me he was going to claim the book. I know we agreed he'd keep me out of it, but I deserved to know something like that.'

Isabel suspects he didn't tell Sam because he didn't want to tell her about Martin Thompson's threats. She can see what he's doing: claiming the book undermines Thompson's attempts at blackmail and therefore makes Leo a less likely suspect, with the added side effect of drawing attention to the abolitionist movement and establishing himself as a part of it. It's unlikely to change people's minds about Espera overnight, but maybe, down the line, it'll help.

Right now, though, it's brought trouble to their door – and that's assuming the guilds aren't still hunting for the author, and won't send someone after Leo.

Isabel sneaks a peek through the curtains, trying to gauge the damage. The street is rammed, cameras and microphones warring for space with protest signs. SEND THEM BACK is a popular one, and DON'T FALL FOR ESPERAN LIES suggests Leo's declaration hasn't converted everyone to their cause. But there's another faction there too: NO TRADE SANCTIONS. SUPPORT ESPERAN STRIKES. Isabel points that sign out to Sam.

'They must read the Free Press,' says the kid. 'None of the outsider journalists are reporting on the strikes. That's good news, that'll help with the fundraising, if—' She breaks off. 'If Leo can still do that. With everything that's happening.'

'It'll be okay,' begins Isabel, but a second later something hits the window and she flinches back, the curtain falling closed as she reaches uselessly for a non-existent weapon. The glass holds, and when she recovers her nerve enough to look, she sees a broken egg, nothing worse. The yolk leaves a yellow smear as it slides down the pane.

Sam pulls her away from the window. 'Blackout protocols,' she says.

'What?'

'Ant said, if people came, we had to put cardboard in the windows.' She's already on her knees, pulling out sheets of cardboard – dismantled packaging – from under the sofa. 'In case they start throwing things worse than eggs.' She hands one of the pieces to Isabel and starts rummaging in the drawer under the coffee table until she finds a roll of duct tape. 'Well, come on, don't just stand there.'

'Ant's got … protocols for this?' says Isabel, shaking herself out of it and steadying the cardboard while Sam slides it behind the curtain and tapes it to the window. 'Since when? Why didn't I know?'

'Since we arrived, and because you don't talk to Ant and he doesn't trust you.' She clambers onto the windowsill, taping the top of the cardboard. 'We'll need to do upstairs too.'

She shouldn't have to do this, thinks Isabel unhappily. The whole point of getting Sam out of Espera was to give her a better life, a safer life – one where she wouldn't have to hide. But here they are, once more blocking out the sun.

'Let's get this one done first,' Isabel says aloud, trying

to keep her voice steady, and together they cover the front window. Sam's gathering the remaining cardboard to march upstairs when they hear someone rattling the back door. Isabel swears. 'If that's another journalist ...'

Sam's already gone to check, peeping out of the kitchen window at the tiny back yard. 'It's Leo,' she calls, with some relief, and Isabel hears the rattle of the security chain as she unlocks the door and lets him in.

'Good work on the blackouts,' he says, sounding exhausted, and sits on the stairs to unlace his trainers. 'It's chaos out there.'

'I can't believe you,' says Sam, before Isabel can speak. 'How long have you been planning this?'

Leo glances at Isabel, then tells Sam, 'Since the guy threatening to reveal it got murdered and fingers started pointing at Esperans.'

The kid gapes. 'Wait, he – he was *what*? How did he know?'

'No idea,' says Leo. 'One of his colleagues told the police he used to joke about his blackmail notebook, kept it on him at all times. It's missing. No,' he adds, when Isabel opens her mouth to ask a question, 'I didn't get arrested. I heard this from a friend whose brother works in catering down at the station. So, yeah, it's hearsay, but it sounds plausible.'

Isabel thinks of Martin Thompson's torn pocket. Something was taken. It could have been a notebook. Could quite easily have been a notebook, and that means this wasn't a random, opportunistic killing: this was somebody in trouble, trying to get out of it. 'Shit,' she says. 'So they're looking for it?'

'Turning his place upside down, apparently. He'd have

more on me than what he wrote in that little book, so I knew I needed to get ahead of the story before they figured out I was one of his targets. Change the narrative.' Leo scrubs his hands over his face. 'Wasn't going to do it today, but I got to work and they told me there's food rationing in Espera now. We're already almost out of supplies, and our money's practically gone, and if they put up physical blockades it'll be a nightmare trying to get anything into the city. I needed to remind the outsiders that there are civilians in there – and I needed to get people's attention.'

'Of course you did,' says Isabel. 'But you could have warned us before every journalist in the city showed up here.'

He flicks a glance towards the door. 'Did you talk to any of them?'

'I opened the door,' she admits. 'The first one. I didn't know it would be a journalist.'

'They got a photo?' he asks, and when Isabel nods grimly, he swears. 'Well, that cat's out of the bag, then.'

'How did they even find us?' asks Sam.

'Search me. Probably keeping tabs on us for a while, waiting for us to do something interesting.' He looks at his phone. 'Ant's held up at work, so hopefully they'll be gone by the time he gets back. In the meantime, we're stuck here.'

They all instinctively duck as another egg hits the front window; the cardboard can't block out the wet sound of the shell shattering. 'That's a waste of eggs,' says Sam. 'You could make cakes with those.'

Isabel's not sure if Sam loves baking because she gets cake

out of it, because she enjoys the process, or simply because it wasn't something she could do in the library basement and now she's making up for lost time, but her indignation prompts a tired smile from Leo.

'Yeah, I think we'd all be better off if they made cakes instead of protest signs,' he says. 'But I doubt we can convince them of that, so we might need to make the cakes ourselves. Want to help, Isabel?'

Her instinct is to refuse, but she stops herself. What else is she going to do this afternoon – hide in her room and wait for the mob to leave? 'Sure,' she says. 'I'll help.'

Sam lets out a whoop of delight. 'Chocolate cake!' she says, already clambering on the kitchen counter to rifle through the cupboard. She brandishes a bag of gluten-free flour triumphantly. 'Isabel-safe chocolate cake!'

Leo steps carefully out of the firing line and brushes flour off his nose. 'Your wish is my command,' he says, retrieving the recipe book from the shelf, and Isabel takes that as her cue to submit to their culinary overlordship.

For the next half-hour, she lets them boss her around, weighing out ingredients with the exactitude she'd have used in a lab. It's a gentler chemistry than she's used to, and the kitchen kinder than any lab, especially with Leo constantly cracking jokes like they're not under siege. It's almost possible to forget that they're doing this in a blacked-out house with a horde of journalists outside – almost, but not quite.

She can't remember baking a cake before. She's a competent cook, used to adapting recipes to suit her temperamental immune system, but her goal is always fuel, not pleasure. Baking is ... frivolous. And messy – she manages to wipe a smear of cake batter all down her face, and when Sam laughs at her, she retaliates by flicking cocoa at her, which goes in Sam's mouth and makes her splutter with its bitterness.

'No food fights in my kitchen,' says Leo, and sets Isabel to greasing and lining the baking tins as penance. 'There are enough people throwing eggs without you two making it worse.'

Once the cakes are in the oven and all that's left to do is wait – and wash up the mountain of dishes they've created – Leo puts his arm around Isabel's shoulder. It's the first time he's touched her since he dragged her out of the garage bar, and Isabel tenses, but lets it happen.

'They might get angry that you're here,' he says, in that quiet, earnest tone of his. 'Say we shouldn't have taken you in, or whatever. But they're wrong. This is your home, and you belong here. I *want* you here. I hope you know that.'

It's an apology for threatening to send her away, and it's a plea not to give him a reason to regret it. Isabel decides that now is not the time to tell him she thinks somebody's trying to frame her, and just leans a little closer, pressing her cheek against his shoulder. 'I know,' she says, and to her surprise, finds she means it. She might not believe herself lovable, but she believes Leo capable of loving even people who aren't, and that, in the end, is what matters: her faith in him.

When she left Espera, she was running to nothing – running *away*, without believing there was anything or anyone waiting for her on the other side. She's not sure she expected to survive. But that hopeless act brought her here: to Leo and Sam and Ant, to cake, to a house with cardboard on the inside of the windows and a bolt on the door, a haven against a world full of hate.

And Isabel is going to do everything in her power to keep them safe.

21

REKUNIĜITA (REUNITED)

Two barriers stand in the way of Isabel's murder investigation: the journalists and protesters camping outside their door, and Leo, who doesn't want her investigating at all.

'Please,' he says earnestly, a few days into the siege, 'I need to know that you're safe. The police will find the murderer. Just stay out of it.'

This would be more convincing coming from anyone except Leo. 'Wow,' says Isabel, with a forced laugh. 'Leo Jura, advocating for the police. Fame's really gone to your head.'

'Isabel ...' he begins, as though he's about to say he's not famous, when even now he's late for another televised interview about the book. He's been fielding media requests for days. Ant should be thrilled – it's what he wanted all along – but he's as tense as Isabel, and Leo's not a fan of the spotlight, either. They've all grown up knowing that drawing attention gets you killed, and that feels as true in Leeds as it did in Espera.

'Look,' says Isabel, 'I get it, you want me to stay out of this. But trying to convince me you trust the police to solve it? To be on our side? Come on.'

'It's different here,' he tries.

'Yeah, here we're automatically suspects by virtue of being Esperan. That's worse.' But they haven't got time to argue about this properly. 'Go do your interview. Get the world on our side. I promise I won't do anything rash while you're gone.'

And she doesn't. But she does borrow Sam's phone to call the community centre and get Catharine's number, and from Catharine she gets Maggie's, and from Maggie she gets James's. Then she texts all three of them:

> Not dead, not in jail, but basically under house arrest until the journalists get bored of us. Any news?

The answers come almost simultaneously.

> **James**
> Heard the army's trying to get the sanctions lifted for their own benefit. Could prove unpopular.

214

Isabel reads all three messages, then puts the phone down. She'll have to tell Leo about Pher's money – and about the army's efforts to undermine both the abolitionist blockades and the government sanctions, though what he can do about that, she doesn't know.

But Catharine's message is just for her.

She's still staring into space when Sam comes looking for her. 'I think I've found something,' she says, looking very serious, her laptop tucked under her arm. 'It might not help with the investigation. But I thought you should know.'

Isabel nudges one of the empty chairs out with her foot, gesturing for Sam to sit down. 'What is it?'

Sam sits, chewing her lip as though she's not sure how to say this. 'The impostor,' she says. 'The person people mistook for you. And the fake Moth. I think they might be the same person.'

This is not what Isabel was expecting her to say. 'Talk me through it.'

Sam opens the laptop. She's got several windows open: the

215

Esperan data dump, the sightings of Isabel, the latest headlines on the murder. 'They've stopped killing,' she says. 'The fake Moth, I mean. Nothing since the tenth of July. But there have been fake sightings of you every night since the sixteenth, and I *know* you haven't been out, because you're here. Sometimes multiple sightings in a night – same club, same stories, different people posting.'

'Okay . . .' begins Isabel slowly, not sure where this is going.

Sam sees her confusion, and explains, 'People in Espera knew you were the Moth. So whoever Comma got to replace you, they must have looked like you. Now whoever that is has stopped killing, *and* there's someone here who looks like you. Don't you think those things are connected?

When she puts it like that, it feels more likely that they're connected than that there are *two* people pretending to be Isabel. But— 'Are you saying Comma sent someone to pretend to be me to frame me for Martin Thompson's murder? Or that they sent the fake Moth to kill him?'

That makes no sense. It was too messy to be a guild hit, and Martin Thompson's not important enough for them to kill, anyway. Besides, if it was an external job, the fake Moth would have headed straight back to Espera to collect their commission; they wouldn't be hanging around in Leeds, drawing attention to themselves.

'I don't know if it's related to Martin Thompson,' says Sam uncertainly. 'You heard what Leo said. He was a blackmailer. Lots of people have secrets, and maybe one of them killed him. Maybe nobody's trying to frame you.'

'But then why would the fake Moth be here?'

'You're here,' Sam points out. 'What if Comma forced someone to take your place but they didn't want to do it, so they ran away like you did?'

'That's—' *Unlikely*, Isabel's about to say, or maybe *ridiculous*, but it's no more ridiculous than the fact that she fled, is it? She can see Ronan doing that: pulling a young agent from training and telling them they're the Moth now, and they'd better fall in line, just like Isabel did.

And maybe it *is* related, even if they're not trying to frame her – maybe Martin Thompson was in the wrong place at the wrong time and ran into a killer who hadn't yet learned to put down their knives, or maybe he was blackmailing them too and they were eliminating a threat. But that would leave the fake Moth here, in Leeds – armed and on the run and careless enough to drop clues, bringing suspicion down on the heads of every Esperan in the city. Desperate and dangerous.

'Fuck,' says Isabel, and skims through the sightings again. The kid's right: there are more of them, and they're convincing. Even if the impostor is an innocent lookalike who's got nothing to do with Espera or the murder, if this many people think they're Isabel, it won't be long before somebody else goes looking for them. That could get messy.

'We need to find them,' she says eventually. 'Figure out if they're really the fake Moth, if they had anything to do with the murder, all of it.'

'That's what I thought,' says Sam, and pulls up a map with half a dozen locations marked on it. 'So I cross-referenced all the sightings to find the ones that were most convincing, and which I knew definitely weren't you. Then I put them all on the map. They're pretty close together, so the impostor must be somewhere around here.'

Isabel clicks on a couple of the pins, pulling up the half-familiar names of bars she might have stumbled in or out of at some point. One of them is the Roxy, where Catharine first spotted her doppelgänger. The rest are all within half a mile of there.

She looks at Sam. 'Has anyone ever told you that you're a genius?'

Sam shrugs. 'A few times, yeah,' she says, and nods towards the screen. 'I don't know if they'll go back to those places. It looks like they don't often make repeat visits. But if you wanted to look for them, that's where I would start.' She adds, thoughtfully, 'It's probably not very safe, but I can help you.'

'Help me how?' asks Isabel, because yes, of course she wants to look for them, needs to look for them.

'Well, Leo won't want you to go. And you can't go without money, or a bus pass. But I can steal those for you. He and Ant are both working tomorrow night,' she adds. 'Or should be.'

Tomorrow night. Isabel wants to go *now*, but she knows they need time to plan. Even tomorrow night might be too soon – but any longer, and they might miss their chance. 'Okay,' she says. 'Tomorrow it is.'

'I would like to come with you,' says Sam, frowning down

at the computer. 'But I know you'll say no, so I'll have to run the op from here.'

Isabel hates herself for thinking it, but Hummingbird really missed a trick when they didn't recruit Sam too.

'I could take your phone,' she suggests. 'If it's secure.'

Sam gives the phone a disdainful look. 'It's not at the moment. I doubt anyone's tracking it, but I can make it safe. I haven't, because Leo says I'm not supposed to do illegal stuff any more, but I *can*.'

'If you can secure it, I can take it, and that way you can let me know if Leo comes home early, or something.' A new emotion swells in Isabel's chest, unfamiliar and strange: hope. 'This could work.'

'Yes. But we need to plan it *properly*. We need—'

The sound of the front door closing startles them both. 'Shit,' says Isabel, slamming the laptop closed. 'Let's ... let's pretend I've been, um ...'

'Teaching me Esperanto,' supplies Sam quickly, sliding the laptop into its sleeve. 'Mi estas bonega studento.' *I'm an excellent student.*

It's hardly surprising that Sam speaks Esperanto – she might have been raised civilian, but Isabel would've been more surprised if the kid didn't bother to pick up a few words while she lived in the library basement. Little point hacking the guilds if she couldn't read their files, after all. But she does wonder if Leo knows, or if Sam's hidden this skill from him so she can understand him when he thinks he's talking behind her back.

'Of course you are,' Isabel tells her, and by the time Leo comes into the living room, she's pretending to explain the finer details of a verb to Sam, who probably already understands it better than she does.

Leo smiles when he sees them together. 'Language lessons?' he says, with an arched eyebrow. 'I never thought of you as a teacher, Isabel.'

'Clearly, you underestimate me,' she says, trying to keep her tone light. 'How was your interview? Touch anyone's hearts today, change any minds?'

His smile fades. 'Hard to say,' he admits. 'Lot of questions about why I didn't claim authorship sooner, and I still haven't got a good answer. And I got a message from Jem, who says things in Espera are getting tougher. The guilds are trying to renegotiate some of their international trade deals to make up for the lost supplies here, but there are already riots about the food rationing.'

Sam swings her feet, her heels thudding against the leg of the chair. 'We should be doing more,' she says. 'There's got to be another way of getting food to them.'

'If there was, we'd be doing it,' says Leo. 'I'm hoping all the publicity will help with the fundraising. Beyond that, I don't know what else we can do. But we won't let them starve. This can't last – something's got to give.'

But Isabel can't help feeling it'll be the people who give long before the city does. Espera doesn't bend. Espera doesn't break. Espera just drives its people into the ground and leaves them for dead. That's how it's always done things.

'I promise,' says Leo, in response to something Sam said that Isabel missed. 'Things will get better.'

Sometimes, Isabel thinks, he's the best liar of them all.

Sam spends hours fiddling with the phone, swearing in creative ways (Isabel hadn't realised the kid *knew* some of those words). Finally, she drops the device onto the settee. 'I can't do it,' she says. 'I don't know if they've changed the software or I'm getting worse at this, but nothing's working.'

'I'll go without it,' says Isabel. 'It'll be fine. I'll watch my back.' She knows these clubs and bars, these student-crammed streets and cheap drinking haunts, even if she doesn't know why their target is spending time there. She's hoping the novelty of seeing her again might loosen some tongues.

She never used to bother dressing up when she went out clubbing, but she makes half an effort tonight, picking out the pair of jeans she knows make her butt look best and a T-shirt cut low enough to show the edges of her tattoos. Then she shrugs her jacket over the top, grateful that the sticky July heat has mellowed into something cooler, and heads into town.

The first club gets her no answers; the second earns her a dirty look and a shove from somebody she doesn't catch. In the third, she hears her name circulating before she's even opened her mouth to ask questions, and leaves before somebody makes a scene. These brightly lit havens of self-destruction aren't as welcoming as they used to be, no longer folding her into their anonymous embrace.

Isabel rounds the corner just as the heavy summer sky

begins to spit down rain, and there's Maggie's garage bar, right ahead of her.

She didn't meant to come here; she doesn't want to get distracted. But the door's open, the lights and music spilling out, and it looks welcoming in a way that none of the other clubs did. Her feet take her to the door before she's even really made the decision to go there, and she hesitates on the threshold.

'Hey, Isabel,' says Pher, lurking in the doorway with a bucket and a stamp for people's hands. She's not used to people here calling her by her real name; it catches her by surprise. 'We're fundraising tonight, did Maggie tell you? Cover charge to the Esperan liberation fund.'

He's sweet. She appreciates him. She wants to introduce him to Leo – but not tonight. 'I'm looking for someone,' she says. 'I've heard rumours. A girl with an Esperan accent. Some people have mistaken her for me. You seen anyone?'

Pher twists his lips. 'She hasn't been here,' he says, and Isabel's about to give up and resume her dispiriting search, but then he says, 'But my housemate Jay saw her. She's been up and down the clubs around here. Looking for something, losing herself, I don't know. When they told me, I showed them a picture of you, but they said she doesn't look that much like you up close. Dyed hair, yeah, but they said her eyes are blue.'

Isabel's surprised Pher's paid enough attention to notice her dark eyes. 'Do you know where I can find her?'

'We think she might be sleeping in the park up the top of the street. She was there a couple of days ago. But she could've

222

moved on by now.' Pher looks back over his shoulder, as though he's about to call someone out of the club to talk to her. 'I can get Maggie, she'll—'

'It's fine,' says Isabel. 'I can't stay.' She glances up the road, already impatient to be gone. 'This park,' she says. 'Point me towards it?'

Pher looks at her like he wants to ask if this is really a good idea, but in the end he just points, giving Isabel a brief string of directions. 'Like I said, she might be gone by now. But that's the best lead I can offer.'

'Thanks,' says Isabel, and offers him her best attempt at a smile.

'Be careful,' he says as she leaves. 'Heard that girl's dangerous.'

So am I, thinks Isabel, and sets off on her mission.

The park is small, barely worthy of the name: an oversized garden viciously fenced in with elderly iron railings, overshadowed by a few large, mature trees. The orange streetlights glimmer on the leaves, wet with rain, and in the faint pools of light the park is empty of anything except shadows.

Then Isabel sees the body.

Her feet slip on the wet pavement as she runs, never stopping to question whether heading straight for a body is a good idea. If they catch her with a corpse again, it won't be the Esperan Liaison Officers they send for her – but she doesn't care. She needs to know, needs answers, and if somebody else is dead then that's a *clue* . . .

The body moves, and Isabel skids to a halt, slipping on loose gravel from the meandering path. *They're still alive.*

What she'd taken for a corpse is a small, sleeping figure, hunched beneath an inadequate raincoat on a bench that must be hard as stone. They've woken at the sound of Isabel's approach, shifting beneath the makeshift blanket. Before she can speak, they push themselves to their feet, their hood shielding their face and hair. It looks like they're about to run.

'Wait—' begins Isabel, and at the sound of her voice, the figure stops and turns. Isabel pushes back her damp hair, exposing her face. 'I'm not here to hurt you,' she says. 'I'm looking for someone. For you, maybe.'

It's a girl, she thinks, slender and shaking, but Isabel can't be sure it's who she's looking for. 'For me?' says the girl, in a hoarse voice ruined by late nights shouting over loud music. 'You police?'

'No.' Isabel takes a step forward, into the weak orange light of the streetlight. 'Are you from Espera?'

The girl freezes. For a second, Isabel thinks it's the question that startled her, sending her into a panic at the thought of her cover blown and her identity exposed. The decision to come here unarmed begins to feel like a misjudgement; any assassin's first instinct after being caught would be to eliminate the witness.

But then the girl reaches up and pushes back her hood, exposing badly dyed hair and a face Isabel knows, a face she'd know anywhere.

Her bright smiles and sunny denial are gone, her lies and masks abandoned: Laura is thin, almost gaunt, her fair hair vanished under an onslaught of coloured dye and pulled roughly back into a ponytail, her clothes ragged and grey with dirt. For a moment, she looks like the ghost Isabel would have assumed her to be – a hallucination, impossible and alien.

But she's alive.

Isabel feels like she's been punched in the gut. *A girl from Espera. False names and changing stories. Lies and masks and guild-trained and dangerous.*

And Laura was a spy.

And Laura is alive.

Why did it never occur to her that Laura could be alive? Why did she never consider this eventuality? Only that Isabel has stopped believing in the possibility of miracles, and this can't be anything else, because Laura who was dead is here, standing in front of her.

She needs to say something, but faced with the girl she thought she'd lost – abandoned – her words have fled. She wants to ask, *Did you kill Martin Thompson?*, but right now she doesn't care what the answer is, because it makes no difference. As if she would ever turn Laura in, after failing her once. She's not making the same mistake again.

Finally, she just says, 'Laura.'

Her voice breaks the spell. Laura takes several hesitant steps forward, closing the gap between them. With shaking hands, she reaches out to trace Isabel's face, as though she doesn't believe it's real. She's abandoned her ragged raincoat on the bench and her T-shirt is soaked through, but it doesn't seem like she cares.

Laura touches her cheeks, her mouth, her eyebrows, the dull brown of her hair, and finally she breathes, 'Isabel.' A ragged hitch of her breath like she's trying not to cry, and a look in her eyes that threatens to undo Isabel.

And then Laura's arms are around her, holding her as though she's the only thing keeping them both upright, and for the first time since she left Espera, Isabel doesn't feel like something's missing.

22

ROMPIĜEMA (FRAGILE)

They go back to the bar, because there's no way Isabel can get Laura home by herself. Not on foot, with the warm rain still falling.

Pher's still at the door with his fundraising bucket and hand-stamps. 'Shit,' he says, dropping them immediately. 'You found her. I'll get Maggie.'

This time Isabel doesn't argue. They wait in the shelter of the doorway, Laura gripping Isabel's hand. They don't speak. They've got everything to talk about and none of it matters more than the whisper of their names on each other's lips and the wondering way that Laura touched her face as though it's a sight she thought she'd never see again, and the fact that *Laura's alive, and she's here.*

It's hard to believe Laura could be the killer, but Isabel wouldn't care if she was. All she cares about is getting Laura home safe.

Pher reappears with Maggie in tow. She gives them a once-over and asks, efficiently, 'Your place or mine?'

'Mine,' says Isabel. 'If you've a car. I don't think she can walk that far.'

Maggie holds up her keys. 'It's a shitbox, but it runs. Let's go.'

It is, indeed, a shitbox. It takes three attempts before the engine roars into life, and when it does, it's deafening compared to the ubiquitous electric vehicles of Espera. Laura doesn't react. She folded herself into the back seat at Isabel's coaxing, and now she's sitting there, unmoving, waiting for it all to be over.

It frightens Isabel because it's a little too familiar.

She sits beside Laura, still holding her hand. Maggie asks for the address, but otherwise keeps her questions to herself. When they're almost at Leo's, she says, 'If you need backup . . .'

'I'll call you,' says Isabel, meaning it. 'Thank you. Really. I—'

'Don't thank me,' says Maggie. 'But be careful. Please.'

She doesn't ask who Laura is, but it's clear she's guessed some of what Isabel hasn't said. It's a testament to her endless supply of second chances that she's driving them home anyway.

'I will,' Isabel promises, and shoots a glance at Laura.

She hasn't moved, or volunteered any information, or acknowledged the sound of their voices.

Maggie pulls up outside Leo's house and puts the handbrake on, leaving the engine running. 'I won't stop,' she says, 'or I might never get this thing going again. You'll be all right from here?'

Isabel unbuckles Laura's seatbelt. 'I hope so. Thank you.'

It's late – late enough that Leo will be home from work, and Sam will have told him where Isabel's gone, because that was the deal. If she didn't come back, Sam would tell him the truth. It's hard to tell if the lights are on behind the cardboard, but someone must be listening for them, because the front door opens before Isabel can get the spare keys out of her pocket.

Leo opens his mouth to speak, no doubt to berate her for sneaking out again, and then the light falls on the figure beside her and his words abandon him.

'Please,' says Isabel. 'She needs to come in. She needs to be somewhere safe.'

Leo only met Laura once, and Isabel doesn't know if he even recognises her, with the hair dye and the dirt and the ravages of the last couple of months stealing her polished glamour away. But he looks at them both, and then out at the street, where Maggie's car is still idling at the kerb, waiting to be sure they make it safely inside.

'Fuck,' he says at last, and opens the door wider to let them in.

In the warm light of the front room, Laura looks even worse.

Her once-bright hair is unwashed and ragged, cut short in an approximation of Isabel's style and dyed in colours that don't suit her. Her face is pinched, and she's lost weight, her collarbones and wrists unnervingly sharp. Leo finds her a blanket, and Sam puts the kettle on, but Isabel can't bear to do anything that requires moving more than a few inches away from Laura. She's afraid that if she closes her eyes, the other girl will vanish like the mirage she must be.

Laura curls up on the sofa, eyes wide and empty of understanding. Her brow creases at the sight of Sam, more than a lack of recognition.

'Sam,' says Isabel quietly, realising the confusion. 'This is Sam. Suzie's sister.'

Laura doesn't acknowledge her words, but her frown relaxes a little. She takes the mug of tea she's offered and sips it, her fingernails black with dirt against the white china mug.

Leo is dumbstruck, and Isabel can't blame him. Whatever he expected when Sam told him about Isabel's mission, it wasn't for her to return with the shattered remnants of her flatmate. The way Laura stares blankly into space, her silence on the journey here . . . Isabel knows it's how she behaved when they brought her here, and that's enough to worry anyone.

Eventually, Leo goes into the kitchen, gesturing for Isabel to follow. She hesitates, but Sam says, 'Go, I'll stay with her,' so Isabel does as she's told.

With the door firmly closed, he says, 'Please tell me she's not the killer.'

Isabel looks down at the floor. 'I don't know,' she says

230

honestly. 'She's not ... I don't know why she would ... She's a spy, not a field agent, and she'd have had no reason to do it.'

There's a long pause. Leo says, 'Let me get this straight. You didn't ask her if she was the killer before you brought her here and *left her alone with Sam*. And what do you mean, she's a spy?'

It only occurs to Isabel then that she never told Leo the truth about Laura. It hadn't seemed important, when she thought her flatmate was dead, and when he hardly knew her anyway. 'She wouldn't hurt Sam,' she says, because that's the important bit. 'She was Hummingbird. She knew Suzie. She's—' Isabel is doing a terrible job of explaining this. 'She was working for my mother.'

Leo passes his hand over his face and then says, 'Okay. I won't ask. But if she killed Thompson, if the police come ...'

'I don't believe she killed him,' says Isabel, which is as definite as she can be about it right now. 'Look at her. She's scared shitless. I don't know how long ago she got out, but she's obviously had nowhere safe to go since then. She's been sleeping in a park. I don't even know how she escaped Espera.'

'Or how she got here without being detained,' says Leo. Isabel hadn't thought of that, but he's right: Laura must have made it into Leeds without being noticed, or she'd have been taken to the detention centre like Isabel. 'Somebody must have helped her. Can't be Jem or Beth, because they'd have told us, but that doesn't mean anything. There are dozens of factions inside the city.' He lets out a long breath. 'Okay, well, we won't solve any mysteries tonight. First things first, she needs a meal and a good night's sleep.'

'She can have my bed,' says Isabel immediately. 'I'll take the floor.'

'I was going to suggest the couch, but ...' Leo glances towards the living room. 'She'll probably feel safer upstairs, with a door that closes. I'll find you a spare pillow.' He's taking this better than she expected, given everything; Isabel's once again overwhelmingly grateful for Leo's unquenchable goodness.

'Thank you,' she says, inadequately. 'For letting her stay.'

Leo looks briefly surprised, but he nods. 'Yeah, well, we'll talk about this, but right now ...'

Right now they've got higher priorities: Laura's empty stare and shaking hands and too-thin face. Isabel goes back into the living room, where nothing about the scene has changed except that Sam's retrieved the empty mug from Laura's unsteady grip.

'Hey,' begins Isabel, in the gentlest voice she can manage. 'So, this is Leo's house, where I live, and we're safe now, okay? And you need to get some sleep. Let's go upstairs, and I'll find you something to wear.'

Laura says nothing, but when Isabel holds out her hand, she takes it and allows herself to be led upstairs. She sits meekly on the edge of the bed while Isabel goes to the bathroom for a bowl of water and a flannel, and lets herself be sponged clean. The water turns a murky grey, and still there's dirt under her fingernails.

'Here,' says Isabel, handing her a pair of pyjamas. 'You wanna change alone, or shall I help you?'

Laura doesn't answer, but she shucks off her own clothes and changes into the pyjamas without complaint. Her body is bruised yellow and green, and there are half-healed grazes on her arms and legs. Isabel bites her lip and doesn't ask. There'll be time for that later, when Laura's safe, when she believes she's safe.

'Get some rest,' she suggests. 'You must be exhausted.'

Laura looks up at her. 'Isabel,' she says, the first word she's spoken since the park.

'It's me,' Isabel agrees, perching beside her on the bed. 'And I'm not going anywhere. So get some sleep, and when you wake up, I'll be here.'

Obediently, Laura climbs into the bed and allows Isabel to tuck the sheets in around her, but when Isabel gets up to leave, she snatches at her hand, pulling her back.

Okay.

Isabel lies down beside her, on the very edge of the single bed, at risk of depositing herself on the carpet with one wrong move. Her fingers are still interlaced with Laura's. 'This better?' she says.

Laura nods. The fear and uncertainty looks wrong on her face. Laura was a liar, everything Isabel knew about her a mask, but still she finds it impossible to reconcile this haunted expression with the carefree civilian she thought she lived with for so long.

'Not going anywhere,' Isabel promises her again, and watches as Laura finally, finally surrenders to her exhaustion.

She doubts she'll be able to sleep herself, braced against the edge of the bed, all her attention on the steady rasp of Laura's breathing. But gradually she must doze off, because she's fast asleep when somebody grabs her hand so hard it jolts her past *awake* into *alert and afraid*.

Laura is rigid, her back against the wall, looking at Isabel with terror. Her grip is so tight it hurts, and she's looking at her hand as though she doesn't understand that it's clutching a real life human being.

'I'm real,' says Isabel, mouth dry and fuzzy with sleep. It's the only thing she can think of to say. 'I'm real. It's really me. Can you – ow – can you maybe loosen your grip?'

Laura releases her, and she rubs her wrist gratefully. The other girl's still shaking, and Isabel can only guess what kind of nightmare she'd been having.

'You're safe,' says Isabel. She feels useless. She should be an expert in this kind of thing – the post-Espera trauma, the nightmares and the doubting reality and the flashbacks – but she's got no idea how to help Laura, how to pull her back to the present or convince her this is real. Doesn't know enough about what Laura's remembering to know what to say to her. 'You're safe. I'm here. Leo's next door, and Sam's upstairs. Ant will probably be home soon. Do you remember Ant? No, of course you don't, you never met. He's nice, Laura, they're all nice. You're safe.' She's rambling, but the words aren't important, not in the way that the tone of her voice is. 'Tomorrow we'll get you cleaned up and find you some more clothes, yeah? You're safe now. We won't let them hurt you again.' Isabel doesn't even know who *they* are. 'I'm not leaving you, Laura.' *Not again.*

Laura's terrified gaze finally fixes on her face, as though trying to memorise it. She says, again, 'Isabel.'

'That's me,' Isabel confirms, wondering if she deserves to be that reassurance, the one who convinces someone else they're safe, when for so long she was the face of people's nightmares. 'The one and only.'

Laura smiles, a cracked and bloody smile. 'I found you,' she says, and then, 'I thought I wouldn't. They said you were there but you never came.'

You never came. Isabel wants to think she's talking about the clubs – that she was following Isabel's trail across Leeds, using the only intel she could get her hands on. Because if she's not, then she held out for Isabel to come back, to rescue her. And Isabel failed her.

'I'm sorry,' she begins, but Laura's asleep again.

The pattern continues for what's left of the night, and Isabel switches off her morning alarms, reluctant to wake Laura from her last bout of fitful sleep. Sometime in the mid-morning, Leo comes in with a pair of mugs on a tray.

'Sam put honey in this one,' he says. 'Thought it might help Laura.'

Isabel nods, but doesn't move to wake Laura up just yet.

'Isabel,' begins Leo, in the tone of voice that means he's going to say something she won't like, 'I don't know if she can stay here long-term.'

It's predictable, but it still hurts. 'She's got nowhere else to go.' Already, Isabel's scrambling for solutions. Maybe they can find somewhere together, her and Laura, somewhere they won't have to be alone. Maybe Maggie can help.

'We need to tell the authorities. She needs ... paperwork. Documents. I can vouch for her the way I vouched for you, but I don't know if that will stand up this time, when I'm a known agitator and she might be a murder suspect. They'll—'

'I don't think she's the killer,' says Isabel, determined.

'She's a Hummingbird spy, we've got no idea how long she's been in the city, and we've got no idea what she traded to get out,' Leo returns. 'I know you want to believe she's not, but we've got no *proof.*'

And the thing is, he's right. A pit of fear opens in Isabel's stomach. Laura's hair has been cut and dyed to look like Isabel's. She's traumatised as fuck by whatever she's been through. And what was Sam's theory? That the fake Moth was someone who never wanted to do it, was forced into it, and fled the city to get away from the name and the obligations that came with it.

Isabel abandoned Laura in a building owned by Comma, under attack from Hummingbird. She left her flatmate *helpless* in the hands of the guilds, and was so convinced Laura was dead that she never stopped to think what other uses they might have for a spy who got a little too close to her target.

It wouldn't have been hard to make a killer of Laura. She completed basic as part of Project Emerald, and managed to tail Isabel for weeks without giving herself away, learning her behaviours and idiosyncrasies. And Isabel's fought her. She knows she's not bad with a knife.

Somebody must have helped her get out of Espera. If Martin Thompson's death was the price of that help, can she really believe Laura would hesitate to pay it?

'I don't think she did it,' Isabel repeats, but it's less certain this time.

'I want to believe you,' says Leo. 'But nobody else will, without evidence. Until she's well enough to tell us what happened, she can stay here, but once she can talk . . .'

'You want to interrogate her.'

Leo looks very tired. 'I want us to be safe,' he says. 'I want *her* to be safe. That means we need to know who the killer really is, and what they're trying to achieve. That's all, Isabel, okay?'

She didn't mean to accuse him; she knows he's right. Isabel takes her mug and wraps her hands around it, a proxy for human contact. 'Sorry,' she says. 'She just looks so helpless.'

'I know.' He looks helpless too, in a different way – less fragile, more exhausted. She feels inordinately guilty for all the trouble she's heaped on his head. 'And we'll help her as much as we can, in whatever way we can. But that's all I can promise.'

It's more than either of them deserves, but that doesn't mean it's enough.

23

UZITA (USED)

Days pass, and Laura doesn't speak. She sleeps badly, waking repeatedly from nightmares to grip Isabel's hand like a rope thrown to a drowning man, and spends most of the day curled up in bed or on the settee, staring into space. Gradually, her bruises fade and colour returns to her wasted cheeks, but she offers no explanations for how she's here.

'She can't stay here,' says Ant, after three days of this. 'It'll fuck us all over if they find out. She hasn't got the papers—'

'And where else is she meant to go?' Isabel retorts, glancing at Laura, who shows no more interest in the argument than in anything else.

'You could at least ask her how she got here.' He snaps his

fingers in front of Laura's face; she blinks, but doesn't move. 'Hey. I'm talking to you. How did you get out of Espera?'

Laura curls herself into a tighter ball, and doesn't answer. Ant swears, and Sam says, 'Leave her alone, Anthony. You're being mean.'

Mean is one word for it: he's been short-tempered ever since the murder, hardly able to keep a civil tongue in his head, though he makes more of an effort when it's Sam he's talking to. Isabel gets it: they're all anxious, frayed to breaking point by the blackmail and the pointing fingers and the state of Espera. But it makes him unpleasant to be around, and it's a relief whenever he storms out of an argument and heads to work, not coming back until the early hours; if he takes on any more overtime, he'll hardly be home at all.

But he's not wrong: they *do* need answers from Laura. Isabel just doesn't know how to ask, overwhelmed by guilt about their parting. And she knows there must be more to Laura's current shell-shocked state than that alone, because Laura's been through plenty and come out smiling, so whatever destroyed her must have been worse.

Leo doesn't push her, despite the urgent need to know the extent of Laura's involvement – or hopefully lack thereof – in the death of Martin Thompson; he's concerned that Laura will retreat even further inside her shell if she feels threatened. But they can't wait for ever, and since Isabel's the only one Laura's spoken to so far, she's got to be the one to break the silence.

She waits until it's dark, because at night they understand each other better. The daytime hours are a tentative stalemate,

Isabel trying to maintain a shadow of her usual routine. She doesn't go to the gym, but she works out in the living room, using Sam's schoolbooks as weights while the kid watches and giggles. She teaches Sam some German to go with her Esperanto, and supervises her baking sessions so that nothing blows up, always with one eye on Laura. Sometimes she thinks her friend is watching them, trying to reconcile Isabel-the-killer with Isabel-the-teacher, but she never catches her at it.

Night time is different, though. At night it's just the two of them, door closed, lying in Isabel's bed. Laura stays close to the wall, and Isabel lies with her back to the door, shielding Laura with her body. Tonight Laura isn't sleeping, her eyes glittering in the small amount of light seeping under the door, and Isabel plucks up the courage to speak.

'Mi pensis, ke vi mortis,' she says; *I thought you died.* They never spoke Esperanto to each other before, but it feels right: back to guild business, their shared heritage of death. Here in this strange outside world, they're finally telling each other the truth, stripped of lies and civilian façades. 'I don't understand how ... I ... you were dying in Espera, I left you in Espera, you died in *Espera*. I left you.'

Silence. She shouldn't have expected anything else. Even her own voice, her own breath, feels too loud in this illusory cocoon of safety. But finally, Laura whispers back, 'Mi ne mortis.' *I didn't die.*

As if that wasn't overwhelmingly obvious. 'I don't understand,' Isabel says. 'There were too many of them. You couldn't have got out of there. We both knew that. That's why you told me to go.'

'I know,' Laura agrees. 'I couldn't have got out. Not alone.' Idly, she runs one of her fingertips over the back of Isabel's hand. It should be a tender gesture, but it feels more like she's tracing the bones to know which of them to snap. 'But Ronan Atwood decided I was more useful alive.'

Whatever explanation Isabel expected, it wasn't this. '*Ronan* saved you?'

Laura shrugs, as best she can while lying on her side. 'Guess he thought there was more I could tell them than I already had. All those months watching the Moth . . .' It's the most she's spoken since arriving here, and the words don't come easily, though her Esperanto is fluent enough. Her accent's almost as natural as Isabel's – Laura may not have joined Hummingbird as young as Isabel joined Comma, but it's still a part of her.

'Was there?' Isabel asks. 'More that you could tell them?'

Laura lets go of her hand and rolls onto her back, staring at the ceiling. 'Ronan can be very persuasive.'

Isabel knows all too well how persuasive Ronan can be, offering choices that leave you stranded between death and the betrayal of your truest self.

'What did he do to you, Laura?' she whispers. She can barely speak the question aloud.

The other girl shifts a little, but doesn't look back at her or reach for her hand. Isabel wishes she hadn't let go. 'Asked a lot of pointed questions. Didn't give me much choice about whether to answer.'

241

'That's not enough.'

'Enough for what?' Laura turns her head. 'You think he should have pulled out my fingernails?'

Isabel shakes her head. 'That wouldn't have been enough to leave you like this.' She *knows* Laura. Betraying Hummingbird wouldn't have broken her – she was already working for Judith behind their backs. And she wouldn't have left Espera unless she had absolutely no other choice, because when Isabel begged her to, she said no.

'Like what?'

Now Isabel's the one who looks away. 'Scared,' she says. Laura's trembling even now, when they're safe and warm and alone, in the only place either of them ever truly stops looking over their shoulder. 'Scared and quiet. The Laura I remember was never quiet, not like this.'

'Maybe that's because you left that Laura for dead.'

She says it without aggression or animosity, but it cuts deep. Isabel hasn't stopped feeling guilty since the day she arrived in Leeds, but grief overshadowed it, greyed out the edges of the pain. Now it rushes back, nauseating and bitter.

She swallows the lump in her throat and the taste of self-hatred and says, 'You weren't scared when you were bleeding to death, or when I was about to leave you. And now you have nightmares. Every night. Now you won't let me out of your sight.'

'So?'

'So something happened. Something you haven't told me about.'

Laura is silent for several minutes, and Isabel thinks she's pushed it too far. She's about to roll over and try to sleep when her flatmate finally says, 'You want to know exactly how guilty you should feel? How much to hate yourself for leaving instead of fighting until you died at the foot of my bed?'

That's exactly what Isabel wants to know, even though it makes no difference, because she'll never forgive herself. Instead, she reaches out and touches Laura's hair, the faded dye grey in the half-light. Laura moves as though to push her away, but doesn't.

'I want to know what happened to your hair,' says Isabel.

Silence, again. She's beginning to hate silence, and the way Laura retreats inside it, the one place Isabel can't reach her.

Laura says, 'I think you already know, don't you?'

Maybe. She was hoping she was wrong. 'I saw the obits,' says Isabel. 'The revolutionaries. The abolitionists. They said it was the Moth. But I was here.'

'Yeah.' Laura's still lying on her back, looking up at the ceiling, only a hint of her profile visible in the darkness. 'But people didn't know that. There were rumours. A confrontation in Lutton. Nobody knew what happened to you after that.'

'And Comma needed the city to think the Moth was still around.' A threat to keep people in line, especially young people, and young people are always the angriest, the most likely to rise up. They needed to know there was someone out there who didn't distinguish between legitimate targets and children, and with Isabel gone . . .

'I guess by that point I'd exhausted my usefulness in spilling

243

Hummingbird intel,' says Laura, unemotionally. 'It was clear to both me and Ronan that they'd never take me back. And he knew I'd been trailing you, studying you long enough to know your methods. I was Daphne, after all. If anyone could be mistaken for the Moth, it was the spy who'd lived in her shadow for months.'

She imagines Laura leaving Isabel's calling cards, putting on a mask, and still it doesn't explain the broken person in front of her. 'But you'd killed before, hadn't you?'

'In training,' says Laura. 'My grad assignment. But not much, and not the way the Moth did.'

And there it is.

Because the Moth was the worst of them: a threat, a horror story, a deterrent. The Moth killed children, the elderly, without remorse. The Moth could never, ever be bargained with. And the city, which had always known that, was forcibly reminded of it when Suzie died, a sign that nobody in Espera was safe.

And Isabel ... Isabel was fucked up enough to do those things. But Laura wasn't. Laura was better than that.

Laura says, 'The abolitionists were one thing. I didn't want to do it, but I had to. But there were others, kills that didn't get reported. Hummingbird agents, trainees, associates – people who knew me well enough to let down their guard around me. I *knew* them. And all the while, Ronan held it over me that Hummingbird would never take me back after what I'd told Comma, and nobody in Comma would come to Daphne's defence if he decided I wasn't useful enough to keep alive. So I didn't have anyone. Not a single person on my side.'

At least Isabel had had Daragh. At least she'd had Mortimer. At least she'd never been alone, no matter how much it felt like it.

'I'm sorry.' Her voice sounds scratched and hoarse.

'Yeah. You should be.'

'What did you . . . what did you do?'

'As I was told. For long enough to lose sight of who I was before that.'

And it wouldn't have been simple contracts they asked her to fulfil. Suzie's death was a rarity, but if Comma wanted to make a point and convince people the Moth was still in the city, those rarities would be exactly what they'd rely on to send the message. Suzie wasn't the only Project Emerald recruit, just the youngest.

Killing a child was bad enough when she was a stranger, but for Laura, who'd worked with them . . .

'The children?' asks Isabel.

'I didn't do it.' Laura swallows; Isabel hears it. 'They sent me to finish the job, to go back to that house and leave it empty, but I couldn't.' She turns her head, and even in the darkness Isabel sees that the expression on her face isn't bitterness or disgust. It's . . . pity. Sorrow. 'I don't know what you went through,' she says, 'that made you able to do those jobs. I don't know what they did to you for it to seem like your best option. But whatever you experienced to numb you to that, it must have been bad. And I'm sorry that it happened.'

Laura doesn't get to apologise to Isabel. Not like this, not for this. She doesn't get to play the forgiveness game and make out like this wasn't Isabel's fault, when it must have been. She was numb to her own atrocities because that's who she is – a rotten thing, all violence and rage inside her bones. For Laura to suggest otherwise means she believes Isabel once had the potential to be something else.

'I don't really remember,' says Isabel slowly, 'what it's like to be a child. I guess that helps.' But it doesn't excuse it – any of it. And Laura doesn't get to pity her, when all she's proved is that faced with the same choices as Isabel, she made a different call.

Laura's a liar and a killer and she's still a better person than Isabel.

'I'm sorry,' says Laura, like she's got anything to be sorry for. Isabel wants to push her away, to get out of bed and go, because she needs not to be here any more, where everyone seems determined to forgive her for things she should never be forgiven for. Why is she the only one who can see it? What's wrong with them, that they keep acting like she's the kind of person who can be redeemed or whatever the fuck they're trying to achieve? She wants to believe they're good people, but good people wouldn't be tolerating her.

But she doesn't get up. And Laura moves a little closer to her, no longer wedged right up against the wall.

'That's when I knew I had to leave,' she says. 'Ronan wasn't going to let me live, and it wouldn't have been pretty when he killed me, either.' Laura huffs out her breath. 'Would've been a lot harder without the protests, but Comma were distracted. Found a smuggler who could get me out.'

Isabel wets her lips. 'What did you ...?' she begins, then hesitates. Does she want to know the answer? Yes. She needs to know. 'What did you offer them in exchange?'

'Intel,' says Laura, calmly. 'Only thing I've ever been good for. Intel I should never have had in the first place, but I'm a fucking great spy, so I knew. Margaret Strange's address, and the security there.' She adds, a little bleakly, 'I haven't kept up with the news, so I don't know if they've killed her yet.'

For a moment, Isabel can only lie there, staring into the darkness, as she processes this. Laura had Margaret Strange's address. Laura handed over *the Director of Hummingbird* to escape. A death like that will ignite the city, create a power vacuum, send Hummingbird into chaos right at the time the guild most needs to be strong, and Laura gave it to them.

And now – now she needs to know for sure. 'When did you leave?' she asks.

There's a pause, like Laura's thinking, and then she says, 'Sixteenth of July. Late morning.'

The day Martin Thompson was killed. Too late to have been involved in his death.

Hope blossoms inside Isabel. 'The smugglers who got you out, would they swear to that? Were they with you?'

'I don't know. Somebody would know, probably.' Laura's unemotional tone has given way to puzzlement. 'Does it matter?'

'It means you've got an alibi,' says Isabel. 'It means you're safe, and they can't take you away from us, and it's going to be okay.' She almost laughs, soft and relieved, until she

247

remembers that it won't fix any of what was done to Laura. Instead, she reaches out and takes her flatmate's hand, squeezing it in hers. 'This helps. I promise you, this helps.'

If Laura hasn't kept up with the news, she probably doesn't even know what she needs an alibi for. But she says, 'Okay,' and laces her fingers with Isabel's, like she trusts her, even after everything.

24

ÎIFRITA (ENCRYPTED)

Laura may have broken her silence, but the chatty flatmate Isabel remembers is long gone. Maybe it's unfair of Isabel to expect anything more than silence and empty stares, knowing how she behaved when she first came here, but it bothers her to see Laura a shell of herself, and she doesn't know how to fix it.

Leo seems keen for Isabel to keep teaching Sam languages, like that'll keep them both out of trouble, so she does. They spend hours together in the front room while Laura looks on, exchanging Esperan conversation for German grammar and back again when Sam grows too restless. They've begun work on the Cyrillic alphabet, too, though this is going slowly, more because of Sam's restlessness than a lack of ability. Isabel can't blame her. She's tried, once or twice, to go back to the books

Leo bought her, but her focus skitters away before she can get through more than a sentence or two.

'I've been working on the investigation,' begins Sam one day, when Laura leaves the room to use the toilet, 'and—'

Isabel looks up in surprise; Sam's expression is serious. 'You're still investigating?'

'We didn't solve the mystery,' says Sam. 'You found the fake Moth, the impostor – so what? People still suspect us. They won't stop until we find the killer.'

The protesters have become such a fixture of their street, their SEND THEM BACK signs growing tatty with use, that Isabel's practically stopped noticing them. She's scarcely left the house since finding Laura, and Martin Thompson's death has slipped down her mental list of priorities.

With a pang of guilt at having left Sam to investigate alone, she says, 'Have you found something?'

'It's . . .' Sam hesitates. 'Well. First I wanted to show you this.' She exits the dictionary tab they were using for their lesson and pulls up the *Bulletin*. 'After what you told us Laura said about how she got out of Espera, I checked. And I found this.'

She turns the screen towards Isabel so she can read the headline:

MARGARET STRANGE IS DEAD

It's very straightforward. No tricks or puns or misdirection.

'So somebody took Laura's intel and used it,' says Isabel,

250

already scanning the page: dated yesterday, words like *power vacuum* and *chaos* and *weakened* littering the article. 'How does this help us?'

Sam shrugs. 'With the strikes, a lot. With solving the murder, not so much. Except . . .' She flips tabs to the Esperan data dump, unformatted as ever, new obits and death figures at the bottom of the list. 'This site. The *Bulletin* published the news about Margaret Strange before they did, which doesn't tell us much, only that the Free Press found out before whoever runs this. But that seemed weird to me, since this site is just data and the Free Press had to write a whole article, so I went poking around, and I managed to break through enough of their security to work out why. This site isn't being maintained from within Espera.'

It takes Isabel a minute to process the significance of this. 'You're saying an outsider's got this information and is sharing it. Somebody who isn't getting it from the Free Press.'

'Right. Which isn't that surprising, because there are a lot of abolitionist factions out there, and some of them are more radical than others. One of them used to meet at the library until Jem kicked them out for drawing too much attention, and they were always talking about assassinating guild directors and stuff like that. It could've been one of them who killed Margaret Strange, and the same one or another who's informing whoever this is. *But*,' she adds, in a dramatic tone of voice, 'this isn't the whole website.'

Isabel watches as Sam pulls up the code for the page, adds a line or two – as if it's easy – and the website reconfigures itself entirely. Messages, Isabel realises, scanning the lines of text – in code, but clearly communications of some sort, hosted on the site's servers.

Given time, squared paper, and determination, Isabel might be able to break the cipher. But Sam, who hacked the guilds at the age of ten, won't need that. 'Have you decoded them yet?' she asks.

Sam grins, pleased that somebody's recognising her skills. 'About half,' she says, and her smile fades a little. 'Which was enough to prove that whoever runs this website killed Martin Thompson.'

'Wait, what?' Isabel leans forward, as though proximity will help her untangle the encryption and read the messages for herself, but of course they remain a jumble of meaningless code. 'Are you sure?'

'Yes,' says Sam, and her tone is such that Isabel doesn't doubt her for a moment. The kid points to some of the messages. 'This person is in Leeds. This person,' she says, pointing to some of the other messages, 'is actually a radical abolitionist group in Espera. Thompson was blackmailing the killer and they were asking for help. The Esperan faction told them to confront and threaten him. They did, it escalated, he's dead. This message,' she adds, highlighting one of them, 'is them panicking about it. And this one is the reply from inside Espera, saying some of their people got killed and they're going dark. They haven't sent any messages since then.'

Isabel stares at the screen. 'Fuck,' she says. She thought Sam

252

was going to give her vague theories, not written evidence that whoever killed the man *was* working directly with Espera.

'Yup,' says Sam, popping the 'p'.

'So, wait, they killed him by accident?' That would explain a lot: the mess, the inefficiency, the evidence. 'But they went there armed, because they planned to threaten him . . .'

'Seems like it,' says Sam. She adds petulantly, 'They switched their codes partway through. I've only broken the newest one, so I don't know if they said what the blackmail was about. I'm working on that.'

Knowing what Thompson had on this person would help with figuring out who they are. But if Sam was able to get this far into the website, maybe there's a simpler solution. 'Can you use this to track them? If they're still updating the site . . .'

Sam nods, like she'd been thinking this too. 'I'm trying. They've got a complex system of proxies set up, but I'll break through it eventually.'

From the doorway, Laura says, 'Who are you trying to find?'

They both turn to look at her, startled by the interruption. 'A murderer,' says Isabel. 'Killed a journalist. Connected in some way to a radical faction inside Espera, though probably not the same one that got you out of the city. Speaking of which, is there anything you can tell us about them?'

She hadn't liked to ask before now; it clearly wasn't an easy journey. But Laura takes the question at face value, thinking for a moment, and then says, 'Very little. I never even got a name, let alone any idea how many people they were working with. I met with one guy, twice, and he drove me out of the city in the boot of a car. I think they switched drivers part way, but I never saw the second one.'

It sounds like a fucking awful way to escape – and it also sounds like Laura's alibi might be hard to confirm. But if her rescuers could *drive* out of the city ... well, either the gates are less secure than before, they've got forged guild permits to get them past the checkpoints, or there's a guild turncoat on their team with a valid exit visa. That could be useful information, if Isabel can figure out how to use it.

'Why don't you think it's the same group?' Laura asks. She sounds curious.

It's the first time she's displayed interest in anything since she came here. Isabel answers her honestly: 'Because they've had other priorities.' She turns the laptop so Laura can see the headline:

MARGARET STRANGE IS DEAD

Laura doesn't flinch. 'Well then,' she says. 'Is it bad? The city?'

'Probably not great,' says Isabel. 'How was it before you left?'

She grimaces, looking away. 'Hard to say. I was insulated from the worst of it, only leaving Comma to do Ronan's jobs. But volatile. The strikes were spreading and the protests with them, and nothing the guilds did was helping. Sending me to wipe out their leaders, taking hostages ...'

'Hostages?' repeats Isabel.

'Both guilds were at it. Abolitionists and union leaders.

Take them prisoner, say you'll release them if people go back to work, kill them if the strikes continue. Bluffing, at first, because making martyrs would only inflame the situation, but of course they were all ready to die for the movement, and they'd told their people to hold the line, whatever the guilds did. So that failed, too.'

Hostages have never been part of the guilds' strategies. They're just not *useful*, unless somebody values the hostage's life above whatever points they're trying to score, and it's rare in Espera for anybody's life to be valued that highly. Katipo tried it, but only because it was Isabel they wanted; Comma would never have given in.

But using them against civilians – yes, Isabel can imagine that would have worked, if people didn't have something bigger than themselves to warrant the sacrifice.

'And now Margaret Strange is dead,' says Sam, 'and Hummingbird will all be fighting over who gets to be in charge, won't they?'

Isabel glances at Laura, who knows best how the other guild organises itself. 'Maybe,' says Laura. 'Normally, there'd be a succession plan, because a director can be assassinated at any time. But right now, with everything the way it is . . .' She shrugs. 'I think it'll add an element of unpredictability to the board that won't de-escalate anything, that's for sure.'

'If the abolitionists want to take down Hummingbird, now's the moment,' says Isabel, and goes to the window, pulling aside the cardboard shutters to stare out at the street. Not too many protesters today; perhaps the August drizzle is keeping them at home. 'Would it help, though, if they did? Even after all Leo's interviews, all the attention he's brought to the abolitionists, the outside world still doesn't care about the protests. They'll keep starving Espera anyway.'

'And if Hummingbird falls, and Comma doesn't ...' says Laura. 'Well, I'll tell you something. Ronan Atwood will find a way to survive this. He won't be the one starving.'

Isabel agrees. She can imagine Ronan taking emergency control of the industrials and sending in his remaining loyal guild members to break the factory strikes, keep his people fed. When she thinks about Espera, she's got to face the fact that the people who were kindest to her are dead, and all their kindness has gone with them. Without Daragh to blunt his edges, Ronan's a knife, bloody and unrestrained.

'So this journalist that was killed,' says Laura, 'what happened?'

Sam gives her a summary, from Isabel finding the body and the Esperan shilling to the hidden messages on the website. Laura frowns at that, taking a seat beside them and scrolling through the website for herself.

'Sloppy,' she concludes, when she's seen whatever she needed to see. 'Definitely not guild-trained. No Intelligence training at all, as far as I can tell, or there's no way they'd be putting this on an unsecured site.'

'It wasn't exactly unsecured,' admits Sam, and then they're off talking about encryption and security, arguing about the relative merits of this system or that, far beyond Isabel's knowledge of programming and old-fashioned text-based codes.

Laura was a spy. How easy it is to forget that, until the moment it isn't.

While they talk, Isabel's mind drifts back to the body. Now she knows it was a threat that went too far, and not premeditated murder, it's easier to make sense of the evidence. The torn pocket, the stolen notebook – that fits, if Thompson was blackmailing them. If the killer were sensible, they'd have destroyed it as soon as they left the crime scene, and it'll be ash in the wind by now. But they're sufficiently clueless to have run panicking about the murder to their Esperan contacts, so there's a chance the notebook still exists. Proof, of a kind these outsider police might actually accept.

'. . . use that to trace it,' finishes Laura, and Sam nods.

'It'll be slow, but I can do it,' she says. 'And then what, we tell the police?'

This is directed at Isabel, who drags herself back into the conversation with some effort. 'We find the killer,' she says. '*Then* we tell the police.'

'But—' begins Sam.

'I think they still have Martin Thompson's notebook,' she says, and watches understanding dawn on Sam's face. She spells it out anyway: 'Nobody will believe a twelve-year-old hacker and two known murderers without hard proof. Laura's not even supposed to be here. The website helps, but it's not conclusive unless we can place the killer at the scene. So we find them, we find the notebook, and *then* we turn them in.'

'Or we could just deal with it ourselves,' says Laura casually.

'If by deal with it you mean kill them ...' begins Isabel, about to explain why that's a bad idea.

'I mean do whatever we need to do to keep this' – Laura gestures to the house – 'you, Sam, Leo, whatever, safe.'

'I didn't know you cared,' says Sam, without rancour.

Laura opens her mouth and closes it again, before finally saying, 'I knew your sister.'

This doesn't go down as well as she might have hoped; Sam's got no love for Hummingbird, or anyone she associates with the organisation that took her sister from her. But all she says is, 'Until an hour ago, you didn't show any signs of caring about anything or anyone. Now you're trying to help us solve a murder you didn't even know about. But Isabel's right – we can't kill someone. That will only make this worse.'

She's got a point. If Isabel had realised all it would take was a murder investigation to get Laura to engage with the world again, she'd have brought this up days ago. But maybe it's the same desperate need to be useful, to be part of something, that she's felt herself. Laura isn't *better* now that she's focused on this: it's just given her something to think about that isn't all the ways she's deeply fucked in the head.

Laura says, 'Then what do you propose?'

Isabel's still figuring out the finer details; she's never known how to solve problems without violence. 'First step is to identify the killer,' she says. 'Then we'll know what we're dealing with, and how much of a threat they are. If you can trace that website ...'

'Already on it,' says Sam.

'Then I'll ask Ant about the different abolitionist factions in the city. Try to figure out who's on the other end of those messages.' Ant, she suspects, will know more about them than Leo. Leo is Free Press and a pacifist through and through, his politics shaped by love, but Ant lived in that basement for three years, and he must have seen every group that came through there.

'And me?' says Laura.

Isabel wants to say: *You should focus on getting better.* But she remembers how it felt to be aimless, wandering, lost in her own memories, and it fucking sucked.

'You're a spy,' she says instead. 'You're going to help me figure out how to keep all this a secret from Leo.'

25

MALKURAĜA (COWARDLY)

That night, Laura falls asleep long before Isabel does. Isabel lies beside her, unmoving, trying to match her breathing to Laura's, but sleep remains elusive. Laura's words are echoing in her head, bringing the past back with them: *Ronan Atwood will find a way to survive this.*

Isabel hasn't thought much about Ronan since leaving Espera. He's an irrelevance, a danger no longer applicable to her current circumstances. It wasn't until it was gone that she realised how heavily his presence weighed on her, but now it's back. Not because she thinks he can reach her here, but because all her anger with him has nowhere to go.

He hurt Laura. He interrogated her and then he used her, just like he used Isabel, just like he'll continue to use others.

He and his guild will suck the city dry, and they won't care how many civilians die in the process. They were happy to order hits on children to keep their power, so she doesn't doubt they'll do whatever they deem necessary to stop the city from falling.

Isabel thought when she escaped, she'd be safe. But she thought that when she left her father's house, too, and getting out from under his clutches didn't stop him doing the exact same thing to a dozen other kids.

Including Suzie.

She'll never forgive herself for that. For not seeing in the face of her target the memory of the girl she saved.

Over and over again, she learns the same lesson: it's never enough to get herself out. She'll always be leaving someone behind, letting someone suffer in her place. She left Michael to his punishment, left those children in her father's power, and now she's left an entire city to Ronan Atwood and his merciless control.

Can she really turn her back on Espera like this? Walk away like none of it matters now she's on the other side of the wall?

Whatever happens next – whether the outside world invades or Espera splinters from the inside and builds a new future itself – it won't undo the suffering. And Ronan . . . Ronan will weasel his way out. It doesn't matter how much of the blame is his, or how much culpability he should shoulder: he'll never face justice for everything he's done. He'll have an exit plan, a new life waiting for him, and he'll be gone before the fires have finished burning.

Ronan is not the kind of rat who will go down with a sinking ship.

And Isabel can't help. Can't go back, can't make him pay, can't *fix this*.

Very carefully, trying not to wake Laura, Isabel slips out of bed, pulling on her hoodie and slippers and heading downstairs. She's surprised to see a light on in the front room. Sam must have left the lamp on, she thinks, and is about to switch it off when she sees Leo slumped in the armchair, a half-drunk mug of tea in danger of slipping from his hands. He's asleep, head flopped to one side and mouth hanging open.

Isabel creeps forward and takes the mug from him before it can fall. The small movement jars him awake, and he looks up at her with unfocused eyes. 'Hmm?'

'You dozed off.' She keeps her voice low. 'It's two in the morning. You should go to bed.'

Leo glances at the clock, like he doesn't believe her. 'Yeah, probably,' he says, without moving. 'Why are you awake?'

Isabel shrugs. 'Couldn't sleep.' She had the vague idea that a cup of tea might help, something herbal to calm her nerves and the sense of impotent urgency running through her, but now she's down here, she doesn't think it'll be enough. 'Can't stop thinking about Espera.'

Leo tilts his head, sleepy eyes sharpening to appraisal. 'Do you miss it that much?' he asks, after a moment.

'It's not about—' Isabel begins, automatically, and then stops herself. Maybe it is, even if it's not nostalgia that calls to her. It's unfinished business, loose ends, debts left unpaid to

262

the city that raised her. 'It's my home,' she says, inadequately. *And I owe them.* She owes Ronan a knife in the chest and she owes the city a fighting chance at a future.

'It was my home too,' says Leo, the past tense pointed and half a lie. He can't claim to have left it behind when he's in so deep with the smugglers he's at risk of being sent back at any minute, and she'd call him out on the hypocrisy if he didn't look so sleep-fogged and bleary. 'But it's a death sentence.'

As if it was ever anything other than that. 'So that's it, then? We give up, because it's dangerous?'

'Does it look like I'm giving up?' says Leo, and she's got to admit that it doesn't. He's done more than the rest of them: it's his face on the news, his words raising money and sympathy for the Esperan cause. If only it were enough. 'I'm sorry, Isabel. None of us wanted to leave. But we can do good from here. Help the city from the outside.'

'And get blamed for a murder we didn't commit,' she says bitterly.

'They'll find the real killer,' he says. He sounds like he's trying to convince himself, and Isabel almost tells him about their investigation, and what Sam's found. She catches herself just in time. Leo didn't want Isabel involved, let alone Sam; they agreed not to tell him until it's over.

'And that'll fix everything, will it?' she says. 'The trade sanctions, and—'

She breaks off at the sound of footsteps on the path outside. It doesn't sound like Ant coming home: there are several of them. Heavy, booted, moving fast. The protesters? She thought they usually kept daylight hours.

Isabel exchanges a look with Leo. He's sitting up straight and alert: he's heard it too.

The knock on the door comes a few seconds later.

'Knock' is a misnomer: they hammer on the wood like they'll break it down if it's not opened soon. Isabel zips her hoodie to hide her pyjamas and Leo rubs sleep from his eyes before going to open it, squinting into the bright white beams of the torches shining in his face. The reflective stripes on their uniforms glitter in the dim light, and Isabel's stomach plummets to the floor.

Police.

'You Leo Jura?' says the one at the front. Leo nods, still stunned. 'Can you confirm who's present in your household tonight, Mr Jura?'

Leo struggles to form a response. 'Why ... are you ... is this ... ?'

'What he means is,' says Isabel, pushing aside her fear before it overwhelms her, 'on what grounds do you need that information, and is there a reason you want it at two in the morning?'

The officer meets her gaze, unimpressed. 'Isabel Ryans,' he says. 'Is that right?'

She nods, which is possibly a mistake, because he immediately writes that down.

'Mr Jura, Miss Ryans, we've received information that another Esperan is living at this address whose identity has not been disclosed to the authorities and who has not submitted to appropriate border controls or identification processes. This individual does not have a legal right to remain in this city, and under the present circumstances, failing to declare their presence may make you an accessory to murder.'

Shit. No. Laura isn't the killer. She's a defector, like Isabel, she should be protected under the same laws that gave Isabel into Leo's keeping instead of condemning her as a murderer. But if she tells them that, tries to defend Laura's right to be here, that's as good as confirming she's on the premises . . .

Isabel looks desperately at Leo, but he just stares back at her, face full of fear, uncertain and lost. *Double shit.* She's on her own with this one, and she doesn't know how to stop them taking Laura away.

'Let me ask you again,' says the officer, tiring of her frozen silence and Leo's mute panic. 'Can you confirm who's present in your household tonight? This shouldn't be a difficult question,' he adds. 'Mr Jura, if you please.'

If they don't tell the truth, they're fucked: the police will search the house, find Laura, and arrest the lot of them for concealing her. If they declare Laura's presence, *she's* fucked.

'Uh,' begins Leo, playing for time. 'Myself. Isabel. Samantha Davies.' His voice is hoarse. 'Anthony Farley is at work, but he should be home soon.'

'Is that all?'

Leo glances at Isabel in a silent appeal, and she makes the only decision she can. *I'm sorry I'm sorry I'll fix it I'm sorry.* 'No,' she says. 'There's also Laura Clarke.'

The officer raises his eyebrow, perhaps surprised to find her more cooperative than Leo. 'How long has Ms Clarke been in residence here, Miss Ryans?' he asks.

'A little under two weeks. She was sleeping rough, and I brought her home. She arrived in Leeds on the sixteenth of July.' She adds, a little desperately, 'She didn't kill Martin Thompson. He was dead before she got here.'

The officer notes this down with no visible change in his expression. 'And can you describe Ms Clarke?'

Why doesn't he care that Laura's innocent? She wasn't in the city, she's got an alibi, why doesn't this man care? 'About my height. Similar hair. Blue eyes.'

He turns to one of his colleagues. 'That's her.'

So they already knew who they were looking for. If Isabel could only remember the words, the legal terms Emily used, then she'd know how to convince them that Laura's not a threat, that she needs *help*, but—

She takes a deep breath. 'Please,' she says, as calmly as she can. 'She's a defector, and she's traumatised. I thought she'd feel safer here than at the detention centre. I wasn't trying to hide her.'

The officer is implacable and unmoved. 'Please step aside, Mr Jura, Miss Ryans.'

'You can't.' Isabel moves closer to the door, blocking their path. 'You can't burst in there, she'll – you can't.' She can't let them invade the only place Laura feels safe. 'I'll ask her to come down. Please. Let me fetch her.'

He looks suspicious, but he doesn't immediately shove her out of the way. 'Is there a back door?' he asks Leo.

Leo nods, and the man dispatches two officers to cover it, as though he thinks Isabel will make a break for it the second she's out of his sight.

'You've got three minutes, Miss Ryans,' says the officer. 'If you're not down here in that time, we're coming in. Understand?'

Isabel nods, and then she turns and runs.

Laura is difficult to wake, fogged with nightmares, and there's no time to explain properly. Isabel finds herself gabbling apologies as she forces clothes over her friend's pyjamas, pushing her hands through the sleeves of a hoodie.

'They're here to arrest you and there's nothing – I can't stop them, okay? But I'll get you out. I promise I'll get you out. Just tell them what you told me, that you didn't leave until the sixteenth. Don't tell them about the Moth. And I'll get you out. I swear.' She's made promises like that before, and she can't let herself think about how badly she's failed in the past, or she'll never endure this. She's not going to lose Laura like she lost Emma. 'Socks. I can't put these on for you. Please put them on.'

Laura fumbles for the socks. 'I don't understand. Isabel – who's here? Is it Comma?'

'No, we're not in Espera, it's the police, okay? And I've told them you're not the killer, and we're going to prove it. We'll get you out of there.' She hates this. Hates everything about it. But the only way she can help Laura is not to fight it, because if she ends up arrested too, she can't prove either of them innocent. 'You'll be okay.'

Laura nods. She's still unsteady and confused, but she stumbles down the stairs with Isabel and into the hallway, in view of the police officer, who is about to push past Leo and come looking for her.

'This is her?' says the officer. 'You. What's your name?'

Laura flinches at his harsh tone, shrinking back towards Isabel, but she manages to stammer her name.

'You're under arrest for murder. Do you understand what that means?' When he gets no response, the officer looks at Isabel. 'What's wrong with her?'

'I told you,' says Isabel. 'She's traumatised. You're scaring her.' She wants to beg them: *please, don't hurt her any more.* She wants to take Laura a long way away from here and protect her from all of this.

He grunts and gestures. Another officer pushes past them into the house, advancing on Laura with a pair of handcuffs. Isabel looks away as he closes them around her flatmate's wrists. It feels a little too much like abandoning her all over again.

I'll get you out, she thinks. Once they find the real killer, she'll fix this. She's got to fix this.

The police are already marching Laura outside. They're not interested in Leo and Isabel any more, except to offer a cursory threat that Leo could be fined for violating the terms of his settlement here, and that his guardianship of Isabel and Sam could be revoked. At no point do they mention Ant. She wonders if they questioned him at work first.

Laura looks back at Isabel as she's shoved into the police

car: wide-eyed, terrified. There's no accusation in her expression, but Isabel feels the wound of it anyway, and her guilt tastes like bile. *It was the only way*, she tells herself, but she's thought that before, and she's always been wrong.

Cowardice, it seems, is a habit, just like murder: bloody and easy and hateful.

26

PERFIDA (TREACHEROUS)

'What's going on?' Sam, sleepy and pyjama-clad, comes halfway down the stairs and perches on a step. 'Where are they taking Laura?'

'It's okay,' lies Isabel. 'They just need to ask her some questions. We'll get her back soon.'

'But she's not the murderer.' Sam sees through her, as always. 'And they've arrested her anyway. They'll put her in prison, won't they? Because she's from Espera, and she hasn't got anyone to fight for her.'

'That's not true,' says Leo. He clears his throat, trying to recover some of his bravery. 'They're not going to put her in prison, and we'll fight for her.'

'We'll find the real killer, and get her out,' says Isabel – *we will get her out,* like a litany, driving back her despair. 'But in the meantime, I want to know how they knew she was here. We're the only ones who knew.'

'Well, and your friend with the shitty car,' says Leo.

It takes Isabel a moment to recall Maggie driving them here. 'Maggie wouldn't go to the police,' she says, with absolute certainty. 'And you haven't told anyone, have you?'

Leo shakes his head. 'Not even the smugglers, and they wouldn't tell, anyway.'

And Sam hasn't been out, and Isabel's been here too, and all their windows are still covered in cardboard. Even if they weren't, Isabel's room is at the back of the house, so nobody can have seen Laura there.

Which means the only person left is Ant.

The police didn't, she remembers, mention him.

'Ant's been working a lot of night shifts recently,' she says, looking across at the calendar where he keeps track of his hours. 'Pretty sure he should be off tonight, actually, by law.'

Leo follows her gaze. 'You know how things are right now with the sanctions,' he says. 'Everyone's working all hours of the day, and they said they'd pay him extra, so . . .' He trails off. 'Isabel, you don't think . . . ?'

'Nobody else knew about Laura. And *somebody* turned her in.'

'Ant wouldn't do that,' he says, immediately defensive. 'He wouldn't throw another Esperan under the bus.'

'Laura's Hummingbird,' Isabel points out, because there's a difference and she knows it bothered Ant. 'First time I met him, I learned he killed a Hummingbird agent. He's got no reason to care about her, and every reason to turn her in if he thought it would keep him or us safe.' By *us*, she means Leo and Sam, because like fuck would Ant do this to protect Isabel.

'He wouldn't do that,' Leo repeats, but he sounds less sure.

'Somebody turned her in,' repeats Isabel. 'And Ant never wanted her here. Maybe he thought if he handed her over, he wouldn't get in trouble for helping to harbour her.'

Leo's about to argue with this when Sam's laptop, open on the kitchen table, chimes with a notification. They all turn to look at it.

Sam looks at the laptop, then at Leo and Isabel. 'I . . .'

'I've told you to turn that thing off overnight, Sammy,' says Leo, sounding almost normal for the first time in the conversation.

'I had to leave it on, the code—' She breaks off, shooting Isabel a helpless look.

The code. Her trace on the website. 'It's finished?' says Isabel. 'It's found something?'

'It's meant to run until it does.' She darts another guilty look at Leo and then slips lightly down the rest of the stairs, going to the computer and waking the screen. 'It's got two IP addresses. And two sets of coordinates.'

'One in Espera and one outside,' guesses Isabel.

'Wait, what is this?' says Leo. 'What have you been doing?'

'Finding the killer,' says Isabel brusquely, and ignores his spluttering dismay to ask Sam, 'Can you stick those coordinates in a map?'

Sam refrains from rolling her eyes, but only just. She dumps the coordinates into the map and they watch it zoom in: the city, the quarter, the area, the street, the house ...

It finally comes to rest, and they stare at it. Leo says, 'That's our house.'

'Maybe I did it wrong,' says Sam, a slight shakiness in her voice. She pulls up her code, skimming through it, her fingers trembling against the touchpad. Whatever error she's looking for, she doesn't find it. 'I thought ... I mean, I was tracing the messages, it should've found where they were sent from, but ...' Her voice cracks.

Nobody wants to state the obvious, but Isabel has made a career of the unpleasant business of violence that others would prefer to avoid, so she says, 'Ant.'

Sam shakes her head vehemently. 'No,' she says. 'Ant wouldn't do that. We must have been wrong. I must have misunderstood the messages. Maybe he's – maybe he's coordinating for the abolitionist side, or – or ... no. I got it wrong. He's not the killer.'

'Sam,' begins Isabel.

'He's *not* the killer,' Sam says, voice thick with the threat of tears. 'I lived with him for two years and I know him but – but that's what the messages said and if the evidence says it then you've got to listen to the evidence because otherwise what's the point in looking for clues and all of them point to him and you said it yourself, Isabel, you said he's killed someone, and I know he has, he's told me about it, and – and ...'

And Sam chokes on a sob and runs from the room, her feet

thundering on the stairs followed by a slamming door and a sudden, bitter silence.

Leo looks at the map, and says nothing.

Isabel looks at the map, and says nothing.

The house is too quiet, the hum of the fridge the only sound in the silent kitchen. No passing car disrupts the uneasy silence, and Laura's absence yawns wide. Ant's absence yawns wider.

Finally, Leo says, 'There wasn't any ambiguity in these messages, I suppose. Room for interpretation.' He sounds like he's only staying calm by sheer force of will.

Isabel shakes her head, a single jerky movement. 'It was an accident,' she offers. 'A confrontation that escalated. If that helps.'

Leo considers this in silence. 'Morally, a little. Legally ... well, fuck.'

Isabel concurs. She was willing to believe Ant would turn Laura in, but she never suspected him of the murder. An oversight, she realises now: he's got a history of violence, enough combat training to teach Leo to escape an attempt on his life, and every reason to hate Martin Thompson. She doesn't know yet what Thompson blackmailed him with, but she can guess – exposing his and Leo's illegal work for the smugglers would get Sam taken away from them even if they weren't sent straight back to Espera for violating the conditions of their asylum.

She wants to believe there's an error in Sam's code, but she can't, because it makes sense.

She wishes it didn't.

'What now?' she asks.

Leo shakes his head. 'I don't know,' he says bleakly. 'If he's the killer, then it follows that he's trying to frame Laura. Easiest way to divert suspicion.'

'Do you think he'll come back here? Can we confront him, or . . . ?' Part of her doesn't want to, the same part that's trying, against the evidence, to give Ant the benefit of the doubt. Another part of her longs to make him pay for daring to frame Laura.

'Depends if he'll guess we figured it out.' Leo turns on his heel and begins to pace the length of the kitchen. 'If we hand him in, we'll get Laura back, right? If we prove he's the killer and not her, they'll have to release her. Except we can't.'

'We'll find proof,' Isabel begins, but that's not what he means; the look on his face tells her that. With a sinking feeling, she says, 'You mean because he's Esperan.'

'Everything I've done to convince the world we're not a threat . . .' Leo shakes his head. 'Fuck, he's not just Esperan, he's an abolitionist. Proving he's the killer will mean more sanctions against the city, and we'll be lucky if we only end up under house arrest.'

'Then what do we do?' Isabel wants to pace too, but there's only room for one of them to wear holes in the lino. Watching Leo is making her dizzy. 'We can't let Laura take the fall for this, and it wouldn't help if we did. Either way it's an Esperan to blame, and we're fucked.'

Leo nods, and swears again. 'I thought he was our friend,'

275

he says. 'I … I've trusted him for years. He practically raised Sam.'

It's not the first time Isabel's been betrayed by somebody she considered family, but it never gets easier. 'If we knew what Thompson was blackmailing him with …' she begins hopefully. 'I mean, maybe he was trying to protect you.'

'By *killing someone*?' exclaims Leo, as if Isabel didn't kill Kieran Atwood for the exact same reason. She refrains from pointing that out, and he takes several deep breaths, trying to calm himself. 'You're right,' he says at last. 'We need to know before we confront him. It makes a difference.'

Isabel zooms back out on the map, then in again, watching Sam's impenetrable code ticking over in the background: *here, here, here*, it calls, pulling the same information over and over again. 'We won't be able to stay,' she says, unable to look at Leo as she does. 'If we hand him in. The work you've been doing for the smugglers, that'll come out, even if it's not why he did it. They'll take Sam away, they'll send you back, we—'

'Stop,' says Leo. 'I can't think about that now.'

'Then when?' says Isabel. 'What's the alternative, frame somebody else?'

'You tell me!' he retorts. 'What's the alternative to staying?'

Going back to Espera. Isabel opens her mouth to say it, but the words stick in her throat. She wants it and she fears it and she didn't think she was allowed to contemplate it, but if life in Leeds stops being an option, then it's the only path left open to them. *We go back, and we fix it.* She makes Ronan pay. She makes all of Comma pay for what they've done.

Leo reads her thoughts on her face. 'We can't,' he says, earnestly and urgently. 'We can't go back.'

'Give me a better idea,' says Isabel. 'You think you can get Ant off a murder charge and we'll all live happily ever after?' There isn't an option where they come out of this unscathed and with their new lives intact.

'We don't even know for sure it was him yet,' says Leo weakly.

'I'm pretty sure if we search his room, we'll find out.' She's never been inside Ant's room before; it feels like a violation of privacy. But he's an amateur and a desperate man, and Isabel knows what evidence of a killer looks like. If Ant's left any traces, she'll find them. 'Either we sacrifice Laura and leave Espera to starve, or we hand Ant in and blow up this life and deal with the consequences, but there are *no neutral options here.*'

Leo winces at the intensity in her voice. 'Okay,' he says. 'You're right. I know. I just ...' He's just exhausted. Bags under his eyes and difficulty focusing, his words coming slowly. She should have seen it sooner. He needs to rest.

'You're tired. I'm sorry.' Isabel softens her tone. 'You should get some sleep, and we'll figure this out in the morning.' She won't sleep: her guilt and fury will keep her awake. But Leo needs it.

He frowns, but eventually nods. 'You'll check on Sam?'

As if Isabel will be able to comfort her. 'Sure.'

''Kay.' Leo steps forward and envelops Isabel in a hug, without any warning. Cautiously, she wraps her arms around him in return, and feels him sway slightly. 'I'm sorry, Isabel. For all of this. For being so useless. That they took Laura.'

'It's not your fault.'

'I know,' he says. 'But it feels like it is.' He rests his chin on her head. 'Will this ever stop following us?'

She doesn't know what he means by 'this' – Espera or death or the feeling of being a failure or the knowledge that you've let down the people you care about the most. But she asks herself the same question night after night, so she just holds him and says, 'One day, you'll be happy,' because it's the best hope she can offer him.

He doesn't comment on her use of the second person. Maybe he doesn't notice. He stays there a moment longer, then releases her, stumbling towards the stairs and his bed. Isabel watches him go, then locks the front door. If Ant wants to come home tonight, he'll have to get past the deadbolt, but somehow she doubts they'll see him before morning.

Then she makes her way up to the attic, and Sam's room.

Sam's lying face down on her bed. Isabel crouches beside it, trying not to think about how poorly qualified she is for this. 'Hey,' she begins. 'So, I know you don't like the idea that Ant might have lied to you, because you trusted him.'

'He looked after me,' says Sam fiercely, without lifting her head from the pillow. 'For *years*.'

'I know,' says Isabel. 'It sucks when you think you know someone and they do something that proves you didn't. Did I ever tell you about my friend Michael?'

Sam says nothing, but eventually she rolls over to look at Isabel, which she takes as an invitation to continue.

'Michael was Comma, like me,' says Isabel. 'He came to live with me and my parents, and we trained together. He was the closest thing I ever had to a sibling, and after I ran away, he came to find me. I thought he was on my side, but he was always on theirs. He's the one who killed Emma.' Her voice cracks. Almost three years, and she'll never forget looking up and realising Michael wasn't aiming for her. 'It would always have hurt. But the fact that it was Michael, the only person who understood what I'd been through, the only person who really knew me . . . that made it so much worse. I think it's the same for you now, isn't it? You and Ant shared a life that nobody else shared, and now he might have done something terrible.'

Sam rubs defiantly at her tears with the heel of her hand. 'I don't want him to have done it. But it makes sense.'

'I know,' says Isabel. 'And if there's any chance at all that we're wrong, we need to know that before we tell anyone. So do you want to help me search his room?'

'We're going to turn him in?' says Sam. 'To the police?'

They've got no choice. Isabel doesn't like it, and she knows Leo doesn't either, and whatever happens they're screwed, but they can't leave Laura there. 'If he's guilty,' she says, and tries not to think about giving one of their own into the hands of a justice system that wasn't built for them and a world that will always consider them a threat.

'But . . .' begins Sam doubtfully, and then shakes her head. 'Okay. I trust you. Let's look for clues.'

Isabel doesn't deserve to be trusted – not when she let them take Laura. But the next person she betrays is going to deserve it, and if she wants to be absolutely sure of that, she needs Sam's sharp eyes and clever mind.

'Right,' she says, holding out her hand for Sam to take. 'Let's catch ourselves a murderer.'

27

HIPOKRITA (HYPOCRITICAL)

By the time Ant gets home in the late morning, they've got all the evidence they didn't want to find.

He lets himself in as normal, leaving his boots beside the doormat even though Leo's told him to put them on the shoe rack, and heads straight for the kettle. He looks faintly surprised to see Isabel at the kitchen table, even though there's no reason she shouldn't be there at eleven thirty in the morning.

'Long shift,' she says, voice carefully neutral.

'Yeah,' he says. 'There was a whole bunch of paperwork to do. Bureaucracy, you know.'

Yes, she can imagine there's a lot of paperwork when you sell out a friend to save yourself. He must've made some kind of amnesty deal. 'Hope you got paid extra for it.'

He gives a humourless little snort. 'If only. Where are the others?'

'Leo's at work. Sam's in her room.'

Ant nods. 'And Laura?'

Isabel narrows her eyes. 'In my room.'

Is that a flicker of surprise on his face? Or fear? 'Thought she usually came downstairs during the day.'

'She wanted to rest.' Isabel isn't as good a liar as Laura, but she's better than Ant. Even without solid evidence of his guilt, his visible discomfort would confirm it. No wonder he's been avoiding her these last weeks; she'd have seen through him in a heartbeat.

'Rest from *what*?' says Ant, making himself a mug of instant coffee. 'She doesn't do anything.'

'She brought down Margaret Strange,' says Isabel. 'I'd have expected you to be more excited about that.'

Her tone is a little too sweet – maybe that's what tips him off. He turns, about to ask her what she means, but the question falls from his lips before he can voice it. 'Isabel . . .'

She's done with pretending. 'Where's the line, Ant?' she says. 'Guild on one side, you on another. What's the difference, if you're solving problems with a knife too?'

'I'm not—'

'You killed Martin Thompson.' It's not a question. It doesn't need to be, because all the evidence was there in his room: bloody clothes stuffed in a bag; a knife, wiped clean but not disinfected; and most damningly, the notebook, the edges of the pages stained with blood. Anyone with an ounce of sense would have destroyed all of that, but Ant's an amateur, and his mistakes are enough to ruin him.

He puts down the teaspoon and reaches for a knife – but the knife block is empty.

'I took a few precautions,' says Isabel. 'You'll find a marked shortage of sharp objects in this room. Meanwhile I'm both armed and able to kick your arse even if I wasn't, so if you were thinking of trying to fight me, I'd think again.'

His nostrils flare. 'What do you want, Isabel?'

'A confession would be nice,' she says mildly. 'Might speed up the process of exchanging you for Laura. But we don't really need it, so in the meantime, I'll settle for an explanation.'

'Fuck you,' he says. 'I don't owe you anything.'

'No,' she agrees. 'But you owe Sam.' And there's the kid, coming down the stairs, exactly on cue. She hasn't slept and her face is pale, but she's got a look of determination only a pre-teen can wear.

Something about her expression breaks through Ant's façade, and he flinches at the sight of her.

'You turned Laura in,' says Sam. 'You killed a man, and then you framed her for it.'

'She was Hummingbird,' he says. He sounds desperate. 'She was—'

'No worse than the rest of us,' Isabel interrupts. 'A hell of a lot better than me. And running from more than you've ever had to face. Besides which, turning her in screws us all over – or do you really not think they'll blame all Esperans for the actions of one?'

Ant's gaze darts to the door, but he doesn't make a run for it. Yet. 'So you can't turn me in, either,' he says. 'Same deal applies. Turn me in and we all go down.'

'True,' acknowledges Isabel. 'But at least you're actually guilty.' She takes a clear plastic bag from beside her chair and places it on the table. Inside is the evidence, the notebook on top. 'I presume you made some kind of deal in exchange for Laura, which will complicate things. But this will probably be enough to make the police think again.'

'Fuck you,' he says again. 'You don't understand, I—'

'Don't understand what?' says Isabel, cutting him off. 'That you were being blackmailed? As if Leo wasn't threatened by Thompson the same day you killed him, as if that didn't put him top of the list of potential suspects.'

'I didn't *know* about that,' says Ant, and she actually believes him; there's a frantic truth in his voice. 'I would never have . . . I didn't want him to get caught up in this. I just wanted him to claim the fucking book. If he'd done that, Thompson wouldn't have had anything on him.'

'Except that you were both working for the smugglers,' says Isabel. 'Except that you were a killer, back in Espera, a fact you failed to disclose when you applied for Sam's guardianship. Except that you've been violating the terms of your residency every single day.' She taps her finger against the notebook, protected by the plastic bag. 'Nasty little man, wasn't he, collecting secrets? Fuck knows how he got that information, but it's amazing what journalists can figure out. So you went along to threaten him into silence, and you took a nice big knife along with you. Thought you could use his fear of Esperans against him.'

'What would you have done?' says Ant. 'Paid him? Let him get Sam taken away from us? I thought—'

'I wouldn't have tried to deal with it on my own,' says Isabel, cutting off his excuses. 'Fuck, Ant, if you wanted to threaten the guy, why didn't you ask me? You didn't think I might know how to scare someone shitless without killing them?'

He stares at her, like the idea that she might *help* him never crossed his mind. Maybe it didn't.

'You made them hate us,' says Sam. 'You were meant to be getting the journalists to report on the protests, but instead you made them think we're killers.'

'They've thought that for decades,' he says, but his cruel bravado is undercut by doubt. 'They never gave a shit when civilians were getting hurt. But one journalist, and suddenly they're capable of taking action? That was an *excuse*. They've waited years for a reason to cut us off.'

'And you gave it to them,' says Isabel, voice steady. 'You gave them the ammunition to use against our city. Those trade sanctions are hurting people you care about, Ant.'

'Don't start pretending to care now,' he spits. 'If it weren't for the Moth—'

'I fucking know that, Ant,' she says. 'But you ... you were supposed to be better.' Her voice cracks. 'You're an abolitionist. You're not meant to be a killer, too.'

There's a long, hard silence.

Then he says, '*You* don't get to lecture *me* about morals.'

285

He strides forward, and Isabel pushes herself to her feet. It doesn't help: Ant's nearly a foot taller than her. 'You really think hiding all the kitchen knives will protect you, little Moth?'

She's not afraid of him. She's fought bigger men than him. She's got more training than him, faster reflexes, better aim, a knife tucked inside her sleeve.

'If you want me dead, you'll need to join the queue,' she says. Forget Espera and Leeds and the abolitionists and all her enemies – first in line: a lifetime of self-loathing and destructive impulses.

'Don't,' says Sam. Her back's pressed against the fridge and she looks close to tears. 'Ant, don't, leave her alone.'

That wasn't part of the plan. But the girl's terrified voice gets through to Ant, even amidst his rage, and he looks across at her. Takes his attention off Isabel.

She moves. Grabs his arm, wrenches it up behind him, kicks the back of his knees so that he crumples. In seconds, she's got him face down with his arms behind his back and her weight holding him down.

Right on time, she hears sirens approaching.

Whatever Leo told them, the officers waste no time handcuffing Ant and relieving Isabel of the obligation to restrain him, which is a relief; she's not sure how much longer she could hold his struggling body down. 'Anthony Farley, you're under arrest,' they begin.

Ant doesn't fight it. He lets them cuff him, stays silent while they recount his crimes, and only as they're dragging him over the threshold does he speak. 'Fuck you and your Hummingbird girlfriend, Isabel Ryans,' he says, and then they pull him away.

Leo is the responsible adult here, so he'll be the one to go down to the station with the evidence. Isabel hands over the bag and gives his hand a squeeze. 'You'll be okay?' she asks him; his face is drawn tight with anxiety.

He nods, but he says, 'If I'm not back by dinner—'

'You'll be back,' says Isabel fiercely.

'If I'm not back,' he repeats, stubborn and afraid, 'look after Sam. And I'll be in touch as soon as I can.'

She wants to tell him it's going to be okay, and that they're doing the right thing. But even if this works, even if they get Laura back . . . it's the end of everything. There's no way to explain the blackmail without admitting Leo's own illegal activities, and no version of this that doesn't cast Espera in the guilty role.

Isabel doesn't want to think about what's next, like what will happen to Sam if they decide Leo's not a fit guardian any more. What matters is that Ant's the murderer, and Laura isn't, and they've got to prove that. Ant's dangerous, and she never even thought to consider him a threat. Slept rooms away from him, unarmed and helpless, for months.

A mistake.

So she just swallows and says again, 'You'll be back,' as though if she says it firmly enough she can make it true, and Leo offers her a watery smile, takes the bag, and goes.

An uneasy silence settles over the house, weighty with betrayal. Isabel can't let herself think about Laura, and whether she's okay, whether she really understands what's going on. Maybe being slammed back into a traumatic situation will have sharpened her mind to sanity, or maybe she'll be lost in a flashback, convinced she's still in Espera, and there'll be no one there to bring her back to the present.

Isabel's skin feels too small, that familiar itching wrongness that she only knows how to shake through self-destruction. She can't stay here. She can't stay in this house, helpless, waiting for it to be over, but she can't leave Sam alone, either.

She glances at the clock, then across at Sam. 'How do you feel about coming to support group with me?'

The kid shrugs, and sniffs in a way that suggests she's making a considerable effort not to cry. 'Better than staying here.'

'My feelings exactly.'

So they go. Isabel leaves a note in case Leo gets back before they do, and Sam takes her phone in case of emergencies.

Sam's quiet on the way to the community centre. Only when they're almost there does she say, 'I thought solving a mystery would be fun, but it's shit. Completely and utterly shit.'

'I'm sorry,' says Isabel, helplessly.

'I thought we'd catch the killer and it would be great and we'd know we were safe from Espera and everything about it, but instead—'

'Instead it was someone you trusted and you're not safe from anything. I know.' The sting of betrayal is no less bitter for being familiar. 'But turning him in was the right thing to do. We don't know who else he might have hurt.'

Sam scowls. 'I thought doing the right thing would feel better.'

'If being a good person was fun, everyone would do it.' They pause outside the building. They're a few minutes late – group will already have started – but it feels more important to have this conversation than to go inside. 'At least you know you helped Laura.'

'No offence,' says Sam, 'but Ant was my friend way before I met Laura. I don't even ... I don't even *know* her.' Her eyes fill with tears. 'Maybe we shouldn't have turned him in. Especially because they might lock Leo away and I don't want – I don't want them to make me live with outsiders, I don't want that, they said—'

'That's not going to happen,' says Isabel firmly, because she doesn't know what would become of Sam if she ended up in the hands of the state, but she doesn't want either of them to find out. 'I'll take you back to Espera myself before I let that happen.'

Sam stares at her. 'But—'

'We did the right thing,' she insists. 'Ant was a killer. Laura was innocent. And they are not going to send Leo to prison.'

'Laura's a spy,' the kid retorts. '*You're* a killer. You killed Kieran Atwood in the library where I lived!'

'I—' There's really no way to argue with that.

'So why is it different when it's Ant? It was an accident. He didn't even mean to kill Martin Thompson. And now ...' Sam breaks off, sobs. 'Now everything's falling apart.'

'It's not,' says Isabel, but she doesn't even believe it herself.

'Look, it's . . . I know it's complicated. I know we're not good people. And I want to say that it's different, because that was Espera, but—'

'But people are still people,' says Sam. 'Dead is still dead.'

'Yeah.' Isabel reaches out and touches Sam's shoulder, waiting to be shoved away. When the rejection doesn't come, she squeezes gently, the only comfort she knows how to offer. 'I don't know what's going to happen. But you did the right thing. I promise.'

It tastes like a lie, because Sam's right. Ant's a killer, and maybe he deserves to be held responsible for that – punished, brought to justice, whatever will make the people of this city feel safe again. But if that's true, what about Isabel? What justice will there be for what she's done, for the lives she's taken? They're not gone, just because they're on the other side of a high wall. People are still people, even in Espera. And dead is still dead.

Dead is very much still dead.

28

Rezoluta (Determined)

Eventually, Sam calms down enough to consent to going inside. They pause on the threshold, and Maggie looks up and sees them. 'Hey, Tashie,' she says. 'Is that your housemate?'

'One of them,' says Isabel uncertainly. 'This is Sam. Is it okay if she ... I mean, we can go, I just ...'

'Sit down,' says Catharine, with her usual expansiveness. 'It's a small group today. The more the merrier.'

It *is* a small group: Maggie, Dan, James, Catharine, Pher. No unfamiliar faces, nor any of the half-familiar ones whose names Isabel can't recall. She and Sam take adjacent seats; that way they don't have to look each other in the eye.

'Something happened?' asks Dan, sympathetically.

'You could say that,' says Isabel. 'I don't even know where to start.'

'The beginning?' suggests Maggie, but they haven't got all night. Isabel shakes her head and stares down at the floor, like she'll find the words embedded in the dirt between the scuffed floorboards.

'Martin Thompson,' she says finally, not looking up. 'Our housemate killed him.' Pher inhales sharply; the rest of them are tensely silent, waiting for more. 'Then he framed my ... our ... Laura. Got her arrested. So we turned him in. Now Leo's down at the police station trying to pick up the pieces.' How does she always end up here: trading lives, giving up on people? She's sick of having to make these decisions. 'Been a shit few hours, to be honest. Thought if I stayed at home, I'd probably do something stupid, so I'm here.'

There's a long silence while they all process that. Finally, Maggie says, 'Proud of you for coming,' and she sounds like she means it. 'You want to talk any more about the rest?'

'Not particularly,' admits Isabel, but she can't throw something like that at them and expect them not to be curious. 'It's ... complicated. It was an accident. I don't know if that helps.'

'Manslaughter's not murder,' offers James, like this might be helpful. It isn't.

Sam's slumped in her chair, arms folded, every inch the petulant adolescent. 'It was an accident,' she says, 'and we turned him in, and Isabel doesn't want to talk about it because then she'd have to admit she's a *hypocrite*.'

Isabel says, apologetically, 'We haven't exactly found unity on the question of whether turning him in was the right choice. Considering, you know, everything.'

'Because you're the Moth?' says Dan, acutely.

'Because I'm the Moth, because I killed Suzie Davies, because I'm the worst of them.' She doesn't look at Sam as she speaks. 'It's a fair point.'

'Suzie Davies,' echoes Catharine.

Isabel's not sure if it's a question; she doesn't know how much of the Free Press leaks they've all read. 'Sam's sister,' she says. 'She was twelve. Hummingbird were training her.'

There's a pause, and then James says, 'The worst of them.' His tone is thoughtful, and he's watching Isabel closely. 'Hummingbird were training Suzie, and your guild trained you. How old were you?'

She's not here to hash out her childhood trauma for an audience. 'Does it matter?'

'How old?'

'I—'

'Nine, isn't that what you told me? Or ... what was the phrase you used, *born into it*?' He sits back, folding his arms. 'How many people know about that? How many people realise that the Moth was one of the illegal baby assassins?'

Isabel doesn't know what he's getting at. 'I don't know. It doesn't matter.'

'Doesn't it?' James looks across at Sam. 'Maybe not to Sam. Or to Suzie. But to you, and the city ...' He shrugs. 'It doesn't fix anything, and fuck knows the military's been recruiting

293

kids out here for decades and nobody's stopped them yet, but I think if more people knew your guild did that to a child . . . well. I don't think they'd consider you the "worst of them".'

Maybe not. Fuck knows Ronan's earned that title. But she's still done terrible, awful things, and if Espera wants reparations for the guilds' atrocities, they won't overlook that. It doesn't matter that she only became what the city made her. That she, like Espera, was never given a chance. She's still a killer and a mess and every bit as guilty as Ant.

Sam knows that. It's why she can't look at Isabel any more.

Pher says, 'What are you going to do now?'

'I don't know,' Isabel admits. 'Confirmation that the killer is Esperan will only fan the flames, and the city can't take much more. Plus, I don't know if Leeds will let us stay, when Leo and Ant have been working with the smugglers the whole time.'

Sam says, 'Isabel wants to go back.'

'What?' says Isabel, turning to look at her. 'No, I meant—'
I'll take you back to Espera. It was a promise not to give up more than a literal statement, and Sam didn't hear her conversation with Leo last night, so she can't know . . .

'You've wanted it from the beginning,' says Sam. 'You don't care if it kills you. You'd rather die in Espera than live out here.'

'That's not true,' she begins, defiantly. 'If I didn't want to live, I wouldn't have left in the first place.'

Sam shrugs. 'I'm just saying what I know.'

'*Can* you go back?' asks Dan. 'I got the impression that wasn't on the cards.'

294

'It's not,' says Isabel, but maybe that's her cowardice speaking. She's got unfinished business with the city, yes, but she can't shake the feeling the city also has unfinished business with *her*, and she doesn't know if she's strong enough to face it. 'Even if we wanted to, the blockades and the sanctions would make it difficult.'

'Difficult,' says Pher, sitting forward eagerly, 'but not impossible, right? We raised money. Nearly four grand. You could take it back with you.'

Four grand of outsider money won't help them in Espera, but he looks so excited about it, she doesn't point out the currency problem. 'It's dangerous,' she says, trying to convince herself, but she's known it from the moment Leo agreed to hand Ant over: there are no neutral choices. They've burned a bridge, and staying here breathing in the smoke won't help anyone. 'We can't . . .'

Sam gets up, her chair screeching across the floor as she stands. 'We made a mistake,' she says. 'We shouldn't have turned him in.'

'Sam—'

'I want to go home. I want to see Leo.'

Isabel bites her lip. 'Okay,' she says, and looks at the others. 'Sorry. I shouldn't have brought this here. It's our shit to deal with.'

'It's fine,' says Maggie. 'I'll give you a lift home.'

'Oh, it's fine, it's—'

'You're way too recognisable now to be wandering around on your own,' she says firmly. 'I'm giving you a lift whether you like it or not.'

And she does. Isabel sits in the front because she doesn't think Sam wants her company in the back, and tries to figure out what to say to Maggie. *Thank you* is inadequate. *Why did you decide to care about me?* is too pointed. In the end she settles for silence, and the sound of the rackety engine accompanies them across the city.

As they pull up outside Leo's house, Maggie says, 'The girl who was with you before, she's the one who was framed?'

Isabel nods. 'Laura. My flatmate, back in Espera.' *Flatmate* is so inadequate. Friend. Shadow. Laura was spying on her, and she doesn't have a word for that relationship, and it doesn't matter.

Maggie considers this. 'Is she who you were grieving, first time you came to us?'

By which she means, *Is she the reason you threw yourself at me even though it clearly wasn't something you wanted?*

'Among other people,' says Isabel, with a sigh. Maybe it *was* about Laura; maybe she was looking for something to explain the depth of her loss. She didn't find it, though, in any of those hurried kisses or inelegant bathroom encounters.

'Well,' says Maggie. 'I'm glad you got her back, anyway. Be careful, Isabel, won't you?'

Sam shoves open her door, slamming it shut as soon as she's out of the car, and stomps up the path to the front door. Isabel watches her go.

'I should . . .' she begins, but she doesn't know how to fix this. 'Thanks, though,' she says, and gets out of the car herself. 'And you be careful too.'

Maggie gives her an ironic salute. 'Always am,' she says, and pulls away.

Inside the house, Sam disappears into her room and closes the door. Isabel leaves her in peace; she doesn't want to make any of this worse.

Maybe she'll just curl up in the armchair for a few minutes. Rest her legs. Rest her head, too, while she's about it; it's been too long since she slept, and the chair's comfortable to lean against . . .

Isabel wakes when the front door closes, startling her out of the armchair. No light creeps through the gaps in the windows' cardboard shields, and the clock on the mantelpiece tells her it's past eleven at night. She hears the thud of a pair of shoes hitting the mat, and then a second.

Laura appears in the doorway of the front room.

She's pale, still dressed in the mix of pyjamas and clothes that Isabel hastily shoved her into, but she's alert, her expression sharp. She gives Isabel a small smile, and the sight floods through her like fresh water, a blessed relief. 'Hey.'

'I'm sorry,' says Isabel immediately.

Laura shakes her head. 'Wasn't your fault,' she says. 'You had to let them take me. Wouldn't have ended well if you resisted. And let's be honest . . . I've had worse.'

After being interrogated by Ronan Atwood, it makes sense for Laura to be unbothered by the West Yorkshire Police. But Isabel was meant to be keeping her safe, and she still feels like she's failed.

Leo appears behind Laura, a wavering smile on his face. 'We're okay?' Isabel asks, desperate for a glimmer of hope.

'They believe us, at least.' He flops down onto the settee. 'There'll be a hearing, about our residency. But the murder – well, the evidence was indisputable. In the end Ant confessed. Think he realised he'd never get away with it, and admitting guilt sooner rather than later might help his case. There's a chance he'll get off with a manslaughter charge. A small chance, admittedly.' Leo looks like he might fall asleep right there and then. 'Laura's not fully in the clear yet. Gotta do a bunch of paperwork and interviews before they'll grant her asylum, but they agreed she could stay here for now – even if that's only as long as they don't kick *us* out.'

'It's cheaper for them,' adds Laura, 'if they haven't got to feed me. Then they can deport us all together.'

Isabel remembers the detention centre and feels a wave of relief that Laura won't be sent there to await a decision about her fate. Maybe it only felt dark and hopeless because she didn't know there was anything on the other side of it, but she still wouldn't wish that on anyone. 'You think they will?' she says, worried by Leo's sombre expression. 'Deport us?'

'I don't know,' he says heavily. 'You and Sam haven't done anything wrong. But me and Ant . . .' He gives a funny little half-shrug. 'I don't think that's going to help his defence, and I don't know how I feel about that. It's hard to abandon a friend, no matter how badly they screwed up, and hard to convince myself it's fair, when the two of you have killed a lot more people than Ant has.'

It was always going to come back to that. 'Of course it's

not fair,' says Laura, before Isabel can speak. 'None of this ever has been.'

'Yeah,' says Leo. 'I guess that's the problem, isn't it?' He heaves himself off the settee and goes into the kitchen to boil the kettle for tea. 'I know it's about risk. About the danger to others. Ant was unpredictable, and he could have killed again, and I know you won't, but ...' He leans back against the door frame, his head thudding against the wood. 'Maybe it's not justifiable. Maybe there's no way to make this fair inside my head.'

Isabel doesn't have an answer to that. She waits for him to make his tea and come back into the living room, and eventually he does, but his shoulders are still slumped. There's more weighing on him than justice.

'What is it?' she says, in her best attempt at a gentle voice. 'What else has happened?'

With noticeable reluctance, Leo says, 'I got a message. From Beth.'

There's a beat before Isabel processes this. *Jem* is Leo's contact at the library, and they keep comms to a minimum to reduce the chances of somebody realising she's got a line out of the city. If Beth's messaging him instead ...

'Is Jem okay?' It's a stupid question. If Jem was okay, Leo wouldn't look this worried.

He shakes his head, looks up at the ceiling, and blinks a few times, trying not to cry. When he looks back at her, his eyes are dry. 'She was taken by Comma for questioning because of her involvement in the protests. She ... hasn't come back out.'

'Questioning,' Isabel repeats.

'She's a hostage,' says Laura. 'I told you they were doing this. Interrogation, not elimination. Take people they think are key to the resistance movements, offer to release them if people break the strike. If they think your Jem's important enough to take, then she's fucked.'

She's lucid, almost her old self again but with all the edges chipped off, leaving her spiky and uncompromising. She makes no effort to soften her words for the sake of Leo's feelings, but maybe they've already had this conversation.

'But they can't kill people like that,' says Isabel. 'It'll make martyrs of them. The city's a powder keg as it is.'

'They don't announce the deaths,' says Laura. 'Nobody knows for sure if they're alive or dead, but they don't come back out again, because nobody backs down. And nobody dares act, in case there's a chance they're still alive.'

But even if they are, they're unlikely to be living in the lap of luxury: anyone who survives being taken as a hostage by the guilds is likely to wish they didn't.

'Have any of them come out again?' Isabel asks, suspecting she already knows the answer. 'Afterwards?'

Laura's laugh is hollow. 'After what?' she says. 'None of this shit is ending.'

That's a no, then.

And they've got Jem.

'So that's it,' says Isabel, without stopping to think it through. 'Fuck waiting around for them to deport us. We go back, we get Jem out, we make Comma suffer for taking her.

The abolitionists might not be able to get close enough to help her, but they don't know Comma like I do.'

Leo puts his mug down on the coffee table, like he thinks he might need his hands free to restrain her. 'No, Isabel.'

'We knew this was coming,' says Isabel. 'Everything's going to shit here, and we can't – we can't just *leave* Jem there, and let the city burn itself to the ground while we hide and cower and wait to be kicked out. So we go back.'

'I told you,' says Leo. 'We can't go back.'

'Why not?' spits Isabel. 'Because it's dangerous? Because we're meant to be building a new life? What good is a new life if back in Espera the same thing's happening over and over again to everyone we care about? I can't just sit here while good people are dying and people who deserve to be punished are walking away unscathed.'

Leo draws in a breath. 'This is about revenge,' he says. 'Isn't it?'

No. Yes. 'It's about justice.'

'Let me guess. Ronan Atwood.'

Leo knows her too well, knows she's been haunted by the thought of Ronan getting away with this. 'He hurt Laura. He made her—'

'I don't need you to avenge me,' says Laura, cutting her off.

'Tough,' says Isabel. 'I'll do it anyway. He can't—'

'Killing him won't undo what happened,' Leo interrupts. 'Revenge won't change anything. And it won't help Jem.'

It might. It might, and there's a chance, and anyway: 'It'll stop it happening again,' Isabel points out. 'As long as he's in charge, he'll keep doing this. As long as the guilds are allowed to exist, they'll hurt people. Generation after generation, they'll keep fucking people up.'

Leo's laugh is bitter and startling. 'If Espera could hear you now ...' he says. 'The Moth, an abolitionist. Now there's a thing.'

'I'm not ...' Isabel begins, but maybe she is. She always thought the end goal was getting out, but sometimes that's not enough. Sometimes escaping means tearing down the walls, destroying the chains, making sure nobody else can ever be held in the same prison again.

'It won't help Jem if you get yourself killed trying to take Ronan out,' Leo tells her, his voice gentler now. 'And it's not your responsibility to save her, whatever you feel you owe her. She knew the risks, and she made a choice.'

Isabel turns away, but it's hard to avoid someone's gaze by staring out of the window when all the windows have been blacked out with cardboard. 'So we just leave her to die? Because she will die, won't she?'

This remark is directed at Laura, who grimaces. 'Probably,' she admits. 'The timing will depend on how much proof they've got that she's involved in the protests.'

'She's Free Press,' says Isabel. 'I'm pretty sure there's plenty.'

'In that case ...' Laura bites her lip. 'Look, they're being careful about it. They can't risk inflaming the situation. But if she's Free Press, she might already be dead.'

Isabel's faced odds like that before, and it didn't work out too well last time, but she's a sucker for a lost cause. 'But she might not be. And I can get in there – I can do what the abolitionists can't. Besides, if the protesters see the Moth breaking into Comma, and know I'm on their side ...'

'Absolutely not,' says Leo. 'They can't know you're back.' It's the first sign he's given of even entertaining the idea. 'They hate you, Isabel. They drove you out of the city in the first place. You're the reason all of this is happening!'

'Which is why it would be powerful for them to know I'm on their side.'

'They'll kill you.'

'No,' says Laura thoughtfully. 'I don't think they will. Not if she's helping.'

'I go into Comma,' continues Isabel, ignoring them both. 'I get Jem out, show people the guild isn't all-powerful, the tide turns. And maybe, while I'm there, I wipe that fucking smile off Ronan Atwood's face, but the first priority is saving Jem.'

'This is a suicide mission,' says Leo.

It's accepting an inevitability before it crashes down on her head. She survived the worst of Espera half a dozen times already, and there's got to be a reason for that, but she doesn't think she'll find it here. And in the meantime she's done letting the guild take people from her, done letting authorities decide her fate, done being pushed around like a puzzle piece. Leeds doesn't want her; Jem needs her; Espera claims her.

'Tell me you've got a better idea,' she says simply, and Leo can't, because he doesn't.

'Fine,' says Laura. 'I'm coming with you.' She sees Isabel open her mouth to argue and adds, 'I can't stay here, can I?

I don't even have leave to remain. And if you think for one moment I'm letting you abandon me again, Isabel Ryans, you can think again.'

Isabel swallows hard around the lump in her throat. 'I wouldn't – I didn't mean . . .'

The set of Laura's jaw is stubborn and firm. 'So if you intend to stop us, Leo,' she says, 'you can go through the both of us. And we've got a lot more training than you have.'

Leo looks haggard, years older than he should, eyes heavy with surrender. 'The two of you will be the death of me,' he says. 'But fine. You're going back. And I'm coming too, because if I don't, you'll do something insane and get yourselves killed – and there's no way the abolitionists will work with either of you.'

It's a fair argument, but he's forgotten one thing. 'What about Sam?' asks Isabel.

He closes his eyes momentarily and swears. 'Well, Sam will have to come with us as well, I guess.'

'Come with you where?' asks Sam, appearing on the stairs in her dressing gown. 'Are we going somewhere?'

'Home,' says Isabel. 'We're going home.'

29

ŜULDIĜITA (INDEBTED)

That night, it's Isabel's turn to wake sobbing from a nightmare. She dreams of those last hours at Chadwick Green Hospital, terrified for Laura's life, and wakes convinced that the Laura beside her is an impostor, because the girl she knew and cared about is dead. She's a trembling wreck in the corner by the time Laura manages to convince her otherwise; the horror of the dream hasn't faded with wakefulness, only become stranger and harder to dismiss.

She wanted to go back. She's wanted to go back since she came here. But now that it comes to it, Espera is nothing but nightmares in the form of a city.

'We don't need to do this,' Laura tells her. Her brush with danger seems to have broken the haze of confusion that mired her in fogged trauma and uneasy dreams, the familiarity of interrogation and threat easier to bear than kindness. Isabel doesn't want to think about the implications of that, and what it says about Laura's life since she left. 'It's not your job to save everyone.'

'It's my home, Laura. I owe the city something.' Home. A place that wanted her dead. A city of violence. She owes Espera everything, including the revenge she never thought she'd have the opportunity to take.

Ronan needs to pay. He can't be allowed to hurt anyone else.

Leo's made it clear how he feels about that idea, though, so Isabel keeps this to herself. No doubt her radical friends would be equally disappointed to hear her planning to murder someone, though Isabel's pretty sure if any of them had met Ronan Atwood, they'd want him dead too. Since they haven't, they don't get to judge her.

'It's all of our homes,' says Laura, 'but that doesn't mean we've got to go back.' The dye is fading from her hair, the blonde roots showing through, and Isabel wishes she could bleach the lot and bring back the Laura she remembers, free of the shadow of the Moth hanging over them both.

'Maybe we shouldn't have left.' Isabel turns away; this is easier if she doesn't look at Laura. 'Maybe I made a mistake when I ran.' She left Emma. Emma's grave and Emma's art, scattered across the city. She doesn't know why she thinks she deserves friends when she's so good at leaving them behind. 'It took everything in me to go. Even when the whole city wanted me dead, even when there was nothing left for me there, I still didn't want to run.'

'But you wanted to live.' Laura's voice has an edge to it these days, and Isabel doesn't know if that was always there beneath the ditzy veneer she wore like a mask, or if it's new, a product of the violence that's been done to her. 'You don't give yourself enough credit for that. Not many people would have done what you did.'

Not many people would have let themselves become the most hated murderer in the city, either. Not many people would have let their selfish desire to live make a child-killer of them. They'd have run sooner, like Laura did.

'I was a coward,' says Isabel. 'I abandoned you – abandoned everyone – just to save my own skin.'

'You were brave,' Laura corrects. 'I told you to go. And you ran towards a world you'd never seen on the off chance it would give you more options than ours. You were willing to face the unknown for that – and that's not cowardice. Trust me, I've known a lot of cowards. I'm pretty sure I'm one of them myself.'

Well, that's patently untrue. 'It was the easy way out.'

'You just told me it took everything in you.'

Maybe that's a spy trick, using Isabel's own words against her to reveal her lies. 'That doesn't mean it wasn't the easy way out.'

'I think,' says Laura, her tone softer now, 'it was the only way out.' She takes Isabel's hand. Her skin's a little dry, her movements hesitant. 'We don't have to go back,' she says again. 'Not if the mere thought of it is giving you nightmares. You can't save anyone if you're mentally shutting down from trauma.'

Isabel swallows. She's grateful for the low light, the room

illuminated only by the small lamp they leave on so neither of them ever wakes in darkness. 'Do *you* want to go back?' she says. 'Or will that hurt you?'

Laura's laugh is hollow. 'I'm fucked up enough that it won't make a difference, Bel, trust me.'

'That's not an answer,' says Isabel. 'If it'll make you feel worse, if you don't feel safe . . .'

'I don't feel safe here either,' says Laura. 'I won't be safe if you abandon me. If you're going back, then I'm coming with you. That's all there is to it.'

'I would stay,' says Isabel. 'For you, if you asked me to.'

There's a long silence. Laura says, 'I thought you owed Espera to go back.'

'I owe you more.' She owes Laura the chance to get better, to live in this city until the nightmares stop, to learn how to be herself away from Judith Ryans and Hummingbird. She wants to take Laura to the library and show her the colours. Wants to introduce her to Maggie and James and the others – her revolutionary friends, who gave half a shit about her even when she didn't give half a shit about herself.

Laura says, 'This city's changed you,' which isn't at all what Isabel was expecting. 'Look at you. You're practically in touch with your emotions. Daragh would be proud.'

Isabel wants to laugh, but it hurts too much to think about Daragh. 'You say that like you knew him,' she says numbly.

'I did,' Laura points out. 'Briefly. I only needed five minutes to see he'd been trying to make you talk about your feelings for years.'

Which is true, but thinking about it makes Isabel's lungs collapse in her chest and strangles her heart with the ache of knowing he'll never see her get better. Never see her trying to be the person he always thought she was.

'Still doesn't make sense to me that he's dead,' she admits. 'As long as I believed I was never going back to Espera, it was easier, because it almost didn't matter. Alive or dead, they were all *gone*, so sometimes I could pretend they were still alive and just – just not *here*. But when we go back, Daragh will still be dead. Mortimer will still be dead.'

Until she said the words aloud, Isabel hadn't realised that part of her still believed returning to Espera would make everything go back to the way it was. But the Espera she knew growing up is gone, isn't it? The people she loved are dead, and the city is shaping itself into something new. She doesn't know if she'll even recognise her home when she sees it again.

'Yeah,' says Laura, as helpless in the face of Isabel's grief as Isabel is, neither of them wanting to think about the part she played in Mortimer's death. It's not something Isabel ever thought to forgive her for, because she thought Laura was dead too. Now that she's not, it's a hurt she doesn't know how to begin repairing. 'I'm sorry.'

Isabel glances sideways at her. 'Be honest,' she says. 'Do you want to go back?'

Laura shrugs. 'I don't want to be here,' she says, and maybe she means Leeds, and a world she doesn't know. *Hopefully* she means Leeds, because Isabel can deal with that, and it justifies their return. She can't, however, convince Laura it's worth being alive.

'Then we'll go,' says Isabel, because at least if she can get Jem out, she can rest easy knowing she hasn't failed every single one of her friends.

She expects some kind of peace to come with the resolution, but all she can think is that Espera is burning, and she's flying right towards the flames. Will any of them survive this? Once they cross those city walls, will they ever come out again?

Does it matter if they don't?

Laura doesn't seem to notice her apprehension. 'Okay,' she says, and smiles. 'When do we leave?'

Despite the threat of deportation hanging over their heads, and the SEND THEM BACK signs the protesters still carry, nobody actually wants them to leave Leeds – and they *certainly* don't want them crossing into Espera. The city is under trade sanctions, the gates firmly closed, and if they were to drive straight in with the car full of supplies that Pher's fundraising bought for them, they'd be breaking multiple laws. But Leo's spent months working with smugglers who know every illegal way in or out of the city, and none of them got where they are because of a healthy respect for the law. Handing Ant in burned a few bridges, but they still have enough contacts to get past the blockades.

Isabel gets a chance to say goodbye to Maggie, but when it comes to it, she doesn't know what to say. She wants to believe she might come back to Leeds some day, and that returning to Espera doesn't mean giving up on a life in the outside world, but right now it's difficult to convince herself she'll even survive.

'Don't kiss any Esperan girls, Tashie,' says Maggie, with a wry twist of a smile. 'They won't treat you as well as me.'

'I know,' says Isabel, and gives her a hug, one she hopes says everything she can't: *Thank you for not letting me do more things I'd regret.* 'Keep Pher out of trouble. That Esperan obsession's dangerous.'

'Oh, we'll all be looking out for the kitten, don't worry.'

Impulsively, because it might be her last chance, Isabel asks, 'Why do you call him that?'

'Kitten?' says Maggie. 'Because I'm an arsehole.' Then she grins. 'Christopher. Kit. He decided on Pher last year and insisted no one was allowed to call him Kit any more, but he's been Kitten to me since he was twelve. It stuck.'

Solving this small mystery feels like closure, and closure feels like loss, like agreeing that this is over. Isabel swallows her grief, and tries to give Maggie a smile to remember her by.

James isn't around, so she can't say goodbye to him, not without drawing attention. She borrows Sam's phone and texts him, instead:

Won't be at group for a while. Ask Maggie. Sorry.

If it's being bugged, at least there's nothing inherently suspicious about that.

And then they leave. In broad daylight, because it looks less suspicious than creeping around at night, and it makes it easier to meet their contacts outside Leeds to swap cars, distribute the supplies to be smuggled in via another route, and embark on the next stage of their journey. Isabel stares out of the window in wonder, watching the city give way to countryside. It's nothing special: agricultural land, mostly, rolling hills that reveal fields upon fields, all different shades of green and yellow and brown. But it's *new*. She's never had the chance to see the outside world like this.

They're headed for the east wall of the city. It's the furthest from Leeds, but the smugglers assure them it's the most reliable route in, not least because it doesn't open straight into an area currently being picketed by striking workers and regularly raided by the guilds. All the main gates are swarming with law enforcement and the military, enforcing the trade blocks; they've even commandeered an old country house just outside the wall near Sledmere as a temporary garrison, not for the first time in Espera's history. Leo gives these encampments a wide berth: as soon as a soldier asks them for identification, their whole mission is fucked, and they don't particularly want to find out if the guilds have reinstated the snipers on the watchtowers to shoot out the tyres of anyone straying too close, either.

It's strange to see Espera from the outside, with its high walls made higher by strategic use of hills and ridges, hiding the city from the world. They're featureless from here, all grey concrete and barbed wire and faded plaster, with no hint of the art that covers them on the inside, or of the city's beauty. It looks like a prison.

It is. But that isn't *all* it is. They might have called it the City of Hope because they hoped for victory in war, but it's been more than that to desperate people since then, granting safety and asylum to those who couldn't find it anywhere else. Isabel's brief forays into outsider history books proved that Espera's neutrality was a technicality if not an outright lie: the city may not have taken sides, but only because it was supplying both parties in any given conflict. But the lie had a grain of truth, because if people came here, they'd be safe, as long as they left everything behind.

Is it safe now? Are they destroying the only hope of desperate people, or freeing those trapped by lies?

Leo keeps glancing in the rear-view mirror as though he thinks they'll be tailed, but the road remains stubbornly empty.

'Either they haven't noticed we've left,' says Laura, after an hour of unencumbered driving, 'or they really don't care.'

'Oh, they care,' says Leo. 'Whether they can spare the resources to deal with it is another matter. They're probably hoping we'll be killed trying to get into Espera and then we won't be their problem any more.' Which is particularly bleak coming from Leo, whose optimism has always seemed boundless.

'We could just keep driving,' suggests Isabel, without really meaning it. 'Keep going until we find somewhere that feels right enough to stay.'

'We could,' agrees Leo, but his tone makes it clear that he, like Isabel, knows the only place that'll ever feel right is on the other side of that wall. The side with the art, not the side that's grey.

Eventually they make it to the sea, to the cliffs above the stretch of beach the rest of the world shuns. Leo parks the car and switches off the engine, sitting with his hands resting on the wheel as though it's holding him up.

Isabel says, 'You don't have to do this, you know.'

'You're not the only one who abandoned someone,' he says, and looks at Sam. 'Tell me you don't want to go back and we'll stop right here.'

Sam shakes her head. None of them expected anything else.

Leo's phone buzzes. He checks it. 'They're ready when we are.'

As one, they get out of the car. The weather's on the turn, an autumnal breeze coming in off the sea to play with Isabel's hair. It whips the strands into her face and chills her ears, and she flips up her hood, grateful for its meagre protection.

'Here.' Laura holds out a hand. Hesitantly, Isabel takes it. Laura says, 'We didn't leave together, but that doesn't matter. We're going back together.'

Isabel can't speak past the lump in her throat, so she swallows and nods and hopes that it's enough.

Sam links her arm through Leo's, and together the four of them approach the city that raised them.

30

DECIDA (DECISIVE)

It's a steep walk up to the city from where they've parked, and there's little welcome waiting. Half a mile to the south of the eastside gate, a watchtower punctuates the wall, bristling with barbed wire and the threat of cameras and alarms. It's not a friendly sight, but it offers shelter from the wind; they slump down in its shadow with their backs to the concrete wall, worn out by the climb.

'Last chance,' Leo says. 'Speak now or for ever hold your peace.'

'We're going in,' says Isabel. 'We didn't come all this way to turn back.'

He nods, and takes out his phone to message his smuggler contacts. Several minutes pass before the response comes:

The wait is interminable. Isabel's hyper aware of every tiny noise around them: the distant wash of the sea, carrying further than she thought it would; the muffled sound of the city going about its business on the other side of the wall. She feels oddly dislocated, like somebody's pulled her away from the planet and invited her to look back at it from the moon.

Espera was her whole world for two decades, and now she's crouched outside it, eavesdropping on a city's conversations. It shouldn't be possible to step outside your own world like that.

'Five minutes to go,' says Sam. She's not wearing a watch, so it's hard to know how she can be so certain, but Leo doesn't contradict her. She's probably been counting the seconds.

Finally, Leo's phone buzzes, and a moment later, a metal grille Isabel had taken for part of the tower's ventilation slides open, unexpectedly smooth.

'That's us,' he says. 'Come on.'

It's only just large enough to crawl through, and on the other side is a narrow concrete passage no bigger than the door itself, festooned with cobwebs like some kind of arachnid kingdom. Isabel tries, and fails, not to think about spiders crawling in her hair or inside her clothes.

Leo sees her shudder and looks quizzical. 'What are you ... ?'

'Spiders,' she says, and waits for him to laugh at her fear, because he doesn't know about the time she spent in her father's lab with dozens of the poisonous fucking beasties all around her, the moments when her father let them crawl on her skin.

(*Venomous*, corrects a voice in her head that sounds like her father's, and Isabel thinks, *Fuck you*.)

Leo doesn't laugh. He says, 'I'll go first. That way they'll mostly end up on me.'

This, here, is Leo's kindness. He doesn't wait to be thanked before squeezing himself into the passage. Sam follows, Isabel after that, and Laura bringing up the rear. Sure enough, if there are adventurous spiders, they're on Leo, not Isabel; she makes it to the other end unscathed, toppling into a small room just as her elbows are growing sore from crawling.

It's got the dank, unloved feeling of a cellar, a bare bulb illuminating two figures waiting for them. Their balaclavas obscure any glimpse of their faces as they indicate a ladder disappearing into the floor. Leo looks less than enthusiastic about the idea of climbing, but he goes ahead, and the rest of them follow.

The ladder leads into another cellar, stacked high with boxes. Their guides haul aside some crates and slide open a door. The narrow passageway behind it is dark, but the air feels fresher than the damp basement and there are fewer cobwebs. Isabel trails her hand along the wall to feel her way, and is relieved when it opens into a larger space, though her heart sinks at the sight of another ladder.

'Beginning to see why you're not using this path to get supplies in,' says Laura, and Isabel concurs. The tunnel she used to escape wasn't a bundle of laughs, but at least it was mostly *flat*.

'Hatch leads to the base level of the watchtower,' says one of the figures. 'Room's locked, they don't come down there, but noise would disturb them. That's why we wait for the shift changeover. Cellar's ours, so's the passage. We're about fifty yards out from the watchtower now.'

Leo puts his hand on the ladder. 'Guess we're going up this one, then?'

The masked guy shrugs. 'Unless you want to stay here for ever.'

Leo pulls a face. 'I'll take the ladder,' he says, and begins to climb.

The ascent seems endless, and Isabel's grateful for her workouts by the time Leo and Sam disappear above her. She heaves herself up the last few rungs with burning arms before collapsing onto the floor of the room above. It's dark, the windows painted over and the light socket hanging empty above them, but she can just about make out Leo's exhausted expression as he catches his breath.

'Still want to do this?' he asks Isabel.

'No going back now, is there?' she replies, then adds, to lighten the mood, 'Once was enough for me with those ladders.'

'Nearly there,' says the more talkative of their masked guides. 'Agreed rendezvous in about five minutes.'

The dark room belongs to a similarly decrepit house. Their guides lead them through and out onto the street outside, across the road, and up the steps to a slightly less tatty property. The door opens at their approach.

And inside, in the living room, is Beth.

'Fuck, Leo,' they say, wrapping him in a tight hug. 'Jem's going to be *so mad* that you came back.'

Beth, it turns out, arranged their safe passage in exchange for the supplies they'd gathered. That doesn't mean they're thrilled to see the three of them back in the city: Leo and Sam, because they were safer in Leeds, and Isabel, because ... well. The reunion's awkward, little more than a forced smile on both sides, and looks set to continue that way until Beth says, 'So this must be Laura,' and gives them both the small dignity of ending the conversation.

Jem's been gone for several days, and the mood among the gathered abolitionists is pessimistic. Even if Jem isn't already dead – and most of them remain convinced that she's alive – nobody taken by the guild comes back in one piece. Or at all.

'And the longer she's in there,' says Beth, once they're all settled with a cup of tea, 'the higher the chance they'll get something out of her that compromises the whole operation.' They look out of place in dark clothes and a smuggler's hideout, displaced from their books to help a city in revolt. Isabel wonders if the library is even still standing.

'Some people think the best option for the hostages is a sniper,' says Rae. It takes Isabel a moment to place them, their hard features familiar but their name difficult to recall. She gets there in the end, but they haven't so much as glanced in her direction since she arrived, so Isabel hasn't had to figure out how to thank them for giving her a way out of the city.

'A sniper?' repeats Leo. 'What do you mean?'

'A bullet to the brain,' says Laura flatly. 'Before they say anything they shouldn't, and before the guilds hurt them any worse.' She looks at Rae. 'Is that what you think?'

Rae meets Laura's gaze steadily, without asking her who she is, or why she's here, invading this community of people who love each other and their city enough to fight for it. 'I think to do that, we'd have to know where they are,' they say. 'But we don't, so it's a moot point. Jem knows the score. City wide policy. No negotiating. No breaking the line. No capitulation.'

Beth hunches tighter around their cup of tea. 'I want her back. Of course I want her back. But the best we can hope for is a quick death.'

'Oh, Beth,' says Leo, and somehow they're hugging, and the conversation moves on. Those who knew Sam at the library are soon gushing over how much she's grown, and they're all swapping stories of the state of the city.

'Margaret Strange is dead, did you hear?' says Rae eventually. 'And it doesn't seem like Hummingbird have replaced her yet. The guild's in a state of chaos.'

'If we knew where to find Ronan Atwood, we could have a matched pair of headless chickens,' says one of the other abolitionists, an older man Isabel's never met before. 'But after old Marge's death, he's upped his security, and nobody's had a confirmed sighting of him in days. Certainly not at his usual office; we took the Cowlam building last week.'

Isabel's got distinctly mixed recollections of the Comma offices in Cowlam, so she doesn't mourn the loss, but it comes as a surprise that it should have fallen into abolitionist hands.

Leo, too, is startled. 'You've taken the building?'

'It's occupied. Comma won't be reclaiming it any time soon.' The abolitionist looks smug; maybe he had something to do with it. 'So wherever Ronan's hiding, it's not there. Narrows the list of possibilities slightly.'

'Fordon,' says Laura.

Everyone turns to look at her. 'What?' asks Rae.

'They kept me in Fordon. And the hostages, too, in the other building. Ronan's got an office there.'

Isabel's mouth is dry. 'Where in Fordon?' she asks. She's kept quiet until now, extremely conscious that she doesn't belong here; she's done nothing but hurt these people. But if she can help ...

'I don't exactly know the address,' snaps Laura. 'I was a prisoner, not a *guest*.' But when she realises she's got the attention of everyone in the room, she tries to elaborate. 'There were ... three buildings, I think. I never saw inside the third. One of them had long corridors, training rooms inside. Small bedrooms upstairs. That's where they kept me at first, but then they moved me to the other building, and I saw them taking the hostages there. It had a sloped roof, and all the drainpipes were blue, not black. I noticed because it seemed odd for a building like that.'

Blue drainpipes.

There are Comma offices and facilities scattered across the

city, half a dozen of them in Fordon, and they could've taken the hostages anywhere. But only one of their buildings has got a sloped roof and blue drainpipes.

'Cocoon,' says Isabel, and looks at Leo. 'I know that building. If they're keeping Jem there ...'

Beth is eyeing her with something that, while it isn't outright hostility, certainly isn't welcoming delight. 'Got something to contribute, butterfly?' they say.

'I grew up in that building,' Isabel tells them. 'I – wait. Cocoon. Have they ...?'

The abolitionists look blank, which is its own answer. People might *suspect* that Comma were training kids, but Project Emerald's still the only one to have hit the news. Which means no one yet knows that the Moth was one of the kids they trained, and they've got no reason to give Isabel even the slightest benefit of the doubt.

Leo says, 'Isabel, we knew we wouldn't be able to get Jem out.'

'But we can,' Isabel argues. 'They're holding her in the Cocoon complex. I spent years there, I know every inch of that place. And if Ronan is holed up in there too, then I—'

'He is,' cuts in Laura. 'Even before I left, he was consolidating his resources there. After Chadwick Green Hospital fell, the guild started prepping in case they lost other buildings. That site's their most defensible. If he's anywhere that Comma owns, it's there.'

'Sorry,' says the abolitionist Isabel doesn't know, 'but who are you, again? Both of you, for that matter.'

322

'Isabel Ryans,' says Isabel. Quickly, like pulling off a plaster. 'I used to work at the library with Jem but,' she adds, her mouth twisting slightly, 'you probably know me better as the Moth.'

They must not have recognised her, hair faded and piercings gone, softened by the weeks of slowly losing her mind in Leeds and then rebuilding herself piece by piece. But she can see they remember her now, because they look like they want to kick her in the shins – or stab her in the guts.

'Laura Clarke,' says Laura, following her lead. 'Former Hummingbird spy, unwilling defector to Comma, the Moth mark II while Isabel was gone. Not by choice.' *She* doesn't sound apologetic about it, chin held high, daring them to kick her out. 'Ronan kept me prisoner for several weeks and interrogated me inside that complex in Fordon. Said interrogation had a marked impact on my observational and recall skills, but they're still significantly above average, so I can give you a reasonably accurate description of where his office is within the building, should you decide to raid it.'

'No need,' says Isabel. 'I remember.' Her mother was only interim director for three months, until Ronan's predecessor was appointed, but that was long enough. Isabel could sleepwalk to that office. Sometimes does, in her nightmares.

'If you think we're trusting a couple of guild bitches with a mission like this—' says somebody, and the anger that's been simmering beneath the surface of the room finally erupts. The wave of noise from a dozen overlapping conversations sends Isabel reeling, retreating to a corner as though it might be safer there. She catches fragments of the arguments – *two guild members here? – both of them the Moth – Suzie Davies – what were you thinking – can't be trusted –* and she wants to leave, but instead she holds out her hand to Laura and feels her friend entwine their fingers. At least she's got one ally in this room.

'Look,' says Leo, finally cutting through the noise. 'You wanted to know where Ronan Atwood is, and they've brought you that intel. You wanted to know where the hostages are; we know that too. Are you going to act on that and do something useful with it, or are you going to sit here making a fuss about the background of the people who brought it to you?'

'Their *background* is extremely fucking relevant,' says the unknown abolitionist.

'Their background is the reason they're useful to us,' says Leo. 'They're proof that guild members can change, and their intel is valuable.'

More hubbub follows, arguments upon arguments. The noise brings others in from elsewhere in the house, adding their opinions to the mess; Beth leaves for a while, and then comes back, and the whole thing starts again. The gist of it's easy enough to grasp: nobody wants them here, because they're monsters. But because they're monsters, they might be useful, if they can be trusted not to turn traitor.

Eventually, Isabel tires of the circular arguments.

'Have you considered,' she says, in a rare moment of quiet, 'that I want Ronan Atwood dead just as much as you do?' Silence. 'If I can save Jem, I will. She was my friend, even if we had our differences. And I owe her one. I owe her several, probably. But if your priority is taking out the Director of Comma – well, consider me first in the fucking queue. Or didn't you hear me say that I grew up in that building?'

'I don't care—' somebody begins, but Isabel barrels right ahead.

'You're all so outraged about Project Emerald, so here's some fucking *intel* for you. It wasn't the first of its kind. That was Cocoon. I was nine years old, I grew up in Comma, and every time I tried to leave they dragged me right back where I started.' She doesn't wait for a reaction; they haven't got time for disbelief or pity. 'If there's one thing I learned by leaving the city, it's that they'll never stop hurting people until somebody stops them.'

'Assassinating Ronan Atwood won't topple the guild,' says Leo reasonably. He believes that, she knows; he's not only saying it because he doesn't want Isabel turning murderer again. 'Comma will just shift power to the next person. That's what the guilds always do.'

'Hummingbird hasn't,' says Laura quietly, and everyone's attention shifts to her. 'I gave Strange up and she's dead and the guild's weak. Cracked, not destroyed, but with the trade sanctions and the protests, all you need is a crack to drive a wedge into, and the whole thing crumbles.'

'The birdie's got a point,' says Rae grudgingly, and then they're all back to arguing again, but the tone of the discussion has changed.

'We can help,' says Isabel, when she's finally given the chance to speak again. 'Me and Laura. We'll take point. Get

Jem out, find Ronan. We know that building in a way your people don't – let us use that knowledge.'

Everyone looks at Beth, because with Jem gone, they're in charge. They look unwilling to be responsible for this kind of decision, but after a long moment, they say, 'Capture, not kill. If possible.'

'But—' begins Rae.

'Don't you think it would be *useful* to have Ronan Atwood in our power?' says Beth, and looks at Laura and Isabel. 'I don't like this. I don't trust you. But if you can get Jem out, if you can save her . . .' Their expression wavers for a second. 'Fuck, I don't know, just do it.'

And like that, Isabel's won the argument. But the victory brings her only dread, because it means going back to the one place she swore she'd never return to.

31

NESAMA (DIFFERENT)

If Jem's still alive, then every minute lost is a minute she'll be suffering at the hands of Comma. But the Cocoon complex is the guild's last hiding place for a reason, and it's fortified enough that a straightforward physical assault is bound to fail. If this is to work, they need a plan, and they need to be clever about it.

Isabel needs to be clever.

It's lucky, then, that she knows Ronan almost as well as she knows herself.

Urgency thrums through her as the abolitionists argue about logistics. They don't want her acting alone, but that's the only way this is possible at all. She can go places they can't – and if they don't get over their distrust of her, they'll be too late to help Jem.

It's almost dawn by the time they reach an agreement, and still there are some who don't like it. Isabel ignores them, grabbing her jacket and heading straight for the cars they'll be taking to Fordon. The faded guild insignia of the vehicles' former owners are still faintly visible, and she wonders how they got their hands on them, but there isn't time to ask. No time to say goodbye to Leo, either, or to Sam, who has taken over monitoring the abolitionists' communications and seems to be in her element. But that's okay. Saying goodbye would be like admitting she doesn't think she'll come back, and Isabel is determined that this isn't how she dies.

One of the abolitionists is driving, giving Isabel a chance to watch the city pass by. Espera has been irrevocably altered in her absence: graffiti openly declares support for abolitionist causes, lamp posts are plastered with fliers and pamphlets about meetings and protests, and community soup kitchens are operating out of people's houses to stretch rationed food supplies a little further. Even aside from that, there's something about having another city to compare it to that makes it feel different, like Leeds has forever shifted Isabel's understanding of Espera, because it's no longer the only city she's ever known.

In the back seat, Laura is pale and tense, but she waves away Isabel's concern, as though they're not going back to the place where she was imprisoned and tortured. Isabel doesn't push it. She's repressing enough of her own shit to let other people have their lies when they need them.

They park the cars around the corner from the complex.

The early morning is already warm, a flurry of August heat after a few blustery days. Isabel releases and reties her ponytail to keep her hair off her neck, then joins Laura in crouching behind a low brick wall. The others follow suit.

'You guys know how to find the back door?' she asks the abolitionists, whose names she's neither heard nor asked. When they nod, she says, 'Get to the prisoners as quickly as possible. Laura, you're with them. You know where to look for the hostages.'

Laura hesitates, like this isn't the plan they spent hours debating. 'Are you sure about this?' she asks.

Sure about what – the fact she might be walking to her death? No. But she doesn't think she is. She thinks – *hopes* – Comma would hesitate to shoot their prodigal daughter.

'I'll be fine,' says Isabel, with more confidence than she feels.

'What if you're wrong?'

If she's wrong, she's dead. But the guild has always expected her to come running back to them, and she knows Ronan doesn't believe she's got it in her to leave completely. She's counting on that mistake to ruin him.

Though considering that she's here, in the home of her nightmares, maybe he's not wrong.

'I'll be fine,' she says again. 'Wait until you're certain they're distracted, then head straight for the back door.' She's beginning to second-guess her decision to go in unarmed. Her hands itch for the security of a knife, but she knows exactly how she'd get inside that building with a blade in her hands, and it would involve a lot of blood and a lot of death. And those people, she thinks, those ordinary people with their admin jobs, their security jobs, trying to hold things together in a crumbling city . . . they don't deserve to die.

Ronan always told her not to think about it in terms of deserving. But she's got to. She's got to, because out there in the real world, there's nobody to make those calls for her, and nobody to redirect her violence. She needs to decide where to put it herself.

And she's decided: *not here*.

She reaches for Laura's hand and gives it a squeeze, resisting the urge to go over the plan one more time. 'I'll see you on the other side,' she says, and tries not to make it sound like a question.

Laura gives her a small, sad smile. 'Whatever else happens, I'll find you,' she promises, and that's all they can give each other.

Isabel gets to her feet, squares her shoulders, and walks towards the front door.

The floodlights catch her first, picking up the movement and filling the space with a bright white light that outshines the morning daylight. Isabel keeps moving, half blinded and squinting, and wonders how she looks to their cameras, with none of the colour and attitude they remember of the Moth.

But then, Comma knew Isabel Ryans before. They've seen her broken before. None of this is anything new.

Approaching the door takes all her strength. Flashbacks threaten to break through the carefully constructed walls in her mind, every instance of walking through these doors as a child piled on top of each other and tangled with hurt and fear and grief. She tells herself that she isn't a child any more, that her parents are dead, that she got out – more than she ever believed she would, she got *out*. She left the city. And coming back was her choice.

The closer she gets, the less it feels like a choice and more like a magnet, pulling her in.

She wants to look over her shoulder at Laura. She wants to run back to her and hold her and never let go of her again. She wants to back out and return to hiding in bed and pretending she can leave this city behind.

But she's done being a coward, and she's not going to abandon her home.

Beside the door is a camera and a biometric scanner. 'Hello,' says Isabel, smiling at the lens, and places her palm on the scanner. Time to find out if they ever bothered revoking her security clearance. 'Did you miss me?'

The scanner gives an uncertain beep, and then the light turns green and she hears the thud of the locks disengaging.

'Guess I'm still on the books,' she says, and lets herself inside.

The entrance hall is empty. This is unnerving: Isabel expected a heavily armed welcoming committee, or at least a receptionist, ready to direct her to the appropriate department. But the front desk is deserted, cleaned out, and there isn't so much as a security guard waiting for her. Her shoes squeak on the marble floor as she crosses the lobby. She pauses at the convergence of corridors, possibilities unspooling. The left-hand corridor leads to the armoury, and she's tempted, her lack of weapons now feeling foolish rather than strategic. But there'll be time for blades later. She's got higher priorities.

Isabel turns right, instead, and takes the stairs up. The lower floors mainly hold records offices, training suites, nothing useful: the offices are upstairs, and the people who matter will be found in the heart of the building, as far from the outside world as possible.

Nobody stops her.

She was expecting to be stopped by now. She had a plan to get past them – so bloodless even Leo agreed to it – and instead she's walking through empty corridors, unchallenged. If she didn't know Ronan so well, she might think she's in the wrong place, but he's always been testing her, trying to see if she'd come back. Trying to see how far back she'd come.

Even here. Home of her oldest nightmares. She would come back even here.

As she draws closer to her destination, the need for violence grows inside her, furious and consuming. One last bloodstain on her hands, and then it'll be over, and she can rest.

No peace. Just emptiness. But emptiness is something she's learned to live with, and if she can only eliminate this final threat ...

Isabel turns the corner, and comes face to face with half a dozen Comma agents. *Here you are*, she thinks, and stops perfectly still as the six of them raise their weapons. If she had a gun, she could cut a path through them and leave them bleeding and regretful in her wake, but she doesn't, and they haven't opened fire yet, which means they haven't got orders to shoot on sight.

Slowly, she raises her hands. 'I'm unarmed,' she says. 'And I'm here to talk to Ronan Atwood. I think he'll want to see me.'

There's a long, fraught pause, and then the closest agent lowers their weapon, watching her as though they expect an attack the second they drop their guard. She stays where she is, empty hands raised, until they realise she's serious.

They search her for weapons, which she expected. One of them raises a radio to his lips and speaks into it, his code opaque but the meaning easily guessed: *the Moth is here, what the fuck do we do now?* After a second, there's a terse, equally incomprehensible response, and the guards exchange a look before stepping aside to let Isabel pass.

Their expressions aren't friendly: one of them spits at her as she passes, a gobbet of saliva hitting her right cheek. She raises her hand and wipes it away with all the dignity she can muster, and keeps walking. One step. Two steps. Three steps closer to Ronan.

But when she reaches the door, she hesitates.

There aren't enough people on this side of the building. It's been bothering her since she arrived, and it's only getting more noticeable. One hallway of agents in a deserted building – where are the rest? She's meant to be the distraction, but she can't do that if they're not *here*, and if they're not here, then there's every chance they're guarding the back door, or out in the city causing trouble.

Still, it's too late to change the plan now. Isabel reaches out, turns the handle, and opens the office door.

Ronan Atwood is sitting at his desk, waiting for her.

Isabel knows he's waiting for her because there's no paperwork in front of him, no pen in his hand, and the screen of his computer is dark. He's dressed in black, his usual grey darkened to charcoal, and there are lines on his face that weren't there when she last saw him. He raises his gaze, makes eye contact, but doesn't say a word.

She closes the door. Flips the lock. 'A little privacy,' she says. 'For our chat.'

Ronan watches this without anything resembling alarm or surprise. Either he's very confident in his ability to kill her before she can hurt him, or he's entirely unafraid of death. Knowing Ronan, it's likely both.

He continues to regard her as she crosses the room towards him, and finally says, 'Isabel. It's been a while.'

'Did you miss me?' she asks. On top of the filing cabinet is a knife. She picks it up, tests its edge – sharp – and its balance. It's unclear why his guards bothered checking her for weapons if Ronan was going to give her one so easily, but perhaps they haven't realised yet that he plays games with his own life as much as he plays them with everybody else's.

'For a while,' he says pleasantly. 'Your Daphne proved a passable imitation at first, but it seems the demands of the job were too much for her.'

Isabel considers the knife. It's a blade that favours the personal approach, demands intimacy; it can't be thrown with any accuracy, but it'll slip between ribs like a whisper. 'There was a time,' she says, 'when you thought training children was an outrage, and killing them more so.'

'There was a time,' Ronan responds, 'when I needed you.'

Which is as good as admitting he never meant a word he said. But she knew that. She's always been able to see his manipulation for what it is. It's just that once upon a time, his lies still seemed like the best option she was going to get.

'You could use me now,' she says, gesturing in the vague direction of the outside world. 'Whole city demanding change. You need someone to make them afraid.'

'Is that why you came back?' he says mildly. 'To offer your services? I rather thought fleeing the city was your resignation letter.'

'And yet you didn't revoke my security access.' Isabel steps forward. The knife hilt is comfortable in her grip, made for the kind of dirty work she's always been good at. 'Was that because you thought I'd never come back, or because you were certain I would?'

Ronan's lip curls with wry amusement. 'Maybe I wanted to keep my options open.' Then he adds, 'Though I must confess, I didn't expect to see you today. If I'd placed bets on who would visit first, my money would have been on Laura. You made such a fuss of leaving, after all; I rather thought you'd stay gone.' He gives her one of his old knife-thin smiles and inclines his head towards the weapon in her hand. Nothing about his expression or tone changes as he asks, 'Are you going to kill me, little Moth?'

When she looks at him, she sees it all: everything he did to her, all the violence wreaked in his name, his neat signature signing death warrant after death warrant. She sees Laura's shattered expression, Daragh's fatal loyalty, her own deadly bargain made because she had no other choice. And she hates him for it. Of course she does. His hands are soaked in blood that will never wash off.

She came back to this place, the birthplace of her nightmares, because she thought she wanted revenge. She was fully prepared to kill him regardless of Beth's orders, because he deserves it. But standing here, with a knife in her hand and Ronan in front of her, all she can think is that she's spent too much of her life playing the executioner.

Isabel stands, puts the knife back on top of the filing cabinet and says, 'No. I'm not going to kill you.'

Not because he deserves to live. But because she does. Because there are other kinds of justice than the knife in her hands, and there are other kinds of peace than the emptiness of vengeance.

She thinks he understands. There's no triumph on his face, no satisfaction, though she expected him to gloat over her weakness or tell her she's gone soft. Instead, he says, 'We weren't sure whether you'd really got out. But you did, didn't you?'

He isn't talking about the city walls. 'Yes,' says Isabel. 'I got out.'

And it's funny how that only feels true now, right back where she started.

32

MALHONESTA (DISHONEST)

'So,' says Ronan, 'what happens now?'

He still isn't showing any fear. Of course he's not scared of Isabel: he made her. He owned her. He's always had power over her.

She doesn't want to think about the games he's playing, the traps he's setting. If he thought Laura might come back here, why did he leave a knife in easy reach? Because he didn't think she'd have it in her to hurt him, or because he didn't care if she did?

Instead, she asks, 'Jemma Adams. Is she alive?'

Ronan's expression sours, as though he finds the question distasteful. 'The Free Press woman from the library? Yes. Is *that* why you're here? To bargain for her life?'

'I don't make bargains with men like you,' says Isabel, sitting on the edge of his desk. 'I've learned you'll always fuck me over.'

'No bargains, and you won't kill me ...' He steeples his fingers. 'You can't be planning to let me *go*. Perhaps you intend to keep me locked in here for ever, is that it? I wouldn't recommend it. Starvation *would* eventually undermine your noble decision to let me live.'

'Keeping you alive isn't a kindness,' says Isabel; if it's for anyone's benefit, it's not Ronan's. 'You'll pay one way or another.'

'Yes, I'd gathered that.' She wants to slap the smile off his face. She hates that he's finding this entertaining, because it means she's missed something, and she doesn't like not knowing what it is. 'You don't have a plan, do you? You're stalling because you don't know what to do next.' A small laugh. 'I didn't see it until now, but of course. You were planning to kill me. Now that you haven't ...'

Unfortunately, he's right about that. Laura's team get the hostages, Isabel deals with Ronan – and this would've been a lot simpler if she could walk out of here leaving a body behind.

Instead of answering that, she says, 'This building's too empty. Where is everyone?'

'Haven't you heard? The city's in revolt. *Quite* the state of chaos. I'd ask if you had anything to do with Margaret Strange's death, but I know you didn't.'

'No,' agrees Isabel. 'That was the other Moth.' She has the

338

momentary satisfaction of watching his eyes widen in surprise, but that doesn't answer her question. Even if he's dispatched agents across the city to quell the riots, this building shouldn't be silent and empty. There should be admin staff, cleaners. She asks, 'Why did you send everyone away?'

'You assume it was my choice,' he says, and at first Isabel thinks this is more dissembling, but she can't dismiss the possibility that he's telling the truth. That the admin staff have joined the strikes, that his agents have abandoned him, that Comma's really, truly, falling. But why would he sit here in his office and wait for her – for Laura, for whoever would be sent against him – if he knew he was helpless? Yes, Ronan plays games, but not for stupid prizes.

'I don't believe that,' she says, but she can't keep every hint of uncertainty out of her voice. 'Where is everyone?' She needs to know how many people her friends will have to fight their way past.

'Out,' says Ronan simply. 'Having more fun than me, I suspect.'

Isabel exhales, frustrated. She didn't expect him to be helpful, but she thought after everything that's happened, he might at least take her seriously. Looks like she was wrong.

'You're losing,' she tells him. 'Comma. The guilds. You're not going to survive this.'

He shrugs. 'Maybe not.'

'All that ambition and sacrifice and everything you did, this is where it brought you. And you'll die on your knees like a martyr to the revolution.'

Ronan doesn't react. 'Quite possibly,' he agrees, as though he doesn't care at all.

Isabel snaps. 'What is *wrong* with you?' she demands. 'Don't you care that everything you built is crumbling?'

She shivers as Ronan turns his implacable gaze upon her. 'Unlike you,' he says, 'I know when to stop.'

His eyes are so fucking *empty*.

Isabel looks at the knife. It would be so easy to kill him after all – and why shouldn't she? He destroyed her life. There's no nobility in keeping him alive, after all the bodies in her wake; no redemption in shrinking from this particular murder. Ronan's caused so much pain to so many people, and he deserves death far more than anybody he employed her to kill.

But that's the point.

Isabel isn't the only person he's hurt. There's an entire city out there that deserves revenge, or justice, or whatever will start to repair those broken pieces. If she kills him here, she robs them of that. Maybe he'll die in the end, but he'll stand trial, he'll face up to what he's done, and maybe they'll be able to force him to make amends.

A quick death, or even a slow, painful one, is more than he deserves. Ronan owes Espera a debt, and it's not Isabel's job to absolve him of that.

Like she said. This isn't a kindness.

'Get up,' says Isabel finally. 'Keep your hands where I can see them. We're going to take a little walk.'

Ronan gets up. He's lost weight, his black shirt loose on his frame and his wrists sharp where they emerge from his rolled-up sleeves. Is it the riots that have had this effect on him, or is it grief? Perhaps he really did care about his cousin. Perhaps Daragh's absence makes as little sense to him as it does to Isabel.

'Your father always thought you'd thrive outside,' he says thoughtfully. 'I wasn't so sure. But I see now that I underestimated you.'

'You do that a lot,' says Isabel, yanking open Ronan's desk drawers until she finds a pack of zip tie handcuffs – she'd have improvised if she needed to, but she knows him, she knows he's always prepared – and binds his hands with them. Then she shoves him towards the door. 'If your people are out there,' she says, 'you're going to tell them to let us pass. Understand?'

'They're long gone,' says Ronan, and sure enough, when Isabel unlocks the door and gingerly nudges it open, the corridor is deserted. 'See? No sticking power.'

He probably sent them away himself – another game, and once again Isabel's got the nagging sense that not only does she not know where all the pieces are, she's not even sure she can see the board. Why isn't Ronan fighting this? Does he think it'll save him, when the revolution comes and the trials begin, if he cooperated for five minutes? Because it won't. She'll make sure of that.

'Where are you keeping Jem?' Isabel asks, swallowing the urge to demand more complex answers.

'What gem?' he responds, with seemingly sincere confusion.

'Jemma Adams,' she grinds out. 'The "Free Press woman from the library". Where is she?'

Ronan indicates with his head towards the northern side of the site. The old Cocoon training block. 'Don't tell me you're here alone,' he says. 'Haven't your friends already got her out? I assumed that was why you were trying to distract me.'

'You're going to take me to where you're keeping her,' she says, ignoring this, 'and if she or any of the others are still there, you're going to release them.' No time to dwell on the idea that if Jem's still there, it means Laura's team failed and are probably dead. 'Understand?'

'You like giving orders, don't you?' Ronan comments. 'Very confident, too, for someone who doesn't have a weapon. What will you do if I refuse to cooperate?'

Isabel left the knife in his office on purpose. 'I don't need a weapon to hurt you,' she says. 'And I know you know that.'

Ronan is a satisfying person to threaten, because he *does* know that, possibly better than anyone. So although by now it's clear he cares as little for his own safety as he used to for hers, he does as he's told, leading them along the corridors and down a back staircase, towards the courtyard and what used to be Cocoon.

Isabel focuses on Ronan to avoid thinking about the building. Keeping her gaze fixed on his bound hands makes it easier to cross the threshold, though she's braced for the flashbacks anyway.

Inside, though, the building's changed: a new coat of paint, new signage, just enough to disrupt her fractured childhood memories and give them nothing to cling to. She lets out a breath and says, 'Which way?'

She's expecting Ronan to lead her down to some miserable basement, all reinforced concrete and bare bulbs, but he heads upstairs instead. The corridor up here feels more familiar, with peeling paintwork and a few felt bulletin boards nailed up at intervals along the hallway, scarred with the remnants of drawing pins. The old metal radiators are webbed with dust, and she has a sudden, vivid recollection of perching on one of these windowsills, feet resting on a barely warm radiator in the midst of one particularly chilly winter, looking out at falling snow.

Sometimes they let her go home, but sometimes she was here for weeks. This was the corridor she walked in her insomnia, trying to outrun her nightmares. She used to be able to see the stars from one of these windows – not many, hazy with light pollution, but enough to remind her that the world was bigger than this building on nights when that felt hard to believe.

The corridor is, like the rest of the complex, ominously empty, with no sign of Laura or the abolitionists and no indication that anybody has been here recently. Isabel takes her eyes off Ronan long enough to glance out of the window, but there's nobody visible there, either. No agents waiting to surround the building and no rebels waiting to invade it.

'Why are we here?' she asks.

Ronan inclines his head. 'This way.'

Still suspicious, she follows him along the corridor.

'You're supposed to be taking me to Jem. Not on some wild goose chase.'

'Yes, thank you, I did hear that particular instruction.' He stops outside one of the closed doors. 'Here.'

Isabel tries the handle. It's unlocked, giving way easily beneath her grip, and the door swings open to reveal a small bedroom beyond.

Her breath catches. She knows this room.

If anyone had asked her to describe where she slept at Cocoon, she wouldn't have been able to, but the moment she sees it, the memories flood back. The narrow bed against one wall, the small desk against the other: the room is as familiar as the back of her own hand. She knows it's not a nightmare because her parents aren't here, but she's unmoored in time regardless, disappearing within herself, her childhood rushing in, and—

Isabel presses her nails into her unscarred right palm, hard, letting the pain ground her in the present, and evaluates the scene. The room's been swept of dust, but it's bare of ornaments or personal effects.

And there's somebody lying on the bed.

The figure is curled up as though they're sleeping, half covered by the blanket, one hand visible and the glint of a silver manacle binding their wrist to the metal frame of the bed. But when Isabel steps forward, they don't stir, and when she leans over and pulls the blanket aside, there's no response.

Dead.

Heart in her mouth, she pushes the body's shoulder, and they roll onto their back. Jem.

'You told me she was alive,' says Isabel. She looks up at Ronan. 'You said she was alive!'

Ronan shrugs, the movement made awkward by his bound hands. 'I was lying.'

Isabel's knees threaten to give way beneath her. She can't look at Jem's face. She doesn't want to imagine breaking this news to Leo. 'You were lying,' she repeats, because of all the things she thought Ronan would lie about, funnily enough this wasn't one of them. It probably should have been. She sees now that she was unbearably naïve to take him at his word.

But Jem's not supposed to be *dead*. Not like this. If anyone's going to die, it's meant to be dramatic and drawn out, full of speeches and declarations of revolutionary fervour. It's meant to mean something.

Instead, all Isabel's got is a body in her old bed, and absolutely no idea what to do now.

'She was Free Press,' says Ronan. 'Most of them we can afford to let live, but not her.' In an odd, almost gentle tone, he adds, 'The poison was in her evening meal. She went in her sleep.'

Like that's a mercy, and not a last-ditch attempt to avoid the fallout of a bloodier martyring. Like it makes any of this okay.

Maybe Isabel should fall to her knees beside the bed, clasp Jem's hand and beg her to open her eyes. But she can only stand there: numb, lost. None of this is going to plan. And she's forgotten how to exist in Espera, lost the ability to endure in the face of its violence. She's become sensitised to its cruelties again, after all these years.

'You told me she was alive,' she says again, and even though it's Ronan, and she should never let herself show weakness in front of him, she begins to cry.

33

SPEGULIĜITA (MIRRORED)

The abolitionists find them not long after that.

Really, it's Laura who finds them. Laura's the one who tells them to check upstairs. Laura's the one leading them down the corridor, kicking open doors until eventually she reaches the room where Isabel and Ronan are locked in their strange stand-off: Ronan bound but utterly in control, Isabel free and falling apart.

'Down here,' she calls, and suddenly the room's full of people and they're taking Jem's body and Ronan's backed up against the wall and Isabel can sink down to the floor, unnoticed. She thinks somebody asks her a question, but everything's a blur, veiled by hopelessness, and all that matters is that she's not responsible for fixing things any more.

'Hello, Daphne,' says Ronan, and Isabel hears the smack of skin against skin, but she doesn't look up to see Laura slap him again. Her attention's been caught by something under the bed, carpeted in dust until it's almost as grey as the rest. It looks like a shoebox, and something about the shape and the hiding place – only visible to someone crouched on the floor like a scared child – tickles her memory.

As she reaches for it, she hears Laura say, 'I thought you'd like to know that I'm resigning,' and Ronan's reply, equally glib: 'Difficult to resign when we've already decided we no longer require your services.' But Isabel's already tuning them out, ignoring their conversation as she closes her hands around the box. The cardboard is soft with age and furry with dust.

It resists extraction for a moment, slightly too wide for the gap between the metal struts, so she has to reach around to the front of the bed to manoeuvre it out. Then it's in her grasp: a faded black shoebox, smeared with grey dust now patchy with fingerprints. When she lifts the lid, she sees scruffy exercise books, tattered cheap notebooks, bundles of lined paper – anything that could be scrounged or stolen without being noticed. The handwriting's messy and varied, but she recognises it at once.

Because it's hers.

She didn't think she'd left anything behind here. She didn't know her diaries had survived. Her mother burned so many of them, destroying the evidence, but there were always more. She'd thought them lost.

These pages are a record of the things she couldn't say aloud and didn't trust herself to remember, back when her mother was working hard to convince her she couldn't be believed about anything. She wrote them so she'd know, even if nobody else did – so that when she started doubting the truth, she could come back to the words on the page and know what she was being told to forget. After her injury, after Cocoon shut down, she never saw them again, and she assumed they were gone for ever.

But they're exactly where she left them, under this bed she rarely slept in, the cheap paper crisp and crackling with age and damp.

Isabel swallows a sob and reaches for the nearest notebook, just as a gunshot shatters the room.

It takes several seconds with her ears ringing before she processes the sound and what it means, but the moment she does – *Laura* – she's on her feet, looking wildly around for a weapon she can use to protect her friend.

Except Laura is the one holding the gun. Ronan's got his hand to his chest; the spreading stain is almost invisible against his black shirt, but when he lifts his hand away, his fingers are stained scarlet. He looks at them as though astonished to learn that he can bleed, and then he raises his gaze not to Laura, but to Isabel, his mouth curving into a smile.

'It seems you've been replaced, little Moth,' he says, and even the pain in his voice can't disguise the tone of it: smug and unrepentant. 'Shame to have wasted ... the redemption arc ... on me.'

He falls to his knees, and then entirely.

He dies, in the end, like anybody else.

'Why did you do that?!' Isabel didn't mean to scream it, but the words rip themselves from her throat so loudly that Laura flinches and the abolitionists must hear it all the way along the corridor. 'Why would you shoot him?!'

'He deserved to die,' says Laura simply.

Of course he deserved to die, but none of this has ever been about deserving or neither of them would be standing here. 'That wasn't – he was – he was meant to face justice, he was meant to answer for what he'd done, he—'

'This,' says Laura, holding up the gun, 'is the only justice any of us is going to get. Let's go.'

No. There's meant to be more than that, the world's meant to be better than that. Isabel opens her mouth to tell Laura this, to explain why keeping Ronan alive wasn't weakness, but the words fail her. How can she tell Laura she's not allowed revenge, when she's got as much right to it as Isabel does?

'What's that you've found, anyway?' says Laura, jerking her head towards the box.

'It's—' Isabel breaks off. She doesn't know how to explain what she's found, even to Laura, the only person she ever told about her diaries. This is the last scrap of evidence of her own past, and it's *hers*.

'Whatever,' says Laura, losing patience. 'Are you bringing it?'

Before long, this building will be invaded, occupied. These neglected bedrooms will become something else, and Ronan's body will be dragged away and burned, denying him a grave and the chance to be remembered. Any final trace of Cocoon will be gone.

Maybe she should burn the notebooks too – leave the past to the past, cleanse her bad memories with purifying fire, and walk away from all of it. But the notebooks tell a truth that was taken from her, and her mother burned enough of them already. She owes it to the younger Isabel who fought so hard to preserve these memories not to let these go the same way. It's about time she saved a part of her childhood self.

Isabel picks up the box. 'Yes,' she says. 'I'm not leaving it behind.'

Somehow, word gets out that the Moth killed Ronan Atwood.

It spreads through the city the way only rumours can: their greatest killer, turning on her own guild. Before Isabel and Laura are out of Fordon, the news is circling back to meet them, and by the time they get to Leo, there's no stopping it.

The abolitionists are more welcoming this time, and when Laura asks if she can shower, they readily hand her a towel and point her in the direction of the bathroom. She doesn't glance back at Isabel as she goes. It was a silent, awkward journey, Isabel unable to let go of the idea that Ronan shouldn't have died like that, and Laura struggling to see what the problem is. Somewhere around the Grindale border they stopped talking about it, and something between them has fractured. Or perhaps it's only Isabel who's broken, her fragile sanity cracking. She stands shell-shocked in the hallway, still holding the shoebox and unable to process the steps required to do anything else, until Leo emerges from the front room.

'It wasn't you,' he says, after watching her for a moment. 'It was Laura.'

His perceptiveness spares her from having to explain or defend herself or even decide whether to let Leo believe the lie that's so convenient for everyone else. Of course Isabel would murder somebody. Nobody expects anything else from her.

'Yeah,' she says. 'Yeah, I was ... I was going to keep him alive, I was going to ...'

'I know.' He eases the cardboard box from her unsteady grip and places it carefully on the hall table. 'Here. I'm putting this down so you don't drop it, okay? I'm not taking it away.'

Isabel nods. She feels wrung out. She wasn't even aware she was shaking until now.

'Why didn't you tell them?' he asks. 'That it was Laura?'

She doesn't know. Maybe because Laura doesn't deserve to be the Moth, to be hated like that, and this is easier.

'I make a better scapegoat,' she says. 'And it means more. If it's really the Moth.'

Ronan's death changes things. She wants to pretend that means it was the right thing to do, and that she's glad Laura shot him. She wanted him dead, after all, a revenge she didn't feel she was allowed to take, and this way she can be sure he'll never hurt anyone again.

But it doesn't feel like a victory. Not when Jem's dead, and not when the only justice they can offer the city is yet more blood.

'He put Jem in my old room,' she says. She's telling Leo because she's got to tell somebody, because if the words are only inside her head, they'll drive her mad with their circling. 'My old bed.'

'Your old room?' Leo prompts, waiting for more explanation.

'Cocoon.' She shivers at the memory of those corridors. Toni Rolleston found her once on that windowsill, perched like a moth on the wall, a slightly darker shadow in the gloom. So many sleepless nights. She earned her nickname in that building, and it clings to her like grave dust. 'He did it on purpose. He wanted to make me go back there. Wanted to make Laura go back there.'

Which means he kept her there, too, because they've always been mirrors, except Isabel's shattering and Laura's nothing but sharp edges, violence unmaking them both.

'It's over,' says Leo. 'You got out.'

She doesn't feel like she got out. She reaches for the shoebox, but drops her hand before she touches it, unable to bear the thought. 'We didn't save Jem. We didn't . . . we came back to help her and we didn't save her.'

'I know.' He wraps his arms around her and tucks her under his chin. It feels safe. Familiar. 'But you tried. And she was gone before you got there. That's not your fault.'

'I never save anyone.' Her words are muffled, her face pressed against his chest. 'I always think I can save them, but I can't.'

'You saved me,' he says. 'And Sam.' But that's not enough, because Emma's dead, and Jem's dead, and Ant's facing consequences for a crime far lesser than any of Isabel's, and she keeps fucking *failing* people.

Leo disentangles himself and takes her hand, tucking the shoebox under his other arm. 'Come on,' he says. 'Let's get you to bed.'

Isabel doesn't resist as he leads her upstairs to a spare room. The bed is neatly made with generic, faded sheets, no sign of a previous inhabitant. Leo places her box of memories on the bedside table and drapes a blanket around her shoulders.

'Isabel,' he says, 'I know you're upset that today didn't end differently, but nobody blames you.'

But that doesn't mean anything, because it's not about blame, it's about people, and dead is still dead.

Leo must understand that, because he doesn't say anything else. He sits with her in silence for a while, and when he stands to leave, she clutches desperately at his shirt. 'Don't go,' she says. 'Please don't go.' If he leaves her here, she won't be able to take it. Won't know what's real, or where she is, or whether the shadows are really laughing at her.

'I'm just going to turn off the light,' he says, so she lets him, because in the semi-darkness it's easier to hide her face, to curl up next to him and pretend she isn't crying.

And Leo doesn't leave, even when one of the abolitionists comes to the door and tells him he's needed. The Free Press is trying to print a declaration that the Moth killed Ronan Atwood, they say, but they're short on people to distribute it; will he help? Leo tells them to find somebody else, and then he goes right back to holding Isabel, ignoring their stares.

'I could tell them for you,' he says finally, once they're alone again. 'If it would be easier that way. They already know Laura was the Moth too.'

Isabel shakes her head. 'If she wants them to know, she can tell them herself.' She doesn't want to see Laura today, not with the memory of her shooting Ronan still fresh in her mind. It occurs to her that she's never seen Laura kill before. It's a strange thing to be bothered by, when she is who she is, but some part of her never truly accepted that Laura was Hummingbird.

'They got the others out, you know,' Leo says, after a pause. 'Jem wasn't the only hostage in that building. They freed a dozen or so.'

Isabel should be glad they succeeded at something. 'And did it help? With anything?'

Leo's silence sounds a lot like a 'no'. But finally he says, 'Another group targeted Hummingbird tonight, took the last of their buildings that hadn't fallen after Strange died. With Ronan gone, Comma will fall the same way. I think we'll see change in Espera sooner than you think.'

'Thought you said it wasn't enough to kill the directors,' says Isabel. 'That it just creates a power vacuum, someone worse emerges, and the city goes back to slaughter.'

'I know,' says Leo. 'But I think things might be different this time. And tomorrow maybe we'll start to see that taking shape.'

Always the optimist, Leo Jura. Even after everything he's lost.

Isabel presses herself closer to him, seeking warmth, comfort, solidity. He puts his arm around her, and she leans her head on his shoulder, letting her eyes close. She doesn't need to watch the door if Leo's there.

'What's in the box, Isabel?' he asks, when she's on the brink of slipping into sleep.

It takes her a while to figure out how to answer. 'Pieces of myself,' she says finally. 'Pieces I wasn't allowed to keep.'

He doesn't ask her what she means by that. He just holds her as she slows and surrenders to her exhaustion, and she falls asleep still leaning against him.

34

Ikona (Iconic)

'I know you're, like, pissed at me or whatever, Isabel,' says Laura, slamming the door open, 'but you need to see this.'

Still in yesterday's clothes, grimy and aching with the weight of it all, Isabel rubs sleep from her eyes and forces herself out of bed. It's early, the light strange and thin. She fell asleep sitting up, leaning against Leo; he must have dropped off shortly afterwards, if he didn't try to move her into a more comfortable position, and from the way he's rubbing his neck, it did him as much good as it did her.

'See what?' she says, finally persuading her eyes to focus on Laura's figure in the doorway, silhouetted against the light.

Laura jerks her head towards the hallway. 'On the cameras. Sam saw it.'

Isabel pulls on her hoodie before following Laura down to the living room where Sam's peering at a laptop, half a dozen people gathered around her. Beth's among them, eyes red like they've been crying.

They all look up as Isabel enters, and there's a pause, nobody sure how to treat a murderer who has supposedly done more for their movement than they have. 'Laura said something was happening?'

Sam nods. It's easier to remember she's a child when she's surrounded by adults, but she seems completely at ease, and the serious expression on her face makes her look older. 'Come and look.'

Cautiously, Isabel makes her way over, and Beth moves aside so that she can sit down. On the screen are a dozen feeds from cameras across the city – and outside it.

When she realises that's what she's looking at, that the grey concrete visible in the lower corner of the feed is the wall, Isabel doubles back and looks at the other images again. They're mostly from the industrial boroughs: people gathering in the streets, moving towards the wall. And in the final image, she sees that they're not only gathering *inside* the city. They're gathering outside, too.

'What's happening?' she asks.

'Our people took the Fordon site,' says Beth. 'Another faction captured the last Hummingbird office, in Burton. We know they've got small offices scattered about the place, but every major guild building is now under civilian control.' *Civilian*, they say, not *abolitionist*. Interesting. 'They're too fragmented to mount a coordinated defence, and without leaders, that's unlikely to change any time soon. But this . . .' They gesture to the screen. 'This wasn't us.'

'It started early this morning,' says Sam, pulling up a different camera feed. The angle's poor, but it shows another of the industrials, people moving inexorably towards the walls. 'Pretty much once the news broke that the Moth killed Ronan Atwood.'

'Now that people know the guilds are falling, they've moved onto the next target,' says one of the others, a guy Isabel thinks Leo called Charlie. 'They're not afraid any more. And why should they be? Nobody's calling any hits right now, and if the Moth's on our side, that's one less person to fear.'

'They're heading for the walls,' says Laura. She seems disinclined to correct their misapprehension; maybe she's happy for Isabel to keep taking the blame. 'It's hard to tell if anyone's coordinating it or if it's spontaneous, but that's where they're all going.'

Sam indicates the outside feed. 'This camera's on one of the watchtowers.'

'Doesn't get used much,' adds Beth, 'but we put it up a little while back so we'd know if the outside world decided to invade. Leo's texts made it sound like a possibility.'

'It felt like one,' says Leo, who followed Isabel down and has been watching in silence. 'But I'm beginning to think they underestimated Espera.'

'These are your cameras?' asks Isabel. She'd thought they

were guild security, and that Sam was up to her old tricks. 'How long have you had these?'

'Only weeks,' says Beth. 'Desire to keep our people safe finally won out over reluctance to contribute to a surveillance state.'

Isabel supposes if the abolitionists had had cameras longer than that, the Moth's identity would have been revealed sooner. 'But what are they doing?'

'They're going to destroy the walls, of course,' says Sam, lightly, like it's obvious.

Take down the guilds. Eliminate anyone who might stop them. And then break the city apart, and usher in a new and brighter future as part of the outside world.

But the outside world doesn't want us, Isabel wants to say, and, *Who are we without the walls?* – all the questions her radical friends asked that she couldn't answer. She still can't. She hopes somebody else can, because this is too big for her to process, dread and hope warring in her stomach.

Before she can speak, an alert flashes in the corner of Sam's screen. The kid frowns and clicks on it, expanding the feed so she can see what the system has flagged as unusual activity. It's one of the moving cameras, and it takes a second to pan across to whatever triggered the alert.

It must have been the artists who set it off, but they've already scarpered. All that's left is a huge, spray-painted moth across the front doors of the now-empty Comma complex in Fordon, its wings outlined in red and gold like fire.

There's a long moment of silence.

Then Beth says, 'I never thought I'd be asking you this, but how do you feel about becoming a revolutionary?'

With some surprise, Isabel realises they're talking to her. 'What?'

They gesture to the screen. 'I don't approve of your methods, and I didn't want Ronan Atwood dead, but killing him has had quite an impact on your public image. You're practically a symbol of the resistance now. So how do you feel about doing something with all that symbolism?'

Isabel swallows. Now feels like a bad time to tell them she *didn't* kill Ronan. 'I . . . wouldn't know how.'

'Half the work's been done for you,' says maybe-Charlie. 'People are ready to act; we just need to fan the flames.'

'And Leo said you'd had a change of heart, once you were outside the city,' says Beth. 'Started seeing the guilds more like we do.'

She doesn't see them like the abolitionists do. She sees them like somebody who was raised by them and hurt by them and made into something she never wanted to be by them. 'What are you suggesting, that I give some kind of speech?' Her throat closes up in fear at the thought. 'Because I . . . I don't think I can do that.'

'We need something. We need to use this momentum, let it carry us through to the end.' Beth gestures to the crowd on the screens. 'This isn't a political debate in a basement any more. This is the whole city's struggle.'

'And if Espera doesn't drive the change itself, the outside

world will.' This is Leo's contribution, unexpected and thoughtful. 'After Ant, they'll never leave us be.'

Charlie frowns. 'What happened to Ant?' he asks, like he doesn't know.

Leo shoots Beth a look. 'You didn't tell them?' he asks, sounding faintly incredulous.

Beth looks awkward. 'There wasn't time. I thought ...' They shrug. 'Honestly, I was hoping it might turn out to be a mistake.'

'There was *evidence*,' says Leo. 'I told you, he—'

'Evidence of what?' asks another abolitionist impatiently.

Isabel cuts in before the rest of them can drag this out any longer. 'He killed Martin Thompson, the journalist. He was working with a radical faction inside Espera, though the death itself was an accident. He's been arrested.' By now they'll have charged him. Murder, manslaughter ... it might change the sentence, but it won't change how much people hate him.

Charlie swears. 'That was Ant? The murderer was Ant? *Our* Ant?' He looks at Beth, as though hoping they'll contradict this. 'But the trade sanctions – that nearly killed us, he wouldn't ...'

'He did,' says Sam. Her voice is shaking slightly. 'We had to turn him in. But once people out there know the murder was committed by an Esperan, they'll blame all of us.'

'Shit,' says one of the others. 'I thought once they found the killer, they might lift the sanctions. But if it was Ant ...'

'Yeah,' says Isabel tiredly. 'And Leo's right. They won't stop at blockading supplies, and unless we take the lead, this will end with the city being invaded.'

'At which point we'll all be treated to the bureaucratic delight of becoming part of their great country, no doubt,' says Laura, not sounding thrilled by the prospect.

'If they invade—' begins Leo, then breaks off and shakes his head. 'It became abundantly clear to me out there that the outsiders don't distinguish between guild and civilian. They don't see Esperans as people – they see us as killers. Which means if they invade, people will get hurt. *Good* people.'

Isabel doubts becoming a revolutionary figurehead can prevent that, if the wheels are already in motion and the city's fall is imminent. But if there's anything she can do to help the city she's spent so many years hurting . . .

'Look,' she says. 'I'm not the best qualified person to incite the city to revolution. But if you think there's a part I can play . . .'

Beth exchanges a glance with Charlie. 'I think we can put you to use,' they say. 'Symbolically. The optics would be . . . useful. And who knows, maybe it'll mean you don't spend the next forty years locked up for murder.'

Because if the guilds fall, murders previously dismissed as guild business will become crimes to prosecute. A new administration will have to deal with that, track down the agents still alive and bring them to trial. Of course the Moth would be the first on their list.

Unless she helps them.

'You don't need to blackmail me,' says Isabel, suddenly very tired.

'That's not – we're not . . .'

'That's what it sounded like.' She wants to go back to bed and wake up when it's over. She wants to be out there among the crowds, feeling the change sweep through her. She doesn't know what she wants, only that she can't have it in any way that makes sense. 'Look, if you want me to give a speech, I will, but I don't know what I can say that people will listen to.'

'I don't think you need to speak,' says Beth. 'People just need to see you.'

'And know who she is,' interjects Laura. 'But it's not like she's got a Moth-themed supervillain costume. From a distance she could be anyone.'

Up close she could be anyone, too. Up close she could be Laura, because it's that easy to shift the blame: *the Moth did this*, and therefore it was Isabel, and she has never been her own person.

'I don't like this,' says Leo. 'Some public favour may have swayed in Isabel's direction, but there are still people out there in the city who hate her, and having her at the front of the movement puts her at risk.'

'Risk's not new,' Isabel points out. 'If it's worth doing, then it's worth doing regardless.' She looks at Beth. 'Will it really make a difference?'

Beth looks at the screen, the spray-painted moth across the captured Comma buildings. 'It sure looks like it.'

Isabel looks at the moth too. *Disobedience.* Revolution has never been her style: obeying is how she's survived. Even when she defied the guild, she chose *flight*, not *fight*. But if there's anything she can offer the city to make up for some of the damage she's done, doesn't she owe them that?

She remembers Emma painting a portrait of her on a wall that once showed Espera with its gates open, and knows exactly what her friend would have wanted her to do.

'Okay,' she says. 'I'll do it.'

35

REVOLUCIA (REVOLUTIONARY)

Word spreads across the city that the guilds are the weakest they've been in a hundred years, and civilians flock to the wall. There are pedestrians in the road walking five abreast, dancing and shouting with all the abandon of a ceasefire. The atmosphere is electric with the anticipation of change, but the city is split between party and protest: half the crowd's in bright colours, the other half in balaclavas and masks, celebratory flags and protest banners side by side.

Isabel keeps her hood pulled up as she follows Beth through the crowds. Even people who never read the *Bulletin* will have seen her face publicised by now, and the reveal that the Moth is here is best saved until everything's in position.

Just in case it does backfire. Just in case they *did* underestimate how much everybody still hates her.

'Second thoughts?' asks Beth, with a trace of their old smile.

Isabel wonders if her apprehension is really that obvious, or whether Beth expected her to back out from the beginning. 'I said I'd do it,' she replies. 'I keep my promises.'

'Well, remember, as long as you don't blow up the civilians, you're doing fine.'

'Or myself,' comments Isabel.

'Mm. Sure. You remember the plan?'

They spent all bloody day going over the plan, so long that they're at risk of having to do this by the light of the floodlights on the walls.

'Wasn't expecting this many people,' Isabel admits, as the crowds become denser and they're forced to push and plead their way through narrow gaps. Beth slips through easily, Isabel fights to follow them, and Charlie, who volunteered to join them on this leg of the mission, is in danger of being lost in their wake.

'You'll be fine once we get to the wall. It's us poor sods at the bottom who need to worry.' Beth glances both ways to check their path, then forges ahead. Isabel gathers herself and follows. 'At least up there, you've got fewer people to worry about.'

'Not none, though,' says Charlie, as the wall comes into view, and he's right: there are a dozen people already up on the wall, despite the barbed wire and the spikes. One of them waves a brightly coloured towel like a flag. Isabel suspects, from the looseness of their movements, that they're drunk; she hopes somebody can persuade them down before they fall. A handful more are emerging from the watchtower, climbing over the parapet to reach the wall.

Isabel's never seen people on the walls before, except the border patrols with their guns. She wonders what's happened to them: whether they've been called away to deal with more direct threats to the guilds, or whether they're bound and concussed in the tower basements.

'Well, shit,' says Beth, pulling out their phone to text one of their endless contacts. 'I asked them to stop people from heading up there, but I guess there's only so much they can do. I'd planned to take you up via the tower, but it looks like it's time for Plan B. Charlie, where's the nearest ladder team?'

'About two hundred yards south of here,' he says, consulting his phone. 'Smudge's team.'

'Smudge isn't meant to be out today,' says Beth, dismayed. 'I told him to stay— ah, shit, he never listens to me. Well, can't be helped.' The name rings a bell, but Isabel can't place it. 'All right, Isabel, keep up, we're making a detour.'

There are fewer protesters on the streets the further they get from the south-west checkpoint, but Isabel can't relax. Too much of this plan is relying on her, and there are too many ways it could go wrong.

One of the roads has been closed off with makeshift barriers. Beth drags them aside without hesitating, and they slip through. The ladder team is waiting for them behind the barricade: a small group of abolitionists with the tallest ladder they could find at short notice, and a bunch of grappling hooks and ropes to make up the difference. Isabel would feel a lot more confident if the kid leading the group didn't look about fourteen.

'Hey, Smudge,' says Beth, and Isabel finally connects the name to a memory: one of her first meetings with Abbie Miner and the other smugglers. Looks like he managed to avoid staying in school after all. 'Everything in place?'

The kid nods. 'Ready and waiting. We tested the ropes, but no one's gone up ... yet. What's the plan?'

Beth jerks their thumb towards Isabel. 'She's going up. Placing the fuses.'

The boy gives Isabel an unimpressed once-over, but shows no signs of recognition. 'Well, we tested it with my weight, so she should be fine. Best to send the fuses up separately, though. Do you have a plan to get everyone out of the way?'

'Yell at them, mostly,' says Beth, with a half-smile, and claps Isabel on the back. 'You ready for this? Bit flashier than your usual style.'

Isabel doesn't feel at all ready, but she nods, glancing once at Smudge and then back at Beth. 'I didn't know you had kids running ops for you these days,' she says, trying not to sound judgemental.

Beth pulls a face. 'Desperate times. Besides, he's one of our best runners.'

'And I'm not a kid,' says Smudge. 'I'm fifteen.'

Isabel swallows her answer to that and lets him fasten the harness around her waist and clip the rope onto it. 'So this will hold me, right?'

His hesitation doesn't fill her with confidence. 'It'll hold you while you climb,' he says finally, 'but don't fall off. A sudden jolt could dislodge the hooks.'

'And then splat,' says Charlie helpfully. 'Squashed moth.'

'Thanks,' says Isabel. 'That's exactly what I needed right now.' She gives the rope a tentative tug. It *feels* solid, but that doesn't mean it is.

'We'll send the explosives up after you,' Beth promises. 'And we'll make sure you're down before it blows. Just remember, once you're up there, be careful to—'

'I *know* the plan.'

'All right. Just checking.'

Isabel swallows, her mouth suddenly dry as cardboard. It'll be fine. The fuses are long; she'll have plenty of time to get down. And the wall's not that high, really. Wider than it looks, too, easy to walk along if you can ignore the barbed wire and metal spikes and electrified posts disguised as ordinary supports so that you don't know the difference until they shock you.

Steadily, she places one hand on the ladder. Then one foot. And then she begins to climb.

By the time she reaches the top of the ladder, the wind has begun to snatch at her, the smooth plaster-over-concrete of the wall offering little grip to keep her from being dragged sideways. Even with the rope, it feels like the wall's trying to throw her off as she climbs the final section. Isabel scrambles to the top, over the ridged edge, into the little hollow between the two sides, and narrowly avoids cutting herself on barbed wire in the process.

Gingerly, she pokes her head over the edge, and signals to the abolitionists: *I'm up.*

Beth looks very small down below. They give Isabel a thumbs-up and start tying the bag of explosives to one of the ropes, giving it a sharp tug when they're done. Isabel hauls it up, grunting slightly at the effort, and detaches it from the rope once it's safely at the top.

Inside the bag are enough explosives to bring down half the wall.

Some of this will need to be done from the bottom; the abolitionists are already placing charges at intervals along the wall's foundations. But that doesn't provide the opportunity for theatre – drama – the statement they want Isabel to make. So she places the explosives exactly as she was told, counting the paces between them, trying not to lose track as she steps over the barbed wire and weaves between the spikes. When the bag is empty, she makes her way back along to the centre of the targeted area and takes the gun from the holster at her hip.

It's a small gun, and not particularly her style, but it makes a loud enough noise when she raises it above her head and fires three shots into the air – loud enough for the civilians milling around below to turn and look up at the figure silhouetted against the evening sun.

'Get away from the wall,' she calls, as loudly as she can. 'Unless you want to get blown up, get away from the wall. Move back.'

Can they hear her? Maybe not – they're pressing closer,

trying to make out her words, and that's the opposite of what she wants.

'Get back!' she yells. 'Get back or you're going to die.'

To her horror, a couple of the others on the wall are moving towards her, stepping inside the blast zone of the explosives. If they're still up here when it blows, there's no way they'll survive.

If *she's* still up here when it blows, there's no way she'll survive, either.

Isabel tries to warn them away, but the wind whips her words from her mouth. She abandons her position and works her way along the wall to head them off before they get any closer.

'You need to get back,' she tells them, once they're in earshot. 'Get off the wall. The whole thing's going to blow.'

'I heard,' says the woman, and holds something out towards her. 'Here.' Isabel takes it: a megaphone. She looks up in thanks, but the woman waves away her gratitude and her questions. 'You're the Moth, aren't you? You look like her, anyway.'

'Yes,' says Isabel, and for the first time she admits it readily, without fear. She's already reaching into her pocket for the lighter that will set the fuses and mark the point of no return. 'And you should get back. If you don't, you're going to die.'

The woman gives her a nod of solidarity and starts beating a hasty retreat along the wall. Isabel looks down at the megaphone in her hand. She wasn't going to make a speech. She doesn't have the knack of it. But:

'This is the Moth speaking,' she says into the megaphone, and hears her words, amplified, ring out into the anticipatory air. 'People of Espera, please get the fuck away from the wall. This is for your own safety. I repeat, get away from the wall.'

They're looking at her. Her words spark a murmur, a rumble, a shout. *It's the Moth. That girl up there, it's the Moth.* Even as they begin to move back from the wall, she hears her name on their lips, less of a curse and more of a prayer, spoken with hope instead of fear.

She's meant to be a horror story, but right now, outlined in golden light on the top of the wall, she's become something else.

Isabel checks her harness, the rope, the rail she's clipped it to. And then she flicks the lighter into life and watches the fuse catch and the flames lick hungrily at the path to the explosives.

She closes her eyes and jumps, and, for a moment, it's almost like flying.

36

BRULA (BURNING)

The second Isabel's feet hit the ground, she unclips the rope and legs it, trying to put as much distance between herself and the wall as she can. She's still not sure it's far enough as the first thunderous explosions shake the earth and the rumble of shattering concrete sends vibrations thrumming through the ground under her feet. She stumbles, picks herself up, keeps going. Catches the tail end of the fleeing crowd and they're running too, maybe now grasping the urgency of her instructions to move.

The sound of the wall starting to fall is like the world being torn apart.

Isabel's ears throb with the immensity of it, a noise she *feels* as much as hears. She makes it out of the kill strip into the first narrow streets, but she doesn't know how far is far enough, so she keeps running, until she can hardly see the wall over her shoulder.

She doesn't need to see it to know when the first enormous chunks of masonry hit the ground. They probably felt that all the way across the city. The impact triggers the charges in the foundations, and the next wave of thunder sends Isabel to her knees. She slams into the ground, wrist bending in a direction it shouldn't go, and a lance of white-hot pain shoots through her arm. Gritting her teeth, she pulls herself up with her other hand. All she can hear is *noise*: the crumble of destroyed concrete, the ringing in her ears, the roaring of the crowd – in approval, in fear, in anger.

Isabel retches, the pain of her broken wrist flooding in as the adrenaline of the climb and the jump leaves her body, and begins stumbling back the way she came, looking for Beth and Charlie. As she reaches the end of the road, cresting a slight hill, she gets an unobstructed view of the damage for the first time, and stops dead at the sight of the huge, gaping wound in the wall.

The sunset paints the sky a furious red behind the smouldering fires, the twisting smoke, the jagged pillars of concrete with spikes of iron rebar protruding from the chunks – and there in the centre is a space where the whole world can live.

She sinks to her knees.

'She's here! Over here, it's her, she's here!'

For a moment, she thinks it's Beth or Charlie come to fetch her, but it's only another stranger wanting a piece of the

Moth. They bend over her, brushing her hair out of her face, as though they're not afraid of her at all. The crowd grows, the hubbub of their questions muted by her damaged hearing. She catches only fragments: *Are you really the Moth? Why did you turn on the guild? What does this mean? Is Ronan Atwood really dead? What does this mean?*

What does this mean, what does this mean, what does this mean? Isabel wants to know that too. She looks at the hole she's made in the wall and tries to imagine an Espera that's open, but all she sees is destruction. People close in around her, blocking her view. If she had her senses, she'd tell them to leave her alone, and if she had her gun, she'd make them, but she lost both when she jumped, so instead she sits numbly on the ground and waits for it to be over.

'Isabel? Isabel, is that you, are you there?'

Not a stranger's voice. Laura. Isabel raises her head to see her friends pushing through the crowd: Laura and Leo and Sam, all of them uninjured, all of them with shining eyes.

Laura drops down beside her. 'Are you okay? Your wrist – what happened?'

Isabel looks blankly at her left wrist, which is hanging at a worrying angle, unhealthily swollen. 'Fell,' she says, and a hysterical laugh bubbles in her throat. *Jumped off the fucking wall while it was exploding*, she wants to say, *but I broke my wrist stacking it when I tried to run*, except she hasn't got it in her to manage that many words, so she just holds out her other hand to Laura and lets her friend cling to it, desperately, like they haven't seen each other in years.

'It's happening,' says Sam. 'People are climbing through, it's happening.' And sure enough, people aren't only staring at the gap, but climbing over it, through the still-smouldering wreckage. People of Espera, taking their first steps outside the wall, whooping with delight and calling for their friends to join them. Teams gathering to scoop away the rubble, shouting for tools and machinery to be fetched.

'You did that, Isabel,' says Leo, and his smile is tearful but it's real. 'You brought down the wall.'

Isabel shakes her head. It wasn't her. It was the city, which got to the point where this was possible. It was Laura, who killed Ronan; it was the unknown radicals who took out Hummingbird; it was everyone who protested while they were gone. 'Not me,' she says.

'You made it happen,' Laura tells her, squeezing her hand. Then she adds, with a sly, knowing smile, 'The *Moth* made it happen.'

Maybe it's fitting for Espera's liberation to be built on a lie: deception has always held the city together. But it feels no better now than it did the first time someone credited her for Ronan's death.

'Maybe it should've been you,' she says. 'With the lighter.'

Laura laughs and shakes her head. 'Not my style. The revolutionary symbol look's more convincing on you.' She tucks a strand of Isabel's hair behind her ear. 'Besides,' she adds, 'I'd have pissed myself up on the wall like that. I can't believe you *jumped off*.'

Isabel manages a small smile. 'Seemed a better option

than getting blown up.' Less bravery, more her fucked-up self-preservation instincts finally kicking in, but in that brief moment of flight, she realised she wants to live – and this time, it feels like a revelation, not a failing. Not an act of cowardice, not a reason to run, but a reason to stay. *She wants to live.* Wants to see what happens next. Wants to know what this new Espera will do – this city she hardly recognises, brimming with the potential for change.

She always thought Espera was a city so complicit in its own atrocities that it could never turn its back on them. But in the space of days, weeks, months, something new has been born here. Something that belongs to the art on the walls and the solar panels in the roads, defying the shadows who roam the city dealing death and vicious bargains to keep it fed.

And the real fuses, she knows, were laid years before she lit the spark, years before she knew where to look for them. They were there the day she first spoke to Abbie Miner. The day she delivered the *Bulletin* to Mortimer Sark. The day her parents turned their backs on Comma and formed their own guild, undermining a trade deal and exposing the cracks in the city's fragile relationship with the outside world.

Perhaps they've been there longer even than that, fault lines running through Espera's past. And when the structure's faulty, the tiniest push, the tiniest change, can bring it all crashing down.

And a moth can destroy a wall which has stood for decades.

'I want to see what's happening,' says Sam, so Laura helps Isabel up, and she leans on her friend's arm as they cross the wreckage of the kill strip towards the fallen wall, stepping around the rubble and the dust until they can see the path to the outside world. Until they see the citizens of Espera walking out, tentative, taking their first steps on free soil. Until they watch spectators from the outside come forward to take the hands of Esperans, to hug them, to welcome them to a world they've only heard about.

They don't want us, Isabel had thought, but that's not true of everyone. It's not true of the smugglers who fed the city and kept faith with its people, year upon year, and it's not true of the students who agitated and raised money to help them, and it's not true of anyone who's come to bear witness to the city's revolution.

'We should go up there,' says Isabel, pointing to the wall. 'Get a better view.'

'You can't climb,' says Leo. 'Not with that wrist.'

'We could go up the watchtower,' suggests Laura. 'There's only one ladder, and it's short. The rest is stairs.'

So they make their way to the watchtower, climbing the stairs through the guards' lounge and kitchen, the observation station and the armoury, until finally they emerge through the hatch onto the roof with its metal railings and view of the city. To the west, the country stretches on, impossibly large, full of places they've never been. To the east, Espera is awake, every light on, every door flung open. She can hear car horns and music blaring and people shouting, a tapestry of noise that doesn't belong to her city.

Sam leans over the railing. 'Is that Leeds?' she asks, pointing to a distant haze of lights.

'I don't know,' says Leo. 'More likely York. Or somewhere else entirely.'

'What about that?' She's pointing again, made childish in her wonder. 'What's that?'

'I don't know,' says Leo for a second time, and he says it like it's the greatest gift he's ever been given, not to know.

Isabel goes to the eastern edge of the tower and grips the metal railing tightly in her good hand, looking out over the city. Even from here, she can see makeshift flags going up across Grindalythe and beyond – towels and blankets fluttering in the wind, illuminated by streetlights and torches. Towards Lutton, fireworks shatter the sky with colour, sparklers glittering gold in gardens and parks. The solar panels wink and change under people's feet, but for once, nobody's looking down.

One section of the wall has fallen, and the rest will follow. The gates will open, and people will bring their tools to chip away the concrete, fragmenting all those paintings of bright skies and open seas in favour of the real thing. She wonders if anyone will save the art, for so long the city's only beauty. She wonders how many people will choose to stay.

Laura comes to join her, then. She doesn't speak. She leans on the railing by Isabel's side, and they're shadows together, invisible on top of the dark watchtower, while below them, the future is being born.

Not everyone in the outside world wants to hold the Esperans' hands.

They hear the shouting first, and when they cross to the

western side of the tower, they see the flashing lights, the vehicles streaming in: one armoured van after another, the army and riot police come to push back the crowds. It's too late to stop anyone crossing the wall, but they're barking orders anyway, trying to divide people into free citizens and undeserving Esperans to be herded back into their prison. The celebratory mood turns violent, the party becoming a protest.

Leo swears quietly. 'I should go down,' he says. 'Help.'

He doesn't sound like he wants to. He doesn't sound surprised, either, which means the abolitionists anticipated this, and they've got a plan to deal with freedom in a world that doesn't want them.

'I want to stay here,' says Sam.

'Okay.' Leo squeezes her tight, kisses the top of her head. She's getting tall, almost as tall as Isabel; if she keeps growing, he won't be able to do that any more. 'Stay here with Isabel. But come down eventually, will you? My knees can't handle living in a watchtower.'

He doesn't need to ask Isabel if she wants to stay here. Of course she's not going down there, with the law and the military looking for somebody to punish. She'll be lucky if nobody points her out to them – no need to hasten the moment.

Laura stays too. Sam says, 'They can't make us rebuild the wall, can they?'

'No,' says Isabel, more certainly than she feels. 'But I think they'll probably make everyone do a lot of really boring paperwork.' She wishes she believed that was all it would take. But after the politics, after the decision-making, then comes the reckoning – and if the world is ever going to take Espera back, they'll do so only because they think they've brought to justice the people responsible for its atrocities.

Isabel doesn't want to go to prison, and she doesn't want to die.

She turns away from the view and sits on the floor with her back against the railing. Sam joins her, then Laura.

'What is it?' asks Laura.

'Thinking about the future,' says Isabel. She wants to believe the wall has fallen for her. That she could go back to Leeds, and it wouldn't mean exile, and it wouldn't mean abandoning Espera – she could come and go, between the city that made her and the one that remade her. She could go further, travel the world, see the places she's read about and never thought she'd see for real.

But she's the Moth. It doesn't matter that she helped destroy the wall: the only way she'll avoid being put on trial for what she's done is to disappear before anyone can hold her accountable. To become somebody else and start again, cutting off her name, her past, all her connections to anyone she cares about.

She doesn't want to. For better or worse, she's Isabel Ryans, and this city made her. Can't they see that? Can't they understand that she's only ever been what Espera made her?

Give me a chance, she thinks. *I can be better. I swear I can be better. I didn't kill Ronan Atwood, that means something, that means I'm more than a killer, please, I can be more than this.*

Except what she's really saying is: *I want to live, I want to live, I want to live.*

But the city deserves justice; she knew that when she came back here. And she's been living on borrowed time since she was seventeen. Maybe the hour has come to repay her debt.

Isabel takes a deep breath, and forces a smile onto her face. 'A whole new Espera,' she says, trying to sound like she believes that's a good thing. 'A whole new future. And we did that.'

Handed the world the knife it needed to hurt her. Just like she always does.

37

KOMPENSA (REPARATIVE)

The gates fall next, then a mile of the eastern wall.

Isabel is still staying in the abolitionists' guest room in Reighton. They've been kind enough: splinted her broken wrist, found her clothes to wear. They haven't explicitly said she's under house arrest, and on the few occasions she's dared step outside for a walk, nobody has stopped her. But it's been implied, heavily, that she shouldn't go anywhere, because people will want to talk to her.

There's a lot of talking happening. Down in the abolitionists' living room, the radio is always on, faceless voices arguing about the city's future. From this, Isabel learns that the borough councils have formed a provisional government and taken over the administration of the food rationing, since the outside world refuses to lift the trade sanctions. This is a mistake on the outsiders' part, Isabel thinks: it gives people a reason to flee. Every day, dozens more Esperans make it across the rubble of the wall and strike out into the unknown.

And all the while, Espera's future hangs in the balance. There's talk of it maintaining its independence, talk of it becoming part of England, talk of its citizens being dispersed across the country to quell any further resistance ... (This last, proposed by outsiders, is resoundingly and predictably unpopular with Esperans.)

But upstairs, in her room, there's no talk of anything. Isabel can close the curtains and the door and pretend that nothing has changed and nobody is going to come for her.

Around a week after the destruction of the wall, Leo brings home news of the Esperan Re-Integration Committee, or ERIC. It's not the first committee to be proposed, and probably won't be the last; Isabel, already tired of politics, is only half listening as he explains that it's a mixed council of Esperans and outsiders, aiming to ease the city's transition and bring the guilds to justice, giving civilians the closure they need.

'Because of my experience helping the abolitionists on both sides of the wall, I've been asked to join,' says Leo. He sounds proud. Isabel wishes she was too, but all she hears is *bring the guilds to justice*, and it's frozen her blood, filled her with fear again. She knew it was coming, but she didn't think it would come from Leo, who for so long has been the only person among the abolitionists she would truly trust with her life.

'Isabel,' he says, noticing her anxiety, 'this is a good thing.'

'Yeah, of course,' she says, unconvinced. 'I'm happy for you. It's a big honour.'

He rolls his eyes. 'It's a good thing because it means there's at least one person on that committee who is on your side.'

Until then, she hadn't realised he saw through her forced smiles and false optimism. She hasn't told anybody of her dread, because it doesn't seem like their problem. If Espera needs to punish the Moth in order to thrive, then they should do that, and she doesn't deserve to beg them for mercy.

She stares down at her lunch, trying to muster an appetite. They're alone: Laura is out with Sam, the pair of them piecing together a fragile friendship that will never be entirely free of Suzie's shadow. She's glad they're gone, because she can't look either of them in the eye these days.

'It doesn't matter,' she says. 'That you're on my side. They only need to look at the Comma records to know what I've done, and . . . and there's no talking my way out of that. If they want to lock me up . . .' She trails off, looking at him. 'Is that what they're going to do? Prison?'

Leo's mouth is a tight line. 'That's a subject of some debate,' he admits. 'Some of the outsiders want to reinstate the death penalty. Almost all of the Esperans voted against it.'

Isabel nods. No surprise there. James was right: set yourself up with the political power to kill your opponents and congratulations, you've reinvented the guilds. The outsiders wouldn't understand that, but the people of Espera know better.

Still. Part of her thinks a swift execution would be preferable to living the rest of her life behind bars.

Leo adds, 'A significant faction of the committee is of the opinion that punitive justice will only make everything worse. That we need to take a reparative approach.'

These words don't mean much to Isabel. 'And that means ...?'

'They think – *we* think,' he corrects, 'that punishment only perpetuates and recreates harm, rather than repairing it. If we want to build a better future for this city, we need to take a different approach. Find ways to undo the damage and lay the foundations for something better.'

Isabel swallows the lump in her throat, and the huge, indescribable emotion rising up inside her. She doesn't deserve Leo. *Espera* doesn't deserve Leo: doesn't deserve for a man who was shaped by its violence to come out the other side good, and kind, and without a trace of vengeance in him. How does he do it? How can he sit here, and look at the damage the guilds have done, and not want to punish them for it?

Maybe he does – maybe he aches with the need for revenge, but he would never let himself act on it, and Isabel is floored over and over again by that strength of conviction and the fact that somebody who has suffered at the hands of the guilds can keep insisting on people's potential for goodness, and their right to a chance to seek it.

'No one can undo the damage,' says Isabel, as gently as she can, though all her words feel like weapons these days. 'People are dead. I can't bring them back.'

'Yes,' says Leo, 'that's one of the difficulties we're having,' and he gives her a lopsided smile. Then it fades, and he says,

'Most of the adjacents won't be brought to trial. Hard to hold a factory worker responsible, even if they were making weapons. Medical and education, they'll be fine. The higher-level admin staff, though, that's more complicated. Lawyers and accountants and all that. A lot of them have never killed someone, but—'

'Bold assumption,' says Isabel, and shrugs when he glances at her. 'People move departments more than you'd expect. If they did anything beyond basic training, they'll have needed a graduation kill. Just because they're a lawyer now, doesn't mean they always were.' It's one of the ways the guilds keep their people loyal, override their moral qualms. *You're no better than us*, they can say, because it's true. Sometimes she thinks that field agents are the only ones being honest with themselves: at least they admit they're killers.

Leo frowns. 'I didn't know that,' he says. 'I'll have to tell the others.'

'Most of the top levels are dead, anyway.' The reports have been trickling in over the last few days: Ronan Atwood's second was at the Cowlam Comma building when it fell; Margaret Strange's planned successor died early in the protests, unremarked.

'Yes,' Leo agrees. 'They would otherwise have been the highest priority. There's a sense that culpability lies most strongly with the decision-makers, and ...' He shrugs. 'In their absence, I suspect it will be difficult for people to achieve closure.'

Isabel's surprised the committee recognises that much.

Even her patchy knowledge of history tells her it's rarely governments that are held to account for war crimes committed in their names.

'And intelligence?' she asks; her mind fills in *lycaenidae*, Comma's departmental names indelibly marked in her brain no matter how rarely she uses them. 'Codes, research? They compiled the files we used to find our targets, so they're an essential part of every hit.'

'Intelligence is complicated,' Leo admits. 'But the highest priority now that the directors are dead is field agents.'

Nymphalidae. Isabel's department. And the Moth will be top of their list.

'I'm sorry,' he says. 'That's why I wanted to warn you. Why I wanted to be on the committee in the first place. I've been fighting your corner, pointing out that you helped us, and that's something, but Isabel, they . . .' He hesitates, as though whatever he's about to say is somehow worse than the news that she'll be put on trial and nobody can agree what they'll do to her if she's found guilty. 'They can't find any evidence of Cocoon.'

It takes a long moment for that to sink in. 'They what?'

'If we could prove it . . .' He trails off. 'We shouldn't need to. They should be able to do the maths. But there's no record, no evidence that you were a child or that you were coerced. Even your personnel file says nothing about the circumstances of you joining Comma, and you were seventeen by then, so they can pretend it was legit.'

If they've got access to her personnel file, they've broken

into Comma's most secure storage – and *still* they've found nothing about Cocoon. 'And if I wasn't forced into it, I did all of that by choice, so I'm guilty.'

He nods miserably. 'Project Emerald is documented – extensively. Laura will be fine; her work for Comma was also clearly under duress. But right now, the written record claims that you were willing.'

Isabel sits with this knowledge in silence. Ronan must have hidden the records once Project Emerald came out, trying to protect Comma's reputation. She's got the notebooks she rescued from Cocoon, but for the most part she suspects they're a banal record of her parents' abuse, nothing that can be concretely tied to the guild. Small details, perhaps, but not enough to prove the existence of an entire child training programme that's been summarily wiped from record.

And if Ronan didn't hide the files, if he destroyed them . . .

No. He was clever and he was cautious, but Ronan knew the value of that information, and he wouldn't have done anything irreversible. She needs to believe that, because otherwise there's no chance of retrieving it, and no hope for clemency from the committee.

Do you deserve clemency? asks the little voice in her head that still sounds like her mother.

Yes, she roars back. *Yes, I deserve mercy, I deserve another chance, I deserve for them to see what was done to me.* She wants to live. She blew a hole in her own city because she wanted to live.

'I wasn't,' she says flatly, after a long pause, 'and I'll prove it. If you give me time. If I . . .' She hesitates. 'Am I allowed to go out? Properly out, I mean, not just a walk around the block?'

Leo chews his lip. 'Not out of the city,' he says. 'And some would say not out of the borough, but . . . I'll make a case for it. Where do you want to go?'

The abolitionists control all the guild buildings, so they'll have found any paperwork kept there. That means it's off site, and there's only one place she can imagine Ronan considering adequately secure, well-defended and entirely secret.

'You've got the personnel files?' she asks, and watches him nod. 'I need Ronan Atwood's address.'

38

KAŜITA (HIDDEN)

Isabel's expecting grey and glass and metal, so the modest red-brick house with its green front door and drainpipes comes as a surprise. But the keys from Ronan's desk drawer fit the lock, and the door opens with the creak of a deliberately neglected hinge. That sound convinces her she's in the right place: Ronan appreciated prior warning.

Inside, the house is incongruously homey. The décor's all rich blues and vibrant greens, as though monochrome was a disguise Ronan wore to work. Or maybe this house is the mask, a make-believe normal to come back to at the end of the day.

The living room tells her nothing of use, except that Ronan owned at least two cat-themed ornaments, and kept a framed photo of two people on his mantelpiece. His parents, Isabel presumes, giving it a cursory glance. The man has the same cool grey eyes as Ronan, but his face is softer, kind; the woman shares Ronan's nose and thin, curved eyebrows. Isabel doesn't linger. It already feels absurd to be creeping around Ronan's home, when he's only ever existed for her as the personification of his job.

In the kitchen, something makes a plaintive noise. Startled, Isabel snatches up one of the heavier ornaments in her good hand and moves silently across the room. She thought the house was empty: everybody who ever knew this as Ronan's address is dead now, unless there's more she doesn't know about his life.

Isabel slips into the kitchen.

The noise comes again.

There, looking up at her from beside an empty bowl, is a small black cat. Kitten-sized, she'd have thought, but the proportions are wrong, and anyway, she's seen this cat before. It appears to be made entirely of fluff, big eyes staring up at her, one prominent canine poking out of its mouth.

'Hey,' says Isabel, setting the ornament on the table and crouching in front of the beast. She feels foolish, and looks around for any clue as to how to deal with a cat. Nothing. There's a sheet of paper fixed to the fridge with a magnet, but it's only a shopping list: *pasta, tinned tomatoes, food for Rory . . .*

Isabel regards the cat. 'Are you Rory?' she asks it. The name rings a faint bell.

The cat meows again, an anguished sound, and leaves the food bowl in favour of headbutting Isabel's legs.

'I guess you're hungry, aren't you?' Nobody knew about the cat. It's been days since Ronan died, and whatever food he left for it will have been long gone. If Isabel hadn't come here . . .

How hard can it really be to look after a cat, anyway? Ronan managed it, and he wasn't exactly abundant in his capacity for kindness and care. She steps cautiously around the little creature and opens cupboards until she finds something that looks like cat food. Rory yowls at the sight of the bag and seems intent on tripping Isabel before she can get it open, but she manages to deposit a handful of the stuff in the bowl, and the cat practically dives head first into it.

Isabel adds another handful, then takes the other dish to the sink and fills that with water, because it feels like the logical thing to do. 'All right then, beastie,' she says, setting it down. 'What now?'

The cat looks up from the bowl at the sound of her voice and makes a questioning noise, almost a chirp, but its interest isn't held for long; food takes first priority. Understandable, in the circumstances.

'All right,' says Isabel again, and eases herself back up. Wherever Ronan kept those files, it's unlikely to be in the kitchen – or anywhere else the cat could get to them. She needs to look for a closed door, a locked cabinet.

Adding a third handful of food to keep the creature occupied, she rinses her hands and leaves the kitchen. The downstairs of the house is quickly surveyed: living room; kitchen; toilet under the stairs; back room that's really a partially converted conservatory, home to a number of succulents and almost no furniture. She can't imagine Ronan spending much time in a room made significantly of windows, and the lack of furniture suggests she's correct, but perhaps he enjoyed his prickly, low-maintenance plants.

She leaves them and goes to the stairs, which are narrow but well-carpeted. The whole house is elegantly decorated, and she can't help wondering, a little hysterically, whether Ronan chose the colours himself or hired an interior designer. If the former, she thinks the city would have been far better off if he'd indulged his creative passions rather than his murderous organisational skills.

Upstairs is a bedroom: a double bed, pushed against the wall as though occupied by somebody who had zero expectation of ever sharing it, and a wardrobe containing eighty per cent monochrome suits and ties and twenty per cent jeans and warm green and blue jumpers. Isabel is struck by the uncomfortable suspicion that Ronan had favourite colours, which she dislikes, because it comes rather too close to making a person of him. She shuts the wardrobe doors – no files here – and tries the next room, which proves to be a bathroom.

The final door is closed. In most houses of this size, this would be a child's room, or a home office. Unless she's made some wildly incorrect assumptions about Ronan, she's betting on the latter.

The door is locked.

Isabel swears. Ronan's keyring only held the front door

keys, because he's not an amateur, and he'd never keep this key on the same ring. Very few people would have known his address, but secrecy is no substitute for security; she's willing to bet that after Kieran's betrayal, he upped his precautions, and that means this door is definitely trapped.

Taking out the phone Leo loaned her and switching on its torch, Isabel angles it towards the lock and peers inside. Sure enough, there's a fine wire stretched across it, not much thicker than a hair. Could be an alarm, could be an explosive; she's not about to stick something in there and find out. It looks like it's only connected to the lock, though, not the door itself – designed to catch a clumsy intruder, not to hold off a determined one.

She didn't know what to expect from the house, so she brought all the tools the abolitionists would give her. It's not a full kit by any means, but it allows her to rig a length of wire to keep the circuit intact while she manoeuvres her lockpicks around it, painfully aware that if this *is* an explosive, one wrong move could make the whole mission a moot point. The cast on her left hand doesn't help matters, awkward and bulky.

Finally, the lock gives way, and the door opens. Isabel lets out her breath and makes one last sweep with the torch, but no other traps reveal themselves. Doesn't mean they're not there, but she won't find them by looking. She steps inside.

The room is dark, the blind half drawn. One wall consists of floor-to-ceiling bookshelves, filled, to Isabel's amazement, with neatly alphabetised fiction. Most of the books look almost new, but there are tiny hints of wear, small creases in the spines as though somebody tried hard not to bend them but didn't entirely succeed. Books bought by somebody who hadn't always had the money to buy books, and was taking care of them now that he had.

She wishes it wasn't so patently obvious that Ronan lived alone, because this careful man with his modest comforts is so deeply at odds with the bastard she knew and loathed, and it's fucking with her head.

In front of the small window is a desk, layered in dust as though Ronan didn't spend enough time at home to use it. She checks the drawers, but they're home only to miscellaneous stationery and a few bills. He lived here under the name *Séamas Myers*, apparently, which shouldn't surprise her; of course he wouldn't have given the neighbours his real name.

The two metal filing cabinets are promising – locked, again, but the key is in the desk drawer. But when she opens them, they contain only the detritus of Séamas Myers' life, carefully organised: filed bills, bank statements, mortgage paperwork. An entire life lived behind a mask. Was it really Ronan who lived here? Or did he feel like Séamas when he took off his work suit and put on a cosy jumper to spend the evening with his stupid little cat?

(She knows the cat is stupid because it was immediately willing to accept food from Isabel, despite the fact that she's a stranger, and shouldn't be relied upon to be kind to a small animal.)

That leaves only the antique-looking cupboard against the final wall, an edifice of wood too large for the room. Fuck knows where he got it; she can't imagine Ronan at an antique sale, and this must have been imported, because it's older than Espera. Maybe it was seized from a smuggler, although large items of furniture aren't their usual style. Maybe he bought it on one of his rare trips outside the city, just because he could.

There's no key for this cabinet's locked door, either on the keyring or in the desk drawers. Isabel heads briefly back to Ronan's bedroom and checks the drawers of the bedside table, but they're empty, which is something of a relief. Finally, she accepts that if the key is in this house, she's unlikely to find it; it's more likely Ronan had it on him when he died.

She kneels in front of the cabinet. There's no sign of any further traps, and an antique lock like this is more for show than security, easy to pick. But she doesn't trust it. Would Ronan really have relied on that single tripwire to protect his work? If this cabinet contains anything of value ...

But maybe it doesn't. Maybe it's Ronan's baby photos and childhood art projects in this cupboard, or a set of fine china he wanted to keep away from the cat. Maybe the files are already ash in the wind and there's no hope for her.

There's only one way to find out.

The lock's tougher than it looks, and Isabel's broken wrist and lack of practice are painfully apparent as she fumbles her way through picking it. But in the end the door swings open, revealing two cupboards subdivided into shelves and crammed with neat archival boxes. The action also releases a knife; Isabel snatches her hand out of the way the moment she catches the metallic glint at the edge of her vision, but the blade still grazes her cast before hitting the carpet. If not for her broken wrist, she'd be bleeding.

'Any more tricks to offer?' she mutters, eyeing the boxes. The labels are in code, but that's no real challenge for Isabel. *Cocoon, 2021–23*, reads the first; *2024–25* and *2026–termination* beside it. That's all she needs to know.

She doubts Ronan's trapped the shelves too, but he might have done something to the boxes themselves. Unwilling to risk a faceful of anthrax or something equally nasty, Isabel takes a pair of latex gloves and a mask from her bag – the shitty disposable kind, but it was all the abolitionists had – and puts them on. Then she eases the first box out of the cupboard, and lifts the lid.

Well, the files are there. And it looks like she's exhausted Ronan's traps, too; it's paper, harmless, nothing worse than dust and memories to trouble her.

Sliding it back onto the shelf, Isabel takes a careful photo, then turns her attention to the rest of the boxes. One is unlabelled; she tugs it out, untying the string that holds it closed and lifting the lid.

Her own face stares up at her, fifteen years old and unconscious. She's wearing a hospital gown. Even without the date scrawled in the top corner – *March '28* – Isabel would know it was taken after the job gone wrong that left her permanently scarred and precipitated the end of Cocoon.

Swallowing hard, she flicks through a few more of the papers. This, she realises, is her medical record – the *whole* record, not the redacted, sanitised version they kept on file at the hospital. Even a brief glimpse tells her that Ronan knew far more about her than she realised, because there are photos of her scars here, back when they were fresh.

It was documented. All of it. Those diaries she kept, desperately trying to cling to the truth ... why bother? The guild *knew*, always.

Maybe Ronan didn't, when he first met her. Maybe he only got access to this information when he became director. That's possible. She'll give him that, charitably, because she doesn't know how he could ever have expected her to help find her parents after their defection if this file was sitting on his desk at the time.

Fucking hell.

Isabel closes the box, reties the string around it, and returns it to the shelf. She doesn't need to know what's in the other boxes, or who else's suffering is documented here: it's not her place to see those things. It's nobody's place to know this about her, either, but it might save her, so she'll give it to them. All the bloodiest secrets of her childhood, in exchange for her future.

Isabel takes a photo of the whole cabinet and texts it to Leo.

Send your people to get these.
Upstairs back room.

By the time they get here to take them, she'll be long gone.

The muted thump of small feet on the stairs distracts her, and she barely has time to close the cabinet doors before the small bundle of fluff Ronan called a cat barrels into her, trying to climb into her lap. Isabel swears softly and then, tentatively, touches the creature's head.

Rory chirps in delight and proceeds to shove its entire face into her hand.

'You,' she tells it, 'are an incredibly stupid creature, you know that?'

But the cat lived with Ronan Atwood for fuck knows how long, so it must have become desensitised to the Eau de Murderer accompanying its chosen humans. And she can't leave it here, abandoned and forgotten, to be trampled by the abolitionists when they come to clear the papers from this house. Maybe the cat was the only thing on earth Ronan knew how to care about, but he's gone, so somebody else will have to do it now.

Uncertainly, because she doesn't know how to grip a cat without hurting it, Isabel lifts the creature up and stands. It yowls at being dislodged from her lap, but seems content to huddle in her arms, warm and soft, once she's up. She sustains her uneasy petting of its head, and is startled when it begins to vibrate. *Purr*, she remembers, from what she's read about cats. It's purring.

Well. She must be doing something right.

'Shall we go and see Leo?' she asks it, and listens to its answering chirp. 'Yeah, you're right. He'll know what to do with you. Find you somewhere to go.'

Right now the cat seems to want to go inside Isabel's clothes; she lets it snuggle into her jacket, keeping it supported with one arm, and says sternly, 'Behave. I gave you food. You owe me one.'

Mrrp, says Rory, and Isabel accepts this as agreement.

She lets herself out of the house, gripping the cat as tightly as she dares, and closes the door behind her. So that was Ronan's house. And this is Ronan's cat. And she might, possibly, have stolen it.

Well, Ronan took enough from her, so maybe he owes her this.

She looks down at Rory's vacant little face, poking out of her partially unzipped jacket. 'Leo will know what to do,' she says, and with her good hand cupped around Rory's head to shield the small creature from the world, she sets off to find him.

39

TENERA (LOVING)

The trial is interminable.

It's not all about Isabel – she's only a figurehead, a scapegoat for Comma's crimes. That detail, and Leo's persuasive meddling, granted her the small mercy of being tried in absentia, which is a relief: there's no way she'd get through the showing of the Cocoon evidence without having a panic attack, and the jury would doubtless read that as manipulation. She stays at home, instead, accompanied by Rory the cat, since nobody knows what to do with the beastie either. Leo is smitten, Sam is allergic, and Laura is wary, which is understandable, since Rory has taken a dislike to her. Isabel, terrified at all times of doing something wrong and hurting the cat, is growing slowly used to having a soft, warm little body curled up against her as she sits at home and reads, trying to forget that the city is deliberating her fate.

The abolitionists found them a house, previously guild-owned, so Isabel's got a room now – one that feels a little less like a guest room and naggingly like a prison, despite the yellow curtains and colourful rugs. In theory, she's allowed to go out, but not alone, even with the ankle monitor they forced her to agree to wearing. In reality, the outside world holds little appeal; she can't go two streets without being recognised. Nobody can decide if the Moth is the hero or the villain of the piece, and Isabel doesn't like gambling on the answer every time she meets someone.

'Cocoon's hit the news,' says Laura, on the eighth endless day of the trials. 'Want the highlights?'

Isabel looks up from her book, her other hand resting absently on Rory's small head. 'Not particularly,' she responds. 'But Leo will tell me anyway, so you might as well get it over with.'

Laura sits down on the settee beside her, a development Rory does not appreciate. The cat hisses in her direction, fiercely ready to defend Isabel.

'Calm down, little beast,' says Isabel, rubbing the spot between the cat's ears until Rory settles down. When she looks up, Laura arches an eyebrow. 'What?'

'I can't tell if you've adopted the cat or the cat has adopted you,' says Laura. 'Do you think she knows I'm the one who killed Ronan?'

At the sound of Ronan's name, Rory's ears flick forward.

'Don't know,' says Isabel. 'She's a cat. I've got no idea what they know.' It's plain, however, that Rory does not count Laura among her favoured humans.

Laura continues to look doubtful and keep her distance. 'Well, surprise, surprise, public opinion is divided. Almost universal condemnation of Cocoon, barring a few nuts claiming it's basically cadets and *they* turned out fine after doing rifle drills as a twelve-year-old.'

'Clearly they did not turn out fine,' says Isabel, 'if they're justifying teaching children to kill people.'

'Agreed,' says Laura. 'Most people are firmly on the negative side, though. No reports of the actual abuse so far – don't know if they've reached the medical records and have closed the court to reporters, or if they haven't got that far. You'd have to ask Leo.' Laura doesn't ask how Isabel feels about her personal medical history being used as evidence. They don't have those kinds of conversations any more, even though they're living together, and even though Laura was the Moth. Ronan's death and the lies around it are a heavy burden on their friendship.

'But?' prompts Isabel; there's always a but.

'But a lot of people are coming down on the side of having had a shit childhood without turning into serial killers,' says Laura baldly. 'Hard to judge how this might go. Even if they can prove coercion, that doesn't necessarily remove all culpability.'

Of course it doesn't. And even if they exonerated Isabel of the guild murders, what about the rest? Ian Crampton, Nick Larrington, Kieran Atwood?

'Great,' says Isabel, without enthusiasm. 'I look forward to Leo being sad but optimistic over dinner.' She's the test case, the chance for ERIC and the courts to decide where they'll go from here. The outsider suggestion of the death penalty was thrown out on the first day in court – nobody wants to see Espera slip back into a murderous cycle – but the punitive and reparative factions, as Leo calls them, can't agree on what justice means. Everyone wants a better future for the city, but nobody knows what that looks like in reality.

Laura watches Isabel and Rory for a moment, and then says, 'I think I need to confess.'

'Confess what?' asks Isabel absently, and then, when her brain catches up with her: 'Oh, about Ronan? Why?'

'Because even though half the city thinks you're a hero, the other half is ready to hold it against you.' She twists her hands together. 'The way they see it, you left the city, seemed to make progress, then came back and enacted vigilante justice against a man who should have stood trial, so clearly you can't change. If they lock you up because of a lie, because of *my* lie . . .'

It's the first time Laura has verbally acknowledged that killing Ronan might have created as many problems as it solved. Isabel wants to tell her that of course she should confess, she's the one who did it, but—

But Isabel was *going* to. Up until the moment she stepped into that room, her intention was to kill him. Does it matter that she changed her mind? Maybe the city is right to think she'll never change.

I did change, though, says the small, stubborn voice in her mind. *And it does matter.*

'They'll only put you on trial as well,' she says.

Laura shrugs. 'He interrogated me, and there are records of that. Besides, police records from Leeds show I was a mess, unable to make sane judgements. If they don't let me off entirely, they'll definitely go light on the sentencing.'

'You don't know that,' Isabel objects.

'I know I'm not letting you take the fall for my lie.' Laura reaches out a tentative hand, but Rory swipes at it with her claws out. 'Look, even the fucking cat knows I'm guilty.'

The cat. Isabel can't keep Rory for ever, but they haven't found another home for her, and if Isabel is taken away ...

'Okay,' she says eventually. 'But talk to Leo first. See if it would help or harm my case not to be the person who killed Ronan.'

Laura nods, accepting the compromise, and is silent for a long minute.

'I don't regret it,' she says eventually. 'I'd kill him again, given the chance. But ... but I understand why you didn't. And I don't think it was weak. I think it might be one of the bravest things you've ever done.'

Isabel looks down at Rory, blinking back the moisture in her eyes. She didn't realise anyone understood the leap of faith it took to believe, momentarily, in a world where Isabel Ryans wasn't a killer and justice was something that could be hoped for. Letting Ronan live was an act of self-belief that Isabel feels entirely incapable of living up to, not least because nobody else believes she can do it, either.

Maybe she is what people think she is. But on good days, when hope feels real, she believes she's more than that.

'Thanks,' she says inadequately, and scoops the cat out of the way so she can reach for Laura's hand.

The day her medical records are shown in court, Leo comes back blank-faced and shaking and insists on giving Isabel a hug: a long, tight embrace like he never plans to let her go.

The day Laura confesses to killing Ronan Atwood is the same day her father's notes go public – a lifetime after she decoded them, untangling his formulae and the records of the poisons he tested on her – and somebody makes a group online: *Justice for Isabel Ryans*. Sam's eyes shine as she tells Isabel about it, as though it's enough to exonerate her, even though it isn't.

And the day Oliver Roe's family give testimony against her, Laura forbids Isabel from using the internet, in case she sees what people are saying about her. In case she finds out why Oliver was killed and what she was complicit in.

But the day set aside for testimonies in her favour ... that day, Leo says, 'I think you should come with us this time,' and because he asked, she goes.

She's not expecting much. She expected Leo – of course he'd speak for her – and Sam, who plays up her own youth and makes sure to emphasise Isabel's language teaching, trying to soften her image. She talks about Suzie, too: about Isabel trying to save her. She knows enough about Katipo that her sister must have talked to her about it, because even Isabel didn't have those details.

More surprising as a witness is Beth, who talks first about Isabel's time as a library assistant, and then about the part she played in the revolution – coming back to help Jem, bringing down the wall. And Rae, whose testimony is brief and business-like, describes Isabel risking her life to help smuggle Leo and Sam out of the city.

Then to her astonishment, Maggie comes to the stand.

It's wrong to see her there. Both because the courtroom is clean and glossy and Maggie belongs to the garage bar and the faded community centre, places so close to their roots they've never grown past them, and because she shouldn't be in Espera at all. But she looks steadily around at the gathered crowd and the waiting jury, and then down at her notes.

'I met Isabel at rock bottom,' she says. 'She was grieving. And almost the first thing I realised about her was that she turned that pain inwards before she ever let it touch anyone else. She'd have destroyed herself rather than hurt somebody.' Maggie hesitates, wetting her lips. 'I can't claim to have saved her, or done anything more than give her a place to exist as herself, but I can tell you this: Isabel Ryans came to me for help, because she wanted to get better. That's all she ever asked of the world. A chance to get better.'

Isabel is grateful, then, that Leo found her a seat high up in the shadows of the closed public gallery, so that nobody can see her crying.

When Maggie steps back, it's James who takes her place.

'Like Maggie, I met Isabel when she was in a bad place. The difference is that I was in a pretty rough state myself, too.'

He looks around, like he's trying to spot Isabel in the crowd, but when he fails, he looks back at the lectern. 'I hated her at first. I saw her as a symbol of everything Esperan that ever hurt me – and I lost my best friend to an Esperan bomb. But the more time I spent with her, the more I realised it wasn't like that. If Isabel's a symbol of anything, it's of all the ways people get hurt by a world that values weapons over children. Truth is, she's like me, and I'm like her. We were just kids. Coerced or not, free or not, we were soldiers before we were people. And the real crime there was committed by the people who made us that way.'

He raises his eyes to the gallery and she sees the moment he spots her, a smile lifting the corners of his mouth.

'Having Isabel Ryans in my support group is the best thing that happened to me since I got out of the army,' he says. 'I don't think she knew she was helping me. I'm fairly sure she didn't think she was even helping herself. But after all the guilt and my attempts to deflect it by blaming everyone else, it was Isabel who taught me that survival is a gift as much as a burden, and for the first time, I thought maybe I was allowed to want to live.'

She doesn't hear the rest. Isabel slips out of the gallery and into the toilets, locking herself in a cubicle so that she can sob unobserved. Leo's down in the committee box, so he won't come looking for her; she's got time to figure out how to put herself back together again.

She didn't know her friends from Leeds would speak for her. She didn't think she'd ever see them again. James looks well. His hair's growing out. He's still got his military posture, but he'll always have that, and there's something softer about the angles of his face that speaks of change.

She's like me, and I'm like her. She's never been alone, even when it felt like it.

She waits (hides) in the toilets until she hears people leaving the courtroom, and then she splashes water on her face and goes down to the hallway where Leo said he'd meet her. He takes one look at her face and says, 'Okay. Let's go home.'

Wordlessly, she follows him to the car. It's a short journey from the central court to their house, and it passes in silence. Isabel's afraid that if she tries to speak, her voice will crack and fail her, and she won't be able to stop herself from crying.

Only when they reach the house and Leo's turned off the engine does he break the silence himself. 'You haven't got to believe me,' he says, 'and you haven't got to say anything, but I want you to know that as far as I'm concerned, every single word spoken about you today was true. You are everything we see in you. You are loyal, and you are brave, and you are trying so hard to be more than what they made you. And if you can't see that about yourself, then let us see it for you, and tell you over and over again that you deserved better.'

Isabel swallows hard and says, 'I would have deserved better even if I wasn't all of those things.' She doesn't mean it as a rebuke, but she's suddenly afraid it might have sounded like one.

But Leo's face cracks into a smile, broad and genuine. 'Yes,' he says. 'You would. I didn't know if you could see that.'

Isabel looks away, hiding her expression. 'Emma told me that,' she says. 'I didn't believe her then. I didn't know how to. But I think . . . I think I believe her now.'

Three years too late, but she believes her now. *I deserved to be safe.* And she wasn't. But maybe, eventually, when all of this is over – maybe she will be.

40

Espera (Hopeful)

The day the court is due to pass judgement on Isabel's future, neither Leo nor Isabel is allowed in. Their presence will be required for the sentencing, the specifics, but today they're to keep away, in case their presence is off-putting to the jury. Leo offers to wait outside the door until the verdict, but Isabel asks him if he'll escort her to the cemetery instead. If this is her last day of freedom, then there are some people she needs to visit.

She hasn't been to the cemetery since before she fled the city. They go to Emma's grave first: Emma and Toni and Jean, still in their neat line. Leo spreads out his picnic blanket, even though it's firmly autumn now and too damp for picnicking, and Isabel sits down beside him. He's got a thermos of mint tea in his bag, and a box of cakes that Sam and Isabel baked.

'Hi, Emma,' says Isabel. 'Have you heard the news? Everything's changing.'

They share the story between them, unable to agree on which are the most important parts. They talk about Leeds, and Isabel makes sure to describe the library, because she thinks Emma would want to know about the colours and the tiles and the art. Leo tells the story of the revolution, and makes Isabel sound like a hero. They laugh and they cry and they tell her everything she's missed, and they do it together, passing the thermos back and forth, sharing the cakes.

When they've run out of stories, Isabel says, 'I don't know what's going to happen next. But if I can visit you again, I will. You know I will, don't you?'

'She knows,' says Leo, and puts his arm around her, a sideways hug. 'Of course she knows.'

He's brought secateurs and gardening gloves with him, so Isabel trims the grass while he pulls up the weeds. When they eventually brush the detritus away from the three graves, they're starting to look cared-for again.

Leo says, 'There's another grave I thought you might want to see. I looked up where it was.'

Isabel nods and follows him along the paths, fallen leaves mushy beneath her feet. He stops in front of a simple white marker stone.

DARAGH BENJAMIN VERNANT
13TH FEBRUARY 1994–27TH APRIL 2032
A GOOD MAN.

She stares at it for several long seconds. 'Who . . . ?' she begins.

'Ronan, I think,' says Leo. 'I did some research. He was listed as Daragh's next of kin.'

A good man. Such a simple understatement, almost impersonal in its distance. No 'beloved cousin', and he was nobody's brother, and his parents must be dead if Ronan was all he had left.

'Hi, Daragh,' she says, and this time her voice does crack. She had time to come to terms with Emma's death; she never really made sense of Daragh's. Not without him there to hold her through it.

Blinking back tears, she looks away from the grave, but the trouble with cemeteries is that there's nothing to look at but more graves. And the one next to Daragh's is another pale marble stone:

CHRISTOPHER JOSEPH WILKES
19TH SEPTEMBER 1993–8TH JULY 2022
ARTIST, BROTHER, PARTNER, AND FRIEND:

THE COLOURS WILL FADE BUT
HIS MEMORY WILL LIVE ON.

Christopher.

This must be Daragh's Christopher, by his side at last. If Ronan arranged Daragh's burial, it wasn't the Ronan Isabel knew. It was the one Daragh knew: the one who kept that neat little house and fed Rory and lived for years under somebody else's name. And he chose this spot with care, because he didn't want his cousin to be alone.

There's nothing on Daragh's gravestone to suggest he was ever a member of Comma and that, too, is an act of love.

Isabel doesn't know what to say to Daragh. That he was right, and she really did need to talk about her feelings? That he should have left when he had the chance, been someone better, stayed alive? She would love to tell him not to be dead, but the words stick in her throat.

So she looks at Leo instead. 'Is Mortimer ...?' she tries, unable to finish the question.

'Not here,' he tells her. 'There's a small cemetery on the border between Newton and Heslerton, where the abolitionists bury their dead. They took him there.'

She nods. That's okay. At least he's somewhere. At least somebody who cared for him took his body, and gave him a gravestone, and didn't forget about him. But she wishes, perhaps irrationally, that he could have been here, with Daragh. Beloved, and not alone.

Isabel takes Leo's hand, and they wander the quiet paths until they find a bench that's mostly clear of fallen leaves, where they can sit and breathe the closest thing to country air they'll find inside Espera.

'I know you don't like thinking about the future,' says Leo, after a few moments of silence, 'but indulge me. If they acquit you, if you go free, what will you do next? What do you *want* to do?'

Isabel hasn't allowed herself to think about this because

416

she's so afraid she won't get it. 'I'd like to travel, I think,' she says finally. It's terrifying to say it aloud, as though voicing it means admitting she wants it, and ensures it'll never be hers. 'Go to France, Germany. See how my language skills hold up in person. And I – I wouldn't kill anyone.'

'I was taking that as read,' says Leo, because he doesn't understand.

'My father.' It's a struggle to get the words out. 'He taught me languages for one purpose and one purpose only. Not so that I could go to cafés and museums and take photos of ... of nice bridges, and be a tourist, and see the world. But if I could do that, then I'd know I wasn't what he wanted me to be. I'd know I was free.' She stares down at her boots. 'I don't think I'll ever be that free, will I? Even if they don't send me to prison, I'll never have a passport, or be allowed to travel. Nobody would trust me with that.'

When she sneaks a glance at Leo, his lips are pressed tightly together, his eyes too bright, as though he's trying not to cry. Eventually he swallows, and says, 'I want you to have that. Those cafés and museums and bridges. If I can make it happen ...'

'You've done enough for me already.'

'All I've ever done is be your friend.'

Isabel manages a smile. 'Exactly,' she says. 'Far more than I deserved.' Then she has to look away again, because the sight of Leo crying is about to set her off. 'If I can't travel, I guess I want to be ... useful. I liked working at the library. Maybe I could do that again. Help with the archive, like Jem originally wanted me to. Nobody will let me teach, but—'

'You don't know that,' he interrupts.

'Leo,' she says, pitying his naïvety. 'I'm a murderer. No matter what else happens after this, nobody will ever want me near their children.' She scuffs the muddy ground with her boots. 'But I could teach adults, maybe. Languages. Self-defence. I don't know. Something Comma would never have asked me to do, something I wasn't trained for. I haven't got any qualifications, though,' she adds. 'I don't know if anyone would let me get any.'

'If it's what you want,' says Leo, 'then we will find a way. I promise.'

And she believes him. He wants her to have a future that her parents would never have imagined for her, if only she can imagine it for herself.

'Yeah, well,' she says, shrugging it off; dreams are easier if she convinces herself she doesn't really want them. 'I might spend the next fifty years in prison, so let's not get ahead of ourselves.' Maybe they've already decided that. She's surprised they let her out of their sight, but the ankle monitor and the abolitionists tailing them make locked doors unnecessary. They let her wander the city because they know there's nowhere she can go.

'Don't say that,' says Leo, but his protest lacks strength, because no matter what else he promises, he can't promise that Espera will give her the chance to make amends and be part of their better future. Maybe the damage she's done is just too great, and nobody will ever be able to see past it.

The sense of time slipping away is unavoidable, and the

urgency gives Isabel the strength to ask the question she's been avoiding now for weeks. 'What will happen to Ant?'

Leo bites his lip. 'I don't know,' he admits. 'He's not Espera's to punish or to pardon any more, and his trial hasn't ended. If the city walls still stood, maybe they'd send him back here and consider that punishment enough, but since they don't . . .' His shrug is awkward, heavy with grief. 'Most likely prison.'

'That's not fair,' Isabel observes.

'Maybe not,' says Leo. 'But there's nothing I can do. If they'll let me, I'll visit him. I'll write to him. I—' He stops, swallows, says, 'It doesn't feel right. But he did kill someone.'

He did. And he doesn't have Isabel's background, her extenuating circumstances, but does that matter? Aren't they all as bad as each other?

When I had the chance to kill someone in Leeds, Isabel reminds herself, *I didn't take it.* But that's a small comfort after everything she *has* done. She imagines the judge and jury poring over that tally right now: adding up the good and the bad, weighing her heart on their scales. Finding it lacking, inevitably, in redemptive goodness.

She's about to suggest they go home when Leo's phone rings, shrill in the quiet cemetery. He pulls it out and his eyes widen at the number on the screen. 'I've got to take this,' he says, and she knows it's someone from the courthouse, calling with news.

Isabel doesn't try to listen in. She wanders back through the cemetery to Emma's grave, because whatever news Leo is

419

about to give her, she doesn't want to be alone when she gets it. Without the picnic blanket, the grass is cold and damp, but that's okay. She might not get to feel the cold earth when they lock her away.

He's on the phone for a long time. Maybe he's arguing, begging them to reconsider, because he really thought they'd choose kindness and instead they've done exactly what Isabel would have done in their place. Condemned her for being what other people made her, trapped her in a corner without any real way out.

When he finally comes to find her, his voice cracks as he tells her the verdict.

Isabel closes her eyes. Leans her head back against the gravestone. Says, 'Tell me again.'

Leo says something about needing to return to the courthouse for the sentencing. About rules. Limitations. *In recognition of your assistance*, he says, and *In light of your circumstances*, and all the legal terms that hedge their judgement in justifications and defences.

She says, 'Not that part.'

And he says, 'You're free.'

It's easier, with her eyes closed, to believe him. 'Hear that, Emma?' she says to the cold marble, the damp earth. 'I got out.'

Maybe this time it'll stick, and she can stay out, and she won't have to be somebody else to live a new life: she can be herself, always and only herself, but instead of being the worst version of Isabel Ryans, she can be the version Leo believes in. The version Emma believed in.

She stays there for a long time, and then she takes a deep breath and opens her eyes.

Leo holds out his hand. 'We should go home,' he says. 'Tell the others.' And he doesn't say, although she can tell he's itching to, that this sets an important precedent, or that it's a stride forward for his reparative faction, or that it's a sign of Espera finally working to repair damage and not inflict it. But he doesn't need to, because she knows that.

Isabel Ryans is free, and the guilds are gone, and the violence of the past will not be allowed to lay the foundations for the future. Amidst all the pain, the shed blood, the lost friends, the city is lighting candles, dragging them all out of the darkness. One tiny flame at a time. One outstretched hand at a time. One second chance at a time.

Isabel stands amidst the beloved dead of the city of Espera, and breathes in the scent of hope.

FINO

AUTHOR'S NOTE

This book, more than the first two, offers a mixture of reality and fiction: our world alongside the fictional city of Espera. Leeds is, of course, a real place, but I've taken considerable liberties with its geography, and most of the locations depicted in this book – like Maggie and Dan's garage bar, and the club where Isabel meets Kate – are fictional. After all, this book takes place in 2032, in an alternate timeline; it's not *our* Leeds, though it may resemble it. The one exception is Leeds Central Library, where Sam's book club meets, which is very real. The Tiled Hall Café, shared by the library and Leeds Art Gallery, is every bit as beautiful as described here, and the library itself is a gorgeous building full of stained glass, coloured tiles, and columns galore. It also has wonderfully friendly staff (although Oreolu is purely fictional), who didn't bat an eyelid when I took countless photos of extremely random details during my visit in April 2023. Special thanks are owed to Nat

Barnes, who took me on a behind-the-scenes tour and showed me parts of the library not usually open to the public. If you're ever in the area, I highly recommend a visit.

Fiction and reality overlap here in less concrete ways, too. Across the world, people are grappling with questions of justice, whether fighting against occupation, campaigning for prison abolition or an end to the death penalty, or struggling for resolution and peace in their own everyday lives. What does it mean to repair harm, when the damage that has been done can't be undone? What value, if any, can be found in punishment? Our own society is trapped in punitive cycles of violence: hurting those who are hurt, robbing the poor and enriching the rich, incarcerating the marginalised and allowing the unrepentant wealthy to walk away untouched. I wanted to explore what it means to break those cycles, and how we might build a world where hope and healing can replace hurt and hatred.

I drew here on peace and reconciliation movements throughout history, as well as the work of activists today: real efforts to repair societies fractured by deep injustices, and the ways in which those efforts have succeeded or failed. Often, we can learn as much from failure as from success. Among other examples, I looked at Germany after the Second World War, Northern Ireland and the Good Friday Agreement, and South Africa after apartheid. I drew also on revolutions and uprisings across the former USSR, and the ways in which countries and communities have worked to shape their own futures. I didn't want to show Espera being 'saved' by outsiders: I wanted it to determine its own future, and for that movement to be led by ordinary people, by workers and civilians. I wanted it to be a revolution, not a coup.

Violence can seem unavoidable, an essential part of change. Even here, some of the key turning points in the city's struggle for self-determination are acts of violence. Others, though, are acts of force – an important distinction. Pacifism and justice must be active movements, or they will be passive and unjust. Much of my thinking about pacifism has been shaped by Judith Butler's *The Force of Nonviolence*, a book which disrupts the common understanding of pacifism as a passive avoidance of violence, and advocates for the active and forceful disruption of violent systems in order to create a more just and equal world. I highly recommend it to all who are struggling to understand what it means to wage peace in a violent world. In considering the question of repentance, redemption, and repairing harm, I also found Rabbi Danya Ruttenberg's *On Repentance and Repair: Making Amends in an Unapologetic World* to be a useful insight into a Jewish way of thinking about these topics.

I do believe there are acts which are unforgiveable. But I don't believe there are people who are beyond redemption. Everybody has the capacity to put goodness into the world, no matter how much bad they have put into it – even if that goodness will never outweigh the bad and certainly can't wipe it away. That doesn't mean anyone is obliged to forgive them, or that they should be given the opportunity to continue doing harm. This book is partly about exploring those tensions, both in the form of characters who are given another chance, and those who aren't. It's not intended to be a depiction of perfect justice or a bloodless revolution (it's certainly not that), but a hopeful exploration of messy humans trying to do better.

As I said in my author's note for *The Butterfly Assassin*, too many of the details in this trilogy are real. Teenagers are recruited into the military every day. Violence is normalised throughout society. The arms industry thrives in the UK and worldwide, perpetuating and worsening conflicts and enabling human rights abuses. But just as Espera can't be saved from the outside in, nobody is going to fix this world for us. It's up to us to build the future we want to live in – a kinder world, a more just and equal world, community rather than conflict.

It's a big task, though. As individuals, it's easy to feel like our contributions make no difference, and nothing will ever change. But while it's tempting to set everything on fire and watch it burn, sometimes all we can do is light a single candle, and then another, and then another. Small lights in the darkness, until one day we look around and realise it's light enough to see. We aren't all called to start a revolution, but we can bring light into the world anyway, in our own way.

This book is, I hope, one of the candles I'm lighting. A story that says, *one day, you'll be happy.* A story that says, *you deserve safety.* A story that says, *together we can be better than this.*

Outstretched hands and tired smiles and the endless solidarity of the hurt and the marginalised and the forgotten: *you have never been alone, even when it feels like it.* That's the heart of this trilogy, in the end: not the murder, not the city, not even the colours and the art. But love, in all its weird and messy forms: friendship and found family and solidarity. Because that, when it comes to it, is a force that can change the world.

In friendship,
Finn
October 2023

Acknowledgements

This book marks the end of the trilogy that I've been working on for my entire adult life. I have been shaped and influenced and supported by so many people in that time, more of them than I can possibly name, and I am indebted to all of them. I'm terrified of forgetting somebody and I'll never be able to say all the thanks I need to, but I'll try.

First of all, the team behind the scenes who made this a real book. To Jessica Hare, my long-suffering agent, who handles my plot problems, online enemies, and unexpected new novels with equal aplomb. To Amina Youssef, my editor, who acquired this series and carried it through from *The Butterfly Assassin* almost to the end of editing *Moth to a Flame*. To Ali Dougal, who picked up where Amina left off, and to everyone else at S&S, including: Olive, Olivia, Miya, David, Laura, Dani, Leanne, Maud, Basia, Nicholas and Zoe. Thank you all.

Unusually, this book had no beta readers. But I'm

nevertheless enormously grateful to all those who have beta-read parts of this trilogy in the past and helped me refine and develop my ideas: Eleanor, Caspian, Torin, Cathryn, Jonathan, Richard, C.G., Emily, and others. In particular, Caspian and Eleanor have dealt with a lot of my 'plotting via 2 a.m. essays in the group chat' over the years, and I am immensely grateful for their patience and contributions.

I am also extremely grateful to everyone who helped this series find its feet in the world, including the wonderful booksellers and librarians who helped it find its readers, and every reader and reviewer who has bought my books, read my books, told their friends about my books … I am not kissing you on the mouth, because I don't like kissing and because there is still a pandemic, but metaphorically, that is the energy here. I love you. Thank you.

Further thanks to everyone who aided in my research process, especially my parents, who took me to Leeds and 'Espera' for a research trip in April 2023. Thank you again to Nat Barnes for the tour of Leeds Central Library, and thank you to Simon Varwell, my Esperanto consultant, and Rachel Fletcher, tame lexicographer and one-time housemate, both of whom have put up with far too many weird queries about words.

Thanks to FiBS/Bragelonne for the stunning French editions of *The Butterfly Assassin* and *The Hummingbird Killer*.

As ever, I'm an unrepentant name thief. *Moth to a Flame* features names stolen from Rory Power, Emily Miner, Natasha Hastings, Ally Wilkes, Kate Thompson, Nat Reeve, Janice Davis, Alison Weatherby, and no doubt innumerable others I've forgotten. I'm sorry if the person who got your name was terrible. I promise this is not a reflection of my regard for you personally, but simply the result of me being terribly unimaginative with names. Thank you also to Alison Stockham, who helped name the Roxy.

I also need to thank those who – indirectly – ensured this book wasn't the absolutely bleak, hopeless story I originally planned back in c. 2015. This encompasses everyone from Judith Butler to people I met at Quaker meetings whose names I never learned, and many authors and friends and counsellors in between. But in particular, I want to thank the authors of the 200k+ Bucky Barnes recovery fics who taught me that sometimes the most narratively interesting thing you can do with a deeply traumatised ex-assassin is allow them to heal. To silentwalrus and owlet in particular: you will probably never read this, but you are part of the reason that Isabel has a future, rather than a gravestone. Thank you. (The names 'James' and 'Natasha' were not deliberate references, but I kept them once I realised what I'd done. Hey, sometimes you gotta acknowledge your influences, even if those influences diverged from their own source material's canon somewhere around 2015.)

Finally, I must offer the usual group chat thanks to: the Muddle Ages; Strap In Patricia; Debut 2022s; Write Club; Gasbags & Gondolas; and the Virtual London Tea Rooms. And to all of my friends and family who have come to my launches, shared my books, and otherwise been there for me over the last three (or ten, or twenty-eight) years: thank you.

Or, as Isabel might say: *Dankegon.*

FINN LONGMAN is an author and medievalist, originally from London. They've spent most of their adult life alternating between working in libraries and studying for increasingly niche degrees in medieval literature, and can usually be found in the vicinity of a pile of books. Finn is currently a PhD student at the University of Cambridge, researching friendship in the late Ulster Cycle.

HAVE YOU READ THE FIRST TWO BOOKS IN THE TRILOGY?

'AN ELECTRIFYING DEBUT!'
CHELSEA PITCHER, *This Lie Will Kill You*

INNOCENT BY DAY   KILLER BY NIGHT

THE **BUTTERFLY ASSASSIN**

FINN LONGMAN

'A DARK, ENTHRALLING THRILLER'
The Guardian

FRIEND BY DAY   TRAITOR BY NIGHT

THE **HUMMINGBIRD KILLER**

FINN LONGMAN